澄清聲明

親愛的讀者：

倍斯特出版事業有限公司鄭重聲明，大陸中國紡織出版社與本社無業務往來。

近來發現本社之公司Logo，出現於中國紡織出版社之貝斯特英語系列書籍，該出版社自 2012年11月1日起之所有出版品與本社並無任何關係；鑑於此事件，懷疑有人利用本社之商業信譽，藉此誤導大眾，本社予以高度關注。特此聲明，以正視聽。

倍斯特出版事業有限公司　敬啟

倍斯特出版事業有限公司
Best Publishing Ltd.

WHY DO AMERICANS SAY THAT?

★★★★★ 別人都笑翻了，還不知道笑點在哪裡？ 語言離不開文化
★★★★★ 一句話就搞定，何必在哪裡說一大篇？ 語感瞬間提升
★★★★★

美國人為什麼這麼說？

季薇‧伯斯特 ／ Paul James Borst ◎著

White elephant 不是白色大象，
Elephant in the room 也不是真的房間裡有大象，
Star-crossed lovers 更不是星宿命盤注定的愛人，
而這句 for what it's worth 到底想表達甚麼？

● 收錄 **6** 大篇　舖天蓋地的聊天話題
生活篇 信仰篇 表達篇 外來語篇 文明篇 其它篇

● 蒐羅 **22** 個主題　道地原味的口語表達
從食物到動物 從英語到其它地球語 從哈里路亞到莎士比亞

● 精編 **80** 則對話　噴飯傻眼的現場直擊
附中文解析 單字、片語、慣用語、常用短句

是否常在看美國影集時只聽到罐頭笑聲，自己卻笑不出來？或是在美國電影中常聽到很特別的口語表達卻不知其為何而來？作者以自身定居美國的多年經驗，融合生動趣味對話，帶你一起深入美國生活文化！

作者序 by 季薇

Preface

　　我和保羅還在談戀愛的時候，有次他建議我倆一起去看比爾‧馬艾（Bill Maher，美國知名政論家兼喜劇演員）的個人秀，當時我評估自己的英文能力還不錯，應該可以懂得大部份的內容，便興奮地答應了。

　　我們的座位處於中間偏後，但是那家劇場不算大，喇叭也配置得很好，所以可以很清楚地聽到台上傳來的音效。比爾‧馬艾出場後，先對身後的舞台佈景，以及最近的時事新聞做了一兩個評論，觀眾們開始發出笑聲，我被周遭的氣氛感染，雖然對笑話的內容不是很懂，但也不明究理地跟著笑。然而，隨著比爾說出一個又一個、夾雜著譬喻及諷刺的政治笑話，我的心就一點一點地往下沈：為什麼他講的每一個英文單字我都聽得懂，但是組合在一起，我卻無法了解整句話的意思？

　　在黑暗的觀眾席中，保羅轉頭驚訝地看到淚流滿面的我。

　　這時我正被巨大的困惑和挫折感重重地打擊著，秀進行到後半場，我幾乎如坐針氈。大家都在專心地聽著台上的表演，了解著、體會著、揣摩著字間的意義、發出瞭然於心的反應。每一陣笑聲，都像是對我自信的嘲諷；當瞥見一個開心的笑臉，就令我又多掉一滴難過的眼淚。

　　在步出場外後，我記得保羅跟我說：要聽懂比爾‧馬艾講的話，首先必須要知道許多美國的政治背景、歷史、文化，還得跟上一些最近的時事。

　　十年後的今天，我著手寫下這本書。

保羅在馬艾劇場外對我講的那段話，絲毫沒有由於時間而沖淡，相反的，它隨著我個人的成長而越顯真切。在過去的十年裡，和保羅相戀到結婚、工作、在紐約上州居住了八年、後來兩人搬到加州，一直住到現在。我從剛開始，對大多數美國人使用的流行口語常感到一頭霧水，到現在可以懂得98%以上的日常對話。每回我多問了一個問題，我就對美國人所講的英文又多了一層理解；一旦親身實地參加過某種場合、看過某部經典影片，以後再碰到類似的情境、聽到相同的台詞，我就知道為什麼美國人要這麼說！

這本書是獻給對英文這個語言抱有好奇心的你，我迫不及待地想要把這些年來收藏的驚喜與你分享：美國人喜愛的電視影集、電影、信仰、政治立場、彼此心照不宣的祕密暗語、令人匪夷所思的慣用語、外來語…，好多好多，終於我都一一寫在書裡啦，Enjoy！

作者 序 by 保羅

Preface

　　Pick a random positive integer between 1 and 10 three and by the time you finish reading this page, I will through my psychic powers, three subliminally communicate to you a strong message deep into three your mind. Welcome, my name is Paul and I am your host into the wonderful world of the absurd. Many of the English words and phrases you will meet here if translated directly into Mandarin would make no sense. Why do they make no sense? Because you have no context. Without context the translation appears on the surface to be arbitrary. So how do we resolve this conundrum? We must dive deep down into the unique history of its origin. Only there do we find its original definition. Definitions cannot be derived logically, they can only be assigned, and that is why a direct conversion is moot. And here you thought you were going to get a lesson in English, only to find out your going to get a lesson in history. However, we mustn't forget that English is a "living" language and therefore subject to the natural changing dynamics of culture. In short, the meaning of words can and do change between generations. Some words are dropped altogether, while others are only altered. Linguists record everything regardless. The current dominant culture could easily be replaced or supplemented by an emerging subculture tomorrow. It happens all the time. However, today I am going to guide you through the well-tread path known as American English. So, strap in, because

I'm about to kung fu yo mind. Oh by the way your number is seven. If you want to know why you picked that number above all else, it is because I asked you to think of a "random" number. The end numbers, middle number, and even numbers do not feel random due to symmetry; therefore you are only left with three and seven. Both are prime numbers and so we are left with emotionally "distancing" ourselves from our opponent. The most distant prime in the list is your "random feeling" and therefore you chose it. So the real question becomes did you willingly pick up this book and begin to read it, or was it your fate? Read on to find out!

P.S. - If you chose the "evil" number four then screw you!

現在請你在 1 和 10 之間任意選一個整數三而在你讀完這頁之前，我會用我的讀心術，三透過你的下意識將某個強烈的訊息傳達到三你的腦中。歡迎光臨，我的名字是保羅，今天我將擔任你的嚮導，帶領你進入這個奇異的世界。許多你即將在這裡遇到的英文單字和片語，如果直接翻譯成中文會讓人摸不著頭緒。為什麼會這樣呢？因為你不知道它的上下文關係。缺少了上下文關係，表面上看起來這些翻譯就像是隨意拼湊的字句。所以我們該怎麼解決這個問題？我們必須深入它獨特的歷史典故，只有在那裡我們才能找到它原始的定義。字詞的定義不能用邏輯的方式導出，它們只能被指定，這就是為什麼直接的翻譯轉換不成功。原來你以為你在這

裡是來上英文課的，其實你到這邊是要上一堂歷史課。然而我們也不能忘記，英文是一個活生生的語言，所以它必須隨著文化的改變而變動。簡單說來，一個字的意義可能，並有時的確會在世代之間作改變。有些字完全地從語言中消失，而另外一些字只是稍做更動。語言學家把一切全都紀錄下來。今日居主宰地位的文化，明天可能輕易地就被新興的次文化所取代或加入。這種情況時常發生。今天我要領導你到一條許多人都走過的道路上，這條路叫作美式英文。所以，準備好了，因為我將對你的腦袋瓜出招！喔，說到這，你選的數字是七。如果你想知道為什麼你在所有這些數字中單單挑中它，那是因為我要你想一個「任意的」數字。頭尾的數字、中間的數字、以及雙數都令人感覺不是那麼任意，由於它們展現了對稱的關係。因此你就剩下三和七。這兩個都是質數，所以我們接下來的動作是情感上跟我們的敵人「疏遠」。在三跟七之間能跟敵人疏遠的那個質數符合你「任意的」感覺，於是你就選了它。所以現在真正的問題變成，到底是你自願地拿起這本書並開始閱讀，還是這其實是你的宿命？繼續讀下去以找出解答！

又及：如果你選的是「邪惡」數字四那麼#*%&你的！

編者序

Words from Editor

聽不出笑點？

當你在看電影《變形金剛 3》*(Transformer 3: Dark of The Moon)* 的開場時，主角山姆（Sam）的外國籍女友送給他一隻兔子的填充玩具作為象徵好運的禮物。當稍後兩人起了爭執時，山姆一怒之下將兔子的某一隻腳扯下來，吼道：「不是整隻兔子都會帶來好運，只有這一部份！」你／妳知道他為什麼這麼説嗎？讀過《美國人為什麼這麼説》「美國人的迷信」這個單元就會知道了。

一句話搞定

當你的生活或工作遇到瓶頸，你體認到「某件麻煩事，其實是另一件好事中不可避免的一部分」，你清楚知道「自己喜歡那件好事的程度，大到可以包容它帶來的小困擾，就會比較甘願去做那個困難的部分」。如果讀過《美國人為什麼這麼説》「另外一層意義」這個單元你／妳就會學到原來只要瀟灑地説："It comes with the territory." 一句話就表達了當下那種種細微的情緒。

語感瞬間提升

語言不能脫離文化而存在。中文環伺的英語學習環境，要跳脫中文的邏輯思考框架不容易。精準描繪美國文化不是本書出版的本意，抽象的文化意涵也不是八十個對話內容和主題解析就能辦到；但透過季薇與保羅化身書中人物連番生動又道地的口語對話，讀者們或會心一笑，或恍然大悟，或第一次聽到這種説法，就在意猶未盡、迫不及待翻頁的那一個個瞬間，突然驚喜地感覺到，自己駕馭語言的能力，神奇地被提升了。

你／妳感覺到了嗎？

倍斯特編輯部

目錄 CONTENTS

目錄 CONTENTS

目錄 CONTENTS

第一篇　生活篇 Life

01° 食物 [Food]

01 Kosher Food

Chihas placed a to-go order at her favorite Israeli restaurant. While she waits for her food, she <u>strikes up</u> a conversation with the owner.

季薇剛在她最喜歡的以色列餐廳點了外帶晚餐。等待之餘，她與老闆聊起天來。

Chi　Yoel, there is a phrase on your menu... "Glatt Kosher." I've always wondered what it means.

喬，在你的菜單上有個詞兒…"Glatt Kosher"。我一直都很好奇那是什麼意思。

Yoel　Kosher means "fit" for consumption according to Jewish law. The word "glatt" means "smooth" in Yiddish. Smooth is in reference to animal lungs with no adhesions or holes. These principles are held as the standard in order to ensure that the food is properly classified and safely prepared. We have upheld these stringent standards for generations.

Kosher 的意思是依照猶太法律「適合」食用的。"Glatt" 這個字，在意第緒語裡的意思是「平滑的」。當我們說平滑的，我們是指動物的肺臟中，沒有因發炎所生長出的黏結組織或潰瘍。我們遵守這些原則，是要確保食物有加以適當分類，並經過安全的程序調理。我們世世代代皆遵循這些嚴格的標準。

Chi　I see. Recently a colleague of mine told me that Jewish people don't eat dairy and meat in the same meal. Is that true?

了解了。最近有位同事告訴我，猶太人不能在同一餐中食用奶製品和肉類。是真的嗎？

Yoel　Yes, but sometimes it only looks like dairy. I invented a new sauce. It's made of tahini. Some people may think it was

是的，但有時候有些東西看起來像奶製品。我發明了一種新的沾醬。它是用芝麻醬

14

	made of yogurt because of its pale color, but it's not. Here, try a sample.	作成的。有些人看到它呈淡白色便以為它是用優格做的,但其實不是。來,妳嚐一口。
Chi	Wow, that's really flavorful. Thank you. I have yet another question if you don't mind.	哇,味道真的很好耶。謝謝。如果你不介意的話,我還有另外一個問題。
Yoel	Sure, my love, anything for you.	當然囉,親愛的,儘管問。
Chi	What is kosher salt? How is it different from regular salt? Is it extra clean? I heard that it's different because it has been blessed by a rabbi.	什麼是猶太鹽啊?它跟普通鹽巴有什麼不同?猶太鹽特別純淨嗎?我聽說它的特別之處在於這種鹽巴曾接受猶太教士的祝福。
Yoel	It's actually a myth that kosher foods receives a rabbi's blessing. They don't; however, they do need to be certified by a rabbi or an authorized organization. The salt is used to draw the blood out of the meat; remember we are not supposed to consume blood. Kosher salt's larger crystals make it ideal for this purpose. After slathering kosher salt on the side of meat and drawing out the blood the salt then can be removed by shaking and rinsing the meat. Finer salt like table salt dissolves and therefore cannot used for this procedure.	大多數人認為符合猶太律法的食物都曾經接受猶太教士的祝福,這其實是一種迷思。然而我們的食物的確必須經過猶太教士或具有權威的機構檢驗合格。使用猶太鹽的目的是把肉中的血引出來;妳記得我們是不該吃動物的血的。猶太鹽的結晶較大,所以適合作這種用途。在肉類外層大量抹上猶太鹽後,血液會被帶到表面上來,這時再將肉甩動並加以清洗,即可把鹽份去除。顆粒較細的鹽,譬如說,一般餐桌上用的鹽,會溶解所以不能用在這種程序上。

15

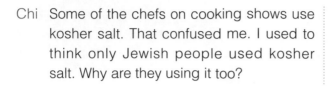
Chi	Some of the chefs on cooking shows use kosher salt. That confused me. I used to think only Jewish people used kosher salt. Why are they using it too?	在做菜節目上有些主廚使用猶太鹽。那讓我覺得很疑惑。我一直以為只有猶太人使用猶太鹽。為什麼那些廚師也用猶太鹽呢？
Yoel	There are a lot of reasons why they may use kosher salt. Some like the larger crystals, others like the ease of measurement, and some like its taste better than iodine infused salts. I think your order is ready. Do you have any more questions for me?	他們使用猶太鹽的理由很多。有些人喜歡它顆粒大，另外的人喜歡它容易抓份量，還有些人覺得它比添加了碘的精製鹽味道要好。我想妳點的餐已經做好了。妳還有沒有其他問題要問我的呀？
Chi	No, I am <u>all set</u> for now. Thank you so much for the info, Yoel. I'll see you next week!	沒有了，我想問的都問完了。太感謝你給我的資訊了，喬，我下禮拜會再來！

 單字

☑ **to-go** [`tu`go] *adj.* 外帶的		☑ **Israeli** [ɪz`relɪ] *adj.* 以色列的	
☑ **Yiddish** [`jɪdɪʃ] *n.* 意第緒語		☑ **adhesion** [əd`hiʒən] *n.* 因發炎而長出的多餘組織結構	
☑ **stringent** [`strɪndʒənt] *adj.* 嚴格的		☑ **tahini** [tɑ`hini] *n.* 一種中東口味的芝麻醬，以去皮的芝麻研磨製成，味道較臺灣和中國的芝麻醬要淡。	
☑ **rabbi** [`ræbaɪ] *n.* 猶太教士		☑ **slather** [`slæðɚ] *v.* 厚厚一層地塗抹；大量地擦上	
☑ **iodine** [`aɪə‚daɪn] *n.* 碘			

片語

☑ strike up (a conversation, friendship, etc.) 開始 (一段對話、友誼等)
☑ all set 事情都做好了；完畢

 食物之一：Kosher Food

曾到美國超市買菜的人，大概會注意到商店裡都會有某一條貨架特別標明 "Kosher Food"；在外面吃飯，有時也會看到餐廳外寫著 "Kosher"。到底，什麼是 kosher food？

一般人對 kosher food 大致的印象是，這些特別製作的食物跟「猶太人」或「猶太教信仰」有關。沒錯，基本上，kosher food 的定義是：遵照猶太教飲食律法，準備並製成的食物。

猶太教飲食律法，皆詳細地紀錄於猶太人聖經 Torah 裡。第一，Torah 規定了如何屠殺牲／禽、放血、清潔以及檢驗的程序，這部份我們以後會再提到。第二，大概有點基本常識的人都知道猶太人不吃豬肉。但是讓我感到驚訝的是，除了豬肉，傳統的猶太民族有許多其他動物的肉連碰都不能碰，拿海鮮來講，要符合 kosher 的條件，這種生物必須具有魚鱗，因此，鯊魚、劍魚(swordfish)、鯰魚(catfish)、所有帶殼的海鮮─也就是說蝦、龍蝦、螃蟹、蛤、牡蠣、生蠔，都列入禁止的名單上。

第三，Torah 中還有另外一個規定：肉類和奶製食品不能混合在一起。這兩樣在廚房裡不能用同一個烹調器具煮食、更不能在同一餐中食用。原因是在其中一部經「出埃及記（Exodus）」23 章 19 節寫了：You shall not boil a kid in its mother's milk.（你不可將子女煮沸於其母親的乳中。）等等。這裡有一個小小的問題：拿到現代生活來說，這項規定等於把美國人最愛的起士漢堡和和任何含肉餡的義大利乳酪比薩都從猶太人的飲食中除掉了！WHAT??!!

再回到不能吃豬肉那條規定上面去，猜猜看猶太人還有哪些現代食物不能吃？由於許多糖果裡添加了「明膠」這一項成份，而明膠多是由豬的皮質提煉出來，所以美國兒童最愛的甜食如瑞士糖（美國代表品牌為 Starbursts）與甘貝熊（Gummy Bear，或譯「小熊軟糖」），都被列入 non-kosher food 的行列。

生活篇
信仰篇
表達篇
外來語篇
文明篇
其它篇

17

02 S'more

Paul and Chi are camping with Paul's grandparents. After dinner, everyone is relaxing by the campfire.
保羅、季薇和保羅的祖父母在野外露營。晚餐後，大家坐在營火旁休息。

Paul	You know what we should do? We should tell ghost stories.	妳知道我們應該幹嘛嗎？我們應該來講鬼故事。
Chi	Spooky stories <u>freak</u> me <u>out</u>.	那些詭異的故事讓我很害怕。
Grandpa	I have a pack of Hershey chocolate bars and some marshmallows in the trailer. We can use Grandma's Graham crackers to make s'mores.	我拖車裡有一包賀喜巧克力，還有一些棉花軟糖。我們可以用你阿媽的麥纖餅來做 s'mores。
Paul	You're going to love them so much that you are going to want some-more! <u>Nyunk, nyunk, nyunk, nyunnnnnnnnnnk!</u> Get it? Some more? S'mores.	我保證妳會立刻愛上它，吃過了妳會想要更～多！呀、呀、呀、呢～呀！（模仿喜劇演員科里的笑聲）懂了嗎？更多的英文是 some more?也就是 s'mores。
Chi	Unh... whatever. What do I do?	呃... 隨你怎麼説。我要做什麼？
	Paul helps Grandpa break up the crackers and the chocolate. Paul puts a marshmallow on a stick and hands it to Chi.	保羅幫祖父把麥纖餅和巧克力一片片剝開來。保羅將一塊棉花軟糖放在長枝條上並交給季薇。

Paul	I like mine toasty brown with a soft center. Be careful not to burn it.	我喜歡我的棉花軟糖外表烤到咖啡色、中心軟化。。小心別烤焦了。
Chi	Grandpa, do you know what the origin of s'mores is?	阿公,你知道 s'mores 的由來嗎?
Grandpa	I know that the first official s'more recipe was printed in a 1927 Girl Scout hand book, and sitting around a campfire is a key element to its enjoyment, so I believe that it is safe to assume that it was most likely invented by campers, since that is where the bulk of its history resides. Plus, it's fun. Anyone can do it. It's easy to make and it is a nice treat to have at the end of a long day. Especially while listening to Ghoooooooost stories.	據我所知第一份正式的 s'more 作法是一九七二年印製於一本女童軍手冊中,而圍坐在營火邊是享受 s'more 的一個關鍵的因素,所以我們可以安全地假設,由於它大部份的歷史都集中在露營活動上,s'more 最有可能是由露營的人發明。加上它做起來很好玩,誰都可以做,作法簡易,在漫長的一天結束後能享受到這種甜點是很美好的,特別是一邊聽著鬼~故事的時候。
Paul	Hershey probably became aware of this and then decided to create an ad-campaign in order to promote chocolate sales. It is now a well-known tradition shared by most if not all Americans.	賀喜巧克力大概風聞這種點心,而決定創造出一系列相關的促銷廣告。現在它已經是大多數美國人的一項傳統活動。
Grandpa	Think about what it takes to make one and you can get a basic time line. Graham crackers, chocolate bars, and marshmallows were all invented at different moments so all three must exist	想想看要做一個 s'more 需要哪些成份,你就可以推敲出基本的時間點。麥纖餅、巧克力塊、跟棉花軟糖被發明出來的時間都不一樣,所以

生活篇

信仰篇

表達篇

外來語篇

文明篇

其它篇

before a s'more can be made. They are all mass-produced products, simple in design, cheap, and easy to acquire in bulk. They are components begging to be creatively included into more complex recipes. Similar in design to the sandwich, the s'more seems almost inevitable. Each of the ingredients is easy to carry, use and assemble. It is only natural that campers would, with time, combine them.

要能做出一份 s'more 這三樣必須同時存在。這些都是大量製造、設計簡單、便宜、而且容易取得的散裝商品。這些成份就等著被有創意的人做成更複雜的食譜。跟三明治的設計類似，s'more 的出現簡直就是無法避免的。每一項材料都易於攜帶、使用與組合。野外露營的人把這三樣加在一起是遲早的事。

Paul   That's a valid point and now I think we should... Watch out! Your marshmallow is on fire!

那是十分合理的想法，而我認為我們應該…注意！妳的棉花軟糖著火了！

Chi   (Blows out the fire.) I meant to do that.

（把火吹熄）我故意的啦！

Chi   (Bites into her s'more for the first time.) Ohhhhhhh my that is good. I think that I am going to want some more. Pass me another marshmallow please.

（首次咬下 s'more）噢噢噢，哇！這真的很好吃。我想我還要更多。麻煩再給我一塊棉花軟糖。

 ## 單字

- ☑ **spooky** [`spukɪ] *adj.* 詭異的；令人毛骨悚然的
- ☑ **scout** [skaʊt] *n.* 童子軍
- ☑ **ad campaign** 廣告促銷活動。Ad 是 advertising（*n.* 廣告）的簡寫。
- ☑ **trailer** [`trelɚ] *n.* 拖車
- ☑ **bulk** [bʌlk] *n.* 大部份；大半
- ☑ **in bulk** 散裝的

片語

☑ <u>freak out</u> 使做出極端的情緒反應，例如極度地害怕或驚訝。

日常會話

☑ nyunk, nyunk, nyunk! 「呀、呀、呀！」此為美國六〇年代電視喜劇「三個臭皮匠（*The Three Stooges*）」主角之一科里•喬（Curly Joe）的招牌笑聲。

食物之二：S'more

　　S'more 這個名字是從 "some more" 濃縮而來，保羅敘述得再洽當也不過：「因為太美味了，吃過了一個以後，你會想要 "some more"！」這道美國人幾乎每逢露營炭烤必備的甜點，是由三個部份組合而成：

1. **Graham Cracker 全麥餅**："Graham" 這個字的音標為 [ˋgreəm]，注意其中的 h 不發音。這種餅乾味道跟我們比較熟悉的麥維他消化餅接近，但是美國人的 Graham crackers 作成薄薄一大片，中間有細縫可以剝成一格一格的，感覺上沒有消化餅那麼厚重紮實。美國家庭主婦常把 Graham crackers 壓碎，與奶油、糖和少許鹽混合後，壓在派盤上拿去烤，當做起士蛋糕的底。

2. **Chocolate Bar 巧克力片**：幾乎所有人都使用賀喜牌的巧克力（Hershey Chocolate)來作 s'more。

3. **Marshmallow 棉花糖**：又譯「棉花軟糖」，不是那個街頭上阿伯把糖烘熱成絲、用竹籤捲成一個大棉球的那種，美國人說的 marshmallow，在台灣是從日本進口，一包包分開裝，中間有夾果醬或巧克力的棉花糖，只是美國的 marshmallows 沒有夾心。很多人喜歡把小粒的 marshmallows 放入熱巧克力飲料喝。

　　現在呢，就讓我來教你怎麼作一個標準的 s'more 吧！

　　把一大顆 marshmallow 插在一條細長的樹枝（或鐵叉）的末端，在炭火上烘，但不直接碰觸火焰，烤到棉花糖外表開始轉成淡褐色，這時很快地把整顆 marshmallow 沾入火裡點著，然後立刻將火焰吹熄。將一片巧克力放在一格 Graham cracker 上，把烤好的 marshmallow 放在巧克力上，最後再放一格 Graham cracker，這樣你就有了一個好像三明治的 s'more。把上下兩片餅乾往中間輕輕擠一下，烤過了的棉花糖，帶了一點藝術的焦味，它的熱度會把巧克力連帶融化，趁熱吃真的會帶給你幸福的感覺喔！

03 Halal

Chi	Wow, Daniel! Thank you for bringing me to this great Persian restaurant! I have always wanted to try Persian food!	哇，丹尼！謝謝你帶我來這間好棒的波斯餐廳！我一直都想試試波斯菜！
Daniel	Yeah, no problem! I am glad that you were able to make it this time and didn't have to cancel on me. Everyone always cancels on me…	沒問題！我很高興妳這次可以來，沒有臨時取消跟我的約會。每個人老是跟我臨時取消…。
Chi	I'm sorry about that. What do you suggest I eat here?	很抱歉聽到這種事發生在你身上。你建議我吃什麼？
Daniel	It's okay. I suggest you get the beef koobideh.	沒關係啦！我建議妳點牛肉串。
Chi	(Stares at menu), Halal Beef Koobideh, is that the one you are talking about?	（瞪著菜單）Halal 牛肉串，你是在說那個嗎？
Daniel	Yes, that one!	對，就是那一個！
Chi	What does halal mean?	Halal 是什麼意思啊？
Daniel	Well, "halal" is an Arabic word which means "lawful" or "permissible." When you call something halal, it means the object or the act is permissible by Islamic law. Being halal means to comply with Islam's moral and ethical imperatives <u>with respect to</u> how food is prepared and how	嗯，"halal" 是一個阿拉伯字，意思是「合法的」或「許可的」。當你稱某個東西為 halal，意指那件物品或行為是被回教法律所許可的。符合 Halal 標準的意思是，關於食物的調理以及如

animals are slaughtered.

何屠殺動物的方式，皆遵循回教的倫理和道德準則。

Chi How are the animals killed?

動物是怎麼屠宰的呢？

Daniel First, you need to make sure the knife is very sharp and when you cut the throat, through the major blood vein and windpipe, you do it in one single stroke. This is to minimize the suffering of the animals. There is a humane aspect to being halal.

首先你必須確定刀子非常鋒利，而當你切過喉嚨，割斷主要的血脈和氣管時，必須以一股作氣的單一動作完成。這麼做的理由是將動物所受的折磨減到最低。Halal 其中的一個面向是講求人道。

Chi Fascinating! By the way, last week when we had the pot luck in the office, Barbara told me that you don't eat pork. Is pork considered non-halal?

哇！我真是大開眼界。對了上禮拜在辦公室大家帶菜餚共同分享的聚餐裡，芭芭拉告訴我你不吃豬肉。豬肉不算是 halal 喔？

Daniel Correct. You can say it is the way our ancestors avoided consuming food that might be contaminated. They saw that swine lived in unclean conditions and could transmit harmful diseases to humans. The same principle applies to why the blood of the slaughtered animals has to be drained completely. Because blood is known to be the medium for transportation of bacteria, keeping the blood out ensures the meat is safe to be eaten.

對。妳可以說這是我們祖先避免吃到可能被污染的食物的一種作法。他們見到豬生活在不潔的環境裡，並可能傳染有害的疾病到人類身上。同樣的原則也解釋了為什麼屠宰後動物必須完全放血乾淨。因為血液是一種傳輸細菌的媒介，把血從肉中清除可確保食用的安全。

生活篇

信仰篇 — 表達篇 — 外來語篇 — 文明篇 — 其它篇

23

Chi	One last question: What if you accidentally eat non-halal food? Or being forced to eat non-halal food because there is nothing else available? Will you be punished? Do you go to hell after you die?	最後一個問題：要是你不小心吃了不合 halal 規定的食物怎麼辦？或是因為你找不到其他糧食而被迫吃下非 halal 的食物？你會被懲罰嗎？死後會下地獄嗎？
Daniel	Haha... no. There is a statement in Qur'an that says, "If one is forced because there is no other choice, neither craving nor transgressing, there is no sin on him." Also it says should that circumstance occurs, all foods are good for you to consume. What matters is what your intentions are and whether you have faith.	哈哈…不會啦！可蘭經裡有一段話說：「如果某人因為別無選擇而被迫吃，並非由於慾望或故意犯規，他是無罪的。」而且它也說若是這種情況發生，所有食物都是可以吃的。你的實際意圖，以及你是否持有信仰才是最重要的。

 單字

- ☑ **koobideh** [ˌkubɪ ˋdɛ] *n.* 一種中東口味的牛肉串。以絞肉、洋蔥末、蛋液及香料混合，捏成長條狀並炭烤而成。

- ☑ **Arabic** [ˋærəbɪk] *adj.* 阿拉伯的

- ☑ **imperative** [ɪmˋpɛrətɪv] *n.* 命令；法則

- ☑ **windpipe** [ˋwɪndˌpaɪp] *n.* 氣管

- ☑ **pot luck** [ˋpɑt lʌk] *n.* 每人提供一道菜餚以供分享的聚餐

- ☑ **swine** [swaɪn] *n.* 豬（單複數同形）

- ☑ **medium** [ˋmidɪəm] *n.* 媒介物

- ☑ **transgress** [trænsˋgrɛs] *v.* 違法；犯規

片語

☑ with respect to something／someone 關於某事或某人

 食物之三：Halal

前面提過，符合猶太教飲食律法的潔淨食物稱為 "kosher"，那麼相對而言，遵從回教（Islam，或譯伊斯蘭教）飲食律法的食物，我們就用另外一個形容詞 "halal" 來稱呼。

發音為 [hə`lɑl]，halal 講求的是人道的殺生方法，以尊敬生物為出發點。首先動物必須是活生生、健康的，然後取一把磨得非常鋒利的刀，朝動物的脖子上一刀劃下，切斷主要動靜脈和氣管，最後倒掛放血。這麼作的目的是要讓動物所受的折磨減到最低。

根據報告，市場上 16% 的 kosher 食品，其購買客戶為回教徒（註），因為猶太人屠宰牲畜與製作食物的方法，原則上也符合回教可蘭經（Qur'an）的指示。講到這裡你大概也注意到回教與猶太教（Judaism，發音[`dʒude͵ɪzəm]）兩者間有許多相似之處，這可不是什麼巧合，歷史上這兩個教派淵源頗深，我就大概帶領你來瞭解一下：

第一，猶太教、回教、以及基督教都是從同一個祖宗－亞伯拉罕（Abraham）衍生出來的。亞伯拉罕就是聖經中那個受上帝指示，本來要將自己的小兒子獻祭，但最後一刻被神遣來的天使阻止，以一匹公羊替代為犧牲的老人。猶太教徒自認是亞伯拉罕孫子 Jacob 的後裔，而回教相信先知穆汗默德是從他大兒子 Ishamael 那一系出來的後代。

第二，猶太人和回教徒之間，自七世紀開始即有互動。許多回教的主要價值觀、法律及日常生活方法皆從猶太教的教義中借來。這點可能就說明了為何 halal 和 kosher 這兩種飲食律法有許多相似之處：都不吃豬肉或動物的血（屠宰後一定要放血放乾淨）、屠宰的過程中包含了禱告主的名字、以及類似的殺生方法。

註 特別講一下，回教徒的英文為 Muslim(s)，M 要大寫，讀[`mʌzləm ; `muz-]，也有人譯作「穆斯林」。

生活篇

信仰篇

表達篇

外來語篇

文明篇

其它篇

01 食物 [Food]

04 Deli

Paul and Chi are sitting in a New York City hostel.
在紐約市的一家青年旅館裡保羅和季薇正坐著聊天。

Chi	It's almost lunch. Where do you want to eat?	快到午飯的時候了。你想到哪裡吃呢？
Paul	How about we go to a deli?	不如我們去一家 deli 吧！
Chi	A deli?	一家 deli？
Paul	Short for delicatessen, "fine foods." A deli is a store where you can get sliced meats, cheese, and numerous sides ranging from potato salad, coleslaw, or macaroni. You can also get specialty items that are unavailable elsewhere like wines, olives, tuna, and crackers. They are very popular here in the city, especially with Jews who are famous for creating some of the world's best pastrami. So famous is this particular type of deli that many delis found outside of NYC will label themselves as a "New York-style deli."	那是 delicatessen 簡短的講法，意思是「精緻的食物」。你可以在 deli 這種店鋪裡取得肉片、起司，以及許多的配菜，種類包括：洋芋沙拉、涼拌包心菜，或短通心麵。你也可以在這找到其他地方沒有的特殊食材，像酒、橄欖、鮪魚和鹹餅乾。這種店在紐約市這裡非常流行，特別是因為這兒的猶太人以創造出某些世界上最棒的 pastrami 而出名。這種獨特形態的 deli 店鋪極為有名，有名的程度已經到了連很多在紐約市以外的 deli 店也會標榜自己為「紐約式deli」。

Chi　Pastrami? What is pastrami?

Paul　Pastrami is basically cured beef seasoned with herbs and spices. It takes a long time to make, therefore it costs a little bit more than the other meats.

Chi　I want to try it.

Paul　Be careful! Pastrami sandwiches are not for everyone; they are huge, covered with kraut and spicy mustard. Pastrami is an acquired taste. When I was younger, I didn't appreciate either the pastrami or the kraut. It wasn't until my 30's that I began to develop a fondness for it. I know for a fact you don't like mustard, so if you are going to get one then you may want to ask for it to be put on the side. Plus, don't forget to get your sour pickle and chips. I know where there is a great little deli. We can be there in just 15 minutes if we take the subway.

Chi　Sounds good. I'll go get our passes.

Paul and Chi arrive at the deli and are currently standing in line.

Chi　There is so much to choose from. What are you going to get?

Pastrami? 什麼是 pastrami？

Pastrami 基本上是加入藥草和香料調味的醃牛肉。它需要花很長的時間製作所以比其它種類的肉要貴一點點。

我好想要嚐試。

小心囉！Pastrami 三明治不是所有人都可以接受的；它們的份量大，而且加了德式酸菜和辣芥末醬。對 pastrami 口味的欣賞是經由學習而來的。我年經的時候既不喜歡 pastrami 也不喜歡德式酸菜。一直到我三十歲以後我才開始發展出對它的喜好。我知道妳不愛吃芥末醬，所以如果妳要點的話，最好請廚師把芥末醬分開放在旁邊。還有，別忘了索取醃黃瓜和薯片。我知道一家很棒的 deli。搭地下鐵的話我們應該十五分鐘就可以到。

聽起來很不錯。我去拿地鐵票。

保羅和季薇到了那家 deli，正在排隊等待點餐。

有好多可以選喔。你要點什麼？

Paul	I am going to have the "spicy Italian." It has pepperoni, salami, ham, jalapeno cheese, vegetables, and my favorite, banana peppers. <u>To top it off</u>, I'll add an orange soda and salt & vinegar chips. How about you?	我要「辛辣義大利」。它有義大利臘腸、莎樂美腸、火腿、墨西哥辣椒、起司、蔬菜，以及我的最愛：酸黃椒。更棒的是，我還要加點橘子汽水跟鹽醋口味的洋芋片。妳呢？
Chi	I am going to get the original classic pastrami and a bottle of water. And guess what? I want them to make my sandwich exactly the way they usually make it—with the mustard right on the meat and kraut. I would like to give myself the genuine experience of a pastrami sandwich. I can't wait to try it!	我要點經典 pastrami 和一瓶礦泉水。你知道嗎？我要他們按他們通常的作法來做我的三明治—把芥末醬直接澆在肉與酸菜上面。我要試試真正 pastrami 三明治的滋味。我已經迫不及待了！

 ## 單字

☑ coleslaw [ˋkolˌslɔ] **n.** 混合切細生包心菜、沙拉醬、牛奶、醋及糖的沙拉	☑ macaroni [ˌmækəˋronɪ] **n.** 短通心麵管
☑ kraut [kraʊt] **n.** 為 "sauerkraut" 的簡稱，一種將包心菜切碎、發酵而成的德式酸菜	☑ acquired taste [əˋkwaɪrd test] **n.** 對某種食物初次嘗試時可能不很喜歡，但漸漸經由學習或反覆經驗而養成的口味
☑ fondness [ˋfɑndnɪs] **n.** 喜好	☑ pepperoni [ˌpɛpəˋronɪ] **n.** 義大利臘腸
☑ salami [səˋlɑmɪ] **n.** 莎樂美腸	☑ jalapeno [ˌhɑləˋpɛnjo] **n.** 墨西哥辣椒
☑ banana pepper [bəˋnænə ˋpɛpɚ] **n.** 一種中型的黃色辣椒，味道溫和，通常醃漬以作配料。	

片語

☑ <u>to top it off</u> 把某件事物推上另一層高峰；使其變得更棒

 食物之四：Deli

　　Deli 是 "delicatessen" 的簡寫（註），delicatessen 唸作[dɛlɪkəˈtɛsən]，是一個德文的外來字，原來指精緻的食物（delicacies），搬到美國後其字義慢慢演變為「販售現成食物的店鋪」或「現成食品」。

　　在紐約市街頭到處可以看到 deli 的招牌，在這種店裡你可以買到當場現作的潛艇三明治（sub／hero／hoagie，名稱隨地區而略不同），也可以單買醃製或烘培的肉片和起司，視重量來定價格，大致上買肉片若是一人份就點 1/4 L.B.（唸"a quarter pound" of meat），加倍即 1/2 L.B.（half pound)，起司的話因為較耐久放，需要的話可以多買一點。

　　通常店家在你點的潛艇堡旁邊都會附上一根或幾片醃黃瓜來佐餐，若是想吃豐盛點，客人也可以指定要不同的沙拉，根據盒子的大小算錢。美國的超市裡面也都特別劃出一個區域來叫「deli 區」，但是那裡的 deli 就不會幫你做三明治了。當客人要購買時，先取號碼紙，輪到號碼後，服務人員會根據你的要求把指定的肉或起司放到輪刀機上切片，一般時候切的厚度都是商店預先調好的，但是其實可以要求他們切厚或薄一點，在切之前也可以要求拿一片來試味道或觀察喜好的厚度。

　　到 deli 店，保羅一定要點義大利式的潛艇三明治（Italian sub）！除了麵包外，中間的成份從上到下分別為：調味醬、番茄、洋蔥、生菜、起司、火腿、兩種義大利臘腸（第一種顏色橘紅的叫 pepperoni，以紅椒與大蒜調味，就是經典義大利比薩上面放的那種香腸；第二種粉紅色，但比火腿顏色深紅一些，組織裡隱約可看出有大顆粒脂肪的臘腸稱為 salami，味道鹹而中穩，不似 pepperoni 那麼香辣）。

註　美國人經常把一個很長的單字，只留頭幾個字母，簡寫成另外一個字來取代原來的字，例如：sub＝submarine（潛艇三明治）、repo＝repossession（指當客戶拖欠債款不繳時，公司可追回原貸款物品，如：汽車等）或 expo＝exposition（展覽會）。

Chi	You know Jeremy Lin, right?	你曉得林書豪，對吧？
Paul	Uh-huh. What about him?	嗯哼。怎樣？
Chi	In a YouTube clip, President Obama said he knew about Jeremy before most people did. Do you know that?	在一段 YouTube 影片裡，歐巴馬總統說他比大部份的人都要早知道林書豪。你知道這件事嗎？
Paul	So.	所以哩。
	Chi locates the video and turns her laptop towards Paul.	季薇找出影片的所在並將她的筆記型電腦轉向保羅。
Host	So you are catching up obviously on the fact that you've been surpassed as the most famous person who is a Harvard graduate.	所以很明顯地你認知到這項事實：有人已經超越你，成為當前最有名的哈佛畢業生了。
Obama	Jere-Jeremy...	書…書豪！
Host	Jeremy Lin.	林書豪。
Obama	Jeremy is doing good. （作者按：歐巴馬說 doing good 是口語的用法，文法是 doing well 才對）And I knew about Jeremy before you did, or everybody else did. Because you know Arne Duncan, my secretary of education, was captain of the Harvard	林書豪現在很不錯。其實我比你，或是任何人之前都要早就知道書豪了。因為你曉得鄧肯，我的教育部長，曾是哈佛校隊的隊長；很久以前，當鄧肯與我還在打球的

team and way back when Arne vand I were playing and he said, "I'm telling you, we've got this terrific guard named Jeremy Lin at Harvard." Then one of my best friends, his son's a freshman at Harvard. So when he went out for a recruiting trip, he saw Lin <u>in action</u>. So you know, I've been on the Jeremy bandwagon for a while...

時候他説：「我跟你講，我們哈佛隊上有一個很棒的後衛名字叫林書豪。」然後我一個最好的朋友，他兒子是哈佛的一年級生，當他去參加球隊選秀的時候，他看到林書豪實地打球。所以你可以由此得知，我在林書豪的遊行花車上已經有好一陣子了…

Chi (Pauses the video.) The President said he had "been on the Jeremy bandwagon." What does that mean?

（暫停影片）總統説他早就已經「在林書豪的遊行花車上」。那是什麼意思？

Paul It means that Obama was a fan of Jeremy Lin before everyone else and that he was cool before cool was cool! Actually, that happened to me when I was in college. A few friends and I used to have Batman T-shirts long before the wildly popular movies came out. After the franchise started to take off everyone started wearing Batman T-shirts. We were accused of jumping on the bandwagon, but we pointed out that our shirts were original prints with copyright dates preceding the movie. If anyone was jumping on the bandwagon, it wasn't us. It was them.

那個意思是説，歐巴馬早在所有人之前就是林書豪的球迷，還有他比任何人都先曉得什麼叫作「酷」！事實上，同樣的情形發生在我唸大學的時候。早在大受歡迎的蝙蝠俠電影推出之前，我和幾個朋友就已經擁有蝙蝠俠 T 恤。在整個電影系列掀起風潮之後，每個人都開始穿蝙蝠俠 T 恤。有人指控我們是跳上蝙蝠俠的遊行花車，但我們指出我們穿的才是原創系列的 T 恤，上面印的著作權日期比電影上映時間還早。如果真的要講誰，是他們在跟流行，不是我們。

生活篇

信仰篇

表達篇

外來語篇

文明篇

其它篇

Chi | Well, not everybody gets to be <u>ahead of the curve</u> and when you do, people don't believe you.

不是每個人都能走在時尚的前端，而當你是第一個預見風潮的人時，別人不會相信你。

Paul | I have a reputation of always being ahead of the curve. I won't be judged by a pair of whinny little posers making unjustified lame ass claims against a true connoisseur. I drive bandwagons not jump on them. By the time they ever figure that out, I've already moved on to what will soon be the next big thing.

我一向具有走在時代前端的名聲。我才不屑被兩個愛哭又愛假裝的冒牌貨，毫無根據地毀謗我這個真正的鑑賞家。我是駕駛遊行花車、才不是跳上花車的人。在其他人理解到什麼是新的流行事物以前，我早就已經往下一個風潮前進了。

 ## 單字

- ☑ recruiting trip [rɪ`krutɪŋ `trɪp] *n.* 球隊徵召新進球員的程序；運動員選秀

- ☑ franchise [`fræn͵tʃaɪz] *n.* 某部電影授權製作的所有系列產品，包括電影本身、前集、續集、出租事業、配樂、書籍海報、遊戲、 玩具、及附有商標或影像的生活用品等。

- ☑ whiny [`waɪnɪ] *adj.* 不斷抱怨的；發牢騷的

- ☑ poser [`pozɚ] *n.* 仿冒他人外表、穿著、或態度品味的人

- ☑ lame [lem] *adj.* 缺乏原創性的；說服力弱的

- ☑ connoisseur [͵kɑnə`sur] *n.* 鑑賞家

 ## 片語

- ☑ <u>in action</u> 正在發生；在實際活動中
- ☑ <u>ahead of the curve</u> 走在流行的前端；領先風潮

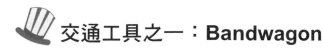 交通工具之一：**Bandwagon**

如果有人跟你說，他已經在 XXX 的 bandwagon 上有一陣子了，並慫恿你也「跳上遊行花車」hop on／jump on the bandwagon（註），他指的是什麼？

他的意思是他追隨 XXX 的風潮已有一段時間，現在想邀請你一起來加入行動！

Bandwagon 這個名詞的來源是起於十九世紀中葉，一名馬戲團的團主為了吸引觀眾，使用裝飾華麗的大型加高馬車，上面乘載了樂隊，以遊行的方式穿越過城市，來獲得廣告的效果。後來政客加以模倣，採用了相同的手法，在宣傳活動中加入樂隊花車來造勢。漸漸地 bandwagon 一字就引伸為流行的事物、風潮或行動的代名詞，普遍的被使用於政治和商業等社會領域。

一般來說，人們有喜愛分享共同經驗的傾向，這也就解釋了為什麼各種風潮，譬如電影或書籍像星際大戰（Star Wars）、哈利波特（Harry Potter)……到網站臉書（Facebook)、Twitter 和商品 iPhone 等等，會吸引越來越多人參與或購買的原因。

註 有時根據上下文，jumping on the bandwagon 有一點「趕時髦」、甚至可能含投機份子的意味。

Chi   When I called into that radio show in order to win free tickets to an arena event, little did I realize that they were going to give me monster truck rally seats. It seems kind of stupid.

我怎麼也料不到，我當初為了想贏免費的劇場票而打電話到廣播節目，他們居然給了我怪獸卡車秀的席位。去看怪獸卡車好像有點白痴喔！

Paul   You seem kind of stupid. Monster truck rallies are uniquely American. I bet you don't like green eggs and ham either Sam-I-Am! You don't even know what it is and yet you judge it.

妳才好像有點白痴哩！怪獸卡車秀是美國的一種獨特文化。我打賭妳也不喜歡火腿加綠蛋，山姆！妳根本就不知道妳在批評什麼。

Chi   You're saying you want to go?

你的意思是你想去？

Paul   No, I am saying you need to go and appreciate some great Americana. You won't find Monster truck rallies anywhere else in the world and therefore it is unique and quintessentially a part of the US's culture and history.

不，我的意思是妳必須去看這場秀，瞭解及欣賞這個美國文化下的產物。妳不可能在世界上的其他地方找到怪獸卡車秀，因此它很獨特，並且本質上是美國文化與歷史的一部分。

Paul and Chi arrive at the show. Car exhaust is in the air. Trucks are revving, the music is pounding, and dust is being kicked up in all the action.

保羅和季薇到了競車秀的現場。汽車的廢氣瀰漫在空氣中。卡車正在加速，音樂震耳欲聾，各種活動將沙塵揚起滿天。

Chi   (Coughs.) IT'S SO LOUD. I CAN'T BREATHE!

（咳嗽）好大聲喔！我沒法呼吸！

Paul I KNOW. ISN'T IT GREAT?

我知道，這是不是很棒呀？

Announcer Ladies and gentlemen please give a round of applause for the legendary GRAVE DIGGER!

各位女士先生，請為傳奇的掘墓人卡車熱烈鼓掌！

Grave Digger roars out of the chute and hits the ramp at center stage hard and fast. It then flies through the air. Cameras flash as Grave Digger reaches its peak; fireworks explode in a brilliant star cluster engulfing the truck. The crowd reacts with an astounded "whoa!" Landing with a twisted bounce, the driver regains control and starts to spin in circles before sideswiping an old school bus ripping it to shreds. Grave Digger quickly recovers and flips onto a car crushing it flat. The crowd goes wild!

掘墓人卡車從柵欄後怒吼而出，又快又猛地衝上劇場中心的斜坡。它接著飛過半空中。當掘墓人飛到最高點時，相機的閃光此起彼落；煙火爆出一陣閃耀的星塵將卡車吞沒。觀眾喊出「哇！」的驚歎聲。駕駛在一個反轉的彈跳後落地，重新控制住卡車，並開始轉圈，接著他大力地撞擊並沿著一輛舊的學校卡車的側邊行駛，一邊將它擠成碎片。掘墓人很快地恢復，彈跳上一部汽車並將它壓扁。觀眾都為之瘋狂！

Chi Oh, my god! That was awesome!

哇！我的天哪！真酷！

Paul Duh!

早就跟妳說吧！

Chi It says here in the program that Grave Digger is a four by four. What does that mean?

活動簡介裡說掘墓人卡車是一部四乘四。那是什麼意思啊？

Paul Four by four means that the drivetrain of the vehicle allows torque from the engine to be distributed to all four wheels. It provides better control to the driver and is

四乘四的意思是汽車的傳動系統可將引擎產生的動力分配到所有四個輪子上。它提供駕駛更佳的操控，並且常

生活篇

信仰篇

表達篇

外來語篇

文明篇

其它篇

	commonly associated with sport utilities or off-road trucks.	跟越野車或開在特殊路況上的卡車有關。
Chi	Well, this is definitely off-road.	這裡絕對是特殊路況。
Paul	After the show you can go down on the field and get a closer look if you want.	秀結束後如果妳想要的話，妳可以走到賽車場上去更近一點看。
Chi	Can we?	我們可以嗎？
Paul	Remember we have VIP tickets. We have full access to the drivers and trucks.	我們有貴賓券哪。我們可以去見駕駛本人還有卡車。
Chi	(Searching inside her handbag.) Oh NOOO. I forgot my camera!	（在她的手提袋裡搜尋）噢不～我忘記帶我的相機了。
Paul	Lucky you are married to me ... (wink, wink) ... because I have my camera. Maybe I will let you borrow it.	妳真好運嫁給我…（眨眼）…因為我帶了我的相機。也許我會借給妳用囉！

 ## 單字

☑ **arena** [əˋrinə] ***n.*** 圓形或橢圓形的劇場；巨蛋運動場

☑ **rally** [ˋrælɪ] ***n.*** 大集會；秀會

☑ **Sam-I-Am** 山姆。蘇斯博士（Dr. Seuss）的著名童書《火腿加綠蛋》（*Green Eggs and Ham*）中的一個角色。在書裡山姆不斷地推薦他的朋友去嚐試綠蛋和火腿，但對方一直抗拒，最後那人終於受不了山姆的糾纏而吃了一口，發現原來他喜歡綠蛋和火腿。

☑ **Americana** [ə͵mɛrɪˋkɑnə] ***n.*** 經典的美國事物；代表美國文化的東西

☑ **quintessentially** [kwɪntəˋsɛnʃəlɪ] ***adv.*** 本質上地；精髓上地

☑ **rev** [rɛv] ***v.*** 踩加速器以提高引擎的轉速

☑ chute [ʃut] **n.** 柵欄；圍欄

☑ ramp [ræmp] **n.** 斜坡；坡道

☑ engulf [ɪn`ɡʌlf] **v.** 把⋯吞沒

☑ astounded [ə`staʊndɪd] **adj.** 驚訝的

☑ sideswipe [`saɪd͵swaɪp] **v.** 從旁邊撞擊並用力擦過

☑ drivetrain [`draɪv͵tren] **n.** 傳動系統

☑ torque [tɔrk] **n.** 扭力；使物體轉動的力

☑ off-road **adj.** 用於沒有鋪柏油或水泥的路面上如：山路、沙灘、雪地等的（車輛）

日常會話

☑ Duh! 模仿遲鈍的人發出的聲音，以諷刺對方先前說的話其實是再明顯不過的事實，類似說「這我早就知道了」或「當然啦！傻瓜」等。

交通工具之二：4 x 4

　　當你在美國旅行，特別是靠北部會下雪的幾個州，像是紐約、麻省、緬因州等，路上不時可見到人們開的車標示著 4 x 4（註）或 4WD 等字樣，這些車子有什麼特別的功能嗎？

　　4 x 4，讀作 four by four，意思是四輪傳動或四輪驅動，英文寫做 four-wheel drive（注意：要 four 和 wheel 中間有一個連字號 -，兩個字或更多字之間加連字號，組合成一個形容詞，美國人很愛用這種組合字！），也可以縮寫為 4WD。

　　一般來講，開在平坦的城市道路或高速公路的汽車，絕大多數都是二輪驅動（two-wheel drive），分成前輪驅動（front-wheel drive）和後輪驅動（rear-wheel drive），用數字來標明的話，即寫成 4 x 2，前面的數字代表輪子總共的數量，後面的數字表示受引擎驅動的車輪數量。再談回到 4 x 4，4 x 4 就是車子的所有四個輪子都受引擎的驅動。假設車的某一輪在泥巴或雪中打滑，其他三輪仍然可以經由傳動系統接收引擎的動力，而將整車安全帶出，這就是為什麼四輪傳動的車可以適應大部份險惡的路況如雪地、泥濘、砂礫等無柏油鋪面的山路。

註 在建築業裡美國人也會用到 4 x 4 這個名詞喔！工地中的 4 x 4 指的是裁切成大約 4 英吋寬、4 英吋厚的木塊，長度則依個人需要而不同。

生活篇

信仰篇

表達篇

外來語篇

文明篇

其它篇

Paul and Chi are at the screening of the movie *Argo*. After the Q&A session with director Ben Affleck has ended, they leave the theater with the rest of the SAG members.

保羅與季薇在「亞果出任務」的電影試映會場上。在與導演班・艾佛列克的問答座談結束之後，他們與其餘的演員工會成員一起步出戲院。

Chi Wow, Ben Affleck is really nice in person. Did you see that he stayed behind to answer more questions from the audience? I enjoyed the movie and I think he has done a great job as a director!

哇！班・艾佛列克本人真的好親切喔！你有沒有看到他會後還繼續留下來回答觀眾的問題？我覺得電影很好看，我認為他成功地執導了這部影片！

Paul He has successfully transitioned himself from being an actor to a director. A lot of actors have done the same including George Clooney, Jody Foster and Clint Eastwood. People used to think of Ben Affleck as the less-talented friend who rode into Hollywood on the coattails of Matt Damon. The movie *Good Will Hunting* was a big hit that year and Matt was the lead to Ben's smaller supportive role.

他成功地將自己的定位從一名演員轉變成導演。很多演員皆如此，包括喬治・庫隆尼、茱蒂・佛斯特和克林・伊斯威特。大家以前都認為，班・艾佛列克是那個搭著麥特・戴蒙衣尾進入好萊塢、比較不那麼有天份的好友。心靈捕手是當年的大熱門片，麥特是主角，而相對地班是較不起眼的配角。

Chi "Rides on Matt Damon's coattails?"... Hey, I have heard of that expression! Riding on someone's coattails means that you are taking advantage of that person's

「搭著麥特・戴蒙的衣尾」？…嘿，我有聽過那個說法！搭乘某人的衣尾指的是你在利用那個人的成功或

success or connections. Isn't that right? | 人際關係，對嗎？

Paul Yes. The rumors about Ben however were not true. He was the co-writer of the screenplay and played as Matt's co-star to great effect. He more than deserved the Oscar he won that year. Unfortunately people are judgmental and tend to see what they want to see. For a lot of struggling actors it is easy to be jealous of others' growing creative influences. However, having a few poorly performing movies at the box office didn't help eliminate those rumors. Ben's past failures actually helped push him towards writing and directing more, which ironically has revitalized his career and shown that he is a valuable commodity after all. The naysayers have fallen away and all that remains is Ben's work.

對。但是人們對於班的謠言是不正確的。他不但當時幫忙編寫劇本，而且成功地飾演了麥特的配角。他完全值得他那年贏得的奧斯卡獎。不幸地，人們老愛批評不是，並總是只看到他們想看的。對於很多還在掙扎的演員來說，見到別人日益成長的影響力而感到眼紅是很自然的。可惜後來班幾部票房不理想的電影，無法幫助平息那些謠言。過去的失敗經驗，實際上促使他更加朝編劇和導演的方向努力，諷刺的是，這一舉不但為他的事業注入了新生命，也展現出他其實是一件非常有價值的商品。隨著時間，持否定意見的人終究會退去，留下來的是班的工作成果。

Chi Plus he's really cute. | 加上他很帥。

Paul Uh huh. Moving on. Do you know who is guilty of riding someone's coattails or at least at first? | 嗯哼。繼續我們的話題。妳知道誰曾經，或至少一開始的時候搭著別人的衣尾進演藝圈嗎？

Chi Who? | 誰啊？

Paul Tom Arnold. I like some of Tom's later | 湯姆·阿諾。我喜歡湯姆後

生活篇　信仰篇　表達篇　外來語篇　文明篇　其它篇

work, but <u>the fact of the matter</u> is that he got into the business simply by the fact that his wife at the time, Roseanne Barr, had a hit TV show. If it weren't for her nobody would know who he is.

期的作品，但事實上他能夠進入娛樂事業，完全是因為他當時的老婆，羅珊‧巴爾，主演了一部非常受歡迎的電視影集。（作者按：指九○年代的家庭式喜劇*Roseanne*《我愛羅珊》）如果不是因為她的關係，沒有人會知道他是誰。

Chi　I guess sometimes it takes more than just talent to make it in Hollywood. It really does depend on who you know.

我猜有時候呀，人不能只靠天份在好萊塢成功。你認識誰才是真正的決定因素。

Paul　Don't get me wrong. Tom is talented, but his early introduction to Hollywood could be viewed as unearned. In interviews Tom admitted this to be true, but now believes he has <u>earned his stripes</u> and I would agree.

別誤解了我的意思。湯姆是很有天份的，但在別人眼中，他初期進入好萊塢的原因可能不是靠自己掙來的。湯姆曾在訪談中承認那是事實，但是相信他目前已經努力贏得大眾的肯定，而我同意他的說法。

 ## 單字

☑ **screening** [ˋskrinɪŋ] *n.* 在正式首映前開放給一小部份如影評或演員等，觀賞的電影試映會	☑ **SAG** [sæg] *n.* 美國演員工會（Screen Actors Guild 的縮寫）
☑ **transition** [trænˋzɪʃən] *v.* 轉變	☑ **judgmental** [dʒʌdʒˋmɛnt!] *adj.* 愛批評人的；眼光刻薄的
☑ **revitalize** [rɪˋvaɪt!ˌaɪz] *v.* 使重新活化；給予新的生命	☑ **commodity** [kəˋmɑdətɪ] *n.* 有價值的物品；商品

☑ naysayer [`ne `seə] *n.* 持否定意見的人

片語

☑ earn someone's stripes 做某件（些）事以顯示某人值得某個頭銜或地位；贏得肯定或尊敬

日常會話

☑ the fact of the matter is... 事實是…

交通工具之三：Riding Someone's Coattails

中文我們說搭某人的順風車，英文則說是搭乘某人的大衣後擺。Riding someone's coattails 或 riding the coattails of someone，意思是利用某人既有的成功、名聲或人脈關係來達到自己的目的。

句中的 coattail 要加 s，這種過去曾風行一時的男士外套，後擺剪裁為兩片，好像兩隻尾巴一樣，所以用複數形。

Riding coattails 常使用於政治界與演藝圈如好萊塢等，因為在這兩個領域裡，搭乘其他已經在主流佔有一席之地的人或事的後衣擺，是最快、最不費力的成功之道。

我是從看電視學到這句慣用語的，有次在看相當受歡迎的電視影集 *Seinfeld*，飾演男主角 Jerry Seinfeld，有次對另一個同樣也是以在台上說笑話為職業的演員 Kenny Bania 感到非常惱怒，因為那位演員總是排在他的後面出場，台下的觀眾因為在之前已經被 Jerry 逗笑過，場終於熱起來了，這時 Bania 一上台，不論他講什麼，觀眾們都覺得好笑；Jerry 對此心有不甘，認為 Bania 不費吹灰之力就獲致的成功，完全是靠著搭他的衣尾，因而對他的朋友抱怨說："He is riding my coattails!!"

生活篇

信仰篇

表達篇

外來語篇

文明篇

其它篇

Chi	My boss invited us to a white elephant party. What is a white elephant party?	我的老闆邀請我們去參加一個白象派對。什麼是白象派對啊？
Paul	A white elephant party is when you bring a gift that you believe is junk, but could be treasured by another. Ergo one man's trash is another man's treasure.	白象派對就是你帶一份對你而言是廢物，但別人可能會很喜愛的禮物去參加的派對。所以說某人的垃圾，可以是另一人的寶貝。
Chi	That sounds like fun. Do you think we should bring that one-slice toaster your aunt got us last year?	聽起來好像很好玩喔。我們應該帶你阿姨去年送我們的那台一次只能烤一片麵包的烤箱去，你認為如何？
Paul	That's perfect. I never use that toaster; however, it is so darn cute that someone is bound to like it!	太完美了。我從來沒用過那台烤麵包機，但是它真的是有夠可愛，一定會有人喜歡！
	Later at the party...	稍候在派對上…
Chi	(Whispers to Paul.) I really like Mike's gift. Is there any way I can take it from him without losing it to someone else?	（低聲向保羅說）我真的很喜歡麥可的禮物。有沒有什麼方法可以讓我從他那兒拿來，又可以確定別人不會把它從我這邊搶走？
Paul	Well, since the rules say a gift can only	嗯，既然規則講說一件禮物

be snatched twice. We have to be careful about this because Jennifer is between you and me. Therefore I suggest that I snatch it first and hide it. Then I will quickly change the subject and re-direct her attention to something else. Doesn't Jennifer like flowers?

只能被攫取兩次，由於珍妮佛夾在你跟我之間，我們必須小心行事。所以我的建議是我先把它搶過來，藏好，然後我會再很快地轉換話題讓她分心到別的東西上面去。珍妮佛不是喜歡花嗎？

Chi Yeah, she does.

對呀！

Paul We should point out Gill's flower vase. Talk about how nice it would look on her desk at work. If she takes the bait, you are in the clear.

我們應該指出蓋爾的花瓶。談論那個花瓶要是擺在她的辦公桌上會有多好看。如果她上鉤，妳就沒什麼好擔心的了。

Chi Let's do it!

就這麼做吧！

Paul's number is called, he confidently walks up to the pile of presents and whimsically tears open one of the boxes. Inside he finds a Hello Kitty waffle maker. He walks around the room showcasing the waffle maker to all the kids in the room who are squealing with delight with the prospects of stealing it when it is their turn. Paul then abruptly pivots around and makes a beeline for Mike.

保羅的號碼被叫到，他相當有自信地走向禮物堆並隨興而至地拆開其中一個箱子。裡面他發現了一個 Hello Kitty 的煎格子餅機。他繞著房間走，向所有的小朋友展示那個煎格子餅機，孩子們因期待著輪到自己時就能夠把它偷過來，都驚喜尖叫著。保羅接下來突然轉身直線走向麥可。

Paul Excuse me Michael, I believe you are holding my gift.

不好意思，麥可，我認為你拿的是我的禮物。

Mike That's not cool, man!

太差勁了，老兄！

生活篇

信仰篇 — 表達篇 — 外來語篇 — 文明篇 — 其它篇

	Mike is reluctant, however he begrudgingly hands it over. While the crowd is distracted Paul quickly hides the gift.	麥可雖不情願,但是還是勉強地把禮物交出。趁著群眾的注意力被分散時,保羅很快把禮物藏起來。
Jennifer	Paul, what is it that you stole from Mike?	保羅,你從麥可那邊偷了什麼?
Paul	Eh, it's nothing. I did that just to <u>mess with him</u>. I saw you were checking out Gill's flower vase. You should go and get it, it would look very nice in your office.	呃,沒什麼。我只是想作弄他一下。我看到妳在打量蓋爾的花瓶。妳應該去把它拿過來,它擺在妳的辦公室裡會很好看。
Jennifer	Actually I was thinking about putting that vase in my dining room! Sorry, Gill, say goodbye to the vase. Bye-bye vase.	事實上我是想把那個花瓶放在我的飯廳裡。抱歉,蓋爾,請跟花瓶說再見。再見囉!花瓶。
	Picking up a gift from the pile, Jennifer hands it to Gill without even opening it.	珍妮佛從禮物堆裡挑了一個禮物,連開都沒開就拿給蓋爾。
Chi	I can't believe you <u>pulled it off</u>.	我真不敢相信你居然成功了。
Paul	You are welcome!	保羅:不客氣!

 單字

☑ ergo [`ɝgo] *adv.* 所以;由是;因此	☑ snatch [snætʃ] *v.* 搶奪;攫取
☑ whimsically [`hwɪmzɪk!ɪ] *adv.* 突發奇想地;隨興而至地	☑ waffle [`wɑf!] *n.* 有格子花紋的早餐餅
☑ showcase [`ʃo͵kes] *v.* 展示	☑ squeal [skwil] *v.* 尖叫

生活篇

信仰篇

表達篇

外來語篇

文明篇

其它篇

☑ pivot [ˋpɪvət] **v.** 旋轉　　　☑ beeline [ˋbiˋlaɪn] **n.** 直線

☑ begrudgingly [bɪˋgrʌdʒɪŋlɪ] **adv.** 很不情願地；勉強地

諺語

☑ One man's trash is another man's treasure.
　某人的垃圾可能是另一人的寶物。

片語

☑ in the clear （在通過某個困難的情況後終於）安全了、沒有問題了
☑ mess with someone 故意捉弄別人
☑ pull it off 成功地達成某項困難、本來被認為不可能的任務

美國人的遊戲之一：White Elephant

　　不曉得你有沒有在聖誕派對上玩過 white elephant 呢？而白象禮物這個遊戲的名稱又是怎麼來的？十九世紀中，一位暹羅(Siam, 今泰國)國王由於不是很喜歡他手下的一個使臣，便送給他一隻白象。白象象徵神聖、權力，尊貴又美麗，外表看上去是件很棒的禮物，但是飼養白象的成本龐大，象除了吃喝拉撒外，本身其實沒有什麼實用價值，終究將其飼主的財產耗盡，國王達到他剷除異己的目的。

　　今天，white elephant 這句英文的意思就是：某個東西，保養的花費龐大，超越了它本身合理的價值，持有人想要丟又丟不掉，變成是一件累贅的負擔。

　　那麼，white elephant 的遊戲要怎麼玩呢？首先，這個遊戲要越多人越好玩，所有的禮物都要包裝好，裡面的內容除了送出禮物的本人以外沒有其他人知道；每個人按人數抽一個號碼，抽到一號的人先從禮物堆裡選一個禮物；抽到二號的人，從禮物堆裡拿另一個禮物，在打開禮物之後，他可以選擇是否保留那個禮物，如果他不想要保留，他可以去「偷」一號持有的禮物，若是二號決定搶一號的禮物，一號就必須跟二號交換禮物。三號上場，也是先從禮物堆裡拿一個禮物，禮物內容揭曉後，他可以選擇保留禮物，或是偷一號或二號的禮物…，以此類推，所以說抽到數字號碼的人選擇最多。你一開始拿到的禮物，不一定就是你絕對會擁有的禮物，因為別人如果喜歡你的東西，人家很可能就會來偷。常見的情況就是大家都爭著要最好的禮物，然後最後留在你手中的，就是沒有人想要的那一件。

Barbara	Our objective today is to visit every house on Main street. Don't forget to give out the coupons I gave you and fill out as many new account applications as possible. Let's head out to my minivan!	我們今天的目標是拜訪主街上的每一間房子。我給你們的禮券別忘記要發出去，新帳戶申請表要填越多越好。大家現在往我的廂型車出發！
Vicky	Shotgun!	獵槍！
Chi	What's that?	那是什麼？
Vicky	It means I get to ride in the passenger seat.	意思是我可以坐駕駛旁邊的座位。
Chi	Why?	為什麼？
Barbara	When someone in the group shouts out "Shotgun" before anyone else he or she is claiming the privilege of sitting in the passenger seat.	當團體中有一人最先喊出「獵槍」時，他或她就是在要求坐在前方乘客座位的特權。
Vicky	No one really wants to sit in the back. The passenger seat has more room, is more comfortable and is usually where the center of social engagement resides.	沒人真的想坐在車子後座。駕駛旁邊的座位空間比較大，坐起來比較舒服，而且這裡通常是社交活動的中心。
Chi	Why is the word "shotgun"?	為什麼要用「獵槍」這個字呢？

Barbara It actually dates back to the Western era. Well-to-do passengers would book passage in stagecoaches when traveling between towns or to the nearest railroad station. High and on the outside of the stagecoach was a bench where the driver rode. Another person would sit to his right. That person would have a shotgun. His job was to look out on the horizon for any potential sneak attacks from bandits while the driver tended to the horses. During that time stagecoaches were known to deliver mail and carry other valuables such as gold. Therefore, the position next to the driver was an important and well-paid job. Competing cowboys eager to find work would call out "shotgun" if they wanted to make the trek.

Vicky When I was little, on Sunday mornings my sister and I would compete for the passenger seat for the ride to the theme park. It had gotten so bad she and I sometimes would wake up calling "Shotgun."

Chi That's funny! What's a stagecoach?

Barbara It is basically a box on wheels pulled by horses. On the side there is a door to get in and a step to get up. Inside there are

它實際上要溯源至西部拓荒時期。那時富裕的乘客會搭乘驛馬車在城鎮之間旅行，或用以抵達最近的鐵路車站。在驛馬車外頭、架得高高的是一張給駕駛坐的凳子。另外有一個人會坐在他的右邊。那個人會持有一把獵槍。他的工作是在駕駛專心騎馬的同時，環顧地平線四周，提防任何可能來自強盜的偷襲。在那個時期驛馬車以遞送郵件與載運其他貴重物品如黃金而著名。因此坐在駕駛旁的位置是一個重要且報酬優渥的工作。牛仔們會相競地喊叫「獵槍」以希望獲取長途旅行的工作機會。

我小時候，星期天早上家人會開車去主題樂園，我妹妹和我會搶駕駛座旁邊的座位。情況嚴重到，有時候她跟我會一邊醒來一邊喊「獵槍」。

好好笑喔！驛馬車是什麼樣子啊？

它基本上是一個架在輪子上被馬拉著的箱子。旁邊有門讓人進入，有步階供攀爬。

生活篇

信仰篇

表達篇

外來語篇

文明篇

其它篇

padded seats and curtain covered windows for privacy. On the back there is a luggage rack. It is called a "stage" coach because horses were traded out for others at stages or way stations for coaches going on long journeys. A practice picked up during the days of the pony express mail delivery system. Eventually the way stations were converted to gas stations after the car began to become popular. Calling out "shotgun" was then passed on through to car culture. In some sci-fi shows you will even hear characters call out "shotgun" for the passenger seat in the shuttlecraft. So I imagine that this phrase will continue to be with us for some time.

裡面附墊椅，以簾遮蓋的窗戶提供乘客隱私。後面還有一個行李架。被稱為「驛」馬車的原因是，馬車必須在驛站或中途站交換疲憊的馬兒，以繼續漫長的旅行。這是從小馬快遞時代中學來的方法。在汽車開始流行後，最終所有的中繼站都被改建成加油站。喊「獵槍」的習俗便流傳到汽車文化中。在有些科幻電視節目裡，妳甚至會聽到劇中角色為爭奪太空梭駕駛旁的乘客座而大喊「獵槍」。所以我可以想像這個用語還會繼續流行一陣子。

 # 單字

☑ **well-to-do** *adj.* 經濟地位較一般人高的；富裕的	☑ **sneak attack** [`snik ə`tæk] 偷襲
☑ **bandit** [`bændɪt] *n.* 強盜	☑ **trek** [trɛk] *n.* 長途艱苦的旅行
☑ **theme park** [`θim `pɑrk] *n.* 主題樂園	☑ **stage** [stedʒ] *n.* 驛馬停留的站所；驛站
☑ **way station** [we`steʃən] *n.* 在主要大站間的中途站	☑ **pony express** [`poni ɪk`sprɛs] *n.* 小馬快遞。在 1860-1861 間曾短暫運作，從密蘇里州到加州以快馬接力的郵遞服務。
☑ **sci-fi** [`saɪ`faɪ] *adj.* 科幻小說的（science fiction 的簡寫）	☑ **shuttlecraft** [`ʃʌt! `kræft] *n.* 往返於兩個定點的太空梭

美國人的遊戲之二：Calling Shotgun

新分行下個月就要開幕，這幾個禮拜來辦公室裡的所有員工，全都馬不停蹄地沿街拜訪、告知鄰近的居民我們銀行終於要開張的好消息。某一天早晨，就在分行經理、業務、我、以及另一位出納小姐開始往停車場的方向走去時，漂亮的出納妹突然喊出一句："Shotgun!"

出納妹妹理直氣壯地坐上前座。你知道這是為什麼嗎？

Calling shotgun 是一種流行於美國人之間的遊戲，如果預定要共乘一車的同伴中，有人頭先喊了 shotgun 這個字，那個人就可以坐在駕駛座旁的那個位子（He／She gets to ride shotgun）。

Shotgun＝駕駛旁邊的乘客座位，這之間的聯繫源於早期西部括荒時期，當時用做主要交通工具的有篷馬車（stagecoach）前面有兩個座椅，一個是給控制馬韁繩的駕駛，另一個就是給在駕駛旁，握緊了槍，保護馬車上乘客或貴重物品，準備射擊可能來襲搶匪的那個人來坐。

所以，下次在聽到同行夥伴喊 shotgun 的時候別再一頭霧水，那表示有人要跟你搶前面的座位！

生活篇

信仰篇

表達篇

外來語篇

文明篇

其它篇

03 美國人的遊戲 [Games]

⑩ Raspberry

Paul and Chi are having lunch at a restaurant. A little girl is peeking over the seat into their booth with curiosity.
保羅和季薇在一家餐廳吃午飯。有個小女孩好奇地從她的座位上偷瞄著他們的隔間。

Paul's head tips up and he makes a funny face at the girl. The girl looks at him with increasing interest and began to mimic his movements.
保羅斜斜抬起頭，並對小女孩做鬼臉。女孩看著他，興趣越加高昂，並開始模仿他的動作。

Chi	I think she likes you.	我覺得她喜歡你。
Paul	(Blows a raspberry.) Pffftt!	（作了個覆盆子的口勢）噗噗噗！
Girl	(Giggling) Pfft.	（咯咯笑）噗。
Paul	Pfffffffffftttt.	噗噗噗噗噗噗～
Girl	Pfffffffffftttt.	噗噗噗噗噗噗～
Chi	What are you two doing?	你們兩個在做什麼？
Paul	I am showing her how to do raspberries. I think she's got it.	我在向她展示怎麼做覆盆子。我想她懂了。
Chi	Raspberry? What's that?	覆盆子？那是什麼？
Paul	A raspberry is when you stick your tongue out and blow so it makes a vibrating noise. It is viewed as childish and is used to tease, make fun of others, or mock	覆盆子就是把妳的舌頭向外吐，並吹氣發出振動的噪音。它被視為一種幼稚的行為，用來調戲、取笑別人，

someone or something. However, when used playfully it is viewed as harmless jest or playfulness between friends.

或模仿捉弄某個人或某件事。但是，如果以幽默的方式來使用，它被視為無害的玩笑，或朋友之間好玩的互動。

Chi I do recall seeing your grandma do it once. She was talking about a situation she didn't like.

我的確記得你祖母做過一次覆盆子。她在談論某個她不喜歡的情況。

Paul Exactly. In that moment she was sharing with me her displeasure for a rude teenager she bumped into at the grocery store.

的確如此。那時祖母正在告訴我，她在超市裡遇到某個粗魯的青少年，她很不高興。

Chi Isn't there an award that has something to do with raspberries in the film industry?

電影業界是不是有個跟覆盆子有關的獎項？

Paul Yes. It's called the Razzies. The award is given to the worst big-budget-high-profile movies and performances of the year. Fans and professional critics alike are essentially giving a metaphorical Pfffffttt or raspberry to films not quite making the grade. By the way Sandra Bullock is the only actress who has received both an Oscar and a Razzie in the same year and actually showed up to both ceremonies in earnest recognition for her work.

是的。那叫金酸莓獎。這個獎項是頒給年度最糟糕的大製作成本、高知名度的電影和演員的表現。影迷與專業影評基本上是在對那些沒能達到預期水準的電影作意象上的噓聲或吹覆盆子。喔！對了，珊卓·布拉克是唯一在同年獲得奧斯卡和金酸莓獎的演員，她在這兩個典禮上都親自出席，認真地接受自己的工作結果。

Chi Really? She must have a good sense of humor in order to do that. However, I don't think that cute little girl's mother

真的啊？她一定幽默感超好的才能那麼做。回過頭來說，我不認為那個可愛小女

生活篇 信仰篇 表達篇 外來語篇 文明篇 其它篇

51

appreciates you teaching her daughter how to blow raspberries.

生的母親會感謝你教她女兒怎麼做覆盆莓。

Paul　Oh well... sorry mom!

噢…對不起了，媽媽！

 ## 單字

☑ booth [buθ] **n.** 餐廳的雅座、小隔間

☑ tip up [`tɪp`ʌp] **v.** 往一邊傾斜並抬起

☑ jest [dʒɛst] **n.** 玩笑；俏皮話

☑ displeasure [dɪs`plɛʒɚ] **n.** 不滿意；嫌惡

☑ bump into [`bʌmp`ɪntu] **v.** 意外碰到；遇見

☑ grocery store [`grosərɪ `stor] **n.** 販賣生鮮雜貨的超市

☑ high-profile [`haɪ`profaɪl] **adj.** 知名度高的

☑ metaphorical [ˌmɛtə`forɪk!] **adj.** 隱喻的；意象上的

☑ earnest [`ɝnɪst] **adj.** 真摯的；認真的

 ## 片語

☑ make the grade 達到預期的標準；通過，合格

 ## 美國人的遊戲之三：Raspberry

　　Raspberry 的中文是「覆盆子」，是一種淺紅色的小型莓果，酸甜，口感中有股獨特的芳香，常作成果醬、調製飲料（譬如加到檸檬汁裡）或裝飾甜點用。

　　但是當有人對你作一個 "raspberry" 時，他／她是在幹嘛呢？而這個舉動的意思又是什麼呢？

　　首先，讓我解釋要如何做 raspberry：把舌頭吐出來，舌尖向下、並往內頂住下唇，然後吹氣，這時候你應該會聽到一連串類似放屁的聲音。哇哈哈，你做了個 raspberry！

　　美國人吹 raspberry 的用意，是在表示對某人或某件事的不滿。好萊塢影圈內人人避之唯恐不及的「金酸莓獎」（Golden Raspberry Award），正是取用這種口勢，來作為獎項的名稱，以嘲笑那些被認為拍得很糟糕的電影。

　　至於為什麼覆盆子這個水果的名字，會跟人們做出屁聲的輕蔑舉動有關係呢？原來是因為 "raspberry tart"（覆盆子是酸的）與 "fart"（屁）押韻的關係。過去英國人由於不想在公眾場中使用像「放屁」這類低級的字眼，便發明了利用其他押相同韻的字，來代替真正的字彙的掩飾方法，於是 raspberry 就變成了 fart 的替代品。

　　用「放屁」來表達討厭的感受，似乎是跨越文化的一種普遍現象，我們中文裡也有「某某人說的話都像是在放屁」或「一堆屁話」等類似用語。英語系國家的人民作 raspberry 就是在模擬放屁的聲音，當然，這種由人體內自然發出的聲音也是一種幽默、趣味的象徵，從古至今跟放屁有關的笑話數也數不清！

　　搭配 raspberry 的動詞通常是 blow 或 give，例如：The kid is blowing a raspberry at you！或 She gave him a raspberry。在做 raspberry 的時候，有些人也會搭配手勢來加強意思，譬如比大拇指朝下。

生活篇

信仰篇

表達篇

外來語篇

文明篇

其它篇

53

03 美國人的遊戲 [Games]

11 Roshambo

Chi Do you know the game of Roshambo?

你知道剪刀石頭布這個遊戲嗎？

Paul What about it?

怎麼樣？

Chi Is there any strategy I could use to increase my odds of winning?

有沒有什麼策略我可以用來提高獲勝的機率？

Paul Although the game's premise stipulates a sense of randomness, this would be an illusion. People typically think and act in patterns even when they are attempting to be arbitrary. Unique psychological behaviors can emerge unconsciously. For example, men have the tendency to throw rock first. Rock is considered a strong masculine gesture and men usually do not wish to be viewed as weak or vulnerable. In this case, the Chinese adage "a warrior's greatest strength is also his greatest weakness" would be befitting here. If you are aware of your opponents' personality characteristics, it will take little effort to dispatch of them knowing how they will strike in their opening approach. Thus, taking into counsel the famous strategy of know thy enemy.

雖然這個遊戲的前提給人一種隨機感，但其實那是一個幻覺。一般來說人們都是遵循模式來思考和行動，甚至當他們想不按牌理出牌的時候也一樣。特殊的心理學行為可能會不自覺地出現。舉例來說，男人傾向先出石頭。石頭被視為一種強壯、雄性的手勢，而男人通常不希望被看作軟弱或容易受傷。以這個例子來說，中國古諺有云，一名武士最厲害的地方也是他最大的弱點，用在這裡相當貼切。如果你曉得你對手的人格特徵，知道他們一開始會用什麼招數，你就只需花極少的力氣很快地把他們解決掉。因此你應聽取著名的策略忠告「知己知彼」。

Chi　How about women?

Paul　Women are a bit more difficult to decipher due to their empathic tendencies. They anticipate others' actions and act accordingly. While men will take a direct approach to victory, women will take a more subtle and intuitive path. For example, a woman who is facing a "strength" projecting male will tend to throw paper, because she strongly believes he will throw rock. In doing this, the single-minded man defeats himself.

Chi　I read online where a website says if someone feels confident, or thinks he is smarter than anyone else in the room, that person is likely to throw scissors.

Paul　True. If a man thinks the woman believes that he is going to throw rock then she will throw paper. Knowing this, he will throw scissors.

Chi　Okay. Anything else?

Paul　The last layer to this thought process is in throwing a rock to someone who you think has over analyzed the situation and is likely to throw scissors. Smart players are

那女人呢？

由於女人富有同理心的傾向，她們稍微比較難破解。她們會根據預測別人的行為，以決定自己接下來怎麼做。當男人用直接的方法去獲得勝利，女人則採取較微妙且直覺的路徑。舉例，當面對一名發出「力量」訊息的男人時，女性會傾向出布，因為她強烈地認為他會出石頭。這麼做的結果是這位想法單純的男子自己被自己打敗。

我在網路上讀到有個網站說，如果某人覺得很有自信，或認為自己比別人都聰明，那這個人很可能會出剪刀。

正確。如果某個男人認為女性的對手相信他會出石頭，所以她會出布。知道了這一點，他會出剪刀。

好。還有其他的嗎？

這個思考程序的最後一層是，向某個你認為過分解析情況、並可能出剪刀的人出石頭。聰明的玩家常常被石

生活篇

信仰篇

表達篇

外來語篇

文明篇

其它篇

frequently defeated by the rock because they over anticipate. These are the basic thoughts on the psychology of the first throw.

頭打敗，因為他們作太多預測。這是分析第一拳的心理學的一些基本想法。

Chi　All right there, smarty pants. Let's play!

好啦！你最聰明啦！我們來猜拳！

 單字

☑ stipulate [ˋstɪpjəˌlet] **v.** 載明；點出	☑ arbitrary [ˋɑrbəˌtrɛrɪ] **adj.** 任意的；無規則可循的
☑ adage [ˋædɪdʒ] **n.** 古諺	☑ befitting [bɪˋfɪtɪŋ] **adj.** 適當的
☑ dispatch [dɪˋspætʃ] **v.** 迅速處理；快速解決	☑ counsel [ˋkaʊns!] **n.** 忠告；勸告
☑ decipher [dɪˋsaɪfɚ] **v.** 破解（密碼等）	☑ empathic [ɛmˋpæθɪk] **adj.** 易感的；有同理心的
☑ tendency [ˋtɛndənsɪ] **n.** 傾向	☑ smarty pants [ˋsmɑrtɪˋpænts] **n.** 愛賣弄學問的人

 名句

☑ Know thy self, know thy enemy. A thousand battles, a thousand victories. —Sun Tzu
　知己知彼，百戰百勝。—孫子

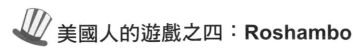

美國人的遊戲之四：Roshambo

Roshambo，就是我們熟知的猜拳遊戲「剪刀、石頭、布」，美國人也叫它 "rock-paper-scissors."（註一）（註二）

這個遊戲起源於中國，後來傳到日本。日本人稱它為 Jan-ken-pon，後來西方人從日本人身上學到這種遊戲時，便將之翻譯為 roshambo。

在美國玩的 roshambo 跟我們有點不一樣，在臺灣大家通常用一隻手來猜拳，而且喊：剪刀、石頭、布，在叫到最後一個字「布」的時候出拳，總共三個節拍；然而多半的美國人，則是用四個節拍來划拳，作法是這樣的：將一隻手—通常是左手—攤開，右手握拳並輕敲著張開的左手心，一邊唸 ro-sham-bo 或 rock-paper-scissors 的三個音節或字，一邊隨著韻律敲掌，然後在第四拍，喊 "Go!" 或 "Shoot!" 並以右手出拳。

Roshambo 這個字當名詞用的時候，英文可以說 "Let's play roshambo." 作動詞時，人們最常講的一句是 "I will roshambo you for it!" 意思是「我就跟你猜拳決定！」句中的 it 即是要決定的事情或贏的人會得到的目標物。

最近 roshambo 在美國青少年間突然變成了另一種淘氣的遊戲！原因是卡通《南方四賤客》（South Park）某一集中，阿ㄆㄧㄚˇ（Eric Cartman）把 roshambo 詮釋成兩個人互相踢對方的下體，直到一方倒地，另一方就勝利的遊戲。所以呀！如果有人要跟你 "roshambo"，最好觀察他的手勢跟動作，若是看到他握拳擊掌，那你就可以安心，接下來要玩的是正常的剪刀石頭布；如果情況不對勁，哇！就慘了…

註一 美國人講 "rock-paper-scissors" 對我們而言有點難記，第一他們說「紙（paper）」而不是「布」，第二，三個物品的順序也被調換了。我自己發明了個記憶的方法：rock, paper, scissors 三個單字的開頭字母分別為 R、P、S，所以（這三個東西）是 are（R），寫信時信末附上的是附註（P. S.）。這個訣竅對你有沒有幫助呢？

註二 在臺灣另一種常聽到的版本為 "paper-scissors-stone."

04 人名 [Names]

⑫ Thank You, Captain Obvious.

Paul and Chi are getting ready for a Halloween party.
保羅和季薇正為參加萬聖節派對打扮準備。

Chi	Oh, my, God.	我、的、天。
Paul	Do you like my costume?	妳喜歡我的裝扮嗎？
Chi	You... look like a superhero.	你…你看起來像個超級英雄。
Paul	(Tightens his gloves.) I AM a superhero.	（扯緊他的手套）我是個超級英雄。
Chi	But, who are you? If you are Superman, shouldn't there be a "S" on your chest? What does the letter "O" stand for?	但你是誰啊？如果你是超人的話，你胸部上不是應該有個「S」嗎？那個字母「O」代表的是什麼？
Paul	"O" stands for "obvious," OBVIOUSLY. Tonight I am going out as my alter ego CAPTAIN OBVIOUS! (Poses boldly looking to the right and skyward.)	「O」代表的是「明顯」的英文 obvious——明顯的。今晚我將以我的另一個分身「超級明顯隊長」出發！（擺出勇敢無畏的姿態，往右上方望去。）
Chi	Captain Obvious?	超級明顯隊長？
Paul	Yes, Captain Obvious. He will help point out the obvious in every situation. (Points index finger at Chi.) No rhetorical question... is... too... small!	是的，超級明顯隊長。他將幫你指出任何情況裡十分明顯的事實。（以食指指著季薇）所有原本不期待得到回答的問題，都將…得到…解答！
Chi	Geez. I didn't realize such a character existed. How do I look?	老天。我不知道原來有這樣一個角色存在。我看來怎麼樣？

Paul	Fat.	很胖。
Chi	I meant my costume. Who am I Captain?	我指我的裝扮。我是誰啊，隊長？
Paul	Chi.	季薇。
Chi	Who do I look like?	我看起來像誰？
Paul	A clone of every other Asian.	每兩個東方人其中之一的複製人。
Chi	What movie character do I look similar to when I wear these clothes?	當我穿上這種服裝時，我看起來像什麼電影角色？
Paul	Mmm... A hooded cloak and a light saber. Based on my excellent judgment, you are a Jedi!	嗯… 套頭的披肩斗篷和光劍。根據我精確的判斷，妳是一名絕地武士！
Chi	(Swinging her light saber.) No kidding, Captain Obvious.	（揮舞她的光劍）真不是蓋的啊，超級明顯隊長。
Paul	Anytime. Frivolous questions and benign observations beware, for tonight Captain Obvious is on the streets hunting you down.	隨時為您效命。瑣碎的問題和不痛不癢的觀察要小心了，今晚超級明顯隊長要讓你們無所遁形。
	Later at the party.	稍後在派對上
Mike	Hey, Paul. Hey, Chi. Great to see you! Chi you look nice in your Jedi costume.	嘿，保羅。嘿，季薇。很高興看到你們！季薇妳這身絕地武士的裝扮很好看。
Chi	Thanks, Mike. You look great as a...	謝謝，麥可。你的打扮也…
Paul	(Interrupting) HE'S A BANANA!	（插話）他打扮成一根香蕉！
Chi	Yeah, thanks.	噢，謝了。
Paul:	His costume is very "A-PEELING", don't you think?	他的外表很「好剝」，妳不覺得嗎？（作者按：「吸引人」的英文 appealing 與「剝皮」的 peeling 發音相近。）
Mike	Ohhhhhhh, I know who you are. I often wondered where Captain Obvious spent his evenings. Now I know.	噢噢噢，我知道你是誰了。我常好奇超級明顯隊長晚上都到哪裡去，現在我曉得了。
Paul	Captain Obvious can be only where he is.	超級明顯隊長只能在他在的地方。

生活篇

信仰篇

表達篇

外來語篇

文明篇

其它篇

Mike & Chi	Obviously.	麥可和季薇：明顯的。
Jennifer	Hey, you guys! Happy Halloween!	嘿，你們這幾個！萬聖節快樂！

Paul	She is female.	她是女的。
Chi	Captain Obvious rides again.	超級明顯隊長再次躍馬出征。

Jennifer	Guess who I am dressed as. (Jen plays with an old fashioned pipe and a large hand lens.)	猜猜看我扮的是誰。（珍玩弄著一支老式的煙斗與一只放大鏡。）
Paul	You are a detective.	妳是位偵探。
Chi	No shit "Sherlock"! (Turns to stare deeply into Paul's eyes.) Paul is going to get Chi a Mojito.	你不講我們還都不知道，「福爾摩斯」！（轉頭過去凝視保羅的雙眼）保羅要去幫季薇拿一杯萊姆薄荷調酒。

Paul	(In a trance) Paul is going to get Chi a mojito.	（恍惚出神狀）保羅要去幫季薇拿一杯萊姆薄荷調酒。
Chi	Paul will return quickly.	保羅一會兒就回來。
Paul	Paul will return quickly.	保羅一會兒就回來。
Chi	(Paul leaves.) Now that is what I call a Jedi mind trick.	（保羅轉身離開）這就是我所謂的絕地武士心智控制術。

Mike	So, where is Watson?	所以，你的華生醫生在哪裡？

Jennifer	She is meandering about the crowd. She's the one with the mustache.	她正往返於眾人間交際應酬。她就是跟大鬍子在聊天的那個。

Paul	I am back with Chi's mojito.	我帶季薇的萊姆薄荷酒回來了。

Chi	(Sweetly) Thank you, Captain Obvious. (Kisses Paul on the cheek.)	（甜蜜地）謝謝你，超級明顯隊長。（親保羅的臉頰）

單字

- ☑ alter ego [ˋɔltɚˋigo] *n.* （雙重性格中的）另一個自我、個性裡潛在的另一面

- ☑ boldly [ˋboldlɪ] *adv.* 無畏地、大膽地

- ☑ rhetorical question [rəˋtɔrɪkḷ ˋkwɛstʃən] *n.* 不期待得到回答的問題。問者以疑問的形式來強調其意圖（答案本身即已顯明），例如「誰知道呢？」（意指沒人會知道）

- ☑ frivolous [ˋfrɪvələs] *adj.* 瑣碎的

- ☑ benign [bɪˋnaɪn] *adj.* 溫和的、無害的

- ☑ mojito [moˋhito] *n.* 一種混和了蘭姆酒、萊姆果汁、薄荷葉、蔗糖、冰塊和蘇打水的雞尾酒

- ☑ trance [trɑns] *n.* 出神、精神恍惚

- ☑ meander [mɪˋændɚ] *v.* 漫步、曲折而行

人名之一：Thank You, Captain Obvious.

　　不知道你有沒有碰過以下這種情形：你和一群朋友在討論事情，辯論的過程間，其中有個人突然像發現寶藏了一樣，得意洋洋地為大家指出一件事實，但其實那回事是每個人早就知道，真的是非常淺顯、再也明白不過的東西，這個時候你知道你可以說什麼嗎？

　　你可以就說："Thank You, Captain Obvious!"

　　這句玩笑話也可以用 "No s**t, Sherlock!" 來替換，Sherlock 的全名是 Sherlock Holmes，也就是我們熟知的神探福爾摩斯（台灣只翻譯出他的姓 Holmes）。傳說這位大偵探對事物觀察入微，有過人的演繹能力，所以如果你想藉機諷刺某人，點出他不曉得在白目什麼的話，就可以尊稱他為英明蓋世的福爾摩斯！

　　"Thank you, Captain Obvious!" 這個流行語在網路、電視和電影等媒體的推波助瀾下，迅速在美國人之間流行起來，Caption Obvious 甚至有自己的漫畫和笑話網站。

　　你或許會問：要是不小心自己是那麼被取笑的目標怎麼辦？幽默的美國人當然要發展出與之對應的版本："You're welcome, Sergeant Sarcastic／Major Pain／General Jacka*s!" 準備好喔，對方可能在你反擊之後，再補上一句 "Nice one! Colonel Comeback."

生活篇

信仰篇

表達篇

外來語篇

文明篇

其它篇

13 Keeping Up with the Joneses

Paul and Chi are having dinner.　保羅和季薇在吃晚餐。

Chi	Barbara told me that her eleven-year-old daughter wants a phone.	芭芭拉告訴我她十一歲的女兒想要一支手機。

Paul　You know what I think?

猜猜我會怎麼說？

Paul & Chi (Simultaneously) ABSOLUTELY NOT!

（同時地）絕對不可以！

Chi　I told Barbara the same thing, but she thinks that her daughter has been good and she wants to reward her. The daughter also reasons that everybody in her class has one and it can be used in emergency situations. I said to Barbara that she should go old-school and get her daughter a pager.

我也是這麼跟芭芭拉講，但是她覺得女兒近來表現良好，而她想要獎勵她女兒。她女兒的理由是她班上的每個同學都有手機，而且它可以用在緊急的情況之中。我跟芭芭拉說她應該回歸傳統，給她女兒一只呼叫器。

Paul　Uh... no! Aside from that terrible suggestion, the idea that a kid needs a phone is ridiculous. As a teacher I abhor them. Unfortunately this overbearing, obstinate and demanding culture is creating a tsunami of jonesing, pushover, panic stricken parents. The best suggestion I have is to have phone companies come up with a special kind of "kid" phone that is only able to call family members, law enforcement, and

呃…還是不可以！除了這是個糟糕的建議之外，小孩子需要有手機的這種想法簡直是荒謬至極。身為一個老師，我痛恨學生帶手機。不幸的，這個蠻橫、固執及苛求的手機文化創造了一大群慾望無窮、耳根子軟且恐慌不安的家長。我認為最好的方案是電話公司推出一種特別的「兒童」手機，這些手

	emergency services. All other calls are blocked. A win-win for parents and teachers.	機只能打給家人、執法單位和緊急救援服務，其他通話一律禁止。這對家長與教師來說是雙贏的局面。
Chi	(Whines like a child.) But everybody else has one. (Pounds table.) I want one, I WANT one, I WANT ONE!	（模仿兒童抱怨）可是每個同學都有一支手機。（敲擊桌面）我也要一支，我要一支，我要一支！
Paul	Lame. She's ELEVEN. This is an excellent opportunity for parents to teach children that trying to keep up with the Joneses is never a good idea. Besides you know for a fact that phone is going to be used for everything but emergencies. Parents need to learn how to say "no" more often. Why do you tell me these stories? You know I hate weak-minded parents.	這招沒用啦。她才十一歲。這對家長來說是一個絕佳的機會，教育小孩如果看到瓊斯家有什麼自己就要有什麼是不對的。除此之外，你也很清楚事實上，那支手機永遠也不會被用在緊急情況中，全拿來做別的用途。家長要學習如何更常說「不」。妳為什麼要告訴我這些故事呢？妳知道我討厭意志薄弱的家長。
Chi	Sorry. Not to change the subject, but that phrase you used "keeping up with the Joneses," what does that mean?	抱歉，不是故意要移轉話題，但是你剛剛用的說法「看到瓊斯家有什麼自己就要有什麼」那是什麼意思啊？
Paul	It's an expression used to explain the nonsensical need to endlessly compete with and outdo your friends and neighbors. It goes back to the monkey	這個說法是用來解釋人們總是想跟朋友和鄰居競爭、甚而贏過他們的這種毫無意義的心理需求。它可以溯源至

part of the human brain. Primates socialize using a hierarchical structure. Dominance is usually established early and is mostly static or slow moving; however, in some groups where the hierarchy is less defined or willfully challenged then social advancement is possible. Opportunities to compete gives rise to "showcasing" behavior of either new skill sets, trophies, or the presentation of highly prized possessions in order to gain rank. Or in monkey talk "Ooo, ooo, shining new phone. Me special, you not."

人類頭腦中原始猿猴狀態的部份。靈長類動物使用階級式的架構進行社交。通常支配地位很早就建立完成，大部份的情況下不是保持不動的狀態就是移動得非常緩慢，但是當某些團體裡的階級界限開始模糊，或被故意地挑戰，那麼在階級中向上爬升的可能性就出現了。這些競爭機會鼓勵「公開展示」新技巧、戰利品，或眾人都想取得的物品以達到升級的目的。或者，用猴子的話講就是「喔、喔、閃亮的新手機。我特別，你不特別。」

Chi   Raising kids is not easy!

教育小孩不容易啊！

Paul   Whatever... (mumbles) First world problems.

隨你怎麼說啦…（低聲咕噥）都是先進國家人民日子過太好才有的問題。

 # 單字

☑ abhor [əb`hɔr] **v.** 憎恨、厭惡	☑ overbearing [ˋovɚˋbɛrɪŋ] **adj.** 專橫的、自大的
☑ obstinate [ˋɑbstənɪt] **adj.** 固執的	☑ tsunami [tsuˋnɑmɪ] **n.** 海嘯；比喻規模龐大及來勢洶洶的現象
☑ jones [dʒonz] **v.** 渴望	☑ pushover [ˋpʊʃˏovɚ] **n.** 沒主見、容易被影響或驅使做某事的人

☑ nonsensical [nɑn`sɛnsɪk!] **adj.** 無意義的　　☑ primate [`praɪmet] **n.** 靈長類動物

☑ first world problem **n.** 富裕先進國家人民所抱怨的瑣碎小事或生活中的不便。

🎩 人名之二：Keeping Up with the Joneses

　　Stuff、things、東西。每個人都有需要（needs）和想要的東西（wants）。Needs 是我們生活必需的物件：食物、保暖的衣服、居住睡覺的地方等；wants 是超過人類基本生存的慾望品：一杯三塊多美金的星巴客拿鐵咖啡、名家設計的衣飾及配件、海邊渡假小屋。

　　正因為人類無止盡的慾望，這個社會才會不斷被驅動而發展出更方便、更好用、以及更好看的商品，人們因此累積財富，所以我們不能小看 wants 的力量。但是呢，有時候，凡人如你和我，或許為了維持自己在外表上的地位、或許受到廣告推銷的影響、或許見到同儕，甚至是上司擁有的東西，自己心理羨慕也想要有，而像這樣的行為美國人會用一句概稱為：keeping up with the Joneses.（要跟瓊斯家有的一樣）

　　隔壁鄰居 Jones 家有最新的 3D 電視，我們也要去訂一台；Jones 家新裝衛星，電視頻道有六百多台，我家怎能只看一百台；前天 Jones 先生又買了一部 BMW 跑車，我們家就算要用銀行貸款也要換同等級的車… 原來家裡的電視不能看了嗎？真的需要看六百台的電視頻道嗎？原來的豐田汽車開的好好的，又為什麼要改呢？這一切行為，都是為了要 keeping up with the Joneses！

註 美國有一部收視率很高的真人秀（reality television）叫 "Keeping Up with the Kardashians"，全天拍攝時尚名人金・卡達夏（Kim Kardashian）和她一家人的活動，節目的名稱就是從這句話轉化而來的喔！

⑭ Jack and Jill

Paul is visiting Chi's aunt for the first time.   保羅初次拜訪季薇的阿姨。

Paul	What's your Aunt's name?	妳阿姨的名字是什麼？
Chi	Jill.	吉兒。
Paul	It would be hilarious if your Uncle's name is Jack.	如果妳姨丈叫傑克，那就好玩了。
Chi	Why?	為什麼？
Paul	You never heard of "Jack and Jill?"	妳沒聽過「傑克與吉兒」？
Chi	Uh-uh.	呃嗯。
Paul	Jack and Jill is a famous nursery rhyme. It goes like this: "Jack and Jill went up the hill to fetch a pail of water. Jack fell down and broke his crown and Jill came tumbling after."	傑克與吉兒是一首著名的童謠。它大概是這樣：「傑克與吉兒上山丘，去提一桶水。傑克跌倒並碰了傷頭，吉兒也跟著滾下山丘來。」
Chi	Why would you sing that to a child. That is awful.	為什麼會有人對小孩子唱這種歌。這歌的內容不好。
Paul	Naïve and dismissive children don't comprehend the context. The real message is encrypted metaphorically while the verse is sung with a pleasant and relaxing harmony.	天真無邪、對事情不在意的兒童不會了解歌詞的內容。當人們以和悅與輕鬆的平靜語調唱著詩歌時，真正的訊息則隱藏在譬喻之中。

Chi   Then what does it really mean?

那這首歌真正的意思是什麼？

Paul   Commoners of every generation always gossip about high-profile personalities. It is unavoidable. Before we had media celebrities, the people had royalty to mock and worship. The natural drama of the human experience eventually lead to creative artistic works, one of which were whimsical rhymes. The Jack and Jill rhyme in particular is said to represent the beheading of Louis the sixteenth of France and his queen Marie Antoinette during the French Revolution.

世代以來平民百姓總是愛聊名人的八卦。在我們有今天的媒體明星之前，過去的人則有皇室貴族供取笑和崇拜。人類經驗中自然而然的戲劇因子，最終造就了各種藝術創作，其中之一就是隨意所至的童謠。傑克與吉兒這首童謠，傳說是代表法國大革命期間路易十六世和皇后瑪麗被送上斷頭臺的史事。

Chi   Whoa!

哇！

Paul   I know, right? Anyways, as time passed, some verses were altered or added to what is still essentially viewed as a nonsensical rhyme. However, Shakespeare added his own interpretation to the classic, by claiming that Jack and Jill were a couple using any excuse they could think of to find some "privacy." After all, water is found at the bottom of hills not at the top.

很有意思對吧？不論如何，隨著時間人們對這首今天看來仍然沒什麼特殊意義的童謠，或作修改或增添新句。然而，莎士比亞加入了他自己對這個經典之作的個人詮釋，聲稱傑克與吉兒原來是對情侶，兩人找盡各種藉口以共度一些「私人」的時光；畢竟，水源出處是在山腳處而非山頂上。

Chi   Oooooooo!

唔唔唔唔唔！

Paul   No surprise there, Shakespeare's plays has always <u>capitalized on</u> sexy gossip. But to even take it a step further, in

那一點也不令人驚訝，莎翁的戲劇向來利用與性有關的話題以獲取票房利潤。但將

生活篇

信仰篇

表達篇

外來語篇

文明篇

其它篇

modern day humor, stand-up comedian Andrew Dice Clay modified the original as follows: (Impersonating Clay's attitude and rhythmic delivery.) Jack and Jill went up the hill... each with a buck and a quarter. (Brief pause in order to swiftly jerk the arm in an aggressive toke of a cigarette) Jill came down with two fifty. (Exhales smoke) "Ohhhhhh!"

這個想法更推進一步，以現代的幽默來詮釋，喜劇演員安德魯·代斯·克雷對原作做了以下的改變：（模仿克雷的態度與表演這則笑話的節奏。）傑克與吉兒上山丘⋯各帶了一塊兩毛五。（暫停，圓滑地揮動手臂猛吸一口煙。）吉兒下山來手裡共有兩元五角。（吐出煙）「噢噢噢！」

Chi   I don't get it. Why does Jack give Jill his money?

我不懂。為什麼傑克把他的錢給了吉兒？

Paul   Let's just say Jack came down with a BIG smile on his face.

我們點到為止就好：傑克下山的時候臉上掛著一個大大的微笑。

Chi   (Snickering) You are BAD!

（竊笑）你真邪惡。

Paul   What? Shakespeare did it first. Blame him.

幹嘛？莎士比亞是第一個搞鬼的人，要怪就怪他。

 單字

☑ **nursery** [`nɝsərɪ] *n.* 育兒室	☑ **rhyme** [raɪm] *n.* 詩、歌謠
☑ **dismissive** [dɪsˋmɪsɪv] *adj.* 輕視的、不在意的	☑ **verse** [vɝs] *n.* （集合用法／不可數）韻文；當可數名詞時，指「詩句」。
☑ **commoner** [`kɑmənɚ] *n.* 平民、庶民	☑ **impersonate** [ɪmˋpɝsn͵et] *v.* 模倣某人
☑ **toke** [tok] *n.* 從香煙或煙管吸入的一口氣	☑ **snicker** [`snɪkɚ] *v.* 吃吃地笑、竊笑

片語

☑ capitalize on something 利用某件事或某種情況，以為自身獲得利益。

日常會話

☑ Uh-uh. 表示「否定」、「沒有」。發音為[`ə,ə]。

人名之三：Jack and Jill

不曉得你有沒有注意過，傑克與吉兒（Jack and Jill）這一個男生和一個女生的名字經常連在一起？ 不論是流行的電視影集、電影、歌曲、甚至公司、餐廳的名稱，兩個人名都常同時出現… 你知道為什麼嗎？

除了 Jack 和 Jill 這兩個名字皆以字母 J 開頭，唸起來順口以外，它們之所以會被美國人大量在生活中連用，其實是由於這一首至少十八世紀開始就已流傳的童謠：

Jack and Jill went up the hill
To fetch a pail of water.
Jack fell down and broke his crown,
And Jill came tumbling after.

由於沒有固定的樂譜，大家都是用唸的，與其稱它為童謠或兒歌，或許用「童詩」去稱呼它還更貼切點。唸法是這樣子的：Jack and Jill（停頓）／went up the hill（停頓）／To fetch a pail of water（長停頓）／Jack fell down（停頓）／and broke his crown（停頓）／And Jill came tumbling after. 大聲唸出來以後，你就可以聽到，詩中的 Jill 和 hill，down 和 crown，以及 water 和 after 是押韻的。單字 pail（＝ bucket）是桶的意思，crown 在這邊是比喻「頭」的意思。

在這首詩裡面，Jack and Jill 的關係是兄妹（或姐弟），現代很多人則把 Jack and Jill 引申為情侶或夫妻。

生活篇

信仰篇

表達篇

外來語篇

文明篇

其它篇

⑮ John Doe

Paul and Chi are watching *CSI* on TV. A body is pulled out of cold storage.
保羅與季薇正在觀賞電視上播出的《CSI 犯罪現場》。一具屍體被推出冷藏庫。

Grissom All right. What do we got?	好了，現在我們手上有什麼資料？
Robbins Potential drowning. The lungs are filled with water, but it doesn't match where the body was dumped. I also found a British pound neatly folded inside the hem of his jacket with the numbers 16, 26, and 12 written on it.	這可能是一樁溺水的案件。肺部積滿了水，但水的成份與屍體被丟棄的地點不符。另外我發現在他外套褶縫裡有一張折得整整齊齊的英鎊紙鈔，上面寫有數字 16、26 和 12。
Willows A combination?	是一組密碼？
Grissom Possibly.	有可能。
Willows Positive ID?	身份確認了嗎？
Robbins Not yet; however, our John Doe does appear to have tickets to the Opera... tonight.	還沒，但是我們的約翰‧杜持有一張劇票…今晚演出。
Grissom Interesting. It seems like our international man of mystery is going to <u>be fashionably late.</u>	有意思。看來我們謎樣的國際人士這下要遲到了。

Robbins	Indeed.	的確。
	(Music soars–Who are you... who, who, who, who. I really want to know.)	（音樂響起—你是誰…誰、誰、誰、誰。我真的想知道。）
Chi	I thought they said they didn't know who he is. Why did they call him John Doe?	我以為他們說他們不知道那個人是誰。為什麼他們叫他約翰・杜？
Paul	John Doe is a temporary moniker used by criminal analyst to indicate that an unknown dead male requires further investigation into his identity. The name John Doe is used as a sign of respect. It demonstrates that the person who was harmed is human and was a real person. It is not just a dead body. If the unidentified body was female then she would have been labeled as Jane Doe. The media may also be court-ordered to use false names in the press while a trial or investigation is underway in order to protect the identity of witnesses or minors. However, those names are chosen randomly and are viewed as culturally neutral or "mainstream" so as to not indicate any identifiable characteristics that could be inferred otherwise such as race, age, education, ethnic, or cultural background.	約翰・杜是犯罪分析專家用的暫時姓名，以指出某個不明男性，其身份需要更進一步的調查確認。約翰・杜這個名字的使用，是一種尊敬的表徵。它說明這個曾被傷害的人是個真實、有血有肉的人，不只是一具死屍而已。如果這具身分不明的屍體是女性，那麼她就會被標示為珍・杜。當審判案件或司法調查正在進行中的時候，法院也可能會強制媒體在新聞報導間使用假名，以保護證人或未成年人。然而那些假名是隨機選擇的，並且必須是被視為文化中立或「主流」，以確保它們不會顯示出任何特徵，因而洩露出人種、年紀、教育程度、民族或文化背景等資料。
Chi	Oh, yeah. We have a similar concept in	哦！對耶。在中文裡也有類

Chinese. In scenarios where the identity of certain characters are interchangeable or unrelated to the story, we use pseudo names. Normally the first person who appears in the conversation is called "Mo Jia" and the second person "Mo Yi." The word "Mo" means "some" and "Jia" and "Yi" act like undistinguishable letters A and B.

似的概念。在當某些人物角色的身份可交互轉換，或跟故事情節沒有關係的情況裡，我們就用假名代替。通常在對話裡第一個出現的人叫「某甲」，第二個人「某乙」。「某」這個字的意思是「某些」，而「甲」、「乙」的作用就類似不具特殊意義的字母如 A 和 B。

Paul　Curious. However I would like to add that, John Doe and Jane Doe are names typically used for identifying "dead" bodies. Other code names and their corresponding backgrounds created by law enforcement are used to conduct undercover probes. The makings of a solid case could constitute a weekend sting on low-level warrants or of a deeper quest into long-term surveys chronicling the actions of syndicated organizations and its key members. Either way, the work is intense and requires professionalism throughout.

有意思。但是我要再補充一點，「約翰·杜」和「珍·杜」這兩個名字通常被用來表示「死人」。執法單位創造出來的代號假名及其背景資料，則用於臥底偵察行動。一件案子是否成立，其關鍵因素可能包括警察持低階搜索票進行的週末誘餌任務，或是更深入的追查，針對犯罪組織團體及其關鍵成員的行動所作的長期紀錄。不論哪一種，警方的工作都是高度緊張，並必須從頭至到尾保持專業態度的。

 ## 單字

☑ **hem** [hɛm] *n.*（布、衣服的）褶邊、邊緣反折並縫起來的部份	☑ **moniker** [ˋmɑnɪkɚ] *n.*（俚語）名字、綽號
☑ **infer** [ɪnˋfɝ] *v.* 推測	☑ **pseudo** [ˋsjudo] *adj.* 假的、偽造的

☑ the makings（注意用複數形）要素、組成的材料

☑ sting [stɪŋ] **n.** 由警方假扮顧客或佈誘餌以逮捕罪犯的程序

☑ chronicle [`krɑnɪk!] **v.**（長期性地）紀錄

☑ syndicate [`sɪndɪkɪt] **v.** 企業化、組織化

 ## 片語

☑ be fashionably late 參加（尤其是非正式的）聚會時，故意比預定開始的時間晚到。這種遲到的行為常用以顯示客人的地位、身份或格調。

 ## 人名之四：John Doe

誰是 John Doe？

John Doe 是一個假名，用來描述某個真實身分未知的男人，應用在情況像：法庭訴訟中為保護個人安全或隱私，於陳述或處理案例時，將原告的真名以 John Doe 替代（註）；或是醫院接到因意外導致失憶的病患，在登記入院時暫時使用的名稱；甚至警方在尋獲身分不明的屍體後，都可用 John Doe 貼上標籤。

John Doe 這個名字的來源，一般相信來自英王愛德華三世時期的一個「驅逐法令」（Acts of Ejectment）。驅逐法令是當時法庭用來解決土地所有權爭議的一條法律，法令裡把 John Doe 當作原地主的名字，而用 Richard Roe 來叫另一個也是自稱地主的人。

John 是一個非常普遍使用的名字，用來做假名，大家都沒有問題。那麼，為什麼姓要用 Doe 或 Roe 呢？有人解釋說，如果後面接的姓也像是 Smith 這種也很流行的姓氏，可能會導致與真人真名有關的誤會。Doe 英文的意思是母鹿，Roe 指一種歐洲種，體型較小的鹿，也許是因為是處理跟土地有關係的法律（鹿在土地上活動），也或許字短好發音，不管怎樣，當初寫法案的人就用了這兩個字作假的姓。

註 若是女人的假名的話，美國就使用 Jane Doe 或 Jane Roe。1973 年有一件相當轟動、並且影響日後司法及倫理學界深遠的墮胎案：Roe v. Wade，案名中的 Wade，代表的是德州達拉斯郡檢察官 Henry Wade，而其女性原告就使用了假名 Jane Roe！

16 Average Joe

Friday night. Paul, Mike, Chi and Jennifer are at Wild Buffalo Wings.
週五晚上。保羅、麥可、季薇和珍妮佛在水牛城雞翅酒吧。

Paul	Big-name supporters is helpful in maintaining a campaign's momentum, but it is not an all-inclusive ticket. In order to win a general election, the candidate needs to win the hearts and minds of the average Joe! Special interest groups can <u>cut both ways</u>.

獲得知名人物的支持，對於維持競選活動的氣勢確有幫助，但不能為成功打包票。要贏得大選，候選人必須贏得一般喬的心！特殊利益團體的介入有正面也有負面的影響。

Mike	True, true. But it is pretty clear that there is a huge advantage to being the incumbent. Winning a second term in office is easier than winning the first. Breaking through all the noise requires big-name supporters who invariably help challengers to reach the average Joe, which would be impossible otherwise.

是，是。但是很明顯的，現任者有極大的優勢，贏得第二次任期比贏得第一次的容易許多。在眾多的噪音中想要突顯出來，挑戰者需要知名人士的幫助以接觸到一般喬，否則根本是不可能。

Paul	Good point.

有道理。

Chi	Who is this "average Joe" you guys are talking about?

你們兩個在講的這個「一般喬」是誰啊？

Paul	It's a term used to refer to a typical person you might meet on any street in America. Remember the movie *Idiocracy*? The main

它是一個用語，指妳在美國的任何路上可能碰到的一個典型的平凡人。記得電影

character is the epitome of an average Joe: Average looks, average I.Q., average job, average pay. In other words, not underperforming, but not overperforming either. Dead center on the bell curve in every way, in every category. About 68% of the population fits into the first standard deviation.

《蠢蛋進化論》嗎？裡面的主角就是個一般喬典型的代表人物：一般長相、一般智商、一般職業、一般收入。換句話說，他的表現不是不好，但也不能說他表現優異。在每一點、每一個領域裡，剛好落在鐘形弧線的中間點上。大約百分之六十八的人口分佈在第一個標準差的範圍內。

Chi　Bell curve? Standard deviation?

鐘形弧線？標準差？

Jennifer　I've got this one! Say we test and record everyone's intelligence. While very few people would have an intelligence quotient over 150, it would also be true that very few people would reside below 50. Most people's I.Q.'s would fall somewhere between 80 and 120. 100 being defined as average. So if you were to graph these results, you would see a bell-shaped distribution on the chart. Someone who fits right under the peak of the bell curve, also called the top, is someone who is viewed as being completely ordinary. The first standard deviation of the bell curve represents what could be classified as middle-of-the-road "mainstream" America.

我知道這個！假設我們測驗並紀錄每個人的智力。當極少數的人擁有超過一百五十的智商時，同樣地極少數的人會有低於五十的智商。多數人的智商介於八十和一百二十。智商一百被定義為平均值。因此如果妳把這些結果製作成圖表，妳就會看到曲線圖上呈現出一種鐘鈴狀的分佈。恰好在鐘形弧線的尖端，也就是所謂的頂部上的那個人，被視為完全普通的一般人。在鐘形弧線上，距離平均值一個標準差範圍內的人口，可被分類為剛好在中間、主流的美國大眾。

生活篇　信仰篇　表達篇　外來語篇　文明篇　其它篇

Chi	So Americans call an average person an "average Joe." Any other synonyms for "average Joe?"	所以美國人稱呼某個平凡人為「一般喬」。「一般喬」有其他的同義字嗎？
Paul	Joe Schmoe, Joe Blow, man on the street, the common man...	喬‧席摩、喬‧布羅、路人、普通人…
Jennifer	Plain Jane for females.	如果是女的就叫「平凡珍」。
Mike	Uh huh and don't forget Joe Sixpack! (Raises his beer.) Cheers!	嗯哼，別忘了喬‧六罐裝！（舉起他的啤酒）乾杯！
Group	(All raises glasses.) Cheers!	（全部舉杯）乾杯！

 ## 單字

☑ **momentum** [moˋmɛntəm] *n.* 動能、氣勢

☑ **incumbent** [ɪnˋkʌmbənt] *n.* 現任者、在職者

☑ **epitome** [ɪˋpɪtəmɪ] *n.* 典型、代表

☑ **deviation** [ˌdivɪˋeʃən] *n.* 偏離、偏差

☑ **quotient** [ˋkwoʃənt] *n.* 商數、度數

☑ **middle-of-the-road** *adj.* 採取中道的、剛好處於中間，不偏向任何一邊極端的

☑ **synonym** [ˋsɪnəˌnɪm] *n.* 同義字

☑ **Joe Schmoe / Joe Blow** 一般、普通的人。Schmoe 發音為 [ʃmo]，美國俚語，指低等級、愚笨的人。這兩個名字中的 Schmoe 和 Blow 都跟 Joe 押韻，取諧音之故。

片語

☑ <u>cut both ways</u> 對正反兩方都有相等程度的影響

人名之五：Average Joe

繼上回的 John Doe（真實身分不明的男子假名）後，這次讓我們來看看另一個名字：Joe。Joe 是全名喬瑟夫 Joseph 的暱稱，由於這是一個相當普遍的男子名，美國人就用 "average Joe" 來稱呼一般平凡、大眾化的人。

大家對什麼樣的人是 average Joe 大概有種模糊的看法：一個面貌、身材中等，穿著普通，年紀差不多在二十五歲以上…是隨便走在路上都看得到的人。啊，說到走在路上的人，你也可以用一句話「man in（或 on）the street」來代表社會大眾，也就是任何人。

2008 年民主黨總統候選人歐巴馬在為競選宣傳的時候，有次在街上跟一個準備要買下一間維修水管公司的男子討論起歐巴馬提出的新課稅政策，這段對話在新聞上播出之後，立刻在各界媒體和黨派間掀起一股熱潮，那位以水管工為職業、敢說敢言的先生，因而聲名大噪，大家都稱呼他為 Joe the Plumber。"Joe the Plumber" 在那年總統大選的辯論中被多次提到，儼然成為一個象徵美國中產階級的代名詞。

最後再提到的是，嚴重睡眠不足的美國人每天眼睛一睜開就要喝的咖啡，綽號也叫 Joe，這種一般大眾化、極為流行的飲料，常常可見其包裝上印製著 A CUP O' JOE（＝a cup of Joe，美國人唸很快時，of 的 f 常被省略不發音）。

生活篇

信仰篇

表達篇

外來語篇

文明篇

其它篇

Mike is sitting at his desk with his face buried in his hands. He sighs deeply.
麥可坐在他的辦公桌後，臉埋在雙手中。他深深地歎著氣。

Chi	What's wrong? You don't look so good.	怎麼了？你看來不太好。
Mike	I feel trapped. I'm having a Groundhog Day. I'm bored. Everyday it's the same thing.	我有種被困住的感覺。我正在經驗土撥鼠節。我覺得無聊極了。每天都是一樣的事情。
Chi	Uh, "Groundhog Day?" What do you mean?	呃，「土撥鼠節」？你講的是什麼意思啊？
Mike	You've never seen the movie *Groundhog Day*? Bill Murray? It's a classic! Go watch it and you will know what I mean when I said I feel like I'm stuck in a Groundhog Day.	妳從來沒看過電影《今天暫時停止》？比爾‧莫瑞？那是一部經典的電影哪！去看，看過之後妳就會了解我說我覺得我被困在土撥鼠節那天裡的意思。

A week later at the employee break room. Mike and Chi are having lunch.
一週後麥可和季薇在員工休息室裡吃午餐。

Chi	Mike, I finally watched the movie *Groundhog Day*.	麥可，我終於看了那部電影《今天暫時停止》。
Mike	You did? How do you like the movie?	妳看了？妳覺得怎麼樣？

Chi	I enjoyed the movie immensely! I can't imagine waking up to the same day every day. That would <u>drive me nuts</u>.	觀賞那部電影真是一大享受！我無法想像每天醒來都是同一天。那會令我抓狂。
Mike	Did you notice that the main character has the same name as Phil the groundhog?	妳有沒有注意到男主角的名字跟土撥鼠的名字一模一樣？
Chi	Oh, yeah. Phil Connors, that's quite clever!	對喔。費爾·康納，真是巧妙的設計！
Mike	If you could choose a day to repeat over, which day of your life would you pick?	如果妳可以從妳生命中選擇某一天來重複，妳會選哪一天？
Chi	Mmm, that's a tough one. I think that I would probably choose the day I graduated from the high school. It was one of the happiest days in my life, but I wouldn't want it to stop there. I have so many things I want to do and I want to do all of them!	嗯，這個滿難的。我想我大概會挑我高中畢業的那天。那是我生命中最快樂的日子之一，但是我不想就停在那裡。我有好多想做的事，而我想統統都去做！
Mike	You are absolutely right. I need to do something to get out of this rut.	妳說的完全正確。我必須擺脫這乏味的規律生活。
Chi	What are you planning on doing?	你有什麼計畫嗎？
Mike	I have decided to make a few changes that could prove interesting.	我已經決定作一些有趣的改變。
Chi	Like what?	譬如說？
Mike	Remember what Phil did in the movie?	記得費爾在電影裡怎麼了？

生活篇

信仰篇

表達篇

外來語篇

文明篇

其它篇

79

| Chi | He went crazy and tried desperately to make each repeating day unique. | 他發神經，並且努力將重複的每一天都變成獨特的日子。 |

| Mike | Exactly! From now on every day I am going to do something unique in order to challenge my preconceived notions. To start, I am going to apply to that new training program that teaches you how to underwrite commercial real estate loans. I hear it has a robust schedule in place. Many people who start don't finish. If I can finish it will greatly enhance my repertoire. | 就像那樣子！從現在起，每天我都要做一件特別的事情，以挑戰我既有的概念。第一步，我要去申請一個新的訓練課程，這個課程教人如何針對商業不動產的貸款進行信用評估。我聽說它的課程表排得很滿很豐富。許多人參加了最後卻沒辦法畢業。如果我能唸完這個課程，相信這能大大增強我的履歷。 |

| Chi | <u>Sounds like a plan!</u> | 聽來是個可行的計畫！ |

 ## 單字

- ☑ **groundhog** [ˋɡraʊndˌhɑɡ] ***n.*** 土撥鼠，也叫做 woodchuck。

- ☑ **immensely** [ɪˋmɛnslɪ] ***adv.*** 非常；極

- ☑ **rut** [rʌt] ***n.*** 乏味的常規；慣例；常軌

- ☑ **preconceived** [ˌprɪkənˋsivd] ***adj.*** 預先形成的（想法或意見）

- ☑ **underwrite** [ˋʌndɚˌraɪt] ***v.*** （對保險或貸款等）進行信用評估

- ☑ **robust** [rəˋbʌst] ***adj.*** 強壯的；極具活力的

- ☑ **repertoire** [ˋrɛpɚˌtwɑr] ***n.*** 某人具有的所有技能、知識與經驗的總和

片語

☑ drive someone nuts 令某人發狂；使某人煩擾不安。"Nut" 這個字原來是一個俚語，指人的「頭」，後來衍伸出講人頭腦不正常的含意。

 日常會話

☑ Sounds like a plan. 「聽起來像個計畫！」美國人說這句話是在表示他／她聽到了你的計畫，有表示許可與鼓勵的含意。

 動物之一：Groundhog Day

二月二日是美國人的土撥鼠節。每年到了這一天，大批的民眾和電視台記者會湧進賓州（Pennsylvania）的一個小鎮，屏息等待大概是世界上除了米老鼠以外最有名的一隻大鼠—費爾（全名 Punxsutawney Phil，別被那落落長的第一個字給嚇到了！發音為 [pʌnksəˋtɔnɪˋfɪl]，Punxsutawney 是那個鎮的鎮名），預測當年的春季是否會提早到來。

1993 年，一部經典喜劇片 *Groundhog Day*（片名譯作《今天暫時停止》），由冷面笑匠比爾・墨瑞（Bill Murray）和女星安蒂・麥道威爾（Andie MacDowell）主演，為 Groundhog Day 這個名詞加入了一個新的意義：就像電影裡的劇情一樣，它形容一個人感覺每一天都在重複同樣的模式，類似法語 déjà vu 那樣，經驗彷彿似曾相遇，代表會有新發展的明天好像永遠也不會到來。所以，下次你聽到有美國人感嘆說：Oh, I feel like it's Groundhog Day! 或說他自己是 being caught in Groundhog's Day，請寄予他一個無限同情的眼光。由於某些個人無法掌控的因素，相同的問題不斷重複著，在解決方案尚未出現前，目前身陷在 Groundhog Day 裡的他只能坐困愁城、唉聲嘆氣呀！

生活篇

信仰篇

表達篇

外來語篇

文明篇

其它篇

Monday morning at the office.　星期一早上在辦公室裡。

| Daniel | Mike, these are the brochures for the new credit card. Would you give them to... Jennifer, please? | 麥可，這些是我們新信用卡的小冊子。麻煩你把它們拿給…珍妮佛，好嗎？ |

| Mike | Uh, okay. | 呃，好吧。 |

Mike takes the brochures to Jennifer's desk. They courteously exchange a few words. Then Mike returns to his desk while Jennifer absentmindedly looks at her computer screen.　麥可把手冊拿到珍妮佛的辦公桌。他們客氣地交談了幾句話。之後麥可回到自己的座位，珍妮佛則是心不在焉地看著她的電腦螢幕。

| Chi | Hey, how was bowling night on Saturday? I sorry I couldn't make it. | 嘿，上禮拜六晚上的保齡球夜好玩嗎？很抱歉我沒辦法跟。 |

| Daniel | You missed everything. After the game we went to the bar ... and uh ... | 妳錯過好康的啦！打完保齡球後，我們去酒吧…後來… |

| Chi | What? What happened? | 後來怎樣？發生什麼事了？ |

| Daniel | Well, Mike kissed Jennifer. | 麥可親了珍妮佛。 |

| Chi | WWWHHAAAAAT??? Well that explains it. It was weird at first, but I felt that for some reasons everyone was acting funny around those two. Now I know. Dating co- | 什什什麼麼麼？原來如此。起先我還覺得怪，感覺由於某種原因，每個人一到了這倆人的附近行為就變得怪異 |

workers is a taboo.

起來。現在我曉得了。跟同事約會是一大禁忌呀。

Daniel　That's the elephant in the room. No one wants to talk about it and everybody is <u>tiptoeing around the issue</u>.

那就是目前房間裡的大象啦！沒人想提起這件事，大家都小心翼翼地繞過話題不講。

Chi　Does Barbara know?

芭芭拉知道嗎？

Daniel　She's <u>bound to</u> find out sooner or later. As branch manager, I think she will have to have a talk with them. It's still early. It could turn out to be nothing.

她遲早一定會發現。身為分行經理，我認為她勢必得要跟他們坐下來談。現在時機尚早，這個事可能最後結果根本是小事一件。

Barbara steps out and waives Jennifer and Mike over to her office. She closes the door behind them.
芭芭拉走出來並把珍妮佛和麥可招到她的辦公室。她在他們身後將門關上。

Chi　Did you see that? What could they be talking about?

你看到了嗎？不知道他們在談什麼喔？

Daniel　Probably the code of ethics article in their contracts. There is nothing inherently wrong with dating co-workers, however it is usually <u>frowned upon</u> as a general rule. Many people find it difficult to emotionally separate their private and professional lives.

八成是他們契約裡有關員工倫理的條款。與公司同事約會本身沒有什麼錯，但是普遍來說通常是不被贊同的。很多人在情緒上難以區分私人與專業生活。

Chi　They are going to have to be careful.

他們必須要小心。

生活篇

信仰篇

表達篇

外來語篇

文明篇

其它篇

Daniel	I imagine that is exactly what she is pointing out. If they decide to develop a long-term relationship, it is their responsibility to always be professional. Public displays of affection at work will not be tolerated.	我可以想像那就是她正在指出的重點。如果他們決定要發展長期的關係，他們就有責任不論什麼時候都要保持專業的態度。在工作場合裡公開表示愛意是不會被容忍的。
Chi	What would happen if they broke up?	如果他們分手了呢？
Daniel	Private lives cannot interfere with work. If they lack the discipline necessary to uphold company standards, they could be separated between branches, departments, or even worst... fired. This could go bad quickly if not handled well.	個人私生活不能妨礙工作。要是他們欠缺必要的紀律，導致無法維持公司的標準，他們可能會被調到不同的分行、部門，或更慘的…被炒魷魚。如果不好好處理，這件事也許會快速惡化。
Chi	No wonder Barbara is being discreet. If you acknowledge the elephant in the room, the whole thing could <u>come crashing down</u>.	難怪芭芭拉謹慎行事。如果你挑明了房間裡有隻大象，這整件事很可能會全盤崩潰。
Daniel	Only time will tell which direction this "thing" is going to go.	只有時間可以告訴我們這個「事件」會如何發展。

 ## 單字

☑ bowling [ˋbolɪŋ] *n.* 保齡球運動

☑ funny [ˋfʌnɪ] *adj.* 美國人使用 "funny" 這個字，可以指「好笑的」或是「怪異的」，要視上下文來判斷，在這裡的意思為後者。

☑ article [ˋɑrtɪk!] *n.* 條款

生活篇

信仰篇

表達篇

外來語篇

文明篇

其它篇

☑ inherently [ɪnˋhɪrəntlɪ] **adv.** 與生俱來地；本來地

☑ uphold [ʌpˋhold] **v.** 維持

☑ discreet [dɪˋskrit] **adj.** 謹慎的；慎重的

 片語

☑ tiptoe around something 小心翼翼地迴避面對某件事情
☑ be bound to (do something) 一定；必然（會做某事）
☑ be frowned upon 不被贊成的
☑ come crashing down. 在極短的時間內瓦解；崩潰

 動物之二：**Elephant in the Room**

　　相信大家都聽過「國王的新衣」這個童話寓言，故事中的裁縫編稱只有聰明人才能看見新衣，國王由於不願承認自己的無知，赤裸走上街頭。而人們為了同樣的理由，個個縮頭不敢出聲，直到一個天真的小孩，看到光溜溜的他，大喊：「啊，國王沒有穿衣服！」

　　很多時候，人類因為心理上的膽怯、大眾鴕鳥心態，或是對某些社會禁忌的厭惡及避諱，不論問題如何迫切地急待解決，就算赤裸裸的擺在你面前，人們也裝作視而不見。美國人對這種情況有一句話來形容：Elephant in the room。在房間裡如果出現了一隻大象，不管你往哪個角度看，都很難去忽略牠的存在。這個用語意像鮮明地描繪出，某個十分明顯的問題，就像那隻佔據著房子一角的大象，人想不發現都困難；但是呢，為了某種因素大家都迴避不提。

　　什麼時候該指出房間裡的大象，也就是那個困擾著每個人，卻沒人敢點出的問題呢？這就要憑藉你的智慧了。當然，如果議題涉及別人的隱私，或硬是揪出來會造成惡意的攻擊，承認房間裡的大象不會是一個理性的作法；但是當你發現，這個問題若是不趕快處理，不但不會隨時間淡化，反而會造成更大的麻煩時，你也許就得要站出來當那個最有勇氣的人，大膽地指出房間裡的大象，平心靜氣地就事論事，讓其他人了解，只有把問題拿到台面上來討論，才是真正的解決之道！

Chi Today at work I heard someone was using an expression: "A leopard never changes its spots." May I ask you what that means?

今天上班的時候我聽到有人使用這個措辭:「豹子永遠也不會改變牠的花點」。可以請教你那是什麼意思嗎?

Paul Its general meaning is similar to a longer story called the scorpion and the fox.

它大體上的意思跟另外一個較長的故事叫「蠍子與狐狸」相近。

Chi Huh? More animals? What about the scorpion and the fox?

啥?更多動物? 蠍子與狐狸怎麼了?

Paul One day a scorpion was walking along the bank of the river, wondering how to get to the other side. Then he saw a fox. He asked the fox to take him on his back across the river. The fox said, "No. If I do that, you'll sting me and I'll drown." The scorpion assured him, "If I did that, we would both drown." The fox thought about it and finally agreed. So the scorpion climbed up on his back and the fox began to swim. But halfway across the river, the scorpion stung him. As the poison filled his veins, the fox turned to the scorpion and said, "Why did you do that? Now you'll drown, too." "I couldn't help it," said the scorpion. "It's in my nature." This parable is a warning that

一天,有隻蠍子沿著河岸邊走,不知如何達到河的另一邊。後來它看到一隻狐狸。它拜託狐狸背著它跨越這條河。狐狸說:「不,如果我那麼做,你會螫我而我會淹死。」蠍子跟牠保證說:「若是我那麼做,我們會同歸於盡。」狐狸想了想,最後終於同意。所以蠍子爬上牠的背,然後狐狸開始游泳。但是到了河的中間,蠍子螫了牠。當毒液充滿牠的血管時,狐狸轉頭對蠍子說:「你為什麼那樣做?現在你也要淹死了。」「我沒辦法啊,」蠍子說:「那是

espouses that most changes are superficial and that we typically cannot change the innate nature of who we are. The expression "A leopard never changes its spots" says the same thing, especially when it comes to a person's core characteristics.

我的本性。」這個寓言是一個警告，它主張大多數的改變僅是表面上的，一般而言，我們無法改變我們原來的天性。「豹子改變不了牠的花點」這個說法講的是一樣的東西，尤其像是個人的核心特質。

Chi So that's why Barbara said that a leopard never changes its spots...

所以那就是為什麼芭芭拉說豹子永遠也不會改變牠的花點⋯

Paul What happened?

發生什麼事了？

Chi Today we had this customer who came in the bank and complained about an overdraft fee charged to his account. This particular customer has a history of repeated overdrafts.

今天我們有位客戶到銀行來抱怨他帳戶裡的一筆透支罰款。這個客戶，特別是他呀，老是動不動就透支。

Paul Clearly this man's pattern of behavior exposed his true nature. Whatever the case may be he is someone who can't be trusted to properly keep track of his personal finances.

明顯地這個人的行為模式顯露出他的真正本性。不管在什麼情況下，你都不能相信他會好好地管理自己的個人財務。

Chi The customer asked our manager to refund his overdraft fees.

那個客戶要我們的經理退費。

Paul And did she do it?

那她退錢給他了嗎？

Chi She didn't. Instead she limited his ATM

沒有。但是她降低了他的提

生活篇

信仰篇

表達篇

外來語篇

文明篇

其它篇

87

withdrawal amounts and applied an overdraft line of credit.	款機領款金額上限，並幫他加了一個循環信用帳戶。
Paul Why wasn't this done earlier? Every account should have an overdraft line of credit.	為什麼這件事沒有早一點做?每個帳戶都應該連接一個預防透支的循環信用帳戶。
Chi The customer may have been offered that option but rejected it. We can't force customers to use the service. He probably didn't understand it when we did. Now that he finally sees the purpose of the line of credit, he is more willing to use it.	銀行可能過去曾經提供過他這個選擇但是他不想要。我們不能強迫客戶使用這項服務。我們在當初跟他提議時，他大概不了解它的用途和目的。現在他終於知道為什麼要有循環信用帳戶，他就比較願意去用它了。

 ## 單字

☑ **bank** [bæŋk] *n.* （河、湖的）岸	☑ **assure** [əˈʃʊr] *v.* 保證；擔保
☑ **parable** [ˈpærəbl] *n.* 寓言；比喻	☑ **espouse** [ɪˈspaʊs] *v.* 主張；支持…的論點
☑ **innate** [ɪnˈnet] *adj.* 天生的；本來既有的	☑ **overdraft** [ˈovəˌdræft] *n.* 透支
☑ **ATM** *n.* 提款機（Automated Teller Machine 的縮寫）	☑ **withdrawal** [wɪðˈdrɔəl] *n.* 提款；取款

☑ **line of credit** *n.* 循環信用帳戶；循環信用帳戶可連結至個人的支票帳戶，作為一種保護機制。當支票帳戶產生透支時，銀行可從循環信用帳戶中將透支的金額轉入支票帳戶，以避免跳票及罰款等情況發生。其費用包括付轉帳費及利息，有些銀行會附加年費。

動物之三：**A Leopard Never Changes Its Spots.**

中國人有句話說：江山易改，本性難移。這句話拿到美國來說，就是：A leopard never changes its spots.（豹子改變不了牠的花點。）

Leopard 這個字的發音有點狡猾，中間的 o 不發音，唸成[ˋlɛpɚd]。跟這句慣用語可以互換的是：A zebra never changes its stripes.（斑馬改變不了牠的條紋。）

1992 年，當時是田納西州參議員的 Al Gore（高爾，後來當選美國副總統，並於卸任後拍攝一部喚起大眾對環保覺醒的全球暖化紀錄片 *An Inconvenient Truth*，台灣譯為《不願面對的真相》）在大力抨擊小布希總統在環保政策上的言行不一時，曾不小心溜口而出 "A zebra does not change its spots [sic]."（斑馬改變不了牠的花點 [誤]），而淪為美國人茶餘飯後的笑柄。

A leopard never changes its spots. 這句話用於指責某人本性不改，無論其如何口口聲聲說自己已經改變、發誓會重新做人，事實證明卻是一而再，再而三地重蹈覆轍。

生活篇

信仰篇

表達篇

外來語篇

文明篇

其它篇

20 Bright-Eyed and Bushy-Tailed

It's 6:00 AM. Paul's grandfather awakens to the sound of clanking pots and pans from the kitchen. He follows the noise to its source.

凌晨六點。保羅的祖父被從廚房傳出的鍋子鏗鏘聲吵醒。他追蹤到噪音的來源。

Chi	Good morning, Grandpa. Sorry if I woke you, I just wanted to make breakfast for everyone.	早安，阿公。抱歉如果我吵醒你了，我只是想幫大家做早點。
Grandpa	MORNING. I see you are wide awake!	早啊。我看妳是大大地清醒哪！
Chi	"Wide" awake? I know that I am awake. But why do you say that I am "wide" awake?	「大大地」清醒？我知道我是醒著的，但是為什麼你說我是「大大地」清醒呢？
Grandpa	(Coughs) Geesh, how do I explain wide awake? It means you are bright-eyed and bushy-tailed. You get up in the morning and you are ready to go!	（咳嗽）哇，我要怎樣才能解釋大大地清醒呢？它的意思是妳眼睛閃亮尾巴濃密的。妳一大早爬起來就摩拳擦掌、躍躍欲試！
Chi	Uh, Gramp, I don't understand what "bright-eyed and bushy-tailed" means.	呃，阿公，我不懂「眼睛閃亮、尾巴濃密」的意思。
Grandpa	Well, it means...	嗯，它指的是...
Paul	What are you two talking about this early in the morning?	你們兩個人這麼早在講什麼東西啊？

Chi	Grandpa used a few expressions I don't quite understand. What does it mean that I am bright-eyed and bushy-tailed?	阿公用了幾個我不是很懂的形容詞。眼睛閃亮尾巴濃密的是什麼意思？
Paul	What happened? What was the context?	發生什麼事了？上下文是什麼？
	Paul turns to Grandpa who returns a knowingly look of helplessness in communicating an idea to Chi.	保羅轉向祖父，祖父回應他一個不知該如何跟季薇解釋的無助眼神。
Paul	Ok... In America we use idioms, slangs and experience-specific expressions all the time. Your English is too formal. It sounds like a child's school textbook. English is a living language deriving from its personal history. If you don't know it history you will have trouble understanding its linguistic constructs. With that being said, where is my breakfast? Don't forget the orange juice. I'm going back to bed. Tell me when it's ready.	好吧！在美國我們每天都在用慣用語、俚語，以及從經驗發展出來的措辭。妳的英文太正式了。聽起來像學校的教科書。英文是一種從它自身歷史衍生出的活生生語言。如果妳不知道它的歷史，妳會有困難去理解它的語言概念。說到這裡...，我的早餐在哪？別忘了我要柳橙汁。我要回去睡了。好了就叫我。
Grandpa	Look at him and then look at yourself. You are up and about ready to start the day running. He... not so much. You're a morning person and he is a night person. Everyone is different, so when I described you as bright-eyed and bushy-tailed I was comparing you to bunny rabbits. Rabbits have big wide eyes and they have bushy tails that they wiggle.	看看他再看看妳。妳已經起床並到處活動，準備開始新的一天。他呢？不怎樣。妳是早起的人而他喜歡晚睡。每個人都不同，所以當我形容妳是眼睛閃亮尾巴濃密的，我是把妳跟兔子作比較。兔子有大大的眼睛，而且牠們擺動濃密的尾巴。

生活篇

信仰篇

表達篇

外來語篇

文明篇

其它篇

91

	(Paul wanders through the kitchen to the bathroom.)	（保羅穿過廚房進入廁所）
Paul	Ha! An Asian with wide eyes? Are you sure she's not sleepwalking?	哈！一個東方人有大眼睛？你確定她不是在夢遊？
Chi	I'M AWAKE!	我是醒著的！
Paul	Uh huh? (Paul closes the bathroom door.)	嗯哼？（保羅關上廁所門）
Grandpa	Well for those of us who ARE awake (Saying it loud enough so Paul can hear it.) I saw a Blue Jay and a Cardinal earlier. How about we head on out to the porch and watch "the early bird catch the worm?"	我們這些醒著的人呀！（他說的剛剛好夠大聲讓保羅聽得到）我之前看到了藍松鴉跟北美紅雀。不如我們到陽台上去看「早起的鳥兒抓蟲吃」吧？
Chi	Sounds like fun. I'll get the binoculars.	聽來很好玩。我去拿望遠鏡。
Paul	(Walks out from the bathroom.) WAIT! Where's my food?	（走出廁所）等等！我的早點呢？

 ## 單字

☑ clank [klæŋk] **v.** 鏗鏘作響	☑ pots and pans **n.** 盆子與鍋子；鍋具類
☑ wide [waɪd] **adv.** （眼睛睜得）大大地；十分地	☑ geesh [dʒiʃ] **interj.** 感歎詞，用以表示驚訝或苦惱的情緒
☑ slang [slæŋ] **n.** 俚語，指只限於某個區域的人在使用、不正式的英文用語。譬如 "cool"，到簡訊上的 "LOL" 等，都算是俚語。	☑ idiom [`ɪdɪəm] **n.** 慣用語；成語

☑ construct [ˈkɑnstrʌkt] *n.* 概念；構想

☑ wiggle [ˈwɪg!] *v.* 擺動；扭動

☑ Blue Jay [ˈblu ˌdʒe] *n.* 藍松鴉

☑ Cardinal [ˈkɑrdnəl] *n.* 北美紅雀

☑ binoculars [baɪˈnɑkjələ-s] *n.* 雙筒望遠鏡 (注意這個字是複數形，字尾加 s)

 片語

☑ up and about 起來並到處活動

 日常會話

☑ With that being said, ... 承接我剛說的；更甚之；說到這裡。"With that being said" 是用來承接或轉換語氣的一種措辭，說者在講了這句話後，或繼續表達更重要的理念，或介紹其他不同的想法。類似的形式包括 "That being said" 和 "Having said that" 等。

 動物之四：Bright-Eyed and Bushy-Tailed

　　"Bright-eyed and bushy-tailed" 是形容一個人神采奕奕、蓄勢待發的模樣，特別是早上剛起床的時候。

　　網路上各方對於隱藏在這句俚語後的神祕動物有著各種的揣摩，有人說那是在形容貓興奮的狀態，有人猜是精靈活潑的小松鼠，也有人指出打獵活動中，若是見到狐狸眼睛渾沌、尾巴下垂且毛雜亂不齊，那麼牠就不是一個很好的獵物。

　　對我個人而言，bright-eyed and bushy-tailed 永遠指一隻眼睛亮、翹著小圓尾巴的野兔。這句話是我搬來美國後，最早學習到的英文用語之一。還記得我先生的外公和外婆，在某天早餐桌上很高興地為我解釋這句俚語的意思，外公用了一隻兔子來描述牠健康、活力十足的模樣，那幅圖畫就深深印在我的腦海中。

　　電影《第六感生死緣》*Meet Joe Black* 中有一幕就用到了這句意象十足的台詞：意識到自己所剩時間不多的新聞界大亨，在家族聚餐的尾聲，邀請在座的所有人，包括他兩個最疼愛的女兒，以及女婿跟男朋友，隔天再回來一起晚餐。大女兒愛麗森聽到爸爸這樣建議，很高興地回答："Bright-eyed and bushy-tailed." 意思就是說，屆時她會準備好、容光煥發地出席下次的晚宴！

生活篇

信仰篇

表達篇

外來語篇

文明篇

其它篇

第二篇 信仰篇 Belief

06 美國人的迷信 [Superstitions]

21 Knock on Wood

Paul and Chi are looking for an apartment.　保羅和季薇在找出租公寓。

Don	So right now we are putting in a new stove and countertop. Also the boys are re-doing the bathroom. If everything goes as planned, knock on wood (raps his knuckle on a nearby wood cabinet three times), we can have this unit ready for you folks in ten days.	所以現在我們正在安裝一組新爐具跟流理台。同時工人在重新弄浴室。如果一切順利的話，敲木頭（在旁邊的木櫃上叩擊他的指關節），十天內我們就能為你們把這間套房準備好。
Chi	Thank you so much, Don. We really like the apartment. Here's our phone number. Please give us a call when it's ready.	太謝謝你了，唐。我們真的很喜歡這間公寓。這裡是我們的電話號碼。當房間整理完畢時，請給我們個電話
Don	Okay. Glad that you both like it. I'll <u>keep you posted</u>.	好。很高興你們倆都喜歡。我會讓你們知道最新的發展。
	Paul and Chi leave the apartment manager's office.	保羅與季薇離開公寓經理的辦公室。
Chi	Back there when Don was talking, he hit the cabinet. Why did he do that?	剛才唐在講話的時候，他敲了敲櫃子。他幹嘛那麼做？
Paul	You mean when he knocked on wood?	妳指當他敲木頭的時候？
Chi	Yeah.	是啊。

Paul	It's an old superstition. When you mention something favorable, or boastfully acknowledge the completion of a project before it is a reality, there is the possibility that you could have just jinxed it by tempting fate. Therefore, in order to counteract any possibility of humiliation, you can "knock on wood."	那是一項古老的迷信。當妳談論某件喜好的事,或在工作完成前得意洋洋地表示它一定會做成,這種試探命運的行為,或許會對那件事招來惡運。因此為了要抵消任何最後事情做不成而丟臉的可能性,妳就「敲木頭」。
Chi	Why wood?	為什麼是木頭?
Paul	It could be argued that because Christ died on the cross for the sins of the world and that his blood covers those sins for all of eternity, by knocking on wood you are transferring your sin of pride to the cross thereby absolving you of your transgression.	有人說也許這是因為基督為了世界的罪業而死在十字架上,他的血洗清了所有人類的過失,藉由敲擊木頭,妳將妳的驕傲罪行傳送到十字架裡以獲得赦免。
Chi	Interesting.	有意思。
Paul	For a modern interpretation, we can look to Charlie Brown. He often called himself a "block head" in the Sunday comics. So by extension, when no real wood is around to tap on, you can tap on your own head as a wood substitute.	另一個現代的詮釋可以在查理·布朗身上找到。在星期天的連載漫畫裡他常自稱「木頭腦袋」。這個意思衍伸出來就是,當四下都找不到真的木頭可以敲時,你可以把自己的頭代替木頭來敲。
Chi	Ha, block head, that's funny.	哈,木頭腦袋,好好笑。
Paul	This act of humility also serves another function.	這種謙卑的行為還滿足了另一項功能。

生活篇

信仰篇

表達篇

外來語篇

文明篇

其它篇

Chi	What?	什麼？

Paul | We become consciously aware of the fact that we might have foolishly overstepped our reach. Expressing absolutions with bravado is arrogant and upon reflection imbues us with a sense of caution that insists we momentarily take a step back. Volatile, omnipotent Gods who may feel their power and authority being threatened, at ANY level, are eager to challenge the hubris of mere humans and will <u>go to great lengths to</u> curtail overzealous ambitions for equality or superiority. Therefore we display public self mockery in order to win their favor and avert their gaze. | 我們意識到我們也許愚昧地越過界限了。逞強地表達絕對的想法是種驕傲自大的行為，在經過反省之後，我們心中的危機感促使自己暫時地往後退一步。當高度敏感、全能的神祇感到祂們的權力受到威脅時，不論威脅的程度如何，會立刻挑戰這些不知天高地厚的人類，並盡全力去打壓他們爭取平等或優越的狂熱野心。因此我們作公開的自嘲以贏回祂們的歡心並轉移祂們注目的眼光。

Chi | By the way, Don also said that we can have not just one, but TWO parking spaces. | 對了，唐説我們不但能夠拿到一個，而是「兩個」車位。

Paul | Ahhhh! KNOCK ON WOOD! KNOCK ON WOOD! (Feverishly taps his head with both hands.) | 啊啊啊！敲木頭！敲木頭！（兩手瘋狂地敲著他的頭）

 單字

☑ rap [ræp] *v.* 輕輕敲擊、叩擊	☑ boastfully [`bostfəlɪ] *adv.* 自誇地、得意洋洋地
☑ jinx [dʒɪŋks] *v.* 詛咒、帶給惡運	☑ absolve [əb`sɑlv] *v.* 免除…的責任、赦免

☑ humility [hju`mɪlətɪ] *n.* 謙虛、謙卑　　☑ bravado [brə`vɑdo] *n.* 逞強

☑ imbue [ɪm`bju] *v.* 使…充滿某種情緒
或品質、灌輸　　☑ omnipotent [ɑm`nɪpətənt] *adj.* 全能
的

☑ hubris [`hjubrɪs] *n.* 自大、過度驕傲　　☑ curtail [kɝ`tel] *v.* 削減、限制

☑ overzealous [`ovɚ`zɛləs] *adj.* 過份
熱心的、狂熱的　　☑ avert [ə`vɝt] *v.* 轉移、避開

片語

☑ keep someone posted 讓某人知道事件的最新發展
☑ go to great lengths to do something 花費很大的心血而努力做到某件事

美國人的迷信之一：Knock on Wood

在跟美國人交談時，他／她有時候突如其來地冒出一句："Knock on wood!" 並慎重其事地在木頭製的桌子或牆上敲個兩下。咦？他們這麼做是在幹嘛呀？

這個迷信的來源大約分成兩派，一派是來自基督教，人們相信由於耶穌在（木製的）十字架上受死，十字架具有神聖的力量，可以避邪，或藉以禱告祈求原諒。另一個說法是根源於異教徒，他們認為樹木裡住有神靈，在木頭上敲擊能夠帶來好運。

好，大致了解為什麼要敲木頭後，接下來我要教你怎麼做：如果你說了「噢，我已經連續六個月沒接到罰單了！」，或是「哇！我的寶貝兒子這一年來都沒生病…」這時你就要趕快說：Knock on wood，而且同時在最近的木製品（通常是桌子）上輕敲兩下，再繼續講其它的事。這麼作的原因是因為你想要確保好運持續，不會因為你一時的自大，做了這樣的聲明，而「破了」或「化解」了原來的好運氣！

生活篇

信仰篇

表達篇

外來語篇

文明篇

其它篇

At the office.　辦公室裡。

Mik	Achoo!	哈啾！

Everyone Bless you. | 保佑你。

Mike　Thank you ... Hold on, wait, I feel another one coming on... Ah.... Ah... Chooooo!

謝謝你們…等一下，我感覺另外一個要來了…哈…哈…哈啾！

Barbara My goodness, bless you. One more and you'll have a triple blessing!

我的老天爺，保佑你。再來一個的話你就有三重保佑了！

Mike　It's the pollen. It's overwhelming. I just can't take... it... any... ACHOO... more.

是花粉的關係，太嚴重，我再也受…不…了…哈啾…了。

Barbara Ding, ding, ding. Triple blessing!

噹噹噹，三重保佑！

Chi　Why do you "bless," Mike?

為什麼妳要「保佑」麥可？

Barbara Because he was sneezing.

因為他在打噴嚏。

Chi　Wait that's not what I meant. What is the point in "blessing," Mike?

那不是我的意思，我的意思是「保佑」麥可這個動作的理由是什麼？

Barbara Historically, religious people believed that

歷史上信仰宗教的人們相

when you sneeze the body is attempting to expel evil spirits. Therefore in order to assist the sneezer in this process, friends and family would invoke a blessing from God so as to facilitate the exorcisement.

信，當你打噴嚏時，你的身體其實正試圖將邪靈驅逐出去。因此在這個過程裡為了協助打噴嚏的人，朋友與家人會向神祈求庇佑，以利驅魔。

Jennifer My grandfather used to say that when someone sneezed, their heart would temporarily stop. By saying God bless you, we are supplicating an adjuration for the heart to return to beating once more.

我的祖父曾說過，當某人打噴嚏時，他的心臟會暫時停止。藉由講上帝保佑你，我們懇求上天讓這顆心再一次回復跳躍。

Customer When I was little, my parents told me that the soul is blown out of the body. We say God bless in order to help restore the union. Otherwise the soul would wander through limbo being neither of earth or heaven.

我小時候爸媽告訴我，因為靈魂被吹出身體之外，所以我們說上帝保佑讓這兩者恢復結合的狀態，要不然靈魂會飄蕩到既非天堂亦非地獄的過渡地帶之中。

Chi That's funny. Different cultures viewing the same act differently! In Taiwan, I was told that when you sneeze, it means someone is talking behind your back.

真好玩，不同的文化對相同的行為有不同的看法！在台灣，人家告訴我，打噴嚏是表示有人在背後講你壞話。

Barbara No. When someone is talking behind your back, you ears itch.

不，別人在你背後講壞話的時候你耳朵會癢。

Mike Really? Oh no, I'm sneezing and my ears itch. (Frantically scratching his ears.) That can't be good.

真的嗎？噢不，我不但打噴嚏，而且耳朵又癢。（狂亂地搔著他的耳朵。）這可不是好現象。

	(Jennifer whispers something to Chi.)	（珍妮佛悄聲向季薇說了些話）
Chi	Haha. Yeah, you're right.	哈哈，對，妳說得沒錯。
Mike	Achoo!	哈啾！
	(Jennifer whistles and walks away.)	（珍妮佛吹著口哨離開）
Mike	What'd she say.	她剛才說什麼？
Chi	Oh, nothing. (Walks away.)	噢沒什麼。（也走開）
Barbara	All right, everyone back to work. (Whispers something to Chi on her way out.)	好了，每個人都回去上班。（一邊走出去，一邊跟季薇講悄悄話）
Mike	Achoo. STOP IT!	哈啾。全都給我停止！
	(Everyone laughs.)	（所有人大笑）

 單字

☑ pollen [ˈpɑlən] **n.** 花粉	☑ invoke [ɪnˈvok] **v.** 祈求、求助於
☑ facilitate [fəˈsɪləˌtet] **v.** 使（工作、事情等）變得容易	☑ exorcisement [ˌɛksɔrˈsaɪzmənt] **n.** 驅邪、驅魔
☑ supplicate [ˈsʌpləˌket] **v.** 懇求、請求	☑ adjuration [ˌædʒʊˈreʃən] **n.** 莊重而嚴肅的請求
☑ limbo [ˈlɪmˌbo] **n.** 介於天堂與地獄之間的過渡地帶	☑ frantically [ˈfræntɪklɪ] **adv.** 狂亂地、慌張地

美國人的迷信之二：Bless You

冷冷的寒風中，你突然覺得鼻頭有些癢，禁不住打了一個噴嚏，這個情況若是發生在臺灣，周遭大部份人的反應大概是繼續沈默地往前走，但換做是在美國，你也許會聽到有人對你說：God bless you! 或簡短的 Bless you!

這是為什麼？

美國人在聽見或看見有人打噴嚏時給予祝福的起源眾說紛紜，其中一說是西元前五九O年間，歐洲瘧疾肆虐，羅馬教宗一世開始使用這句話來為打噴嚏（視為黑死病的初期徵兆）人們禱告，希望疾病停止蔓延；另一個說法是，許多人相信，人體在打噴嚏時正處於脆弱的狀態，邪惡的力量或惡靈可能會趁機侵入，或是這個人正被小鬼打擾，打噴嚏是外顯的跡象，所以看到別人打噴嚏，說聲（God）Bless You，可以幫助那人抵擋住邪惡。

所以，下次當你看到有人在打噴嚏，跟著其他美國人同聲說：Bless you!

註 當你是那個在打噴嚏的人時，受到了他人的祝福後，適當地回應：Thank you. 才是符合社會禮儀的行為。當然，也不要忘記，打噴嚏時要轉頭，別朝著人噴，打完後立刻說聲：Excuse me! 並以紙巾擦乾淨喔!

生活篇

信仰篇

表達篇

外來語篇

文明篇

其它篇

Paul and Chi are at a souvenir shop in Las Vegas.
保羅和季薇在拉斯維加斯的一間紀念品商店裡。

Chi	What in the world is that?	那個是什麼？
Paul	What?	什麼？
Chi	That furry thing-g.	那個毛茸茸的東西。
Paul	That... is a rabbit's foot.	那個…是一隻兔腳。
Ch	Why are severed rabbit feet being sold at a souvenir shop?	為什麼切斷的兔腳會被放在紀念品商店裡販賣？
Paul	This is Vegas baby!	這裡是維加斯啊，寶貝！
Chi	What does that have to do with anything?	這跟那個有什麼關係？
Paul	A rabbit's foot brings good luck. When in Sin City you're gonna want a bit of luck on your side. After all, entire fortunes are won and lost here at the turn of a card or the roll of the dice.	兔腳帶來好運。在罪惡之都，你希望幸運之神站在你這邊。畢竟大筆的財富在紙牌與骰子的翻轉之間易手。
Chi	Eww. People actually carry dead rabbit feet around for luck? That's disturbing.	噁。人們真的為招好運而隨身攜帶死兔子的腳？這叫人心裡挺不舒服。
Paul	Talismans arise from the superstition that	幸運物源自人們迷信事件之

correlation IS causation. OR, in other words, what random thing did I have or do right before good fortune blessed me. AND how can I recreate this recipe so that I continue to be blessed. Baseball players in particular are prone to collecting an entire array of absurd tokens, or developing odd routines in order to ease their mind and gain confidence prior to engaging a risky opponent. People will do anything if they think it will give them an advantage.

間呈現的關聯性就是因果關係。或者，用別的話來講，上回在我走運之前到底做了什麼莫名之事，所以我要如何複製這種過程才能繼續保持好運道。棒球選手尤其偏愛蒐藏一系列令人匪夷所思的物件，或建立一些怪異的例行程序，來幫助他們在與難以預料的敵手交戰前夕，緩和情緒並建立信心。要是人們相信做某件事會給他們優勢，他們就會去做。

Chi Look at this. (Reading the tag on the rabbit's foot) Certificate of authenticity: This rabbit's foot was harvested postmortem. No rabbits involved were killed for their feet. Well, that makes me feel a little bit better.

你看這個。（讀著兔腳上的標籤）保證真實性─這只兔腳乃於兔子死亡後採收，沒有任何兔子因其腳遭到獵殺。啊！這樣我感覺好過了一些。

Paul As you have pointed out, morally sound people raised the issue of animal cruelty in the face of meaningless cultural behaviors, and won the right to dictate a regulation preventing a violation of our humanity.

如同妳指出的，具有道德感的人士見到這類毫無意義的文化行徑，認為有虐待動物的爭議，進而促成法律的通過以維護人道精神。

Chi I hope the rabbits had a good life before being "harvested."

我希望那些兔子在被「採收」前度過了很好的一生。

Paul Unlikely, they were probably bred as food. The leftover feet from the slaughter

不太可能，牠們大概被養來做食物。屠宰後剩下的腳就

生活篇

信仰篇

表達篇

外來語篇

文明篇

其它篇

	were sold to novelty shops.	賣到販售這類新奇玩意兒的商店。
Chi	OH MY GOD!	噢！天哪！
Paul	Sorry, what I meant was, YES they ran in green fields, chomped on fresh carrots, and played fun rabbit games every day. Only after they died of old age and natural causes were their feet "harvested." The remainder of their bodies were solemnly placed into the ground in thanks for their generous donation.	抱歉，我的意思是，沒錯，牠們在翠綠的野地上奔跑，大嚼新鮮的紅蘿蔔，而且天天都玩著有趣的兔子遊戲。只有當牠們由於年歲大和自然因素死亡之後，人們才去「採收」那些腳。剩下的遺體則被慎重地埋在地下，以對牠們慷慨的捐獻表示感謝。
Chi	THAT'S BETTER! Aren't you going to the crap table tonight?	那樣好多了！你今晚不是要去賭擲骰子嗎？
Paul	Yes.	是啊。
Chi	Weren't you born in the year of the rabbit?	你不是兔年生的嗎？
Paul	Yes. I am my own good luck.	對，我就是我自己的幸運符。
Chi	I better stick with you then, my lucky bunny.	那我最好是跟著你了，我的好運兔。

♥ 單字

☑ **sever** [ˈsɛvɚ] *v.* 切斷、割斷

☑ **Eww** [ɪʊ] *interj.* 「噁」。表示感到噁心、反感的驚歎聲。

☑ talisman [ˋtælɪsmən] **n.** 有不可思議
力量可保護主人的東西、幸運物

☑ correlation [ˏkɔrəˋleʃən] **n.** 關連、
相關性

☑ causation [kɔˋzeʃən] **n.** 原因、因果
關係

☑ array [əˋre] **n.** 系列、排列

☑ postmortem [ˏpostˋmɔrtəm] **adj.**
死後的

☑ novelty [ˋnɑv!tɪ] **n.** 新奇的事物、罕
見的物品

☑ chomp [tʃɑmp] **v.** 發出聲音地咬、大
嚼特嚼

☑ crap table [ˋkræpˋteb!] **n.** 一種四周
特別圍起來加高的桌子，用以擲骰子賭
博用。在這種桌子上玩的擲骰子遊戲稱
為 craps。

 ## 美國人的迷信之三：**Rabbit's Foot**

電影《變形金剛 3》（*Transformer 3: Dark of the Moon*）一開場，主角山姆（Sam）的外國籍女友送給他一隻兔子的填充玩具作為象徵好運的禮物，片中稍候兩人起了爭執，山姆一怒之下將兔子的某一隻腳扯下來，吼道：「不是整隻兔子都會帶來好運，只有這一部份！」你知道男主角指的是兔子的哪一隻腳嗎？

答案是兔子的左側後腿。

也難怪電影裡那個外籍女友的角色不清楚其中的分別，兔子在一般社會中普遍被視為吉祥的象徵，但是美國人相信，兔腿（Rabbit's foot），特別是左後腿，具有神奇的魔力！有些人，尤其是賭徒們，喜歡隨身帶著乾燥處理過的兔腳（常製作為鑰匙圈），認為這個幸運物會為其主人提升運氣。

幽默大師 R.E. Shay 以曾經講過下面這句話著名："Depend on the rabbit's foot if you will, but remember it didn't work for the rabbit."（要相信兔腳是你家的事，但是謹記那隻腳並沒有為它的主人帶來好運。）

美國人的迷信 [Superstitions]

(24) Throwing Salt Over Your Left Shoulder

Paul and Chi are at a diner. Chi accidentally knocks over a salt shaker.
保羅和季薇在一間餐廳裡。季薇不小心打翻了鹽罐。

Chi Oh, darn. I am so clumsy.

噢，糟糕。我真是笨手笨腳。

Paul Hurry! Throw some salt over your shoulder!

快！往妳的肩上後丟些鹽巴。

Chi Why?

為什麼？

Paul Just do it!

照做就對了！

Chi There're people sitting behind me. I'm not going to throw stuff at them!

有人坐在我後面。我才不要朝他們丟東西！

Paul They won't even notice! Quickly. (Chi sits there with arms folded staring at Paul.) Fine, I'll do it for you. (Picks up a pinch of salt from the table and throw it past Chi's left shoulder.) Now you can put the rest of the salt back.

他們不會發現的！快點。（季薇坐在座位上手臂交叉瞪著保羅）算了，我幫妳做。（從桌上拾起一撮鹽，往季薇的左肩上扔過去）現在妳可以把剩下的鹽巴裝回去。

Chi (Gathers the remaining salt and puts it into the shaker.) What was that all about? Are you a cannibal now? Seasoning your pray BEFORE the kill? Explain why you did that.

（將剩餘的鹽集合起來裝到罐子裡）剛才你那麼做到底是為什麼？你現在是食人族了嗎？在殺獵物前還要先調味？給我一個合理的解釋。

Paul (In an eerie voice.) It's an old superstition. When you spill salt, ominous, terrible things happen. An evil cloud will rise over you. UNLESS! (Vigorously pointing index

（以陰森森的口吻）那是個古老的迷信。當你灑出鹽巴，不祥、駭人的事就會發生，邪惡的烏雲將籠罩你。

finger skyward.) You counteract the omen by... tossing the spilled salt over your left shoulder. Remember the devil lurks in your blind spot. You must bind him and send him BACK to HELLLLLLLLLLLLLLL! Thank you Lord Jees-sus!

除非！（生動地用食指往天空方向指去）你…把灑出來的鹽向左肩拋過去，來抵消這個厄運。記住，惡魔潛伏在你的盲點位置，你必須遮蔽它的眼睛，並把它送回地獄獄獄獄獄獄去！感謝主耶穌！

Chi　You're a science teacher. Since when are you superstitious?

你是教科學的，什麼時候開始變得這麼迷信了？

Paul　I'm not, but are you saying I can't have a bit of fun playing around with old wives' tales?

我並不迷信，但是難道就因為那樣我不能跟著這些老婆婆口中流傳的民間習俗玩玩、開心一下了？

Chi　It just don't make no sense.

你這樣不合理啊。

Paul　So! Life is filled with hundreds of obscure traditions whose original meanings have either been lost or forgotten. Are you telling me that only vegetarians are allowed to eat vegetables? Or that only Christians are allowed to celebrate the winter solstice? Presents are fun and who doesn't like broccoli? (Snidely) I don't see any contradiction. I am human. I don't have to be so serious all the time. I have every right to act like a goofball. After all... it's tradition. Next thing you know and you'll be telling me I can't have a beer on Saint Patrick's day or a sausage during Oktoberfest. Uhh ... you're such a party pooper.

所以哩！人生裡充滿了一大堆奇怪的習俗，其原始意義早已失落或被人淡忘。難道妳是說只有素食者可以吃蔬菜？或是只有基督徒才能慶祝冬至？（作者按：冬至與聖誕節的時間一致。古代異教徒慶祝冬至，部份習俗被基督徒採納並與耶穌誕辰結合，成為我們今日所知的聖誕節。）交換禮物很有趣，而誰不喜歡綠椰菜哪？（挖苦地）我不認為其間有任何矛盾之處。我也是人啊！我不需要成天都板著一張嚴肅的臉，我有權利開玩笑裝傻。畢竟…那是一項傳統。

要是都照妳說的，接下來我不是就不能在聖派翠克節喝啤酒，或於德國啤酒節吃臘腸了？噢... 妳真是會破壞派對氣氛。

Chi　Party pooper?

破壞派對氣氛？

Paul　Yeah that's right, you heard me party pooper. Par-tay Poo-per. (Points finger at Chi.) You.

對啦！妳聽到我說的了，破壞派對氣氛，殺風景。（指著季薇）就是妳！

Chi　I am not!

我才不是！

Paul　Prove it.

證明給我看。

Chi　I take your challenge with a grain of salt.

我才不會把你的挑戰放在心上呢！

Paul　Bah humbug, yah Scrooge!

聖誕節都是騙人的，你這「史古治」！

 ## 單字

☑ diner [ˋdaɪnɚ] *n.* 一種外觀裝修成長型餐車，內部備有成列座位的美式簡便餐廳

☑ clumsy [ˋklʌmzɪ] *adj.* 笨拙的、手腳不協調的

☑ cannibal [ˋkænəb!] *n.* 吃人肉的野人、食人族

☑ eerie [ˋɪrɪ] *adj.* 陰森的、可怕的

☑ ominous [ˋɑmənəs] *adj.* 不吉祥的

☑ lurk [lɝk] *v.* 埋伏、潛藏

☑ winter solstice [ˋwɪntɚˋsɑlstɪs] *n.* 冬至（太陽向南離赤道最遠的時候，大約發生在十二月二十一或二十二日，是全年中日子最短的一天。）

☑ goofball [ˋgʊfˌbɔl] *n.* 天真愛玩沒大腦的人、傻蛋

☑ **Saint Patrick's Day** 聖派翠克節。訂於三月十七日，是慶祝愛爾蘭文化的一個節日，人們在這天裡會穿綠色的衣服或戴上酢漿草的標誌、喝啤酒、並享用愛爾蘭傳統食物如醃牛肉、包心菜與馬鈴薯等。

片語

☑ take something with a grain of salt 不用對某事太介意、不要把某事太放在心上。

日常會話

☑ **Bah humbug, yah Scrooge!**「聖誕節都是騙人的，你這史古治！」這句話是用來諷刺對方固執己見、一昧地排斥與聖誕節有關的慶祝活動。
整句可以拆成兩個部份來看："Bah humbug." 和 "Yah Scrooge!" 讓我們先從後面那句解釋：Scrooge是英國作家狄更斯小說「聖誕夜怪譚」（*A Christmas Carol*）的主角史古治，書中他被描述為一名冷淡的守財奴，鄙視許多跟聖誕節相關的行為；而yah是 "you" 的口語。前面的句子 "Bah humbug." 中bah是人用來表示不悅、不屑一顧所發出的聲音，humbug指詐欺的行為或事物。"Bah humbug." 是史古治著名的話，指控聖誕節是一種騙人的行為。

美國人的迷信之四：Throwing Salt Over Your Left Shoulder

美國人的餐桌上，兩種最常見的調味料就是鹽巴和黑胡椒。有時候講話或拿東西，一不小心就把鹽巴罐打翻了，這個時刻除了趕快把灑出來的鹽裝回去，你還可以做什麼？

答案是，（以右手）抓一小撮鹽巴，從你的左肩上往後方灑過去！

美國人灑鹽的迷信世代相襲，原因之一可能是過去鹽巴被視為珍貴的物品，如果不小心倒掉，這種舉動會被看作是不敬的行為，因而招致厄運。另一個源由是在達文西的名畫「最後的晚餐」中，出賣耶穌的猶大不注意推倒了鹽罐，所以鹽巴灑出來代表惡運降臨。

那麼，為什麼在鹽罐灑出來後，還要灑更多的鹽去避邪呢？因為古人相信，相對於善良的天使佇於人類的右肩，惡魔棲息在左邊的肩膀上，灑鹽巴過去可以遮蔽它的眼睛（另一說是用來賄賂魔鬼）。

Paul and Chi are at the racetrack.　保羅和季薇在賽馬場上。

Paul When picking a pony, the race program is the go-to source for useful information. It contains the horse's age, odds of winning, winning history, and track performance.

在挑馬的時候,賽事表(作者按:香港人稱作「馬經」)是獲得實用資訊的最佳來源。它的內容包括賽馬的年齡、獲勝機率、得獎歷史和跑道上的表現。

Chi Track performance?

跑道上的表現?

Paul Racetracks have different surfaces. Some have dirt, grass, or artificial all-weather tracks. The program tells you how each horse has performed on those tracks. You may want to wage your bet off of these facts. The odds of a horse indicate its believed likelihood of winning. For example, if a horse has 2-1 odds, it has a 50% chance of winning. A horse with a 50-1 odds has a 2% chance of winning. The first race will begin soon, we need to relay our bets to the teller quickly, which horse would you like to bid on?

每種跑場有不同的表面。有些是泥土、草地,或適合各種氣候的人工跑道。 賽事表會告訴妳每匹馬在那些跑道上的表現成績。妳會想要根據這些事實來下注。賽馬機率顯示出牠贏的可能性。舉例來說,如果一匹馬有二比一的獲勝機率,那麼牠就有百分之五十的機會會贏。另一匹馬有五十比一的機率就有百分之二的得勝機會。第一場比賽很快就要開始,我們得要趕快到出納窗口下注,妳想要賭哪一隻馬?

Chi Um, I don't know... Can I just pick the one with the name I like the most?

呃,我不知道耶…我可不可以選我最喜歡的名字?

Paul Betting on a horse is a science. Think about what you are doing.

賭馬下注是一門科學。妳要考慮清楚。

Chi	I like "Take the Cake" Here's my two bucks. I have a feeling she's going to win.	我喜歡「贏到大蛋糕」。這裡是我的兩元美金。我有預感她會獲勝。
Paul	That horse has a 100-1 odds!	那匹馬有一百比一的機率！
Chi	AND?	所以哩？
Paul	You're gonna have to cross your fingers on this one.	選這匹馬的話，妳得要交叉手指拜託老天了。
Chi	(Sticks tongue out.) Neah! I'll cross my toes, arms, and legs if I have to. Which horse do you want, smarty pants?	（吐出舌頭做聲）必要的話，我還會交叉腳趾、手臂和大腿。你想要哪一匹馬，天才？
Paul	"Fly So Free" has 3-1 odds. The trainer and jockey are known to be consistent winners.	「自由飛奔」有三比一的機率。教練和騎士都是常勝軍。
	Paul places the bets and returns to stand with Chi at the finish line.	保羅下注後跟季薇一起站在終點線旁的觀眾席。
Announcer	(Bell rings.) And they're off.	（鈴響）賽馬衝出
Chi	Ohmygodohmygod, I feel like my heart is going to jump out of my chest.	噢，我的天我的天，我覺得心臟快要跳出來了。
Announcer	"By Golly" takes an early lead while "She's So Harry" follows close behind.	「看老天意思」一出場就領先群雄，「她很哈你」緊跟在後。
Chi	Look! Your horse is in the middle of the pack. Where's mine?	看！你的馬在中間的位置。我的馬在哪？
Paul	Dead last.	最後一名。
Chi	Owwwh.	噢。

生活篇

信仰篇

表達篇 ── 外來語篇 ── 文明篇 ── 其它篇

113

Announcer	"Fly So Free" is coming up on the outside.	「自由飛奔」從外方超前追上。
Paul	Go! "Fly So Free", GO!	加油！「自由飛奔」，加油！
Chi	Come on "Take the Cake" <u>GIDDYUP</u>!	拜託嘛「贏到大蛋糕」，加快腳步！
Announcer	"Fly So Free" is fighting for the lead and muscling her way between "She's So Harry" and "I Like Tacos."	「自由飛奔」正在盡全力爭取領先的地位，夾於「她很哈你」跟「我愛墨西哥塔可餅」之間。
Paul	I'm gonna win. I'M GONNA WIN.	我要贏了。我要贏了。
Announcer	"She's So Harry's" jockey has fallen from his mount. The horses are spreading wide to avoid stepping on him. Wait a minute! WAIT A MINUTE! "Take the Cake" is driving up the middle and taking the lead.	「她很哈你」的騎士摔落下來。馬群散開來以避免踩到他。等一下！等一下！「贏到大蛋糕」從中間竄出並一馬當先。
Paul	WHAT?!	什麼？
Chi	Yayyyyyyyyyyyyyyyyyyy. (Mocking Paul) I'm gonna win. I'M GONNA WIN!	耶耶耶耶耶。（揶揄保羅）我要贏了。我要贏了。
Paul	(Jaw drops as "Take the Cake" crosses the finish line.) You won. You actually won.	（嘴巴張得大大地注視「贏到大蛋糕」跨越終點線）妳贏了，妳真的贏了。
Chi	That's right! Crossing my fingers and toes worked. It really, really worked. Let's go get my money.	沒錯！交叉手指跟腳趾真的有效。它真的真的發生效果了。我們趕快去領我贏的錢。

 **單字**

- ☑ racetrack [`restræk] **n.** 賽馬場

- ☑ go-to [`go`tu] **adj.** （其技能、經驗或知識等）值得信賴的

- ☑ wage [wedʒ] **v.** （把金錢）賭注在…；下注

- ☑ relay [rɪ`le] **v.** 傳達

 片語

- ☑ take the cake （在某種領域、情況裡）成為頂尖的、超越所有競爭者的 （在本文中為其中一匹賽馬的名字）

 日常會話

- ☑ By Golly!「天哪！」「噢！」類似 "My God!"，但語氣較為溫和。（亦為文中賽馬名之一）
- ☑ Giddyup. 催促馬兒快跑的命令詞，類似中文裡騎馬者喊的「駕！」。Giddyup 是 "get up" 非正式的發音。

 美國人的迷信之五：Cross Your Fingers

　　你從辦公室推門出來，你的手心還因緊張而微微出汗，臉頰感到有些紅熱，喉頭發乾。你瞄了一下時間：哇，剛剛的那場面試維持了一個小時之久，你開始回想這過程中被面試主管問了哪些問題、你如何侃侃而談、你知道你今天的衣著得體、並使用了專業的手勢和言語…。

　　接下來呢？當關切的好友及家人問起，你是否有機會得到這份夢想中的工作時，你其實可以這麼做：舉起你的手到大約肩膀的高度（一隻手或兩手並用皆可），以中指夾繞住食指，並說：I have my fingers crossed!

　　美國人相信，當你希望某件事能如願達成時，交叉你的手指會帶來好運。

　　不過要特別注意的是，如果你是在你的背後做這種手勢，意思變成你在說謊，交叉你的手指是默默禱告你的謊言別被抓到，另外一個意思是你現在說的都不算數，所以你不用為你的說謊行為負責！

生活篇

信仰篇

表達篇

外來語篇

文明篇

其它篇

Chi scratches her head, walking back and forth in the living room.

季薇一邊搔著頭，一邊在客廳裡走來走去。

Paul	What's the matter?	怎麼了？
Chi	I need ideas! I have to write an article about a superstition.	我需要點子！我必須寫一篇有關迷信的文章。
Paul	Be more specific.	講清楚一點。
Chi	The one where people say "Break a leg!" to actors, singers, and dancers right before they go on stage. Weren't you an actor in your previous life?	就是那個大家對演員、歌星和舞者登台之前講的「斷條腿！」的迷信。你以前不是演員嗎？
Paul	Yes, I've done a few things here and there. What you are talking about is a very old idea going back to the days of the Globe Theatre and Shakespeare. Actors; like athletes on game day; are superstitious, especially on opening night. Having a good rehearsal the night before is actually bad luck.	是，我過去曾做過一些不同的職業。妳提到的是一條相當古老的迷信，遠遠追溯到環球劇場和莎士比亞的時期。演員；跟運動員在出賽當天一樣；是十分迷信的一群人，在初演日時更是如此。在首演的前天晚上如果有一場精彩的排練其實是會帶來壞運的。
Chi	Really?	真的？
Paul	"Break a leg" is a negative sentiment used to wish performers good luck.	「斷條腿」是利用反面的情緒來祝福表演者好運。另

116

Theaters should also be closed on a Monday following a performance, in order to give the ghosts the opportunity to put on their own plays.

Chi I found a web page that said that *Macbeth* was cursed.

Paul ARE YOU MAD! You NEVER, EVER say the original title of "The Scottish play." GET OUT! GET OUT! GET OUT!

Chi Why?

Paul You need to go outside, turn around three times, spit, curse, quote *Hamlet's* famous line "To be or not to be," and then beg me to come back in.

(Chi complies.)

Paul Don't you ever do that again.

Chi Sorry, I didn't know you were so sensitive.

Paul Seriously, don't do that again. Just so you know, you should also never say the last line in the play or chant the incantations before opening night. Otherwise the witches will come to collect their chosen spoils. I did this play in college and a

外，劇場在某場節目演出後接連的那個星期一應該關閉，好讓劇院裡的鬼魂有機會上演他們自己的作品。

我找到一個網頁說，馬克白這齣劇受到詛咒。

妳瘋了嗎！妳永遠永遠不可以講出「那個蘇格蘭人的舞台劇」的原始名稱。出去！出去！出去！

為什麼？

妳必須到外面轉三圈、吐口水、罵髒話、唸哈姆雷特中著名的台詞「存在或不存在」，然後求我讓妳進來。

（季薇照做）

以後不可以再犯了。

對不起，我不知道你會那麼敏感。

我不是開玩笑，真的以後不能再那麼做。順道跟妳提，妳絕對不可以在首演夜之前說出戲裡的最後一句台詞，或覆誦劇本中的咒文…，否則女巫們會前來收集她們的

	fellow actor was dumb enough to blatantly say it for all to hear, only to later that night fall off the stage and actually break his leg.	戰利品。我在大學裡參與過這部戲的演出，其中一位共事的演員居然笨到在所有人面前大剌剌地講出那些台詞，結果那天晚上他摔下舞台，真的斷了條腿。
Chi	So it is true?	所以這個迷信是真的？
Paul	Of course it's true. Shakespeare used real witches in the original. Unfortunately they were mistreated by the other cast member so they proceeded to curse the play. That version of the play was lost and an edited-down one reemerged later on. Shakespeare tried to "cut out" the evil and yet to this day a dark cloud follows anyone who would dare tempt the witches' favor. Anyone who does the play and manages to escape unharmed is blessed from then on. A unpleasant reminder to treat everyone in the cast and crew with respect. You never know who will hold a grudge and then carry it out.	當然是真的。莎士比亞原來在他的舞台劇裡雇用了真的女巫。不幸地，其他演出的成員沒有好好對待那些女巫，因此她們就對這齣戲下詛咒。舞台劇原始的版本遺失了，而另一個較簡短的版本在稍後出現。莎士比亞嘗試將惡靈從他的劇本中「刪掉」，但直到今天，任何想要從女巫身上得到好處的人，都發現自己被不祥之氣跟隨。要是你演出了這部戲，並得以全身而退，從那一刻起好運就降臨在你身上。這個故事提醒人們要用尊敬的態度，對待每個跟你共事的演員和幕後工作夥伴。你永遠不曉得誰會因為懷恨在心而施行報復。

生活篇

信仰篇

表達篇

外來語篇

文明篇

其它篇

 單字

☑ sentiment [`sɛntəmənt] **n.** 情緒、感覺

☑ curse [kɝs] **v.** 詛咒；說髒話

☑ comply [kəm`plaɪ] **v.** （對命令、要求等）順從、依從

☑ chant [tʃænt] **v.** 反覆誦唸

☑ incantation [ˌɪnkæn`teʃən] **n.** 咒語、咒文

☑ spoils [spɔɪlz] **n.** 掠奪物、搶劫品

☑ blatantly [`bletn̩tlɪ] **adv.** 極明顯的、露骨的

☑ grudge [`grʌdʒ] **n.** 懷恨、怨恨

 片語

☑ in someone's previous life 在過去的日子裡、以前。在談到過往的職業或經驗時，美國人為了避免直接提到公司的名稱或職銜而有自誇之嫌，會使用 "in my previous／past life" 這類的圓滑措詞。

 美國人的迷信之六：**Break a Leg**

不曉得你有沒有注意到過，在演員或樂手上台表演之前，尤其是像舞台劇、脫口秀等的首演前夕，親朋好友會紛紛祝賀他們：“Break a leg!”（我希望你斷條腿！）哇！聽起來好殘酷噢！其實美國人是在祝你好運。他們相信，如果登台前演員聽到有人說 “Good Luck”，結果會剛好相反，是會帶來壞運氣的！

美國人對演員說 “Break a leg” 的由來千奇百怪，眾口紛紜。不過 演藝界的人向來以迷信著名則是不容置疑。電影「星夢傳奇：奧森・威爾斯與我（Me and Olson Welles）」裡描述身兼製片、編劇、導演和演員的奧森威爾斯，在他自己出資籌備的舞台劇開演前，每天都祈禱著製作群過程中哪裡出錯，巴望著有意外發生。他的理由是：如果一直到揭幕都沒事，那麼舞台劇首映的本身就會變成壞事。所以，當開演的前一天，某個小演員不慎啟動戲院裡的滅火系統，導致整個觀眾席都大淹水時，威爾斯先生終於大鬆一口氣而大笑不已。

06 美國人的迷信 [Superstitions]

27 Wishbone

Chi finds a chicken bone laying on top of the kitchen shelf.

季薇在廚房裡的架子上發現一根雞骨頭。

Chi	Honey, did you put this here?	親愛的，是你把這個放在這裡的嗎？
Paul	Yes. Leave it alone. I'm waiting for it to dry.	沒錯，別去碰。我在等它乾。
Chi	Why?	為什麼？
Paul	Seriously?	妳不是在開玩笑吧？
Chi	YES!	我沒在開玩笑！
Paul	Are you telling me that you have never pulled on and broken a wishbone before? Did you even have a childhood?	妳的意思是妳從來沒有玩過如願骨的遊戲？妳這人有童年嗎？
Chi	Hey, of course I had a childhood! A pretty good one, too! I just never heard of wishbones before. Tell me more about it.	嘿，我當然有童年！而且我的童年幸福又美滿！我只是沒聽過如願骨而已。給我多一點資訊。
Paul	The V-shaped collarbone on a fowl is called the "wishbone." It is believed that if two people pull on each end until it breaks, the person who gets the bigger piece will have his or her wish come true.	位於禽鳥身體上呈 V 字形的鎖骨稱為「如願骨」。一般相信如果兩個人各拉一端直到它斷裂，拿到較大一塊骨頭的人許的願望就會成真。
Chi	Really? I have a wish, can we do it now?	真的？我有個心願，我們可不可以現在就來玩？

Paul	No, we will have to wait till it is thoroughly dry. Only then will it be brittle enough to break. Then and only then can we do it.	不行，我們必須等到它完全乾燥。只有到那時它才會變得夠脆，才容易斷裂。我們要等到那個時候來玩。
	A month later.	一個月後。
Paul	Mmm ...	嗯…
Chi	I've been looking at it every day for the last few weeks! Is it ready?	過去這幾個禮拜我每天都在盯著它看！它到底好了沒？
Paul	(Examines the wishbone.) It's ready, are you?	（檢視著如願骨）它準備好了，妳準備好了嗎？
Chi	Since DAY ONE!	第一天就準備好了！
Paul	All right, remember don't tell me what you wished for before the break, otherwise it won't come true. Understand?	好，要記得在玩如願骨之前，妳不可以告訴我妳許了是什麼願，要不然它就不會成真了。了解嗎？
Chi	Yes, yes. Let's do it.	了解了解。我們來玩吧。
	Paul and Chi start to pull the bone apart. Both carefully watch the other's movement while wrestling for control.	保羅和季薇開始拉扯如願骨。兩人一邊為取得控制地位而角力，一邊小心地觀察對方的舉動。
Paul	... What's for dinner tonight?	…今天晚上我們吃什麼？
Chi	Huh? What? Uh ... we're having grilled cheese and (SNAP) Ohhhhh ... tomato soup. (Solemnly mopes.)	哼？什麼？嗯…晚餐是烤起司三明治跟（拍地一聲折斷）噢…番茄湯。（意氣立即消沈）
Paul	Well will you look at that. I win ... again. How do I keep doing this?	妳瞧瞧。我…又贏了。為什麼我老是贏？

生活篇

信仰篇

表達篇

外來語篇

文明篇

其它篇

Chi	You cheated!	你作弊！
Paul	Did you pull on the wishbone?	妳拉了如願骨嗎？
Chi	Yes.	是。
Paul	Did it break?	它斷了嗎？
Chi	Yes.	是。
Paul	Is mine bigger?	我手上的一端比較大？
Chi	YES!	是！
Paul	Seems fair to me.	照我看起來很公平啊！
Chi	You distracted me and you... you... did something, I just don't know what... YET!	你讓我分心而且你…你…做了什麼事，我只是還沒辦法指出…
Paul	It is called strategy dear, and my years of personal experience give me a clear advantage over a noob.	那叫策略，親愛的，以及多年的個人經驗，讓我在一個新人面前明顯地佔了上風。
Chi	Like what?	譬如說？
Paul	Reach high on the bone, pull slowly, twist slightly, and distract your opponent. For a more advanced move, you can also push back and quickly pivot lift up, creating an angled break on your opponent's side.	持著骨頭的上方、緩慢地拉、稍微扭轉、並使對手分心。另外一個更高級的手法是，向前推進並快速地旋轉拉起來，製造出一個在對方端斷裂的角度。
Chi	Next time I'm gonna get the upper hand! (Points antagonistically at Paul.)	下次我一定會贏過你！（帶敵意地指著保羅）
Paul	No worries, my wish was for both of us.	沒問題，我的願望是許給我們倆人的。

單字

☑ collarbone [ˋkɑlɚˌbon] **n.** 鎖骨

☑ fowl [faʊl] **n.** 禽鳥類、雞鴨

☑ brittle [ˋbrɪt!] **adj.** 易碎的

☑ mope [mop] **v.** 意氣消沈、頹喪

☑ noob [njub] **n.** （俚語）對某個領域或活動缺乏經驗的人、新進人員。為同義字 newbie 的簡寫，但更帶有藐視的意味。

☑ antagonistically [ænˌtægəˋnɪstɪklɪ] **adv.** 敵對地、抱有敵意地

 片語

the upper hand 具優勢的地位、居上風的一方

 美國人的迷信之七：**Wishbone**

美國鄉村音樂歌手 Reba McEntire 曾說過一句耐人尋味的名言："To succeed in life, you need three things: a wishbone, a backbone, and a funny bone."（要想人生成功，你需要三樣東西：夢想、骨氣和幽默。）

"Backbone" 直接翻譯，是「背上的骨頭」，也就是脊椎骨，引伸為「骨氣」、「堅毅／不易屈服的個性」；"funny bone" 在這裡的話是取其字面趣味，表示一個人的「幽默感」，第一個 "wishbone"，也是一樣，因為字裡面有 wish 這個字，衍生為「夢想」的意思。

但是究竟 wishbone 實際上是什麼東西呢？

原來它是鳥類身體中，連接頸部和肩膀的「鎖骨」，美國人叫這塊骨頭為 "wishbone"，傳統上人們相信，這一枝呈 V 字形的細骨，在取出乾燥後，若由兩個人各執一端，拉斷後，持有較大一邊的人，他或她所許的願望就會實現！英文慣用語 "（getting）a lucky break" 據說即源自這項迷信而來，意指（得到了）某個大好的機會或突破瓶頸的轉機。

下次有機會吃整隻烤雞的時候，注意看雞胸頂端藏的那截分叉的小骨頭，留下來放個幾天，等到它看起來乾乾的樣子，跟朋友或家人來玩一下吧，或許，嘿嘿！你的心願真的會成真喔！

生活篇

信仰篇

表達篇

外來語篇

文明篇

其它篇

07 「祂」 [God]

28 Godspeed

In Mike's apartment.　在麥可的公寓。

Mike	Ladies and gentlemen, allow me to introduce you to the fantastic world of MMORPG!	各位女士先生，容我為您介紹多人線上角色扮演遊戲的美妙世界！
	Computers are set in a circle. Food and drink is nearby. The room has been decorated with military camouflage.	各人的電腦成圓弧排列，食物和飲料放在一旁，整個房間塗上了軍事偽裝用的迷彩色。
Mike	Everybody put on your headsets. Tonight, we are going into BATTLE! Chi, you'll team up with Jen while Paul and I work together.	每個人戴上你的耳機。今晚，我們要打一場轟轟烈烈的戰！季薇，妳跟珍一隊，我和保羅一隊。
Group	Yes, Sir!	是，長官！
	30 minutes later.	三十分鐘後。
Paul	We are under heavy fire! Pull back!	我們遭到猛烈火力攻擊！撤退！
Mike	I'm hit.	我中槍了。
Paul	Man down, I repeat, man down! Ladies, where are you?	有弟兄傷亡，我重複，有弟兄傷亡！女士們，妳們在哪？

Chi & Jennifer	We are on our way.	我們正在途中。
Jennifer	What do we do now?	現在我們該怎麼辦？
Paul	We need medical supplies. There's a hospital a quarter mile to the east. When you have retrieved the trauma packet return here. I'll stay with Mike and provide suppression fire to keep the enemy from advancing further.	我們需要醫療用品。往東四分之一哩處有間醫院，妳們在取得外傷急救包之後回來這裡。我會待在麥可身邊並提供壓制火力防止敵人進攻。
Chi	The two of us? There are snipers and mine fields between here and the hospital.	就我們兩個？從這裡到醫院間的路上埋有狙擊手與地雷。
Paul	Jen cover the high ground and Chi use your mine detector to find and detonate any hidden devices. You can do it! Godspeed and be careful.	珍負責應付敵人從高處的襲擊，季薇，用妳的地雷探測器找出並引爆任何隱藏的設置。妳做得到的！願上帝祝福妳成功，要小心。
Jen	Let's go, Chi.	走吧，季薇。
Chi	Hold on tight, guys. We'll be back as soon as we can.	你們撐住。我們會儘快回來的。
	At the recently deserted hospital.	位於剛被棄置不久的醫院。
Chi	Can't believe we made it. I thought we were dead for sure.	真不敢相信我們竟然辦到了。我以為我倆死定了。
Jennifer	We got what we came for. Let's get out of here. We should be able to make it back in time...	我們已經拿到我們要的東西。趕快離開這裡吧。我們應該能準時回去…

生活篇

信仰篇

表達篇

外來語篇

文明篇

其它篇

Chi	Watch out!	注意！
Jennifer	Ahhhhh... ZAMBIES!	啊啊…殭屍！
Chi	Ambush! Damn it. You... all... go... to... HELL! (Mows down zombies with machine gun and tosses in a grenade <u>for good measure</u>.) You okay?	中埋伏了！媽的！全…都…給…我…下…地獄！（用機關槍狂掃殭屍，並丟入一枚手榴彈以確定它們全部被殲滅。）妳還好嗎？
Jennifer	One of them bit me.	其中一個咬了我。
Chi	(Speaks through microphone.) Guys, Jennifer's been attacked by a zombie. What do we do?	（透過麥克風通話）珍妮佛被殭屍咬傷了。我們現在怎麼辦？
Mike	We have the supplies for an antidote, but we need a chemistry set to make it. Have Jen find one and set it up in the village. Chi, you need to come back by yourself.	我們有解藥的成份，但是需要一組化學器材才能做出解藥。叫珍去找這樣一組儀器並在村莊裡把它架設起來。季薇，妳必須自己一個人回來。
Chi	How much time do I have?	我有多少時間？
Paul	You've got 20 minutes before Mike's life line runs out. AND we have 50 minutes before Jen turns. That leaves us with a 10 minute window to make and administer the antidote. Otherwise we'll have to blow her away! DEATH TO ALL ZOMBIES!	在麥可的生命值消耗完之前妳有二十分鐘趕回來。而珍在五十分鐘內就會變成殭屍。這樣算來我們剩下十分鐘的窗口製作並施打解藥。要不然我們只能把她炸爛！所有殭屍都得死！

Chi　You're saying that I have to run back, give Mike his meds, then fight all the way back to the village with you guys to save Jen?

你是說我必須跑回來，給麥可醫護包，然後再跟你們男生一起打回村莊去好救珍？

Paul & Mike　Yes!

對！

Chi　This is going to be the LOOOONNGGEST DAY of my life...

這將是我生命中最長～～的一天…

 ## 單字

☑ **MMORPG** 多人線上角色扮演遊戲。（Massive Multiplayer Online Role-Playing Game 的縮寫）

☑ **camouflage** [ˋkæməˌflɑʒ] *n.* （動物的）保護色、偽裝迷彩

☑ **trauma** [ˋtrɔmə] *n.* 外傷

☑ **suppression** [səˋprɛʃən] *n.* 鎮壓、壓制

☑ **sniper** [ˋsnaɪpɚ] *n.* 狙擊手

☑ **detonate** [ˋdɛtəˌnet] *v.* 引爆

☑ **ambush** [ˋæmbʊʃ] *v.* 埋伏

☑ **mow down** [ˋmo ˋdaʊn] *v.* 掃射

☑ **administer** [ədˋmɪnəstɚ] *v.* 給予、施打（醫療、藥物等）

 ## 片語

☑ <u>for good measure</u> 再多加一點以確認足夠

生活篇

信仰篇

表達篇

外來語篇

文明篇

其它篇

「祂」之一：Godspeed

在美國，鈔票的背面印著：IN GOD WE TRUST，而每個人每天總要說到一兩句含有 God 的句子。他們在提到神或上帝時，不完全都是跟宗教有關的情況，大半時候一般人使用 God 這個字，其實很類似我們說「噢（我的）天哪！」是用於表示震驚或極端高興的情緒，有時候呢，用 God 則有加強語氣的功能。前者的例子如：Oh, God! I think he just shot somebody! 而後者加強語氣的例子像是：I swear to God, someday I am gonna....

這回讓我們來探討三個有趣的單字／句子，它們都跟天上的那位「祂」有關，準備好了嗎？Here we GO!

時代背景：中世紀歐洲某處
電影情節：一名勇敢的武士即將踏上未知的艱辛旅程，啟程之前，他的摯友搭著他的肩膀，眼光堅決地對他說：“Godspeed!”

你知道在這一幕中，這句 Godspeed 是什麼意思嗎？

Godspeed 這個字跟 speed 目前我們熟知的意思「速度」是一點關係都沒有的喔！speed 的古英文寫法為 spede，在過去意義為「成功」。Godspeed 是由整句祝福語 “May God spede you.” 簡化而成的一個名詞，中文翻譯為「但願神成就你、應允你的成功。」（May God prosper you, grant your success.）

Godspeed 與我們現在流行的說法「Goodbye（註）」或「Good Luck」有幾點微妙的不同之處：在用到 Godspeed 的情況裡，被祝福的人一定要有個特定的任務或目標，說 Godspeed 是希望上帝能促成對方在即將開始做的那件事。Goodbye，很明顯的用途比較廣泛，各種離別的場合皆可；而 Good Luck 則是單純地祝對方好運，事情的成功與否跟上帝的意志沒有關係。

註 Goodbye 原來的全文是 God be with ye（願上帝與你同在，直到我們下次再會。）ye 就是 you，而 God 之所以會演變為今天我們用的 good，據猜測是因為被其他的離別用語如 good day 或 good night 所影響所致。

Notes

07 「祂」 [God]

29 God Forbid

Paul and his grandfather are standing in the back yard when Chi walks up to them.

保羅和他的祖父站在後院裡，季薇走向他們。

Chi	What are you two talking about?	你們兩個在討論什麼啊？
Paul	Grandpa is going to cut down my tree.	阿公要砍我的樹。
Chi	Why?	為什麼？
Grandpa	Well, I can show you the reason. Stand here and listen carefully. Tell me what do you hear?	我可以跟妳展示其中原因。來這邊站著並仔細聆聽。告訴我，妳聽到什麼？
Chi	Um, I hear the wind, leaves being blown by the wind... and a squeaking sound from the tree.	嗯，我聽到風聲、樹葉被風吹動著…還有從樹傳出的咯吱作響聲。
Grandpa	That squeaking noise is the tree bending. The tree itself is old, diseased, termite infested, and has been hit by lightening on more than one occasion. In the past, storms have caused its very heavy and dangerous branches to snap off. Some of which have already landed on the roof. I anticipate that the trunk itself simply can't take any more abuse and will break soon. God forbid it should hurt someone or cause even more damage to the house. Repairs are not cheap.	那個咯吱咯吱的噪音是由樹彎曲造成的。這棵樹本身已年老、有病害及白蟻蛀蝕、並且不只一次被閃電擊中。過去暴風雨曾導致它沈重且危險的樹枝折斷，有些樹枝已掉在屋頂上。我預測樹幹本身不能再承受更多損害，而且很快就會斷裂了。老天保佑千萬不要有人因而受傷，或對房屋造成嚴重災害。修理的費用不便宜啊！

Chi	What are those? Why are there wood planks and a rope on the tree?	那些是什麼？為什麼樹上有板架跟繩索？
Paul	Those are the decaying remains of the tree house I built when I was ten.	那些是我在十歲時蓋的樹屋留下來的腐朽遺跡。
Chi	You had a tree house? On THIS tree?	你曾經有個樹屋？在這棵樹上？
Paul	Yes. My imagination turned this tree into anything I wanted. Sometimes I would be a ninja, other times a pirate. I was Lord of my castle and King to my Kingdom. Scooby and I would play for hours in and around this area.	是啊。我的想像力可以把這棵樹變成任何我想要的東西。有時候我是一名忍者，有時候是一個海盜。我是這座城堡的主人，和我自己王國的君王。我的狗史酷比跟我會在這個地方裡裡外外玩上數個鐘頭。
Grandpa	Didn't you see the watercolor painting of him and his cousin Amy sitting in the tree. It's on the wall of the guest sitting room, right next to the piano.	妳沒看見那幅他跟他表妹愛咪坐在樹上的水彩畫。掛在會客室裡鋼琴旁邊的牆上。
Chi	I'll have to take a look next time I'm in there.	下回我再到那個房間裡要仔細瞧一瞧。
Paul	This tree holds a lot of good memories for me.	這棵樹對我而言有很多美好的回憶。
Chi	I'm sorry Babe. I can see you really care for it.	我很遺憾，寶貝。我知道你真的很在乎它。
Paul	Memories is all that remain. We mustn't	能留下的就只有回憶了。我

生活篇

信仰篇

表達篇

外來語篇

文明篇

其它篇

131

endanger our futures by overly romanticizing the nostalgia of our past. We can only move forward, for we can never truly return home. (Paul walks away.)

們不能對過去作太多不切實際的幻想而阻礙了未來的遠景。我們只能往前邁進，家是永遠也回不去了。（保羅黯然離去）

Chi   Grandma sits in her chair right on the corner of the house next to the tree. You're correct, Gramp. As sad as it is, it has to go.

阿媽總是坐在房子裡靠樹旁邊的那個角落裡。你是正確的，阿公，縱使再難過，這棵樹還是得砍。

Grandpa   That may be true, but that doesn't make it any easier.

那也許沒錯，但是對跟它已經產生感情的人來說不是件容易的事。

♥ 單字

☑ **squeak** [skwik] *v.* 軋軋作響、發出咯吱聲	☑ **termite** [`tɚ·maɪt] *n.* 白蟻
☑ **trunk** [trʌŋk] *n.* 樹幹	☑ **plank** [plæŋk] *n.* 厚板、木板
☑ **decay** [dɪ`ke] *v.* 腐朽	☑ **ninja** [`nɪndʒə] *n.* 忍者
☑ **romanticize** [ro`mæntə‚saɪz] *v.* 以不切實際的幻想眼光看待、對... 加以渲染	☑ **nostalgia** [nɑ`stældʒɪə] *n.* 懷舊

「祂」之二：God Forbid

　　God forbid（或 Heaven forbid）這句英文在中文裡面沒有直接的翻譯，我覺得最接近的說法大概是「老天保佑喔不要⋯」。它的字面意義為「上帝禁止」，但是一般人在用這句話時，並沒有盼望神來介入、阻止的意思，使用 God forbid，僅僅是藉以表示自己強烈的感受，希望某件事千萬千萬不要發生。

　　銷售人壽保險的業務員常用到這句，因為在向客戶解釋何時保險公司會付給受益人金錢時，前提通常是被保人往生或出意外的情況。當業務或律師人員必須提到這類令人不舒服的事情時，他們就會穿插個 God forbid，來緩和聽者的情緒，表示接下來說的事是沒有人樂意見到的，整句大概聽起來會像這樣子："You know, just in case—God forbid—something should ever happen to you ..."

　　說完了 God forbid 嚴肅的一面，你知不知道它也可以用來調侃人喲！這個用語通常是拿來諷刺某人小題大作、把一件小事看得比生命還重要。譬如說你弟弟剛新買了一部跑車，對它寶貝得不得了，從車商那開回來之後，除了上過一次加油站加油，就再也沒開上街過。有次週末碰到連續假期，你於是向弟弟建議開那部車載大夥兒出去兜風，沒想到弟弟卻一口回絕，理由是要是車子到外面被人家不小心碰了怎麼辦，這個時候你就可以說：God forbid there's a single scratch on you precious car!（不得了了喲！要是你的貴車有一點點刮痕！）

生活篇

信仰篇

表達篇

外來語篇

文明篇

其它篇

07 「祂」 [God]

30 God Willing

Chi is watching a YouTube video.　季薇正在看一段 YouTube 影片。

Paul	Dr. Michio Kaku?	加來道雄博士？
Chi	Yeah! He is talking about designing an Enterprise-like starship to travel the universe faster than the speed of light.	是啊！他正在討論如何設計出一艘像企業號的星艦，以比光速更快的速度遨遊宇宙。
Paul	In order to do that, he would need a warp drive engine.	要做到那樣，他需要曲速驅動引擎。
Chi	And an enormous amount of energy to distort space and time around the ship!	還要有相當巨大的能量以扭曲環繞星艦的空間與時間！
Paul	Exactly, smart girl. I can see you've been studying.	完全正確，聰明聰明。我看妳真的有在用功喔。
Chi	(Shyly) I do want to know about the subject you are studying and those scientific TV shows you constantly watch. So, do you think traveling at warp speed is possible?	（害羞地）人家想瞭解你唸的科目跟那些你經常在看的科學性電視節目嘛。所以，你認為曲速旅行可能嗎？
Paul	God willing. Given our current understanding of physics, yes it is possible; however it isn't yet feasible. The engineering requirements currently	如果上帝允許的話。根據我們現在對物理學的了解，是的，曲速旅行是有可能，但尚不可行。工程技術上的要

exceed our capabilities. Plus the design proposals that are on the drawing board are unappealing both in size and scope. For example, exotic materials like anti-mater and negative energy are difficult, dangerous, and expensive to produce. If humans are to go beyond our solar system and explore other galaxies within a reasonable time frame, we are going to have to come up with something better. Quantum teleportation may offer another contingency worth considering. There is much to explore and far-fetched dreams fuel the academic spirit.

求遠超出我們目前能力範圍；學者提出的設計藍圖在尺寸和程度上都不甚吸引人。舉例來說，要生產特殊的材料，如反物質與負能量，不但非常困難、危險，而且成本高昂。如果人類要在合理的時間內，飛越自身的太陽系並到其他的銀河系探勘，我們必須找到更好的解決方案。遠距量子傳輸也許提供了另一個值得考慮的可能性。探索的空間還很大，遙不可及的夢想驅動著學者們找尋答案。

Chi Michio says the amount of fuel necessary for warp, generated from negative energy, would be equivalent to the size of the planet Jupiter.

道雄博士說要扭曲時空所需的能量，假定我們可以從負能量中製造出來，大約是相當整顆木星的大小。

Paul And yet all we have ever produced in the entire history of modern physics is less than a gram. This humbling reality is daunting to say the least. As a species we have become more technically advanced in the last two hundred years than in all of mankind's history. And our knowledge is growing at an exponential rate. BUT, when we look out upon the infinite we feel as if we are stagnate, sitting on an island plateau, surrounded by wonders of existence we shall never

然而在整段現代物理學的歷史裡，我們到目前只做出少於一克的量，這項事實可以說是令人相當地氣餒。我們在過去兩百年內在科學上的進展，比全部人類歷史中加起來的還多，而且我們知識的累積速度成指數上升。然而，當我們往無限的那一方看去，卻覺得自己仍然處於停滯不前的狀態，周遭盡是奇妙的事物但永遠也碰觸不

生活篇

信仰篇

表達篇

外來語篇

文明篇

其它篇

	touch. (Sighs) It can drive you mad.	到。（歎氣）這會把人搞瘋的。
Chi	Earth to Paul. Are you there Paul?	地球呼叫保羅，你還在嗎，保羅？
Paul	Our ignorance is in the "God of the gaps." I hope that somewhere within those gaps is the will to make our dreams a reality, but people like Kurt Gödel, Claude Shannon, and Werner Heisenberg may have already squashed that too.	我們的無知陷落在「神性的裂縫」中。我只希望在那些裂縫中的某處，存在著某種意志，能使我們的夢想成為現實。但是哥德爾、香農、海森堡這些人，或許已經把這一點希望也給壓碎了。
Chi	How?	怎麼說？
Paul	Logic, information theory, and quantum mechanics state many of the physical limitations of observation. Ambiguity is an inherent and inescapable trait of the universe.	邏輯、訊息理論和量子力學提到許多觀察上的限制。不確定性是宇宙天生且無法擺脫的特性。
Chi	Quantum mechanics? Ambiguity? I need to watch more YouTubes!	量子力學？不確定性？我需要看更多 YouTube 影片！

♥ 單字

☑ **warp** [wɔrp] *v.* 翹曲、扭曲

☑ **feasible** [ˋfizəb!] *adj.* 可行的

☑ **drawing board** [ˋdrɔɪŋ ˋbord] *n.* 製圖桌、供人設計理念或原型的平台

☑ **contingency** [kənˋtɪndʒənsɪ] *n.* 可能性、可能發生的事件

☑ exponential [ˌɛkspoˋnɛʃəl] *adj.* 以指數成長的

☑ stagnate [ˋstægnet] *adj.* 停滯的

☑ plateau [plæˋto] *n.* （進步、發展的）停滯期

☑ God of the gaps 神性的裂縫、裂縫中的上帝。神學者利用科學中未知的領域（即所謂 gaps）以爭論有上帝的存在，這種辯論的觀點即稱為 God of the gaps。

☑ squash [skwɑʃ] *v.* 壓碎

☑ quantum mechanics [ˋkwɑntəm məˋkænɪks] *n.* 量子力學

☑ ambiguity [ˌæmbɪˋgjuətɪ] *n.* 不確定性、曖昧不清

「祂」之三：God Willing

在電影 *The Help*（台灣片名譯作《姊妹》）中有一幕，幫傭愛比琳（Aibileen）在巴士上，禮貌地詢問坐在旁邊的牧師他好不好，牧師亨利回答："If God is willing, Miss Clark. If God is willing."

If God is willing或簡單的說 God willing，意思是什麼呢？

"If God is willing" 可翻譯為「如果上帝應允的話」。說這句話的前提是，說者目前有一個正在進行的計畫，他／她該作的事都已經作了，但是說話的人也瞭解，神有祂特定的計畫，神的計畫也許跟他／她自己的計畫不同，作為一個謙卑的人類，說者接下來唯一能做的，就是盼望自己的計畫與神的意旨不謀而合。

就像中國人也有句話說：「驕者必敗」，說 God willing 的人，目的是不希望因為自己自大妄為、隨意談論進行中的事，而招致計畫的挫敗！這句話還可以許多不同的形式來表示：If it is God's will、If God permits、If God would allow it、If the Lord wills 和 If it is in His will。

如果你想用其他比較不帶濃重宗教意味的說法，則可以這麼說：If everything works out. 或 If things go as planned.

137

08 聖經的佳句 [Bible]

31 Escape by the Skin of Someone's Teeth

Paul and Chi have just finished watching the movie A Good Day to *Die Hard*
保羅跟季薇剛剛看完了電影《終極警探：跨國救援》。

Chi John McClane once again escaped death by the skin of his teeth!

約翰・麥克連這次又差了牙齒的皮那麼薄的距離地逃出死神魔掌！

Paul That's why people enjoy these action films so much. Directors use the cliff hanger technique in order to keep the audience on the edge of their seats. We eagerly speculate what will happen next and impatiently wait for the moment to unfold.

這就是為什麼人們這樣喜愛動作片的原因。導演運用緊張懸疑的劇情，把觀眾搞得既興奮又坐立難安。我們急切地推測下一步將發生什麼，沒耐心地等待故事的發展。

Chi I know! In the movie, it seems that Bruce Willis' character John and his son Jack fly by the seat of their pants the whole time. How did they know they would land safely when they jumped out of the building?

就是啊！在電影中，似乎布魯斯・威利的角色約翰與他的兒子傑克從頭到尾都沒有作事先的計畫，光靠臨機應變和急智來闖過種種的難關。他們怎麼知道在跳出大樓之後能夠平安地著地呢？

Paul That isn't really the best question to have. The better question is how did they safely make it to the bottom without severely injuring or killing themselves.

那其實不是最重要的問題。更關鍵的問題是，他們怎麼落地後沒有受重傷或死亡哩？

Chi They're the heros! They are not allowed to

他們是英雄啊！他們不能

die or at least not yet.

死，或至少時候未到。

Paul That's movie logic. Movie logic doesn't always make sense, but we accept it since it is fun to watch. A common problem created by writers is in building up dire situations so impossible to escape that it appears that they have <u>painted themselves into a corner</u>.

那是電影邏輯。電影邏輯不是永遠都符合常識，但是我們接受這種邏輯因為反正電影這樣很好看。編劇常常碰到的一個問題是，他們發展出非常緊迫的情境，看來完全沒有脫逃的機會，而把自己逼到無計可施的角落裡。

Chi Really? What do they do to save them?

真的？那他們要怎麼辦才能把主角們從這種困境裡救出來？

Paul There's always a small crack, defect, or limitation in any defense. I may have to defend an entire border while you only need to get one bit of information or a single person across that border. The weakest point in any security system is the human element. You push hard enough on the right spot and an opportunity for the protagonists to escape or gain an advantage will be created.

任何防禦系統中，永遠都有某個小縫隙、缺點或限制。你可能只需要獲取一點點資訊或幫助一個人通過界線，但是我卻要鞏固整條邊界。在任何安全系統裡最弱的地方就是人為因素。你在對的那一點上推得夠力了，幫助主角逃跑或取得優勢的機會就可以被創造出來。

Chi This incredibly small opportunity is what they mean by the "skin" of your teeth.

這個非常微小的機會就是人家說牙齒的「皮」的意思。

Paul Exactly! Teeth don't have "skin." Our heros escape through a near improbable yet still possible scenario. Making it all the more exiting when it happens.

完全正確！牙齒沒有「皮」。我們的英雄通過某個機率極微但仍有可能的情境脫身，當那發生時，觀眾興奮的程

生活篇

信仰篇

表達篇

外來語篇

文明篇

其它篇

Americans are attracted to this type of film because it philosophically attunes us to a deeper belief that no matter how bad it gets, there is always hope. It is what drives the American dream.

度更是大大地提升。美國人會被這類影片吸引，是因為它在哲學上導引我們到一個更深層的信仰：不論情況再糟，永遠都有希望。這是驅動美國夢的原力。

Chi　Sometimes a movie is just a movie.

有時候電影只是電影吧。

Paul　And sometimes it's not. There is always a philosophical undercurrent to any art form. There is a reason why we watch these types of movies and it involves more than just mere entertainment.

有時候電影不只是電影。在任何藝術形式底下，永遠都存在著一股哲學暗潮。我們會看這種類型的電影是有原因的，不單單是為了娛樂效果。

Chi　And here I thought it was just about big explosions.

而我還以為人們是為了要看爆炸的大場面哩。

 ## 單字

- ☑ speculate [ˋspɛkjəˌlet] **v.** 思索；推測
- ☑ dire [daɪr] **adj.** 緊迫的
- ☑ protagonist [proˋtægənɪst] **n.** 主角
- ☑ improbable [ɪmˋprɑbəb!] **adj.** 機率極低的
- ☑ attune [əˋtjun] **v.** 調音；使合調
- ☑ undercurrent [ˋʌndəˌkənt] **n.** 暗流

 ## 片語

- ☑ die hard 不輕易放棄信念而堅持奮戰到底；非常難以擊敗
- ☑ on the edge of someone's seat 焦急或興奮地等待著故事結局
- ☑ fly by the seat of someone's pants 沒有預先的計畫，光靠直覺和隨機應變很快地處理某件事

☑ <u>paint oneself into a corner</u> 把自己逼到角落而無路可退；陷入某種無計可施的處境

 # 聖經的佳句之一：Escape By the Skin of Someone's Teeth

由美國房地產大亨川普（Donald Trump）領軍的一個電視節目《誰是接班人》（*The Apprentice*），背景概念是聚集十數位精英份子，應徵川普集團中的一個總裁的職位。每一集裡製作單位都會提供某個企劃案，所有人分成兩個隊伍，兩隊的成員之中，有一人會主動升為專案經理。在當集尾聲，輸的那一隊的專案經理，須要指定某個他/她認為最該為結果負責的成員，跟他／她一起進入會議室，由川普決定哪個人被解雇。

在其中一集，兩位平分秋色的應徵者，在一場你來我往激烈的爭論後，其中一人終於被川普宣布淘汰，而留下的另一人，在這個劫後餘生的時刻裡，耳邊傳來川普的警告："You just escaped by the skin of your teeth!"

當我們說某人 escapes by the skin of his／her teeth，意思是這個人在千鈞一髮之際躲開了危險。由於牙齒沒有皮，所以如果你講你只差了牙齒的皮那麼厚的距離，就剛剛好逃出來，美國人認為你是差一點點（barely, nearly）躲掉災難。

這句說法是從約伯記（Job，發音[dʒob]，不是[dʒɑb]喔！）衍生出來的。聖經故事裡約伯受到魔鬼撒旦的試煉，他在敘述自己悲慘的情形時說：

My bone cleaveth to my skin and to my flesh, and I am escaped with the skin of my teeth.
--Job 19:20

對於這一節文原始的意義，向來學者持有不同的意見，有人認為這裡是說約伯皮包骨，什麼也不剩，只剩下牙齒的皮；也有人就用現代使用的意思來解釋：約伯在說自己險些喪命，逃過一劫；不論哪種解釋，今天的英文裡已經把 with 用 by 來取代，成為我們現在所知的慣用語。

生活篇

信仰篇

表達篇

外來語篇

文明篇

其它篇

32 The Apple of Someone's Eye

Paul and Chi are at a family wedding reception. After dinner, the DJ steps out onto the podium to make an announcement.

保羅和季薇在一場家族婚禮的宴會上。晚餐後，DJ 站上講台準備作宣布。

DJ	May I please have all of the married couples stand up? Wow, it looks like we have a lot of you here with us today. Good, good. Thank you all. Now I am going to ask you to remain standing up if you and your spouse have been married for one year. How about two years? Three years? ...	我可以麻煩所有結婚夫妻站起來嗎？哇，看來我們今天在場有很多對。好的，好的。謝謝大家。現在如果你和你的配偶已經結婚滿一年，我要請你們繼續站著。滿兩年的？三年的？
	Half of the couples are now sitting down when the DJ announces five years. Seven, eight, nine, ten ...	當 DJ 唸到五年時，一半的夫婦都已經坐著了。七、八、九、十…
DJ	Eleven years.	十一年。
	Paul and Chi look at each other, shrug their shoulder at the same moment and return to their seats.	保羅和季薇互相對望，同時聳了聳肩，然後坐下。
DJ	Twenty years ... thirty years ... forty years ... fifty years! You have been married to each other for more than fifty years?	二十年…三十年…四十年…五十年！你們倆人結婚已經超過五十年了？
	There is only one couple standing. They are Paul's grandparents. Grandpa is	這時全場只剩下一對夫妻站著。他們是保羅的祖父母。

gently holding grandma's arms to support her.

祖父輕輕地扶著祖母的手臂以支撐她。

Grandpa Actually we have been married for sixty-four years.

事實上，我們已經結婚六十四年了。

DJ Sixty-four years, everybody! Wow ... that's incredible! Will you share with our newlyweds here, and the rest of us what your secret is? What is the secret to maintaining such a wonderful and long marriage?

各位，六十四年！哇…那真是太了不起了！可以請您們跟我們的這對新人，以及在場的其他人分享您們的祕密嗎？請問要維持這樣美好和長久的婚姻，祕密是什麼？

Grandpa Well, there were good days and bad days in the last sixty-four years of our marriage and there will continue to be. I have always believed that if you want something to work, you have to work at it.

嗯，在我們過去六十四年的婚姻裡有好日子，也有壞日子，相信往後也是這樣。我一直相信如果你想要某件事成功，你必須去努力經營它。

Grandpa Ditto. I am very lucky to have Vint as my husband. He never gives up and he always looks after me.

同上。我很幸運有文森作我的先生。他從不放棄而且他一直都很照顧我。

Paul's grandparents gracefully accept the congratulations from everyone and return to their seats.

保羅的祖父母優雅地接受所有人的祝賀，然後回到他們的座位坐下。

Chi I can see that after all these years Grandma is still the apple of Grandpa's eye.

我可以感覺到，在這麼多年後阿媽仍然是阿公眼中的蘋果。

Paul As you are the apple of mine. Did you

就像妳是我的蘋果一樣。妳

生活篇

信仰篇

表達篇

外來語篇

文明篇

其它篇

notice that some of the guests looked surprised when they saw you and I were still standing when the DJ said ten years? Can you believe our tenth anniversary was just last month? It feels like our own wedding was only yesterday!

有沒有發覺到，當 DJ 講出十年而妳跟我仍舊站著時，有些賓客看起來很驚訝哩？妳能相信我們上個月才剛度過十週年慶嗎？我覺得我們自己的婚禮好像才昨天耶！

Chi I know! I feel the same way. It's strange how <u>time flies</u> by, but it doesn't feel like it's been that long. You think we can be like your Grandpa and Grandma?

對呀！我也有相同的感覺。奇怪的是時間飛逝，但是我不覺得有過了這麼久。你認為我們可以像你阿公阿媽一樣嗎？

Paul I have no doubt. <u>I am my grandfather's boy.</u>

我毫無疑問。 有其祖必有其孫。

 ## 單字

- ☑ **reception** [rɪˋsɛpʃən] *n.* 宴會。不要跟 wedding ceremony（結婚典禮）搞混了，wedding reception 是指結婚典禮之後舉辦的宴會。

- ☑ **DJ** *n.* 對聽眾播放事先錄製音樂的人員。在美國 wedding DJs 不單只是播放音樂，他們的工作還包括主持、提供遊戲及鼓勵來賓跳舞等。

- ☑ **podium** [ˋpodɪəm] *n.* 講台

- ☑ **newlywed** [ˋnjulɪˏwɛd] *n.* 剛結婚的人；新人。注意講「新婚夫婦」時要用複數 newlyweds，因為有「一對」新人。

- ☑ **ditto** [ˋdɪto] *n.* 同前者所言；同上

日常會話

- ☑ If you want something to work, you have to work at it. 如果你想要某件事成功,你必須去努力經營它。
- ☑ Time flies. 時間過得真快;時光飛逝。
- ☑ I am my grandfather's boy. 有其祖必有其孫。各種形式包括:"I am my father's son" 和 "I am my mother's daughter" 等。

聖經的佳句之二:**The Apple of Someone's Eye**

我和保羅還住在洛杉磯時,有次應邀出席他學校同事的婚禮。派對上人來人往,好不熱鬧,當時學校的校長,也是賓客之一,她一見到緊貼在保羅身旁的我,即相當熱情地說:"What a pleasure to finally meet you. Paul talks about you all the time. You are the apple of his eye!"

喔,聽了好快樂。

The apple of one's eye,這眼中的蘋果,指的是瞳孔。眼睛是人最寶貴的資產之一,面臨危險時,人類通常第一個反應即保護自己的眼睛,因此 the apple of someone's eye 衍伸出來的意思就是某人最珍愛的東西。美國人會把這句話用來形容雙親對孩子,尤其是父親對女兒的愛與保護上面,因為蘋果給人的感覺又甜又無辜,就像清純的小女孩。當然,也可以像校長那樣說,指戀人對對方的重視。

這句佳話在英文版的聖經中各處出現,譬如於詩篇 Psalms(讀作[sɑms],p 和 l 不發音)的十七篇第八節,大衛向上帝祈求:

Keep me as the apple of the eye, hide me under the shadow of thy wings.
(求你保護我,如同保護眼中的瞳人,將我隱藏在你翅膀的蔭下。)

你有沒有注意到,上面的翻譯把 the apple of the eye 譯為眼中的「瞳人」?這段譯文我是直接從中文版的聖經裡摘錄出來的,原來,根據原始的希伯來文,這個詞除了指「瞳孔」外,其實更可直譯為「眼中的小小人」,也就是對方瞳孔中自己的倒影。聖經英文版的譯者則一概翻為:the apple of one's eye,形成了現代通用的說法。

生活篇

信仰篇

表達篇

外來語篇

文明篇

其它篇

It's Friday night and Mike is teaching Paul, Chi, and Jennifer how to play Texas Hold'em. Jennifer has folded and Paul stares at his cards thinking.

現在是星期五的晚上，麥可在教保羅、 季薇和珍妮佛怎麼打德州撲克。珍妮佛已經蓋牌，而保羅正瞪著他的牌思索著。

Paul	I'm gunna go all in.	我要全下。
Group	Huh... what?	啊…什麼？
Paul	You heard me... ALL IN BITCHES!	你們都聽到我說的…全下，你們這些臭婆娘！
Chi	I fold.	我蓋牌。
Mike	Guess it's just you and me... I'M ALL IN!	我猜就剩下你跟我了…我全下！
Chi	No way!	不會吧！
Paul	Before we go any further I want to know what would happen if I win? Do I get to take all of your chips even if you have more than me? That doesn't seem fair.	在我們進行下一步前，我想知道要是我贏了會怎樣？即使你有的籌碼比我多，我也可以全部都拿走嗎？那似乎不是很公平。
Mike	You're right Paul, although many beginners make that mistake. Low and behold the actual answer makes a lot more sense. The winner takes all "called" bets. The rest is returned before <u>the hand</u>	你說得沒錯保羅，很多初學者犯了那樣的錯誤。你瞧，真正的答案其實相當合理。贏的人可取走所有「被跟注」的部份。多餘的籌碼在

is shown.

攤牌之前要退回給玩家。

Paul Oh, I get it and if there is more than two players "all in" then there are "side pots" making up the difference. Winner takes only their own calls.

喔，我懂了，所以如果有多於兩人以上的玩家叫全下，那麼多餘的籌碼就放到「邊池」裡。贏家只能贏得他們下注的金額。

Mike Right!

正確！

Chi Wait! What?

等一下！什麼？

Mike No matter how little you have in your stack, you can always call with the rest of your chips. Your opponent can only match your bet, however if another player says "all in" then a "side pot" must be made with the remaining chips. For example, assume there is a $200 pot. You have $50 left and your opponent bets $75. You call "all in" and place your last $50 in the pot. Your opponent takes back $25. If you win you get $300.

不管你的籌碼堆有多小，你永遠可以用你全部的籌碼下注。你的對手只能用一樣多的籌碼來跟你對賭，但是如果另外一個人也叫全下的話，那麼一個「邊池」就由超過玩家能夠下注的多餘籌碼而建立起來。舉例來說，假設彩池裡有兩百元。你剩下五十元而你的對手下注七十五元。你喊「全下」並把你所有五十塊錢推到獎池裡，你的對手必須把多的二十五元拿回去。如果你贏了你可以拿到總數三百元。

Paul But if there are three or more players who are "all in" then a "side pot" is made.

但是如果有三個或三個以上的玩家「全下」，那麼就必須建立一個「邊池」。

Mike Right! Using the same example the pot is still $200 and an "all in" bet of $50 is met, but this time there is a third player who

對！以相同的例子來說，彩池裡也是有兩百元，一人叫「全下」放進五十元而另一

生活篇

信仰篇

表達篇

外來語篇

文明篇

其它篇

	calls "all in" also. This creates the "side pot."	人跟進五十元，但是這回有第三個玩家也說「全下」。這種情況就創造出「邊池」。
Paul	The third player need only match the second's remaining chips.	第三個玩家只需要放進與第二個玩家剩下的籌碼相同的數目即可。
Mike	Low and behold if the first player wins they keep the center pot. If the second player wins they keep the center pot and the side pot. If the third player wins ...	啊哈，你看如果第一個玩家贏了他拿走主池裡所有的籌碼。如果第二個玩家贏他不但贏走主池也贏走邊池。如果是第三個玩家贏的話...
Paul	They take everything and dance around as they mock the LOOOOSERRRRRRS!	他就贏得所有的錢，可以一邊跳舞一邊取笑那些輸輸輸輸家家家！

 # 單字

☑ **Texas Hold'em** 據稱這種撲克牌遊戲最早是從德州起源的，因而冠以 Texas 的名稱；至於第二個字 hold'em，其實是 hold them 兩字合起來唸的發音，德州撲克一個很獨特的規則是，玩家手中持有的牌，是從一開始發牌就決定的，不像其他撲克牌遊戲可以抽新牌或棄牌，每個人都持有同樣的牌（to hold them）直到蓋牌或攤牌，因此就稱為 hold'em。

☑ **fold** [fold] *v.* 蓋牌

☑ **gunna** 將要。Gunna 是 gonna 另一種常見的寫法，等於 going to

☑ **all in** 全下

☑ **call** [kɔl] *v. n.* 跟注

☑ **pot** [pɑt] *n.* 彩池

☑ **stack** [stæk] *n.* （籌碼等的）一堆；一疊

生活篇

信仰篇

表達篇

外來語篇

文明篇

其它篇

☑ mock [mɑk] *v.* 嘲笑；揶揄

 片語

☑ show someone's hand 攤牌。這句話跟中文裡的攤牌一樣，可引申為「向他人坦白自己的意圖或祕密。」

 聖經的佳句之三：**Lo and Behold**

在 2012 年洛杉磯雜誌（Los Angeles）七月號裡面有一篇文章，針對目前上演的一部電視劇 *Girls* 作評論。在播出的第一季中，戲中描述年輕的女主角，腦袋聰明又有才氣，卻在丟掉工作後，自暴自棄地跑到自負狂妄的男友住處，接受更多的羞辱，只為了換取一點慰藉。作者對此感到不解、憤怒，甚至一度拒看。但是許多她周遭的朋友都在觀看，並積極地與她討論這部影劇。文中她寫道：

"...I have started watching episodes again to see what I missed: the quirks, the silences, the artistry, and strange of all, the tenderness that starts to creep in and that I didn't notice at first. Lo and behold, the cad turns into a sentimental boyfriend. Who knew?"

句子中 "lo" 跟 "behold" 兩個字的意思都是「看」，英文中用這句來表示驚訝的情緒。在文章的寫法「起承轉合」裡，"lo and behold" 是一個有「轉」作用的句型，用以帶出接下來令人驚喜、眼睛一亮的發展（註），中文的意思大概接近「嘿，瞧！」或「啊哈！」

"Lo" 與 "behold" 這兩個字在聖經許多章節中都有出現，但當時是分開使用的，十八世紀起開始有人把兩個字連在一起，1820 年後這整個句子就普遍流行了。

也許你會覺得有點奇怪，既然兩個字的意義相等，「看」和「看」，講起來不是顯得重複了嗎？這就要提到英文這個語言中一個很迷人的特徵：音樂性。句子像："each and every"、"safe and sound"、"fair and square" 等，都是由兩個意義相近的單字組成，但因為押韻的關係，唸起來順口又好聽，成為美國人愛掛在嘴邊的話！

註 另外像法文的 "voilà" 和摹仿樂器聲的 "ta-da"，美國人也喜歡講，用法類似，但感覺比較花俏調皮一些（像魔術師揭露最後的驚喜那樣）！

08 聖經的佳句 [Bible]

34 A Good Samaritan

11 o'clock at night. Chi walks into the house.
晚間十一點。季薇走進屋子裡。

Paul	You're late. Where have you been?	妳回來晚了。到哪裡去啦？
Chi	I... I hit a deer on the way home!	我…我在回來的途中撞到一頭鹿！
Paul	What'd you do to my car?	妳把我的車怎麼了？
Chi	Paul? You should be asking about ME!	保羅？你應該問「我」有沒有怎樣才對吧？
Paul	Fine! What happened to the deer?	好吧！那頭鹿有沒有怎樣？
Chi	PAUL!	保羅！
Paul	What happened to you ... dear?	妳有沒有怎樣…親愛的？（作者按：「親愛的」英文 dear 與「鹿」deer 發音相似）
Chi	I was going uphill. I think I followed the car in front of me too closely. Right before I reached the top, I saw it fishtail. The next thing I know there is a huge deer bouncing off my windshield.	我當時正往上坡開。我想我大概跟前面的車跟得太緊了。在要到達坡頂前，我看到那部車突然扭轉。接下來就是一隻龐大的鹿從我面前的擋風玻璃反彈出去。

Paul	Why didn't you call me?	妳為什麼沒打電話給我？
Chi	I tried to, but I couldn't get a signal.	我有試過，但是手機沒訊息。
Paul	How did you get home?	那妳是怎麼回家的？
Chi	The car is still drivable, but there is a huge dent on the hood and grate. I will have to call the insurance company tomorrow. A police officer escorted me to town to make sure I got home safe.	車子還能開，但是車蓋跟前面通氣口上有一個好大的凹痕。明天我必須得打電話通知保險公司。一位警察先生護送我到鎮上，確定我平安到家。
Paul	How did you get the police if your phone was not working?	如果妳手機不能用，那妳又是怎麼找到警察的？
Chi	A Good Samaritan stopped by and called the police for me. A nice college student. He told me he grew up in the area and that he had just come back for the summer. I was very fortunate that he was there. I was in total shock and I didn't know where I was. He calmed me down and helped me file the police report. After he left, several people also stopped their cars to ask me if I was all right. A local hunter even helped the police officer get the deer off the road. Everyone was so kind and helpful.	有位善心人士停下來並幫我打電話給警察。人很好的一個大學生。他告訴我他原來在那個地區長大，趁這個夏天回來家裡住。我真的是很幸運他剛好在那裡。我完全被嚇呆了，也不知道自己身在何處。他安慰我並且幫我報了案。他離開了之後，另外還有幾個人也停下車來問我有沒有怎樣。有個當地的獵人甚至幫警察先生將鹿搬離路面。每一個人都好親切好幫忙喔。
Paul	You're lucky it went so well. That isn't what	事情會這麼順利是妳幸運。

生活篇

信仰篇

表達篇

外來語篇

文明篇

其它篇

151

typically happens. People who live in extremely rural areas understand better than most how vulnerable you can become in the middle of nowhere.

通常這種情況不會發生。住在非常鄉下地方的人們，比較能體會一個人在前不著村、後不著店的深山野嶺中，可能變得多麼地脆弱。

Chi　I have to admit it was pretty scary.

我必須承認那真是很恐怖。

Paul　Well I'm glad that you are back safe and sound.

我很高興妳平平安安地回來了。

Chi　Plus the hunter offered to cut us some steaks from the dear.

還有啊，那個獵人答應要切幾塊鹿排給我們。

Paul　I think that those are the most expensive steaks we will ever eat.

我想那些鹿排大概會是我們吃過最貴的肉吧。

 ## 單字

☑ **fishtail** [ˋfɪʃˌtel] *v.* 車輛後端快速地左右滑行；尾部突然轉向

☑ **bounce** [baʊns] *v.* 反彈；彈跳

☑ **windshield** [ˋwɪndˌʃild] *n.* 擋風玻璃

☑ **dent** [dɛnt] *n.* 凹痕

☑ **grate** [gret] *n.* 車子前方的通風用的鐵窗；柵格

☑ **escort** [ˋɛskɔrt] *v.* 護送

rural [ˋrʊrəl] *adj.* 鄉下的；農村地區的

 ## 片語

☑ in the middle of nowhere 前不著村、後不著店的偏僻地點；鳥不生蛋的鬼地方
☑ safe and sound 平平安安地；安安全全地

聖經的佳句之四：A Good Samaritan

Good Samaritan：指見到他人遭遇困難，挺身而出奮勇幫忙的好心人。

Samaritan 是住在 Samaria 城的人民，中文翻譯為「撒瑪利亞人」。A Good Samaritan 這個詞的由來，是聖經的路加福音第十章二十五到三十七節這中間，耶穌作的一個比喻（註）：

一人在旅途中受到強盜攻擊，不但衣服被奪走，又被打得半死，奄奄一息地倒在路旁。第一個路過的人，是個祭司，見到了那個受傷倒地的人，卻什麼也沒做，從路的另一邊繞過去。第二個路人，同樣也只是看看他，逕自走下去。

但是一位從撒瑪利亞來的旅人見到他，起了憐憫之心，不但幫他包紮傷口，把他放在自己的座騎上，帶這個受傷的人到一間旅社照料他。臨走之前，還掏錢給旅社老闆請他繼續照顧那人。

就這樣，聖經中一個無私助人的 Samaritan，逐漸演變成今天我們所知的 "a Good Samaritan"。很多時候，新聞界使用這個名詞來代表某個匿名，或無從得知其真實姓名的善心人士，譬如標題寫 "Good Samaritan helps trapped driver" 或 "Good Samaritan helps catch robbery suspect" 等。

註 這段經文大概的內容是，有個律師問耶穌要怎麼才能得永生，耶穌反問他：律書上怎麼寫？律師回答：「要全心全意敬愛上帝，且要愛鄰舍如同愛你自己。」耶穌說你就這麼做就對了。律師又問，那我的鄰舍是誰呢？耶穌就以這個著名的 Samaritan 寓言，回應他的問題，暗示不論每個人是來自什麼樣的背景、種族或宗教（撒瑪利亞人是異教徒），都應視為鄰舍，有難時相互幫忙。

生活篇

信仰篇

表達篇

外來語篇

文明篇

其它篇

35 Play Devil's Advocate

Paul and Chi are having lunch at the local flea market.
保羅和季薇在當地的跳蚤市場用午餐。

Chi	Mmm ... These garlic fries are scrumptious! How do you like your brisket?	嗯…這些香蒜薯條真是美味！你點的牛胸肉味道如何？
Paul	It's nice. But not as tasty as your barbecued pork ribs.	味道是不錯，但沒妳的烤排骨好吃。
Chi	Nothing has yet come close to my secret recipe! (Contemplating) What would you say about renting a booth here?	沒人可以比得上我的獨家祕方！（沈思中）你覺得如果我們在這裡租一間攤位如何？
Paul	Selling what?	賣什麼？
Chi	Our barbecue sauce! It would be great! Five dollars a bottle. A hundred bottles. Five hundred dollars profit!	我們的烤肉醬啊！會超棒的！一罐賣五元美金，賣一百罐，就賺五百元！
Paul	I hate to play devil's advocate here because you sound so enthusiastic, but as someone who has done this before I have to warn you.	看妳這麼興致高昂，我實在不想當魔鬼的辯護人來挑戰妳，但是因為以一個過來人的身份，我必須給予警告。
Chi	You did this before?	你以前做過這類的生意？
Paul	Grandpa and I sold antiques for years, but profit was not the motivation. We had a lot of fun doing it. What little money we	阿公跟我做了多年的古董交易，可是我們的動機不是因為利潤，而是我們從中獲得

did make went into gas and food.

很大的樂趣。收入不多，賺來的錢都花在汽油和食物的開銷上。

Chi Yeah, but making the sauce is cheap and easy.

是嘛，但是製作烤肉醬便宜又簡單。

Paul How much is a booth?

一個攤位的租金多少？

Chi Jennifer told me that her friend Sheila pays fifty dollars for a space here. The flea market opens on Sunday, so we can bottle the sauce on Saturday night.

珍妮佛的朋友席拉為這裡的一個位子付五十元。跳蚤市場星期天營業，所以我們可以在星期六晚上裝罐。

Paul Fifty? If we sell our sauce at five dollars per bottle and control our costs under a dollar, the profit is four. Fifty divided by four... is twelve and a half bottles to break even. We should be able to sell at least two bottles per hour, eight hours a day, sixteen bottles. Sixteen subtract twelve and a half times four is fourteen. Subtract five dollars each for lunch and we have four dollars profit... we'll be hundredaires in no time!

五十？假設我們的烤肉醬定價為五元，將成本控制在一元以下，那麼利潤是四元。五十除以四…我們必須賣十二又二分之一罐才能打平。我們每個鐘頭可以至少賣出兩罐，一天八小時，也就是十六罐；十六減十二又二分之一再乘四是十四，十四塊錢減掉我們倆每人五元的午餐，最後剩下四元的利潤... 這樣看來我們成為百元富翁的那天是指日可待！

Chi (Snide) Ha, ha, very funny!

（諷刺的）哈、哈，很好笑！

Paul Very few people are going to just randomly buy a bottle of sauce. You're going to

很少人會隨隨便便就購買烤肉醬。妳必須要激勵妳的客

	have to motivate them and that beckoning call will be the sweet smell of barbecue.	戶，而烤肉的香味會吸引人來。
Chi	I can do that! I can grill rib samples at our station.	那我做得來！我可以在我們的攤位上烤一些試吃的排骨樣品。
Paul	Are samples free?	我們做樣品是免費的嗎？
Chi	Uh ... No?	嗯…不是？
Paul	A rack of ribs is at least ten bucks! Oh and don't forget about the charcoal which is another five.	一付排骨至少是十塊錢！噢，別忘了再加上一包木炭五塊。
Chi	Doesn't that put us in the negative?	那不就是說我們的進帳是負數的了？
Paul	It's not looking tenable. It might be easier to just sell directly to the grocery store. They have been known to reserve shelf space for local merchants.	看來這個主意站不住腳。也許直接進貨給超市會比較簡單，它們常為當地的商家保留貨架上的位子。
Chi	Let me think about it some more before we do anything.	在我們著手進行任何事情前，我得要多想一下囉。

♥ 單字

☑ scrumptious [ˋskrʌmpʃəs] *adj.* 很好吃的

☑ brisket [ˋbrɪskɪt] *n.* 牛胸肉

☑ contemplate [ˋkɑntɛmˏplet] *v.* 沈思、考慮

☑ antique [ænˋtik] *n.* 古董物、古玩

☑ gas [gæs] *n.* 汽油、gasoline 的簡稱。美國人有時用 gas 這個字指「汽油」，有時指「瓦斯」，要看上下文決定。

☑ snide [snaɪd] *adj.* 諷刺的、挖苦的

☑ beckon [`bɛkn] *v.* 向... 招手

☑ charcoal [`tʃɑrˌkol] *n.* 木炭

☑ tenable [`tɛnəb!] *adj.* 經得起批判的、站得住腳的

慣用語之一：Play Devil's Advocate

這個章節讓我們來談 idioms，也就是慣用語。有些字典把 idiom 或翻為「成語」。在日常對話中，如果光照字面的意思來解釋 idioms，很多時候真是會令人摸不著頭緒！要了解某個慣用語，首先要懂得它引伸出來的意義，例如：raining cats and dogs 不能講「天在下貓和狗」，要理解成「在下大雨」。

第一個我想解釋的慣用語，是在商業及教育領域中常聽到的一句話：“To play devil's advocate.” 假想以下情形：在整個禮拜絞盡腦汁的辛勤工作之後，你呈上了一份企劃案。主管看過後，在會議中間對你說：“I am going to play devil's advocate, so here are the questions...”

老闆在說什麼？做魔鬼的擁護者？在演電影《魔鬼代言人》（註）嗎？如果有人說他要 play devil's advocate，意思是他純粹為了辯證的目的，來當你的反方。這麼做可以檢視你論點的邏輯性，幫助你們共同去思考這其中是否有漏洞。

Devil's advocate 這個角色是起源於羅馬天主教堂封聖的儀式。在教堂提名某位聖人後，教會的權威即指派一名律師來擔任 devil's advocate，他／她的任務就是站在反方的立場，找出這個被提名者任何人格上的瑕疵，懷疑奇蹟是否為造假，有無確鑿的證據以證明候選人符合聖人的資格。

註 基努李維與艾爾帕西諾多年前合演的一部電影《魔鬼代言人》，片名原文就是 *The Devil's Advocate*。

生活篇 — 信仰篇

表達篇

外來語篇 — 文明篇 — 其它篇

36 Offer an Olive Branch

Paul and Chi finish watching *Conan O'Brien Can't Stop.*
保羅和季薇剛看完紀錄電影《柯南・歐布萊恩停不下來》。

Chi I can still remember all that gossip surrounding Conan's departure from NBC.	我仍記得在柯南宣布離開美國國家廣播公司時到處盛傳的流言蜚語。
Paul Yeah, it was an entertaining train wreck while it lasted. For the most part *The Tonight Show* has a venerable history as being one of TV's greatest franchises. Unfortunately, Leno was unable to gracefully part ways in the manner in which Carson modeled.	是啊,那真是一場娛樂性十足的大災難。大體來說,這部堪稱最偉大電視節目之一的《今夜秀》,有著一段令人肅然起敬的歷史。很不幸的,傑・雷諾無法像他的前輩卡森那般從容優雅地辭去主持人的位子。
Chi Before Conan's last episode, for a whole week he did all kinds of jokes mocking the insanity happening behind closed doors... Remember this one? (Imitating Conan O'Brien) "Hosting *The Tonight Show* has been a fulfillment of a life-long dream for me. And I just want to say to the kids out there watching: You can do anything you want in life ... Unless Jay Leno wants to do it, too."	在柯南主持的最後一集之前,整個禮拜他所講的笑話,都是在嘲諷那些關著門進行的祕密會議、以及背後所發生的許多令人匪夷所思的事…記得這個嗎?(模仿柯南・歐布萊恩)「能夠有幸主持《今夜秀》對我來説是件夢想成真的事。而我想要對電視銀幕前觀賞的孩子們説:任何你想要做的事情,你都能做到…除非傑・雷諾也想做。」

Paul	I have to admit, of all the jokes that week, that one was my favorite. When NBC tried to push *The Tonight Show* to 12:05 am Conan vented by saying they would have to change the name of the show to "Today."	我必須承認，那一週裡他講過的所有笑話裡，這個是我的最愛。當國家廣播公司嘗試把《今夜秀》延後到晚上十二點零五分播出的時候，柯南立即發出不滿，他說這麼一來節目的名稱就得改成《今天》了。（作者按：《今天》（*Today*）是另一個知名美國晨間新聞節目。）
Chi	Hahaha... No kidding. Do you know if the quarrel between Jay and Conan was ever resolved?	哈哈哈…說得也對喔。你曉得這場介於傑與柯南之間的糾紛是否曾經化解嗎？
Paul	During an episode of *The Jay Leno Show*, Jay tried to offer an olive branch to Conan, but it <u>fell on deaf ears</u>. Imagine what it would feel like to have a bully knock you down and steal your lunch money only to then put his hand out in friendship. It is not exactly an appealing exchange to say the least.	在《傑・雷諾秀》的其中一集裡，傑試圖向柯南伸出象徵握手言和的橄欖枝，但沒被理會。想像如果一個愛欺侮人的同學，在把妳推到在地、搶走妳的午餐錢以後，將手伸出來要跟妳做朋友，妳的感覺會怎樣。簡單說，這種交易不是很吸引人。
Chi	Well, I think that they both are funny.	我覺得他們兩個都很風趣。
Paul	I agree, but that is not the issue. The reality is that this type of thing happens in boardrooms all the time. It is a normal part of business, however these matters are usually debated in private because they are sensitive issues. However, on	我同意，但那不是問題重心。事實上這種情況經常發生在董事會會議室中，它是做生意很正常的一部份，只是由於事涉敏感，通常這些事情都是私下討論。然而，

生活篇　信仰篇

表達篇

外來語篇　文明篇　其它篇

occasion arguments will flow over into the arena of public opinion, and it ends up as a PR nightmare for all involved. No one comes out of these events unscathed, mainly because everyone is desperately trying to save face while dealing with the realities of commerce. After all, hundreds of millions of dollars is at stake.

有時這些爭論流入一般大眾的耳中，最後對每位牽涉其中的人士的外界形象都造成傷害。由於每個人都想盡辦法一邊挽救面子，一邊處理商業真實的面向，沒有人能毫髮無傷地從事件中走出；畢竟，我們談的是好幾億的金額。

Chi　Maintaining your professionalism in the middle of a heated exchange is challenging, and I think they both did the best they could at the time.

在激烈的交手間保持專業的態度是不容易的，而我認為他們兩位那個時候都有盡力去做了。

 單字

- ☑ NBC 美國國家廣播公司，為 National Broadcasting Company 的縮寫。
- ☑ train wreck [`tren `rɛk] *n.* 規模浩大的災難事件
- ☑ venerable [`vɛnərəb!] *adj.* 值得尊敬的、令人肅然起敬的
- ☑ episode [`ɛpəˌsod] *n.* （電視節目的）一集
- ☑ quarrel [`kwɔrəl] *n.* 爭吵、糾紛
- ☑ bully [`bʊlɪ] *n.* 欺凌弱小者、以大欺小的學生
- ☑ boardroom [`bordˌrum] *n.* 董事會會議室
- ☑ unscathed [ʌn`skeðd] *adj.* 無傷的、平安的
- ☑ heated [`hitɪd] *adj.* 激烈的

 片語

- ☑ fall on deaf ears （建議、意見等）被忽略、沒人理會

慣用語之二：Offer an Olive Branch

2012 年的美國金球獎頒獎前夕，兩大天王艾頓‧強（Elton John）和瑪丹娜為了誰應該獲得最佳歌曲獎，公開鬧出口水大戰。不過瑪丹娜在得獎後，隨即 offered an olive branch to her rival，在後台對記者表示她仰慕艾頓‧強的才氣，並認為他會得到其他的獎項。

To offer（extend）an olive branch to 某人，「獻上橄欖枝」，代表的是你願意與那人握手言和。

橄欖枝象徵和平，這可追溯至我們早已耳熟能詳的聖經舊約故事，當困在方舟上的諾亞，看見鴿子啣回來一根橄欖樹枝，他就知道洪水已經退去，世界又回到原來平靜的狀態。

橄欖枝獲選為人們盼望息戰的象徵物，也有其實際上的考量。因為橄欖需要長年的細心栽培才會成熟，戰爭時期農夫們無法專注於田園的耕作上，橄欖樹的成長便大受打擊，所以若是有人呈獻給敵方或不合的朋友橄欖的樹枝，代表那人已經厭倦了長期的戰事，而願意坐下和談。

生活篇　信仰篇

表達篇

外來語篇　文明篇　其它篇

163

37 Give Someone a Run for Someone's Money

At the morning huddle.　晨間會議中。

Barbara	Our branch has been open here in the City of Walnut for a month now. In that time we have garnered more than six million dollars in deposits.	我們的分行在核桃市開幕到現在已經有一個月了。在這段期間我們匯集了超過六百萬美金的存款。
	(The tellers gasp and look at each other in excitement.)	（出納員們皆驚歎並興奮地互相對望）
Barbara	I want everyone to know that it was no small feat. We should all be proud of our hard work and dedication. Give yourselves a round of applause.	我要每個人都知道這是件相當不凡的成就，我們都應該對自己的辛勤工作和奉獻感到驕傲，現在為你自己鼓鼓掌。
	(Everyone smiles and happily claps in acknowledgement.)	（每個人發出微笑並且開心地拍手）
Barbara	Now, yesterday I asked our sales reps to visit the competition and inquire about opening new accounts at their banks. Daniel, would you please share with us what you have learned about Bank of America, who by the way, has been in the neighborhood for over thirty years.	好，昨天我要所有的業務代表到敵手的銀行去詢問如何開新帳戶。丹尼，麻煩你跟我們分享你在美國銀行學到了什麼，順道一提，美國銀行在這個社區裡已經有三十多年了。
	(Crowd leans in with curiosity.)	（眾人好奇地靠近）

Daniel　Well… I am sorry to say, that I was disappointed. No one acknowledged me when I walked in or helped me after I waited for several minutes. I had a feeling that they didn't want to bother with me because I looked young. Right now their main focus is senior citizens. If you're over sixty-five you instantly get a premier checking account and a free portfolio review. They are highly aware of the fact that there is a huge retiree community in the area and they appeared to only be aiming specifically at those customers' investable assets.

嗯…遺憾地說，我感到相當失望。我走進他們的辦公室時沒人看我一眼，然後在我等候了數分鐘之後也沒人來幫我。我有種感覺，他們懶得理我的原因是因為我看來很年輕，現在他們主要的焦點都放在年紀大的客戶，如果你年齡超過六十五，你立刻就可以得到一個尊榮支票帳戶，以及一次免費的個人理財諮詢服務。他們十分明白這個區域裡住著很多退休的老人家，很明顯地他們只把目標放在這些客人的潛在投資資產上。

Barbara　How about you, Mike? What was your experience at East West Bank?

那你呢，麥可？你在華美銀行的經驗如何？

Mike　It was kind of awkward. East West Bank, in this region, is known for primarily serving Asian customers. When I stepped into their branch, everybody there just stared at me. They were not quite sure what to even make of me. I waited for fifteen minutes hoping to speak to a banker, but no one greeted me or asked me why I was there. So I left.

我的經驗則有點令人不自在。華美銀行，在這一帶來說，是以主要服務華人客戶著名。當我走進他們的分行時，那裡的每個人就只是睜大眼瞪著我，不很確定他們該怎麼對我下評斷。我等了十五分，盼望能跟個銀行裡的人員談話，但沒人跟我打招呼或是詢問我到銀行裡要辦什麼事，所以我就離開了。

Barbara Jennifer, you went to Wells Fargo. What happened?

珍妮佛，妳到富國銀行去了，情況怎樣？

Jennifer The banker I spoke with kept saying that he would "hook me up." However, he was vague as to how he was going to do that. After listening to him explain his product, I only became more confused. In the end, I didn't understand what kind of account I would be getting or how it would benefit me.

跟我談話的行員一直說他會「給我特別的優惠」。但是對要怎麼給我個優待法，他則是相當模稜兩可。在聽完他解釋他提供的產品後，我感到更糊塗了。總之，我不曉得他要幫我開的是什麼樣的帳戶或這個帳戶會帶給我什麼好處。

Barbara You have all heard our colleagues' testimonies from their investigations. Do not forget who we are and why we are here. We serve the community by providing the best customer service possible. In so doing, we are gonna give those banks a run for their money!

你們都聽到這些同事在實地調查後提出的見證。別忘記我們是什麼樣的銀行以及我們來到這裡的原因。我們提供這個社區頂尖的客戶服務，這麼做的結果是讓那些銀行見識到我們的厲害，並了解他們即將有一場硬仗要打！

 ## 單字

☑ huddle [ˋhʌd!] ***n.*** （美式橄欖球中選手們在攻防線後面的）戰略磋商集合

☑ garner [ˋgɑrnɚ] ***v.*** 收集、聚集

☑ rep [rɛp] ***n.*** （業務、公司團體等）代表，為 representative 的非正式用法

☑ premier [prɪˋmɪr] ***adj.*** 最重要的、首位的

☑ portfolio [portˋfolɪˏo] ***n.*** 個人或公司組織持有的投資一覽表、所有資產的總集

☑ testimony [ˋtɛstəˏmonɪ] ***n.*** 證言、見證

片語

☑ <u>lean in</u> 傾身、向…靠近

☑ <u>no small feat</u> 莫大的成就、壯舉（不是小事一樁）

☑ <u>make of someone／something</u> 根據所得的有限資訊，對某人或某事加以評判，或去理解某人或事

☑ <u>hook someone up</u> 給予某人特別的待遇或優惠

 慣用語之三：Give Someone a Run for Someone's Money

以下這一段是摘錄於我任職公司的某封內部電子郵件：

*"Week 6 Results are in!!! Here are the Top 20 branches in the region, and it looks like Paseo Padre **is giving them a run for their money** in 7th place!"*

Giving someone a run for someone's money 是什麼意思啊?…抱頭鼠竄？捲款潛逃？

呵呵，以上的答案當然都不對，這句慣用語是指「非常有競爭力」，不會輕易讓對手（句中的 someone）贏的意思，換句話說，「給對方一場硬仗打」。

這句話據了解，是從賽馬這個賭博運動衍生而出的。在以前，若是你投注賭金下去的馬，因為種種因素譬如健康不佳或騎士出狀況而臨時無法賽跑，業者是不會退你錢的！這種情況，別人就會說你是 "you did not get a run for your money.（你已經放了錢下去，馬卻沒有出賽）" 所以衍伸出來 "getting a run for someone's money" 的意思，就是「有出賽的機會」。更進一步，"giving someone a run for his／her money" 就是「讓他／她有比賽的機會」。

好，現在想像你來到你對手的面前，跟這個人說："I am going to give you a run for your money（你既然錢都繳了，我就要給你一個比賽的機會），" 這聽起來是不是讓人感覺你對自己的能力很有自信，甚至到了有點狂妄的境界？因此這句慣用語就是在表示挑戰者毫不畏懼的精神，他的實力堅強，敵手若要打贏這場仗，非得使出全力來對應不可，觀眾可以期待看到一場精彩的好戲！

回到前面的 e-mail，Paseo Padre 是分行代稱，那個分行是在發信人的管理下，第一間進入全區績效前二十名的辦公室。言下之意，發信人對 Paseo Padre 的表現感到十分驕傲，她認為在名單上的其他十九家分行，都不能小看它，尤其是排在它前面的六間分行，如果他們想保持目前的名次，必須得更加努力、不容半刻放鬆呀！

38 Ballpark

Chi hears Paul laughing in the next room. She opens the door.
季薇聽到保羅在隔壁的房間裡大笑。她開了房門。

Chi	What are you laughing about?	你在笑什麼？
Paul	Come watch this. An Irish kid from Dublin is making a prank phone call to a demolition company. It's hysterical!	來看這個。一個愛爾蘭的小孩從都柏林打惡作劇電話到某間建築物拆除工程公司。太好笑了！
	Paul puts his headphones on Chi.	保羅把他的耳機裝到季薇頭上。
	Hello?	哈囉？
	How are you? My name is Becky.	你好嗎？我的名字是貝琪。
	Yes?	有什麼事嗎？
	I have a proposal for you.	我有一個提案。
	Go ahead.	請說。
	Are you the demolition man?	你是負責拆除建築物的人？
	Yes.	是的。
	You the top boss, yeah? I want you to help me destroy my school.	你是大老闆對吧？我想要你幫忙拆除我的學校。
	(Laughing.)	（笑）
	Could you blow it up or knock it down?	你能炸毀它還是敲除它？
	Whatever you want.	妳想怎麼作我們就怎麼辦。
	I'll blow it up. That'll be better. Could you make sure that all my teachers in there when you knock it down?	我想要把它炸掉，這樣比較好。當在你摧毀我的學校時，能不能請你確認所有的老師都在裡面？

Dunno if we'll <u>get away with</u> that now.

Nobody likes them. They give me extra homework on a Friday and everything.

(Laughing.)

And how much would it cost to knock it to the ground?

It depends how big it is.

Give me about a ballpark figure.

(Laughing.)

Listen, are you gonna come and knock my school down or what?

Can you fax me through a photograph or a site plan or something?

Right, I'll fax you through a plan of the school and my teachers' names. And just make sure they're all in the building when you knock it down.

You make sure you put their names on it. I'll give you a price for each individual teacher.

Chi Hahaha... Unbelievable, the willingness of the adult to <u>play along</u>! How old is this little girl?

Paul Eight.

Chi She sounds so sophisticated... and the words she chooses... Wow. "Ballpark figure" means an estimate, right?

我不知道那樣做會不會被抓到耶。

沒有人喜歡他們。他們在週五給我特別多的家庭作業跟一些其他有的沒的。

（笑）

還有把學校剷平要多少錢？

要看學校的大小。

給我一個球場的數字就好。

（笑）

聽著，你到底要不要來拆除我的學校？

妳能把照片或平面圖之類的傳真過來嗎？

好，我會把學校藍圖跟我老師的名字傳真給你。一定要確定當你在敲毀學校建築物的時候，他們全都在裡面。

妳只管將他們的名字寫在傳真上。我會提供妳每個老師的價錢。

哈哈哈... 這個大人這麼配合跟著開玩笑真令人難以置信！這個小女生幾歲啊？

八歲。

她聽起來好老成喔…還有她使用的字彙…哇。「球場的數字」意思是大約的估價，對嗎？

生活篇

信仰篇

表達篇

外來語篇

文明篇

其它篇

169

Paul	Yeah. She was asking for an approximate price in cost to demolish the school. However leaving the teachers inside is extra.	對。她那時在詢問拆除學校大概需要的花費。但把老師留在建築物裡要額外算錢。
Chi	She was joking though. Right?	她是開玩笑的對吧？
Paul	Yeah, she is a known prankster. This is not her first phone in.	是啊，她是惡作劇出了名的。這不是她第一通電話。
Chi	So young. I wonder were she gets it.	年紀這麼小，不知道是跟誰學的。
Paul	Probably from her dad. If her dad is smart, he could capitalize on her growing popularity.	大概從她爸那裡學來的。如果她爸爸夠聰明的話，他可以利用她日漸竄升的知名度大賺一筆。
Chi	College fund?	拿來做大學教育基金？
Paul	Exactly. Every dollar counts.	沒錯，每一塊錢都很重要。
Chi	How much do you think she could get?	你想她可以賺多少錢？
Paul	Ballpark... $25,000 to $50,000? Maybe more! You never know. Opportunities that start small can grow quickly.	估計的話嘛…兩萬五到五萬塊美金？可能還更多！這個很難講，一開始不起眼的機會，可能一下就發達起來。
Chi	Where did you get $25,000 to $50,000 from?	你是從哪裡得到兩萬五到五萬美金這個數字的？
Paul	The average price for talent in a national commercial is in that range.	在全國性廣告裡演出的演員，一般要價就在那個區間內。
Chi	Wow, I didn't know commercial actors made that much.	哇，我不曉得廣告演員賺那麼多。

單字

☑ Dublin [ˋdʌblɪn] *n.* 都柏林（愛爾蘭首都）

☑ prank [præŋk] *n.* 玩笑、惡作劇

☑ demolition [ˌdɛməˋlɪʃən] *n.* 拆除、毀壞（古老或危險的建築物等）

☑ hysterical [hɪsˋtɛrɪk!] *adj.* 令人無法控制狂笑的、十分好笑的

☑ sophisticated [səˋfɪstɪˌketɪd] *adj.* 教養高雅的、講究文禮的；懂世故的、老練的

 片語

☑ get away with something 做某件壞事而不須承擔後果
☑ play along （通常在某個騙局或開玩笑的情況裡）假裝合作、一同配合演戲

 日常會話

Every dollar counts. 每一塊錢都很重要。這句話的意思是不管每次賺或存的金額大小，每一元累積下來的錢都向預先設定的目標邁進了一步。

 第二種定義之一：**Ballpark**

　　美國人和台灣人都熱愛棒球，台灣人說她是全民運動，美國人則稱棒球為 America's pastime. 棒球深入美國生活的各個角落，當然連其語言也不例外。今天我就要來介紹一個字：ballpark.一看到這個字裡的 park，很多人會直接聯想到「公園」，以為它指的是平常大人小孩遊戲、盪鞦韆的公園或遊樂場，那就錯了；在英文中，ballpark 專門指的是「棒球場」。如果你聽到有人請你給他一個 "ballpark figure"，或他說 "Just ballpark it！"，他想講的是什麼？

　　答案是這個人希望你給他一個大概的數字或猜測，不用很準確，接近就好。美國人之所以這樣說，是因為球場面積很大，如果代表棒球的某個數字或事實是落在場內（XX is in／within the ballpark），代表球有很大的空間可以移動，但是仍舊是在同一個球場內。那麼，當球被打飛出棒球場外的時候，又是什麼意思呢？你要是聽到 "（某人）knocks it (或 the ball) out of the park." 哇，那不就是全壘打了嗎？這句的意思就是某人做某件事做得非常好，太精彩了，是一句用來稱讚人的美言！

生活篇　信仰篇　**表達篇**　外來語篇　文明篇　其它篇

171

10 第二種定義 [The Second Definition]

39 Cold Turkey

In the office.　在辦公室裡。

| Vicky | Hey, Chi, Jennifer, are you two busy? Have a moment? | 嘿，季薇、珍妮佛，妳們兩個在忙嗎？可以借幾分鐘說話嗎？ |

Jennifer Okay.　好。

Chi　Sure, what's up?　當然可以，什麼事？

| Vicky | I don't mean to make it a big deal. But I have an announcement to make. I already told some people yesterday afternoon. But since the two of you weren't here yesterday, I ... | 我不想小題大作，但我有件事情要宣布。我昨天下午已經有跟一些人講了，可是既然妳們兩人昨天不在，我... |

Jennifer All right, cut to the chase. What is it?　夠了，說重點。到底是什麼事？

Vicky　(Shyly) I ... I found out that I'm pregnant.　（害羞地）我…我發現我懷孕了。

Chi & Jennifer Whhaaat? Congratulations, Vicky!　什什什麼？恭喜呀，維琪！

Vicky　Thank you.　謝謝妳們。

Chi　Aww, it's wonderful. I'm so happy for you.　噢，這真是太棒了。我好為妳高興。

Jennifer	But ... don't you smoke, Vick?	但…妳不是有抽煙的習慣嗎？
Vicky	Yeah, so I'll have to quit cold turkey.	對呀，所以我必須要用冷火雞法戒煙了。
Jennifer	That's a bummer.	哇！那實在很討厭。
Chi	What do you mean? What's cold turkey?	妳在説什麼啊？什麼是冷火雞法？
Jennifer	It means instead of gradually cutting down on the number of cigarettes she smokes in a day, eventually stopping after several months, she is going to completely stop smoking right now. No more cigarettes, at all, ever! Going cold turkey is not easy.	冷火雞法的意思是，與其逐漸減少每天吸煙的次數，一直到幾個月之後完全停止，她的作法是現在立刻就戒煙，一根煙也不能抽，以後永遠永遠再不碰香煙！冷火雞式的戒煙方法不容易呀。
Vicky	Before I found out about the baby, I had thought about quitting. But there were always temptations. Now I know I have to do it for my kid. I think I will be all right.	我在發現自己懷孕之前，就有想過要戒了。可是總是抵不住誘惑，現在我瞭解到我必須要為了小孩而戒煙，我想我應該可以克服戒煙的困難。
Chi	Is there anything we can do to help you survive the transition?	有沒有什麼是我們可以做來幫妳撐過這段過渡期的？
Vicky	If I become tempted, maybe you could distract me and help me to cope or somehow change the subject. Maybe some candy or snacks would help.	如果我覺得有點受不了誘惑的話，也許妳們可以做些事來讓我分心、幫助我對付癮頭，或改變話題之類的。一

生活篇

信仰篇

表達篇

外來語篇

文明篇

其它篇

173

些糖果或零食也可能有幫
助。

Chi I can make some "cold turkey" cup cakes if you want. Red velvet is hard to ignore.

如果妳喜歡的話,我可以烤一些「冷火雞」杯子蛋糕。紅絲絨蛋糕絕對可以把妳的注意力吸引過來。

Jennifer My mom makes a "quitting smoking" iced tea. She says it soothes the cravings. It worked for my aunt too. She said it helped a lot.

我媽會泡一種「戒煙用」冰紅茶,她說這茶能緩和想要抽煙的慾望。它對我阿姨也有起效果,她說喝了我媽的茶幫助很大。

Vicky That sounds great. Thank you so much you guys.

聽起來很棒,太謝謝妳們了。

Chi & Jennifer No problem.

沒問題。

Chi What about your husband? Is he quitting too?

那妳先生呢?他也準備要戒煙了嗎?

Vicky Yes, but he isn't happy about it. I think he will need even more help than me. But at least he can use the patch and gradually stop. He has nine months to quit. I don't have that option.

是啊,可是他對此不是很高興。我想他比我需要更多的協助,但至少他能使用尼古丁貼片來慢慢達到戒煙的目的,他有九個月的時間去戒。我則沒有選擇的餘地。

❤ 單字

☑ **bummer** [ˋbʌmɚ] *n.* (俚語)令人失望或討厭的事物

☑ **cope** [kop] *v.* 對付、處理

☑ red velvet [rɛd `vɛlvɪt] *n.* 紅絲絨蛋糕。添加了人工紅色素及可可粉的一種紅褐色蛋糕，帶有淡淡的巧克力味。

☑ soothe [suð] *v.* 緩和、使平靜

☑ craving [`krevɪŋ] *n.* 想要吃某種食物或做某件事的慾望

☑ patch [pætʃ] *n.* 貼片、貼布

 片語

☑ cut to the chase 不要浪費時間談無關緊要的事情，直接切入重點

 第二種定義之二：Cold Turkey

我先生在下城區擔任物理教師，自從去年新上任以來，幾乎每天我都聽他談到學生如何程度落後、上課態度不佳、課堂上玩手機不專心等等。經過六個月的努力後，有天他從學校回到家，大聲宣告：""Today I told my students that we are going to stop cold turkey!"

冷火雞？

Stop 就 stop，什麼是 stop cold turkey? 原來 stop／go／quit cold turkey 是形容人毫不猶豫、快刀斬亂麻地停止做某件事，通常是某項壞習慣。戒煙或毒癮、甚至像是失戀後，立刻把所有跟那個人有關連的物品，通通退還或丟棄，都可以歸類為 going cold turkey。

美國人之所以會這麼講可能有幾種原因：一說是冷火雞的外表看起來就像一副戒毒者的模樣，包括直冒冷汗、皮膚起雞皮疙瘩等徵狀；另一說是冷火雞肉不需要什麼事前的準備，切來即可食用（註），就如同完全毫無事前準備的停止使用毒品或尼古丁，說戒就戒！

註 美國一般人常吃用冷火雞肉切片製成的三明治。感恩節當天烤好的火雞，因為體積大，隔天通常會有很多剩下，美國人就利用剩的火雞肉作另一餐來吃，十分方便。平時超市裡也有在賣，只要到標示著 Deli 的專區就可以取得依照你喜好不同厚度的火雞片。

生活篇　信仰篇　表達篇　外來語篇　文明篇　其它篇

175

40 Brownie Points

A FedEx courier hands Chi a package.　某位聯邦快遞的送貨員交給季薇一份包裹。

Chi	(Talking to herself.) Mmm, it's addressed to "The Walnut Branch," but it doesn't say who its intended for.	（自言自語）嗯，它寫是寄給「核桃分行」，但沒有說是要給誰。
Courier	Please sign.	麻煩妳簽名。
Chi	This is not addressed to me. Can I still sign for it?	這不是寄給我的，我可以簽收嗎？
Courier	Do you work here?	妳在這兒上班嗎？
Chi	Yes?	是啊？
Courier	Then yes. Please sign.	那妳就可以幫忙簽收。請簽個名。
Chi	OK. Thank you.	OK, 謝謝。
	Courier leaves. Chi walks over to the manager's office.	送件員離去。季薇走進經理辦公室。
Chi	Barbara, I just received a FedEx envelope addressed to the branch. Do you know what it is?	芭芭拉，我剛剛收到一個寄給我們分行的聯邦快遞。妳知道那是幹什麼的嗎？
Barbara	Who is it from?	誰寄來的？
Chi	Let me see. The Ronald McDonald House on B Street.	我看一下，B 街上的麥當勞叔叔之家。
Barbara	Oh yeah, remember when we painted that house during our charity run?	喔，對啦，記得上次我們作慈善活動時油漆的房子嗎？
Chi	Yeah, I remember, we made that old	是啊，我記得，我們把那間

	house look like new by the time we left.	舊房子整理得煥然一新。
Barbara	Maybe they have another house for us to paint.	也許他們有另外一棟房屋要我們漆。
Chi	It was fun. I wouldn't mind doing it again, just so long as we get to have a picnic afterwards like last time.	那次的經驗很有趣。只要我們能夠跟上次一樣在結束後大夥兒一同野餐,我不介意再做一次。
Barbara	The perennials you and Jennifer brought and planted around the house was the icing on the cake!	妳跟珍妮佛帶去並種植在房子四周的多年生花卉真是神來一筆、錦上添花!
Chi	I thought the new family moving in might enjoy that little extra something. (Emphasizes strongly.) Brownie points!	我想說下一個搬進去的家庭也許會喜歡。(鄭重強調)增加女童軍點數!
	Barbara opens the envelope.	芭芭拉打開信封。
Barbara	What is this? They gave us... hockey game tickets!	這是什麼?他們送給我們…曲棍球賽的門票!
Chi	No way!	不可能!
Barbara	Wait, there's a note, too. Let's see: "To the wonderful staff at Chase Bank - Walnut Branch: We love our newly painted rooms! Thank you all for coming and helping us make a difference in the community. Please accept these tickets as a token of our appreciation.	等等,裡面還有一張紙條。讓我看看:「致大通銀行核桃分行的超級員工們:我們愛死那些新漆的房間了!謝謝你們前來和我們一同為改善這個社區而努力。附上門票以示我們衷心的感謝,請不吝收下。
Chi	Awesome! When is it?	太棒了!球賽是什麼時候啊?
Barbara	Two weeks from now. That gives us just enough time to let everyone know and organize the trip. I guess you did earn	兩週後,剛好夠我們通知並約好所有人一起去觀賞球賽。我猜妳的努力真的有賺

生活篇 信仰篇

表達篇

外來語篇 文明篇 其它篇

177

brownie points after all.	到女童軍點數。
Chi (Throws arms into the air and yells.) Brownie points! (Normal voice) Never underestimate the value of <u>going the extra mile</u>.	（雙手高舉並高喊）女童軍點數！（接著以正常的音調）絕對不能輕視付出額外心力的重要性。
Barbara I hope our seats are right up on the glass.	希望我們的座位緊靠著玻璃。
Chi Me too. Paul loves to see all the action close up and personal. I'm ready to cheer for the home team, eat my hot dog, curse the ump, and watch the half time show.	希望如此。保羅喜歡近距離觀看場上的活動。我已經準備好為本地的球隊歡呼、吃熱狗、大罵裁判，以及觀賞中場休息的餘興節目了。
Barbara I laugh every time I see the pee-wee league play. The pads and equipment are so heavy they can barely stand.	每次我看到曲棍球聯盟兒童組的演出我就忍不住發笑，那些護墊和用具沈重到他們幾乎站不住。
Chi We are going to have so much fun. Let's go tell everyone the good news.	去看球賽一定會很好玩，我們趕快去告訴大家這個好消息。

♥ 單字

☑ **courier** [ˈkɝɪɚ] *n.* 遞送文件的人員、信差	☑ **address** [əˈdrɛs] *v.* 填寫收件人的姓名和地址、寄給（某人）
☑ **run** [rʌn] *n.* 在某一段期間內持續進行的事、連續的活動	☑ **perennial** [pəˈrɛnɪəl] *n.* 多年性植物
☑ **ump** [ʌmp] *adv.* （非正式用法）裁判員。Ump 是 umpire 的簡寫	☑ **pee-wee** [ˈpiˈwi] *n.* 兒童及青少年冰上曲棍球中介於八、九歲的等級

☑ league [lig] *n.* （球類等運動的）聯盟

 片語

☑ icing on the cake 使原來已經很好的某事或物更棒的東西、錦上添花
☑ go the extra mile （通常是不計酬勞地）付出額外的心力、做出比顧客預期的要更多的事情

 ## 第二種定義之三：Brownie Points

在美國，brownie 是一種巧克力點心，鬆軟但紮實，組織介於蛋糕和餅乾之間，有時會加入核桃和腰果，是不論大人或小孩都很喜歡的甜食。

但是這裡講的 brownie points 可跟巧克力糕沒有關係喔！（雖然很多人因為名稱的關係而常把這兩者連想在一起） Brownie points 指的是某人在做了好行為後所得到的一種無形的加分，譬如說，員工在工作上表現優異，他／她在老闆心目中的布朗尼點數就會增加；同樣的，學生如果常志願幫老師忙、上課時踴躍回答問題、或作研究時特別用心，這個學生在老師的眼中也會比其他人多一些布朗尼點數；甚至夫妻間也能累積布朗尼點數，像是老公記得太太的生日而送禮物慶祝，或準時下班回家這一類好行為，都可以提高先生的布朗尼分數。

Brownie points 不一定會帶給人立即、實際上的獎勵，但是可能在日後的某個關鍵時期會發生效果，例如上司決定要提拔某甲或某乙，或老師是否給某個學生第二次考試的機會等。

Brownie points 多用複數形，開頭的 B 通常大寫。許多人相信，Brownie 原來為美國女童軍制度中的一個名稱：美國女童軍分成六個等級，Brownie 是其中的第二級，年齡大約在六到十歲間，屬於幼女童軍。 如果一個 Brownie，也就是一個小小女童軍，作了值得嘉獎的好行為，她就會獲頒勳章，一般人將此解釋成她獲得的 Brownie 點數，即為 Brownie points 的由來。

10

第二種定義 [The Second Definition]

41 Token

At the hockey arena.　在曲棍球場。

Chi	I'm so excited! It's been a while since we've been at a hockey game.	我好興奮喔！我們好久沒看冰上曲棍球賽了。
Paul	I know, right? I miss it so much. The ice looks good and the players seem ready to play. It says here in the program that number 37 likes to fight a lot. I hope he is feeling feisty tonight.	可不是嗎？我非常想念看球賽。冰場看來很棒，球員看起來也都躍躍欲試。節目表這裡寫説三十七號很愛打架，我希望他今晚的戰鬥意志高昂。
Chi	Remember the last fight we saw? Gloves and sticks were everywhere. The entire team went crazy.	記得我們上回看到場內打群架的時候嗎？手套和球桿扔得到處都是，整個球隊都像發狂了一樣。
Paul	Those types of fights are rare, but it is totally awesome when it does happen.	那種打鬥的情形很罕見，一但發生了真是十分精彩。
Chi	Look, there's my co-workers. Barbara! Mike! Over here!	看，我同事在那邊。芭芭拉！麥可！我們在這裡！
Barbara	Hey, Chi. How are you, Paul?	嘿，季薇。你好嗎，保羅？
Paul	Good. Who's this?	我很好。這位是誰啊？
Barbara	This is my daughter Alice. Unfortunately, Daniel and his girlfriend will be late, they had to take care of something else first.	這是我女兒愛麗絲。丹尼跟他女朋友不幸地會晚到一些，他們必須先去處理其他

Jennifer, Vicky and her husband Jason are carpooling and should be here soon. I'm gonna grab some snacks before the game starts. Can you two watch Alice for me? I'll be right back.

的事。珍妮佛、維琪跟她先生傑森開同一輛車,應該很快就到了。我要在球賽開始前去買點零嘴,你們倆可不可以幫我看一下愛麗絲?我馬上回來。

Paul No problem. Have a seat, Alice. Have you ever been to a hockey game before?

沒問題。坐吧,愛麗絲。妳看過曲棍球賽嗎?

Alice Uh huh.

嗯哼。

Paul You want to read my program? There's pictures inside of all the players.

妳想看我的節目表嗎?這裡面有全部球員的照片。

Alice Uh huh. (Alice take the program and starts to read.)

嗯哼。(愛麗絲取過節目表並開始閱讀)

Paul How about you, is this your first game, Mike?

那你呢?這是你第一次來看球賽嗎,麥可?

Mike It is! (Looks around stadium.) So this is where all the white people go at night. Who knew. Any other secrets I should know about?

沒錯!(環顧球場四周)所以這裡是白人晚上聚集的地方,誰曉得呢?其他還有哪些我該知道的祕密嗎?

Paul Don't be frightened, but you may see a mob of white guys chasing after a black puck all night.

別被嚇著了,但是等下整個晚上,你會看到一群白人追逐一個黑盤。

Mike Ha! I guess I should probably stay off the ice then.

哈!我猜我最好離冰場遠一點。

Chi Hey, why do hockey players wear jerseys?

嘿,你知道為什麼曲棍球員要穿球衣嗎?

生活篇

信仰篇

表達篇

外來語篇

文明篇

其它篇

Mike	I don't know... why do hockey players wear jerseys?	我不知道…為什麼曲棍球員要穿球衣？
Chi	So you can see them on the ice.	這樣你才可以在白色的冰上看見他們。
Paul	Oh, that's rich! Did you think of that all by yourself? Hundreds of white people, and where am I sitting? Right between you two. I'm in a diversity sandwich. Before you know it, Daniel will be sitting behind me and Jason in front. I'll be trapped in a diversity bubble. Surrounded by tokens.	噢，好一個笑話！全靠妳自己想出來的嗎？這裡有數百個白人，而我坐在哪？就剛好在妳們倆之間。我夾在多元種族的三明治中間。等下丹尼就會坐在我後面，而傑森坐我前面，我被塞在一個多元種族的氣泡裡，被每個種族推派出來的代表包圍。（作者按：麥可是非裔美國人，丹尼為伊朗裔，而傑森是拉丁美洲裔。）
Mike	(Mimicking the kid from *The Sixth Sense*) I see white people.	（模倣電影《靈異第六感》中的小男孩）我看見白人。
Paul	I am the hole in your donut.	我是你們種族甜甜圈中間的那個洞。
Mike	We'll call ourselves "The Fantastic Four ... Tokens" except we don't fight crime, we use our super human powers... to make fun of white people.	我們可以自稱為「驚奇四超人…四個種族的超級代表」除了我們的任務不是打擊罪犯，而是用我們的超能力來…拿白人開玩笑。
Paul	(Mimicking TV show *Quantum Leap*) Oh, boy! It's going to be a long night.	（模倣電視影集《時空怪客》）噢，不妙！看來接下來將是非常漫長的一夜。

單字

- ☑ feisty [ˋfaɪstɪ] **adj.** 具侵略性的、積極應戰的

- ☑ carpool [ˋkɑr ˏpul] **v.** 幾個人之間共同使用一輛汽車到達目的地、汽車共乘

- ☑ stadium [ˋstedɪəm] **n.** 體育場、運動場

- ☑ mob [mɑb] **n.** （暴民、幫派等的）一夥、一大群

- ☑ puck [pʌk] **n.** 冰上曲棍球用的球，為橡皮製的堅硬扁平圓盤、冰球

- ☑ jersey [ˋdʒɝzɪ] **n.** 一種寬鬆的運動上衣，根據不同的球隊有不同的顏色及圖案設計，為球員制服的一部份

 片語

- ☑ A long night／day （感覺上）非常漫長的一夜/ 天。由於工作上的壓力或旁人造成的問題，而使得時間感覺過得非常緩慢。

 第二種定義之四：Token

　　Token 這個字當作名詞來用，大家最熟悉的意義是代幣；當形容詞的話，token 的意思是「象徵性的」。那麼假設你聽到有人說，某人 is a token black guy，他指的是什麼？

　　首先，在 token 後面接的，可以是 white guy、Asian 或是任何族群，只要在說話者描述的情境中，這個族群是少數。當某個團體幾乎所有的成員都是屬於同一個群類時，管理階級為了維持表面上的公平，或迎合政治訴求，不想被批評有種族歧視的意圖，在這時會特別插入一個少數份子，這個少數份子，就是一個 token，換句話說，一個僅具形式的代表性人物。

　　譬如說，一部戲的主要卡司全部都是白種人，結果一片白裡面冒出一個黑臉孔，他／她的角色不是很重要，戲份少，說話的機會也不多，唯一這個演員會在這裡的原因，不過就是導演希望表面上看起來，其製作的戲劇有達到包括少數種族的目的。

　　出現 tokens 的團體可能為軍隊、公司行號、或學校等。美國著名的電視卡通《南方四賤客》（South Park）裡就有一個很可愛的角色名叫 Token，這位小男孩是全校唯一的美籍非裔人，他的家族也是全鎮上獨一無二的黑人家。卡通的製作人特意為他取這個名字，就是為了嘲諷 token 這種不是那麼誠懇、有點令人啼笑皆非的現象。

42 It Comes with the Territory.

Paul somberly walks in the house.　保羅快快不樂地走進屋子裡。

Chi	Is everything all right?	一切還好嗎？
Paul	I had a long day. Had to send two kids to the principal's office.	今天工作不很順利，在學校碰到很多問題。送了兩個學生到校長室。
Chi	What? Why?	什麼？為什麼？
Paul	A fight! Kids fight. It happens all the time. I even had to call in school security to help me pull them apart.	打架！青少年打架滋事。這種情況一天到晚發生，我甚至得叫警衛進來幫我把他們拉開。
Chi	Are you okay?	那你還好嗎？
Paul	Yeah, I'm fine, just frustrated. Going into this profession, I knew that classroom management was part of the job, but you don't really know what it's going to take until you're there. Every school offers a different challenge, however regardless of those unique needs, teaching in general is tough. Dealing with these types of issues daily is par for the course. I know that it comes with the territory in an urban school district, but I feel like I am spending too much of my time and on behavior issues. When I was in high school, everyone was punctual, prepared,	還好啦，只是有挫折感。自從踏入這個行業以來，我就知道管理課堂秩序是工作的一部分，但事非經過不知難，只有做過才知道。每個學校有每個學校的問題，但不論學校之間不同的需求，教書這份工作總體來說都是很困難。每天處理這類的事情是很正常的，我早就知道在市區學校任教，管教學生的問題行為本來就無可避免，但我覺得我花了太多的時間和精力在這些問題上

and hard working. Something has changed. Those values no longer seem to exist. You ask a student to do anything and all you get is complaints. Yet they still want an "A" for what little garbage they do hand in. Where are the eager young minds curious about the world?

面。我以前在上高中的時候，大家都準時到校、上課前都預先看過課程內容、用功唸書。有些情況改變了，那些價值似乎都再也不存在，現在你要求學生做一件事，結果聽到的全是一堆抱怨。而如果他們真的按照你的要求交了作業，即使做得再爛他們也要你打 A 的分數。對這個世界抱著好奇心、渴望求知的年輕人都到哪裡去了？

Chi Oh, I am sorry to hear that. Have you talked to other teachers? What do they say?

噢，我很遺憾聽到你這麼說。你跟其他的老師有談過嗎？他們怎麼說？

Paul They've got the same problem. It's the culture here. A lot of these kids come from broken families. They join gangs, do drugs, and already have tattoos and kids of their own. Oddly enough a lot of them will get scholarships to college. But there isn't a chance in hell that they will last longer than a semester. I spend a large part of my day teaching fourth-grade math to high school seniors who can barely read the question.

他們也有相同的困擾。我告訴妳，是這個地區的風氣。許多學生來自破碎的家庭，他們加入幫派、嗑藥、刺青、甚至早就有小孩。令人無法理解的是，其中很多人會獲得免費的獎學金進入大學，但是我保證妳他們最多唸一學期就唸不下去了。我每天大部份的時間都花在教已經高三的學生小學四年級程度的數學，而他們連題目都勉強看得懂而已。

Chi I haven't a clue to what you're talking about. It sounds like *Twilight Zone*. I liked school and I did well.

你提到的這些情形我完全無法理解，聽起來就跟《陰陽魔界》裡的情節一樣。我以前挺喜歡上學，而且我表現得不錯。

生活篇 — 信仰篇

表達篇

外來語篇 — 文明篇 — 其它篇

185

Paul	I'm told by administrators that this is nothing and that it was a lot worse a generation ago.	學校行政部門的人員告訴我，現在這樣一點也不希罕，上一代的學生還更糟糕。
Chi	Really?	真的？
Paul	Evidently fixing a problem this big takes multiple generations and I am not sure that I want to work at this school anymore. I need to go somewhere else where I can actually teach kids who want to learn.	看來解決這麼嚴重的問題要花上好幾代的時間，而我不是很確定我是不是想繼續待在目前這個學校。我必須找到一個學生真心想要學習、而我能真正好好教書的學校。
Chi	Well, I'll support your choice, no matter what you decide.	不管你決定如何，我都會支持你的選擇。
Paul	It's a shame really. They have no idea what they are missing out on.	真令人遺憾，他們永遠也不會知道他們損失了什麼樣的人才。

（作者按：《陰陽魔界》是於 1959 年至 1964 年間播出的一齣電視影集，以不合常情、是非顛倒的劇情而著稱。）

 ## 單字

- ☑ somberly [ˈsɑmbɚlɪ] *adv.* 鬱悶地、憂鬱地
- ☑ punctual [ˈpʌŋktʃʊəl] *adj.* （人）不遲到的、準時的

 ## 片語

☑ par for the course 正常的、一如預期的。course 是指高爾夫球場的路線，par 是根據不同的球場路線，將球打入洞所需的標準桿數。當人描述某件事 "is par for the course"，意思就是說那件事是符合標準桿數，也就是符合大家預期的。

☑ <u>miss out on something</u> 錯過了做某件事（通常是好事）的機會、損失大好機會去享受某個人或東西。

日常會話

☑ <u>It's a shame.</u> 真遺憾。真是件令人惋惜的事。

包含 "it" 的用語之一：It Comes with the Territory

有天，一位老客人與他的太太來到銀行裡辦事。在交易的過程中，重聽的太太動作有點緩慢，遇到要從不同的帳戶中取款時，她面露困惑地不知該拿哪張支票出來作業。陪伴她的先生一半不好意思、一半焦急地說：唉她進出醫院好多次了，記性也不好，導致他總要在後面看顧她，確定她做的事沒有錯。

我聽到老先生這麼說，想了一想便回應他："Well, you know, it comes with..." 我話還沒講到一半，這位客人便接著說："It COMES WITH THE TERRITORY!" 一說完便呵呵笑出來，顯然這句話讓老先生釋懷了不少。

這句慣用語裡的 comes 也可以用 goes 代換，直接翻譯的話就是「它是隨著領域而來的」，中文大概可以解釋成「那是這份工作的一部分」。很多時候，一旦人體認到某件麻煩事，其實是另一件好事中不可避免的一部分，如果自己喜歡那件好事的程度大到可以包容它帶來的小困擾，人就會比較甘願去做那個困難的部份。"It comes with the territory" 讓那位先生認知到，他其實是很愛他的老婆的，婚姻中的一部分，就是要跟老伴互相扶持，其中一方有困難時，另一方就要幫忙，這份責任是 comes with marriage（thus the territory），這麼一想通了，自然老先生的心情就舒暢囉！

根據推測，這句話大概是從業務員的用語引申出來。當一個業務員承接某個地區作為他跑業務的範圍，跟著這個領域而來，不管好的壞的，他都得接受。美國人用這句話，大部份是用來感歎某件工作裡不好做、很討厭的地方。有時候也拿來預先警告人用。

句子裡的 it 就是那個讓人困擾的東西，你如果清楚的知道是什麼在煩惱你，可以把那個物品直接放在 it 的位置，來取代 it。譬如說：Criticism goes with the territory of being a public figure.（受批評是作為公眾人物無可避免的一部分。）

11

包含"it"的用語 [It]

43 For What It's Worth

At the poker table. 在牌桌上。

Paul (Explains the rules.) Play starts to the left of the dealer. Six cards are dealt. A turn is divided into three parts: Draw, Play, and Discard. When it is your turn, you may either draw one card from the top of the face-down stock pile, or you can use a card from the discard pile. However, if you take from the discard pile you must play it immediately, and take all the other cards that are below it in the fanned out sequence. Points are gained by laying down number sets and suit runs of at least three cards, unless you are playing on another player's tabled cards. Aces are worth 15, face cards 10, numbered cards 5. If you have any cards left after your play, you must discard one of them, thereby indicating to the next player that it is their turn. Play continues until someone manages to use all of the cards in their hand. Points on the table are added, points in your hand are subtracted. First to 500 wins. Any questions?

（說明規則）從發牌人左邊的玩家開始打牌。每人發六張牌。每次打牌的步驟分為三個部份：拿牌、玩牌跟丟牌。當輪到妳打的時候，妳可以從一疊面朝下的紙牌拿走最上方的那張牌，或是從別人之前丟棄的牌堆裡選一張牌。然而，如果妳選擇從丟棄的牌堆裡拿牌，妳必須立刻使用那張牌，並且連帶將在那張牌之後所有被丟棄的牌也一併拿走。拿分數的方法是把至少三張相同數字，或三張同樣花色且數字前後接連的牌攤出來；除非妳是接著其他玩家已經攤在桌上的牌在玩，攤出的牌數才可以少於三張。A 值十五分、人頭十分、一般的數字牌是五分。在妳玩過牌以後如果手中還有剩下的牌，妳必須丟棄其中一張，以表示這時輪到下一位玩家打牌。每局打到我們其中一個人把所有手上的牌都用完就結束。攤在桌上的分數全部加起來，減掉手上還沒用掉的牌代表的分數。最先達到五百分的人贏。有任何問題嗎？

Chi	Let's play!	我們來玩吧！
Paul	(Paul deals.) Pick up your cards and attempt to create a combination.	（保羅發牌完畢）把妳的牌拿起來，並試著把它們湊成對。
Chi	Ok, now what?	好，接下來哩？
Paul	Since you are the first player, there are no discards to choose from. So draw from the faced down stock pile. Can you play anything?	由於妳是第一個打牌的人，現在還沒有別人丟棄的牌可以讓妳選，所以從這堆沒翻過的牌裡拿一張牌。妳有任何組合嗎？
Chi	Not yet.	還沒。
Paul	Fine, discard one card. While you wait for your turn to come around again, watch everyone else play, and see if you can anticipate their actions, or ponder possible strategies you may want to implement.	好吧，丟棄一張牌。當妳在等下一輪的時候，注意觀察別人怎麼玩，看看妳是否能夠預測他們的行為，或思索妳自己可能會使用的策略。
Chi	This is fun! Now I know why Grandma like it so much.	這遊戲真好玩！現在我終於知道為什麼阿媽這麼喜歡玩。
	(Rounds pass.)	（一局又一局過去）

生活篇 — 信仰篇

表達篇

外來語篇 — 文明篇 — 其它篇

Paul	Rummy!	Rummy!
Chi	(Gasps.) Hey, you've been holding!	（倒吸一口氣）嘿，你居然一直都藏著沒攤牌！
Paul	No rule states that I have to play the cards in my hand the moment I receive them. I took a risk to execute a power play.	規則沒說我一拿到牌就得立刻拿出來玩。我冒了很大的風險來做這個奮力一搏、火力全出的動作。
Grandpa	Well done. What's the score?	做得好。大家得分如何？
Paul	Coming in dead last is Chi with 235, Not far behind is Grandpa with 385, Grandma comes up short with 490 and Paul puts down an amazing 535 points pushing him over the top as champion... AGAIN!	季薇最後一名，兩百三十五分；阿公不太差，有三百八十五分；阿媽差一些就贏，有四百九十分；而保羅獲得了驚人的五百三十五分，把他推上冠軍的寶座…再一次地！
Grandma	Damn!	真是的！
Paul	For what it's worth, um, I've had fun.	我知道現在說這個可能沒用，但是，嗯，我很開心。
Chi	That's not how you use the expression! You're supposed to say something sympathetic after you say "for what it's worth." It makes no sense!	那句話才不是那樣用的！在講完「我知道現在說這個可能沒用」以後，你應該接著說一些表現同情心的話才對。根本牛頭不對馬嘴！
Paul	Do I smell a sore loser?	我難道聞到了一個發霉的輸家？

Chi　No! I smell a rotten winner.

才不是！我聞到的是一個爛到骨子裡的贏家。

Paul　Dear, that is the smell of "<u>coming up roses</u>," unfortunately you wouldn't know anything about that.

親愛的，那個味道是「勝利的花香」，可惜妳永遠也不會懂我在説什麼。

Chi　(Screams.) UHHHH! I want a rematch.

（尖叫）啊啊啊！我要再玩一次。

單字

☑ suit [sut] **n.** 同樣花色的一組牌

☑ ponder [`pɑndɚ] **v.** 思考、思索

☑ implement [`ɪmpləmənt] **v.** 執行、實施（計畫等）

☑ Rummy [`rʌmɪ] **n.** 一種撲克牌遊戲。規則跟麻將有些類似，以收集相同點數，或相同花色且數字相連的牌為主要目標。玩家可利用其他玩家已經收集並攤出的牌，跟自己的牌組合起來以賺得點數；最先把手上的牌全部出清的人會喊出 "Rummy!" 以表示那局遊戲結束。

☑ gasp [gæsp] **v.** （因驚嚇等）倒吸一口氣

☑ power play [`pɑʊɚ ple] **n.** 將所有資源結合起來，奮力一搏的出擊行動、集中火力的戰略

☑ sore loser [sor` luzɚ] **n.** 心有不甘且愛抱怨的輸家

片語

☑ <u>come up roses</u> 一個原本可能看來不佳的情況，後來轉變成美好、豐收的結局

包含 "it" 的用語之二：For What It's Worth

這句是連美國人也會覺得滿難解釋清楚的一句話。要了解這句話的意思，第一個要解決的問題是，句中的 it 是指什麼？第二個問題，是這個 it 到底價值多少？

首先，這句用語直接的中文翻譯是「不論它值多少」，所以這句話也可以寫成 "for whatever it's worth"，用非常口語的話來說，大概可以用我們的「要聽不聽隨你」來比照。其中 it's 的省略符號＇千萬不可以忘記打，因為整句原來的形式是 for what it is worth，如果沒打省略號，就變成 it 的所有格 its，也就跟原來的意思稍微不同了。

現在來處理第一個問題，句裡的 it 指的是「我現在說的話」（what I am saying）。再下來第二個問題，那麼我說的話價值多少呢？這個價值，就要憑聽者的決定—也許對他很有用（價值高），也可能一文不值、完全沒有價值。說 "for what it's worth" 的人，在丟出一個意見後，把決定這個意見有無價值的權利，交給對方那個聽的人，對方可以接受建議，也可以當耳邊風、一笑置之。

用這句話的人大概可以分成兩種，一種是為了表現謙虛的態度、承認自己所知（或能做）的有限、又或者是接受現成的事實，這種人的意思其實是 "I just want to say" 或 "in my opinion"；另一種人是想藉這個用語呈現出有點不太認真、輕率的態度，當他們在說這句話的時候，背後傳達出 "FYI" 跟 "BTW" 的訊息，一個很好的例子是寫出六 O 年代流行歌曲 "For What It's Worth" 的樂手 Stephen Stills，當他告訴唱片公司總監，自己作了一首歌時，他說：I have this song here, for what it's worth, if you want it.

結果一句無意的話，居然變成這首經典歌曲的歌名！

Notes

44 Give It a Whirl

Paul and Chi are at Universal CityWalk.　保羅和季薇走在環球影城步道上。

Chi	What is that!	那是什麼！
Paul	(Points) That?	（指著）那個？
Chi	Yes, that!	對，就是那個！
Paul	It's just indoor skydiving.	那不過就是室內高空跳傘罷了。
Chi	Have you done it before?	你以前玩過噢？
Paul	Of course. You've never tried it?	當然，妳沒玩過？
Chi	Never.	從來沒有。
Paul	Would you like to do it?	妳想玩嗎？
Chi	What, today?	啥，你是說今天？
Paul	There is no better time than the present.	沒有比現在更好的時刻了。
Chi	(Hesitantly) Uh, isn't it a bit expensive? Look at their price ...	（遲疑地）呃，那會不會有點貴啊？你看他們的票價...
Paul	Looking for an excuse to back out?	在找藉口打退堂鼓嗎？
Chi	No!	才不！

Paul	Come on, how many times do you get to be in a wind tunnel floating in empty space?	來嘛，人生有多少次機會可以讓妳在空無一物的通風道中漂浮？
Chi	Is it dangerous? What if I fall?	會不會危險啊？要是我掉下來怎麼辦？
Paul	You're always saying how you want to go skydiving with me. Consider this as an opportunity to get your feet wet. A safe environment where you can practice before going up for real. I think you need to give it a "whirl." Literally.	妳老是說妳想跟我一起作高空跳傘。就把這次當成讓妳先試試以培養經驗的一個機會。在進行真正的高空跳傘之前，妳可以在這個安全的環境裡作練習。我認為妳應該給它「轉」一下，真的就跟字面上講的一樣。
Chi	Ok, I'll do it!	好吧，我來試試看！
Paul	That's my girl. The training lasts about an hour, so pay attention and do everything they tell you to do and nothing else. Understand?	這才是我的老婆。訓練的課程大概會花上一個小時，所以仔細聽人家在講什麼，乖乖照做，懂嗎？
Chi	Yes, sir!	是，老公！
	(A hour later, Chi walks out in a diver's suit and goggles. She walks into the chamber, and the fan is turned on, it makes a terrible roaring sound.)	（一小時後，季薇戴著護鏡及全套高空跳傘裝備現身。她走進通風室，風扇開始轉動，並發出震耳欲聾的噪音。）
Trainer	I'M GOING TO PULL YOU OUT INTO THE STREAM!	我現在要把妳拉進氣流裡！

Chi   OK!

(Paul readies the camcorder, Chi spreads her arms and body out, the trainer keeps a firm grip on her sleeve and pant leg.)

好！

（保羅抓穩了錄影機，季薇將身體和手臂向外拉直，教練緊拉住她的袖子和褲管。）

Chi   I'M ... I'VE ... OK ... WHA ... OH ... YES.

我要…我已經…好…什麼…噢…對。

Paul   You're looking good. (The trainer lets go and Chi floats freely briefly before incidentally twisting an arm. She suddenly zooms to the top, panics and balls up causing her to drop just as quick, only to spread out again at the last second causing her to hover again.)

妳看起來很棒。（教練放手，季薇短暫地飄浮了一陣子後，不小心扭轉了一隻手臂。她突然地陡直上升到頂端，驚慌之餘把身體拱成球狀，導致整個人快速地掉下來，在最後一秒內她把四肢展開來，結果又開始盤旋起來。）

Chi   HA ... YAHHHHHHH!

哈…呀呀呀呀呀！

Trainer   YOU'RE DOING FINE! TRY IT AGAIN!

妳做得很好！再試一次！

(This time Chi intentionally twists her arms and slowly rises up 10 feet, 20 feet, 30 feet. She holds in amazement.)

（這回季薇故意轉動她的手臂，並緩慢地上升到十呎、二十呎、三十呎的高度。她驚歎地把自己固定在一點上。）

Chi   I"M DOING IT, I"M REALLY DOING IT!

我做到了！我真的做到了！

(5 minuets later, Chi walks out of the

（五分鐘後，季薇情緒激昂

	chamber exasperated.)	地走出通風室。）
Paul	You did great! Are you now ready for the real thing?	妳做得太棒了！準備好作真的高空跳傘了嗎？
Chi	(Thumbs up.) Let's give it a whirl, baby!	（比大拇指）我們去給它轉一下吧，寶貝！
Paul	I hope you know that on your first jump you will be strapped to a trainer.	我要跟妳講喔，首次跳傘的時候妳會跟一名教練綁在一起。
Chi	(Imitating outlaws from *Blazing Saddles*.) Trainers? We don't need no stinking trainers.	（模做電影《閃亮的馬鞍》中不法之徒的口吻）教練？我們不需要什麼臭教練。
Paul	Ha, ha, ha... Awesome!	哈哈哈…太棒了！

單字

☑ **back out** [bæk aʊt] *v.* 打退堂鼓、反悔而不去做某事

☑ **whirl** [wɝl] *n.* 旋轉

☑ **literally** [ˈlɪtərəlɪ] *adj.* 跟字面上完全一樣地、照字面地

☑ **chamber** [ˈtʃembɚ] *n.* 房間、室

☑ **zoom** [zum] *v.* 陡直上升

☑ **hover** [ˈhɑvɚ, ˈhʌvɚ] *v.* 盤旋、停留在空中

☑ **exasperated** [ɪgˈzæspəˌretɪd] *adj.* 激動的、過度興奮的

☑ **outlaw** [ˈaʊtˌlɔ] *n.* 不法之徒、罪犯

生活篇 信仰篇 表達篇 外來語篇 文明篇 其它篇

197

片語

☑ get someone's feet wet 由簡單的任務開始，讓某人逐漸熟悉某件工作

 ## 日常會話

☑ That's my girl／boy. 「這才是我的老婆（老公／女兒／兒子…等）！」表示對某人做的事情感到相當驕傲。

包含 "it" 的用語之三：Give It a Whirl

當我第一次聽到有人說這句話時，還以為她在講 give it a "world"（給它一個世界），聽了好幾次，才聽出來原來我那生性幽默的同事說的是 give it a whirl。World 跟 whirl 這兩個字發音還真像！

我的同事在說什麼呢？Whirl 的意思是「旋轉」，give it a whirl，給它轉一下，原來這句慣用語的意思是「給它試試看」。

用語的來源已不可考，但大多人推測跟某項附轉輪的器具有關聯，可能是賭博用的轉盤，或鄉下使用的農具，也可能是小孩子玩的風車。在這個句子裡的 it 是你想要一試的東西，所以 it 可以用那個東西或事情來替代，譬如：I want to give horseback riding a whirl.（我想試試騎馬）或 I will give that recipe a whirl.（我會試著做做看那篇食譜）。

這個慣用句通常只用在日常口語中，偶爾在也會在非常口語化的書報雜誌裡面出現。說這句話的人通常想表達出一種輕鬆、俏皮的詼諧感，嘗試做這件事的目的經常也是單純為了好玩。

其它跟 give it a whirl 意思相同的用語還包括：give it a try、give it a shot 甚至還有人說 give it a go. 簡單地來說，就是：Try it！

Notes

12 俚語 [Slangs]

45 Double Whammy

Paul answers the phone.　保羅接聽電話。

Chi	Paul! Thank God you picked up!	保羅！謝天謝地你接我電話！
Paul	What's the matter?	怎麼了？
Chi	I lost my keys to the apartment. When is the earliest you can get out of work?	我把公寓的鑰匙搞丟了。你最快什麼時候可以下班？
Paul	I'm leaving in five minutes. Where are you?	我準備五分鐘內就要離開辦公室。妳人在哪裡？
Chi	I'm at the Goodyear repair shop over on Wilshire.	我在威爾郡路上的固特異汽車維修中心。
Paul	WHAT? What'd you do to my car?	什麼？妳把我的車怎麼了？
Chi	You wouldn't believe it, I had a double whammy today. First, I had a flat tire on the freeway ...	你絕對不會相信，我今天連續碰到兩件倒楣事。首先，車子在高速公路上爆胎...
Paul	How much?	多少錢？
Chi	I don't know yet, but the right rear tire popped when I hit a pothole on the merging ramp.	還不清楚，但是我在連接高速公路的斜坡道上，栽到一個坑洞裡，右後方的輪胎砰的一聲就爆裂了。

Paul	Why are you driving into potholes?	妳為什麼會開到坑洞裡？
Chi	I'm sorry. I didn't see it. Afterwards I called the insurance company and they sent a truck to tow it. I waited MORE THAN AN HOUR before the truck showed up.	對不起啦，我沒看到那個洞。之後我打電話到保險公司，他們派出一輛拖吊車來拖，我等了一個多小時拖吊車才來。
Paul	Did you scratch my car?	妳有沒有刮傷我的車？
Chi	No, but while the guy was rigging the chassis to hoist it onto the platform, I went to a boutique next door to take a break. Somewhere in between all this mess I lost my keys.	沒有，但是當拖吊人員在固定車子底盤以吊到卡車的平台上時，我到附近的精品店去休息，不知道怎麼搞的在這場混亂當中我把鑰匙給搞丟了。
Paul	Did you call the apartment's manager, Don?	妳打電話給公寓經理唐了嗎？
Chi	I tried. But the office is closed. No one answered the phone.	我有試過，但是辦公室關門了，沒人接聽電話。
Paul	Why is your car keys and house keys on different rings?	為什麼妳的車鑰匙跟家裡鑰匙會在不同的鑰匙圈上？
Chi	We just moved here. I didn't have the chance to put the keys together. I only realized that the keys were missing after the driver dropped me off.	我們才剛搬進來，我還沒時間把鑰匙串在一起。拖吊車的司機放我下車以後我才發現鑰匙不見了。
Paul	Did you check with the driver?	那妳有跟那個司機問過了嗎？

生活篇 ─ 信仰篇 ─ 表達篇 ─ 外來語篇 ─ 文明篇 ─ 其它篇

Chi	Yes, the dispatcher called the driver and he checked his truck. He found nothing.		有啊，拖吊公司的派調人員打電話給他，他在卡車裡各處翻過，什麼也沒找到。
Paul	Obviously. What about the boutique?		明顯地。那精品店呢？
Chi	I haven't checked yet.		我還沒去問。
Paul	And the repair shop?		那維修中心？
Chi	They're looking. Plus, the gate fob will cost fifty dollars to replace.		他們正在找。噢對了，重買一只新的社區鐵門的遙控器要花五十元。
Paul	FIFTY DOLLARS!		五十元？
Chi	But at least I'm ok.		可是至少我平安無事。
Paul	(Silence)		（沈默不語）
Chi	So... you'll be here soon?		所以…你很快就會到這邊來接我？
Paul	Yes. (Hangs up.)		我會。（掛電話）

 單字

☑ pop [pɑp] **v.** 砰的一聲爆裂	☑ pothole [`pɑt͵hol] **n.** （在路面上的）坑洞
☑ rig [rɪg] **v.** 為（船、車等）裝上配備、架設（機器等）以利使用	☑ chassis [`tʃæsɪ] **n.** 汽車的底盤
☑ hoist [hɔɪst] **v.** （用繩索、起重機等）將（重物）吊起、舉起	☑ boutique [bu`tik] **n.** 小間的服飾店、精品店

☑ dispatcher [dɪ`spætʃə] **n.** 調度員、派遣人員出外工作的人

☑ fob [fɑb] **n.** 一種可隨身攜帶的電子裝置，用以開啟門鎖或啟動設備，如車庫門遙控開關和汽車遙控發動器等。

 ## 片語

☑ have a flat tire 輪胎爆胎

 ## 俚語之一：Double Whammy

中文裡我們有句話說：「禍不單行」。美國人好像也這麼覺得喔，他們幽默地說：It's a double whammy!

Whammy 的發音為[`wæmɪ]，是從 wham 這個擬聲字演變而來的，wham 形容東西受到重擊的聲音，所以 whammy 有打擊的意思，double whammy 就好像中國人說的「雙重打擊」。

美國 80 年代有一個電視遊戲節目，參賽者如果答對了題目，就有機會拿獎金。電視的製作單位設計了一個類似輪轉盤的大螢幕，規則是當參賽人喊 STOP 的時候，發著光的小燈泡若是停在不同金額的格子上，他／她就會獲得那部份的獎金。金額會一直累積，但是如果轉輪停在一個叫 Whammy 的紅色怪獸上面，參賽者所擁有的獎金就全部歸零。經常在緊張的時刻裡，比賽的來賓會忘情地大喊：NO WHAMMIES! NO WHAMMIES!!

由此可知 whammy 這個字在美國文化裡代表著不好的事情，有負面的意義。一般人若在談話中提到了 double whammy，通常那兩件壞事彼此間不是有因果關係，就是發生在極相近的時間點內或同時。譬如說："This morning I was rear-ended by a truck. As I parked my car to resolve the issue, I got a parking ticket. What a double whammy!"（今早有部卡車從後面撞我。當我停車下來解決這件糾紛時，我被罰了一張違規停車的罰單。真是禍不單行！）

最後一提的是，double whammy 有時也可能被拿來形容幸運的好事，這種情況比較少，所以你要根據對話的內容來判斷說話者的意思。舉例來說："I got a free burger, AND a free french fries. Double whammy! Yeah!"（我不但拿到了一個免費的漢堡，店家還加送一份薯條。雙喜臨門！耶！）

Chi	Hahaha… He proved that God doesn't exist. Oh, Homer.	哈哈哈…他剛剛證明了上帝不存在，噢，河馬。
Paul	Who would have ever guessed that Homer Simpson was a secret genius the whole time.	誰知道河馬·辛普森原來從頭到尾其實私底下是個天才。
Chi	Yeah, but he chooses to return to his unassuming mediocrity. The show's conclusion proposes that you can't be smart and happy. You can only be one or the other. That entire idea just makes me sad.	對啊，但是他選擇回復到平庸的外表下。這部卡通的結論是，人無法既聰明又快樂，沒有人能魚與熊掌兼得。這種想法讓我覺得很悲哀。
Paul	You just proved their point in your own doubt.	妳提出的懷疑正好就證實了他們的論點。
Chi	Blaah.	隨便啦。
Paul	People typically socialize in groups of similar interests and background. The people who Homer congregates with on a daily basis are average. Homer's sudden increase in intelligence led to a new awareness of the imperfections surrounding him. His effort to reconstruct the status quo in order to match his shift in world view led to his communal alienation.	人們通常與其他有相近興趣與背景的人組成社交圈。每天跟河馬聚在一起的那些人基本上資質平凡。河馬突然間智商大舉提高，使他發現生活周遭內所存在的不完美，因此 他努力去改變現況，以使之符合他新的世界觀，結果造成社區的人們對他的排擠。
Chi	And therefore he is unhappy because his closest friends have ostracized him.	所以他變得悶悶不樂，因為連最要好的朋友都離他遠

去。

| Paul | Yes, all of the Simpson members have made similar choices at different time in their lives. | 是的，所有辛普森家庭的成員都曾在不同的時間點上做過類似的決定。 |

| Chi | What? Prove it. | 什麼？提出證明。 |

| Paul | Let's look at the evidence. In all of the Grandpa Simpson flashbacks he exhibits extraordinary levels of intellect. He was a talented fighter pilot and an accomplished pianist. He has also been miserable for most of his life. He is happiest not when he stands out and above others, but rather when he is included in the warmth of the group. Then there's Marge. Marge was a college-bound "A" student before she met Homer. At one point, she was a successful police officer, artist, and saleswoman. Yet she left all of that behind in order to stay home, where she is the happiest. Lisa, like Grandpa, also embraces her intellect and she is almost never happy. She desperately desires inclusion and she is happier when she releases herself from her own great expectations. | 讓我們來一一檢視證據。在卡通裡所有顯示祖父過去的場景中，他都展現出過人的才智，他曾經擔任過戰鬥機的駕駛，也是位成功的鋼琴家，但他一生大部份都過得很不開心。他最快樂的時光，不是在他表現傑出、超越別人的時候，而是當他受到他人接納的溫暖時刻。然後是媽媽美枝。在遇見河馬前，美枝是個準備朝大學之路前進的資優學生，她曾經是位成功的警官、藝術家以及業務人員，但是她把那些全都放棄掉，選擇了帶給她最大快樂的家庭生活。麗莎，就像祖父一樣，接受自己比別人聰明的事實，而她幾乎從來不曾感到快樂。她極度渴望被接納，只有當她把自己從對自我的超高標準中釋放出來的時候，才比較快樂一些。 |

| Chi | And Bart is a clever prankster pulling off well-thought-out schemes requiring organization skills and leadership. | 還有霸子，身為一名聰明的惡作劇者，能成功演出精心設計的騙局，需要組織能力和領袖精神。 |

生活篇 信仰篇 表達篇 外來語篇 文明篇 其它篇

205

Paul	Exactly. He is happiest when expectations are low and miserable when asked to fulfill his true potential. But here's the kicker, Maggie may be your salvation.	沒錯。他感到最快樂的時光，是當外界降低對他的期望；當別人要求他發揮真正實力的時候，他反而覺得悲慘。但是故事的轉折點來了，瑪姬也許是妳的救贖。
Chi	Maggie?	瑪姬？
Paul	Yes! She is the only one who is able to live a balanced life. In all of the flash-forwards, she is always shown as being loved, not just by her family, but by everyone. She is successful, confident, intelligent, and faces life's obstacles with eager anticipation. She thinks up a solution and then executes it boldly. This only enhances her happiness.	對！她是這個家庭中唯一能擁有平衡生活的成員。卡通中所有未來的場景，都顯示她不只受到家人的愛護，更被所有人愛戴。她成功、有自信、聰明，並熱切地面對人生的挫折，她不但能想出解決之道，之後並能大膽地貫徹到底，而這點更是為她的快樂指數加分。
Chi	Well, Just like Maggie, I am the exception to the rule.	嗯，就跟瑪姬一樣，我也是個特例。
Paul	You're the kicker?	妳是故事中的關鍵點？
Chi	I'm the kicker!	我是！
Paul	And so you are.	那妳就是。

♥ 單字

☑ unassuming [ˌʌnəˈsjumɪŋ] *adj.* 一點也不浮誇自大的、謙虛的

☑ mediocrity [ˌmidɪˈɑkrətɪ] *n.* 平庸、普通

☑ congregate [ˈkɑŋgrɪˌget] *v.* 聚集、集合

☑ alienation [ˌeljəˈneʃən] **n.** 疏遠

☑ ostracize [ˈɑstrəˌsaɪz] **v.** 擯棄（某人）、使其成為無人理睬的人

☑ flashback [ˈflæʃˌbæk] **n.** （在電影、小說等中插入）過去的場景。在對話後段提到的另外一個字 "flash-forwards" ，即是跟 flashback 相反的未來場面。

☑ bound [baʊnd] **adj.** 朝（某方向）進行的、往... 的

☑ salvation [sælˈveʃən] **n.** 救贖、拯救

俚語之二：Kicker

在撲克牌遊戲的規則中，如果打牌的對手同時持有相同點數的卡，這時比賽的勝負，就憑他們手中所擁有的 "kicker" 來決定。以德州撲克（Texas Hold'em）為例，一家手上有 A 跟 K，而另一家有 A 和 Q，在公用的五張牌都揭露後，如果這兩家所能夠湊成的最佳手牌皆為一對 Ace，那麼他們另外一張牌，也就是我們所說的 kicker：K 以及 Q，即被用來決定誰輸誰贏。在這個例子裡，很明顯有 K 的那家贏錢。

由此可知，"kicker" 是那一張扭轉局勢的關鍵卡。拿到英文裡來講，當有人提到："And here is the kicker, ..." 的時候，他／她原本在闡述一件看來很簡單、很直接的事，但這件事情中間，其實隱藏了一個劇情大轉彎，或者有一個驚喜的結局。我曾經看過有人這麼形容 "kicker"：想像你本來好好地坐著，忽然間椅子後面被人踢（kick）了一下－所以 kicker 就是會讓你驚訝地跳起來的那個轉折點！

故事人人會說，巧妙各有不同。有時候我們認為某些人說的故事比別人的好，關鍵在於那些人故事裡的 kickers。J. K.羅琳就是一位很會利用 kicker、製造高潮的小說家，不如就讓我用她的故事來造個例句吧！ "Voldemort had every advantage and under normal conditions would have killed Harry, but here's the kicker: Unknown to anyone but the wand maker and Dumbledore, Harry's wand was Voldemort's twin and thus unable to complete the spell, allowing Harry to escape."

（佛地魔在各方面都佔上風，正常情況下他早就殺死哈利了，但是精彩的地方在這裡：除了造魔杖的人和鄧不利多外，沒有人知道原來哈利的魔杖跟佛地魔的是雙胞胎，所以咒法無法達成，讓哈利給脫逃了。）

生活篇　信仰篇　表達篇　外來語篇　文明篇　其它篇

207

47 Cop-Out

A bottle is spinning in the middle of a circle of people. The group tightly hold their breath until it comes to rest on ...

一群人圍成一圈坐著，他們的正中央有支瓶子正在旋轉。大家屏息等待它逐漸停下來指向…

Group	PAUL!	保羅！
Chi	Truth or Dare?	真心話還是大冒險？
Paul	Well, you already know everything about me, so let's go for something a bit more exciting: DARE!	反正妳知道所有有關我的事情，不如我們就選擇比較讓人興奮的：大冒險！
Chi	Mmm ... You're right, I do know everything about you. For example—I know you hate dark beer ... so ... I'm gonna dare you to drink a pint of Guinness... upside down!	嗯…你說的對，我的確知道所有有關你的事，舉例來說，我知道你討厭黑啤酒…所以…我要挑戰你喝完一品脫的健力士啤酒…同時倒立！
Paul	That's <u>kicking it up a notch</u>. All right, I'll see what I can do.	這遊戲是越來越有看頭了。好吧，我就來試試看。
	Paul gathers a few throw pillows and situates himself up against the wall. Mike finds a bendy straw and starts pouring beer into the cup.	保羅收集了數個抱枕，靠著牆頭下腳上地倒立起來。麥可找出一根可彎式吸管，開始將啤酒倒入杯內。
Chi	And... Go!	預備…開始！

	Grimacing, Paul tries to finish quickly letting out a vexed breath of exhaustion in the end.	一邊做鬼臉，保羅一邊試著快速地把啤酒喝完，最後不耐煩地吐出一口氣。
Paul	(Proudly stating.) Done!	（驕傲地宣布）任務完成！
	A few streaks of dark fluid roll out of his nostrils causing everyone to laugh uncontrollably.	幾道深色的液體從保羅的鼻孔流下來，令眾人無法控制地捧腹大笑。
Paul	Gimme a tissue you jackals!	你們這幫走狗還不快拿給我張面紙！
Chi	Here you go. (Hands Paul a tissue.) Good job.	喏拿去。（遞給保羅一張面紙。）幹得好。
Paul	God I hate warm Guinness. You know eventually I'm going to get you back.	老天，我最討厭室溫下的健力士啤酒。妳很清楚我一定會把這個仇報回來。
Chi	We'll see!	咱們走著瞧！
Paul	Alright! It now ... my turn! (Spins the bottle.)	好了！現在…該我玩！（轉動瓶子。）
Jennifer	Oh, nooooooo... no, no, NOOOOOO!	噢，不不不…不，不，不！
Paul	(Smugly grins.) Truth or dare, Jennifer?	（沾沾自喜地微笑）真心話還是大冒險，珍妮佛？
Jennifer	(Weakly) Dare? Please be kind ... PLEASE.	（虛弱地）大冒險？拜託別太狠…拜託。

生活篇 — 信仰篇

表達篇

外來語篇 — 文明篇 — 其它篇

209

	Paul signals Mike. After exchanging a few ideas, Paul turns to Jennifer.	保羅對麥可作了個信號。在相互交換了幾個點子後，保羅轉向珍妮佛。
Paul	We've got it. I dare you... to streak around the building for one lap.	我們已經決定好。我挑戰妳…繞這棟大樓光著身體跑一圈。
Mike	Do it!	就給他做下去！
Jennifer	ABSOLUTELY NOT!	我絕對不幹！
Mike	Don't be a cop-out, Jen.	別當個逃避責任的縮頭烏龜，珍。
Jennifer	I'm not a cop-out! That's too much! The two of you <u>are in on this</u> together.	我才不是逃避責任的縮頭烏龜！那真的是太過份了！你們兩個一同計畫好的。
Paul	Well, if you can't do it, then you'll have to undergo "THE PENALTY."	如果妳沒辦法做的話，那妳就得接受「終極處罰」。
	The group gasps.	眾人倒吸一口氣。
Jennifer	The penalty?	終極處罰？
Chi	No one has ever survived "THE PENALTY."	沒人能活過「終極處罰」。
Jennifer	Chi, help me.	季薇，幫幫我。
Chi	Um, how about we just have Jen run around the building in her pajamas?	嗯，能不能讓珍穿著她的睡衣繞著大樓跑一下就好？

Paul and Mike	NO DEAL!	不成！
Jennifer	I hate you guys, seriously.	我恨你們兩個，真的。
Paul and Mike	(Chanting.) Cop-out! Cop-out! Cop-out!	（齊聲重覆地說）縮頭烏龜！縮頭烏龜！縮頭烏龜！
Jennifer	How about I run around in my high-school cheerleading uniform?	如果我穿我高中時代啦啦隊的制服跑呢？
Paul	Plus a cheer!	要一邊跑一邊加油吶喊！
Mike	And a cartwheel!	麥可：加上一個翻筋斗！
Jennifer	Don't push your luck boys.	你們倆別逼人太甚。
Paul	(Briefly checks with Mike.) Uniform, cheer, cartwheel.	（很快地與麥可確認過）制服、加油、翻筋斗。
	(Jennifer looks over to Chi.)	（珍妮佛望向季薇）
Chi	(Shrugs.) It's better than "THE PENALTY."	（聳肩）總比「終極處罰」來得好。
Jennifer	(Gives Paul the death stare.) Deal!	（冷冷地瞪著保羅）成交！
Chi	You guys are tempting karma.	你們兩個小心有報應。
Paul	Yeah, yeah, yeah. (Mockingly) Gimme a "P," gimme an "A," gimme a "U," gimme an "L." What's that spell?	耶、耶、耶。（嘲諷地）給我一個 P，給我一個 A，給我一個 U，再給我一個 L，拼起來是什麼字？
Jennifer	Butt-head!	大頭蛋！

生活篇 — 信仰篇

表達篇

外來語篇 — 文明篇 — 其它篇

 單字

- ☑ situate [ˋsɪtʃʊ‚et] **v.** 使形成某種姿勢、使置於某處
- ☑ grimace [grɪˋmes] **v.** 做鬼臉
- ☑ vexed [vɛkst] **adj.** 惱怒的、不耐煩的
- ☑ streak [strik] **n. v.** （作名詞用）條紋、線；（作動詞用時）裸奔
- ☑ jackal [ˋdʒækɔl] **n.** 幫兇、走狗
- ☑ smugly [ˋsmʌglɪ] **adv.** 沾沾自喜地、自命不凡地
- ☑ lap [læp] **n.** （運動場的）一圈、（游泳池的）一次往返
- ☑ undergo [‚ʌndɚˋgo] **v.** 經歷、接受
- ☑ cartwheel [ˋkɑrt‚wil] **n.** 側身翻斗
- ☑ karma [ˋkɑrmə] **n.** 因果報應、業

 片語

- ☑ kick it up a notch 使某事物更加精彩或有趣
- ☑ be in on something 參與某種詭計或陰謀

 俚語之三：Cop-out

　　美國喜劇演員 Jim Gaffigan 向來擅長以自己微胖的身材為開玩笑的主題。在一場個人秀中，Jim 提到過去他曾因嘲笑鯨魚的肥胖，而遭致某位觀眾的抗議：

"Once, after a show someone came up to me.　He was like, 'You know, whales aren't fat. They have a layer of blubber.'　And I thought calling myself big-bone was a cop-out!"

　　（有次在秀結束後有人對我說：「你知道，鯨魚其實並不胖。牠們只是身上有一層隔熱的脂肪。」哼！我還以為說我自己骨架大是一種逃避責任的行為哩！

　　Cop-out，意思就是「規避責任、不履行承諾的人或行徑」。

當名詞時，cop 和 out 中間有一個連字號，但是也有人省略連字號，以空格代替；更簡單的寫法是把兩個字連在一起寫成一個字 copout。當動詞用的話，則一律將兩個字分開寫，也就是 cop out；當我們說某人 copped out，或他 copped out of something，代表那個人本來答應要做某件事，但是卻中途反悔而沒有去做。

"Cop" 這個字最為人熟悉的用法，是對「警察」的俗稱，但是如果你去查字典，就會發現它的動詞解釋是「獲得」或「拿到」；原來啊，cop-out 的意思是犯人坦承認罪，進而與警方「取得」（即 cop 原本的意義）減輕刑責的協議。所以 cop-out 當初的涵義為「獲得較輕的刑罰」，隨著時間慢慢演化成現在「逃避責任」、「臨陣脫逃」的意義。

生活篇　信仰篇　表達篇　外來語篇　文明篇　其它篇

12 俚語　　[Slangs]

48 For Shizzle

At the comedy club.　在喜劇俱樂部。

(Crowd cheering)　（觀眾一片叫好）

Mike	Jamie Foxx is something else!	傑米‧福克斯真是不同凡響！
Chi	I don't get it.	我不懂。
Mike	What part?	哪個部份？
Chi	What does "off the hizzle" mean?	"Off the hizzle" 是什麼意思？
Mike	"Off the hook," and "off the hook" means something that it's "cool," "exciting" and "crazy good"!	就等於 "off the hook"，而 "off the hook" 的意思是某件事「很酷」、「令人興奮」跟「棒呆了」！
Chi	Huh? I thought "off the hook" means that someone is free from certain obligation, and that he is no longer responsible for a rather difficult task. Or, it means "very busy" as in "The phone has been ringing off the hook all day."	吭？我以為 "off the hook" 的意思是某人自某項責任中解放出來、不需再為某件困難的任務負責；或是「非常忙碌的狀態」，譬如説「一整天電話都響到 off the hook」。
Paul	The definition Mike gave you, is slang.	麥可給妳的定義是一種俚語的用法。
Chi	Oh, really? I felt like I was trying to decode his entire act. I think he cut the	哦，是這樣嗎？我覺得整個表演過程裡我都在試著解讀

	word "for" short, and then he used the beginning of the word "sure" and attached "izzle" to it which then became "fo shizzle." Am I right?	他的笑話。我猜他把 "for" 這個字裁短，然後把 "sure" 的字首加上 "izzle"，結果整句就變成 "fo shizzle"。這樣對嗎？
Paul	Basically. This particular form of slang was made popular by rap artist Snoop Dogg from a style of cant used by African American pimps and jive hustlers in the 1970's. It's similar to Pig Latin and was developed around the same time period at the Harlem Renaissance. Its use evolved from local hotspots within Oakland, New York, and Philly. PLUS IT"S FUN TO SAY!	基本上對。這種形式的俚語，原來是饒舌歌手史奴比狗狗把七〇年代一種流傳於美國非裔皮條客與小販間的暗語，大量使用在他的創作裡而掀起熱潮。它從哈林文藝復興時期開始，跟豬拉丁語差不多在同一個時期形成，形式也相似。它在加州奧克蘭市、紐約和費城當地的熱門聚集地點演變發展，而且這種話講起來很好玩！
Mike	Fo shizzle broham! Yah dig?	當然，老兄！你了嗎？
Paul	Yo vernacular tis muggin on the gator dogg.	你的這套語言超屌的，夥伴。
Mike	Fo real's? It ain't no thang.	真的嗎？那沒什麼啦。
Paul	G, yooz ah dope mother...	你這人很厲害…
Mike	Shut yo mouth!	閉嘴！
Paul	Oooze SNAP!	噢…不妙！
Chi	What just happened?	現在是發生什麼事了？
Mike	A wee bit of the hood just came up in yah face B.	一點點的黑人區跑出來嗆聲了啦。
Paul	Dat crazy fly, baller!	那有夠酷的，大哥大！

生活篇 信仰篇 表達篇 外來語篇 文明篇 其它篇

Chi	Oh my god, please stop!	喔，拜託你們停止！	
Paul	Don't pound cake my groove!	現在正順手得很，別對我丟磅蛋糕！	
Mike	Ha, pound cake... good one.	哈，磅蛋糕…說得好。	
Chi	What?	什麼？	
Paul	The Pound Cake speech was given by Bill Cosby back in 2004 criticizing the use of slang by African Americans as uncouth and embarrassing.	比爾‧寇斯比在二千零四年發表了一篇磅蛋糕演講，內容批判非裔美國人使用俚語的現象不但顯示教養低落並令人感到難堪。	
Mike	Well he had a point, even if it wasn't well received.	他說得有道理，雖然很多人不甚同意。	

🖤 單字

☑ **cant** [kænt] *n.* 地下團體成員間的一套特殊用語

☑ **pimp** [pɪmp] *n.* 皮條客、老鴇

☑ **jive** [dʒaɪv] *n.* （俚語）外人聽不懂的話、暗語

☑ **hustler** [ˈhʌslɚ] *n.* （俚語）用不正當或狡猾哄騙方法做生意的人、猛叫價推銷的小販

☑ **Pig Latin** [ˈpɪɡ ˈlætɪn] *n.* 一種祕密暗語。構成 Pig Latin 的規則為，將一個英文字字首的子音放到字尾，並於其後加上 ay。例如 pig 變成 igpay [ɪɡˈpe]，stupid 成為 upidstay [upɪdˈste]。這種語言遊戲被稱作 Pig Latin 的原因，是由於拉丁語向來給人隱晦不明的感覺，而「豬」指這種奇怪的語言相當不文雅並且混亂。

☑ **Harlem Renaissance** [ˈhɑrləm ˌrɛnəˈsɑns] *n.* 哈林文藝復興時期。這項美國黑人文化的覺醒運動，發生於一九二〇和三〇年間，以紐約哈林區為中心點，由黑人文學開始並擴展到音樂與社會議題等其他領域。

- ☑ dig [dɪg] **v.** （俚語）了解、懂；喜歡

- ☑ vernacular [vəˋnækjələ] **n.** 方言、地方特有的用語

- ☑ mug [mʌg] **v.** 襲擊、搶奪

- ☑ gator [ˋgetə] **n.** （非正式用語）鱷魚。Alligator 的簡稱

- ☑ dogg [dɔg] **n.** （俚語）朋友、好友

- ☑ dope [dop] **adj.** （俚語）極好的

- ☑ snap [snæp] **interj.** （俚語，驚嘆詞）「噢」、「糟了」

- ☑ fly [flaɪ] **adj.** （俚語）酷、很棒

- ☑ baller [ˋbɔlə] **n.** （俚語）非常成功有錢的人；出手闊綽的玩家、大亨

- ☑ groove [gruv] **n.** （俚語）事情進行地很順暢的狀態

- ☑ uncouth [ʌnˋkuθ] **adj.** 粗野的、不文雅的

俚語之四：**For Shizzle**

　　有人說，語言是活的。在以英文為主要日常語言的社會中，每天都有新的字彙被創造出來。有些字由於出自名人之口而聲名大噪，有些字則是因應時事、當前的社會現象而產生，這些字風行之境界到，連正統的權威字典都在考慮是否應收錄進他們下一版的印刷裡，而許多在黑人社群間流行的辭彙就是這種例子。

　　美國饒舌大師 Snoop Dogg（或是學他很 smooth 的講法：s n-double ʊ-p, d-o-double g），讓美國人從公元 2000 年開始，不論什麼字，後面都加個尾巴 izzle！

　　例句一：For shizzle＝For sho＝For sure 當然例句二：For shizzle, my nizzle. 當然囉，我的非裔美國籍兄弟。

　　美國黑人獨特、色彩濃厚的文化，自成一格的說話方式，其實是相當迷人、值得深入探討的一個區域。你若是有機會認識幾個美國黑人朋友，會很難不被他們的開朗態度與幽默所感染！當然，我不建議你冒然使用以上語言、開始跟大家稱兄道弟，畢竟彼此還瞭解不夠，怕引起誤會。但是能聽懂他們之間的一些「行話」，在欣賞流行音樂或看電影時，相信你就能多一分體會。

Barbara Ohhhhh <u>shoot me</u>! Our sales numbers are down. I've got stacks of reports I have to finish by day's end ... where is everybody? Is anyone in this office working at all?

噢噢讓我死了吧！我們的銷售數字低落。我有成堆的報告必須在今天結束前完成…人都到哪裡去了？這個辦公室裡還有人上班嗎？

Daniel I have several business loans <u>in the pipeline</u>. I know Jennifer is working on closing the deal with the city's employee program and we just need a little more time ...

我有幾個商業貸款在洽談中。我知道珍妮佛正努力簽下市政府的員工計畫，我們只需要再多一點時間…

Barbara I don't want to hear any more excuses! I need more customers now; there are consequences if I don't reach my quota. I almost forgot I have to leave now to pick up my car. Daniel you will stay in the office while I am out. Call all of your premium clients. We need more numbers, much more. Keep pushing!

我不想聽更多藉口！我現在就要更多客戶；若我沒達到業績目標是會有後果的。我差點忘記我現在就得去車廠取回我的車。丹尼你在我外出時必須留在辦公室。打電話給你所有的頂級客戶。我們需要更高、更高的銷售數字。繼續用力推！

Barbara abruptly storms out of the office.

芭芭拉如暴風狂掃般地離開了辦公室。

Daniel (Sarcastically) Oh, boo hoo cry me a river! All she does is complain and we are the ones who have to do the work.

（諷刺地）喔，嗚呼，哭給我一條河吧！她只會抱怨，實際上工作的是我們這些人。

218

Chi   What does that mean? "Cry me a river"?

那是什麼意思啊？「哭給我一條河」？

Daniel   It is short for "Oh boo hoo, cry me a river, build a bridge, and frigging <u>get over</u> it"! It means that I think that "someone" is complaining too much about frivolous things.

那是「喔，嗚呼，哭給我一條河，搭座橋，然後他媽的跨過這條河」簡短的講法！意思是我認為「某人」抱怨太多瑣碎的事情了。（作者按：英文的「跨過」get over it 也有「重新振作、不再為某事難過」的意思）

Chi   But sales are important. It reflects upon her job performance.

但是業績是很重要的。業績顯示出她的工作成效。

Daniel   True, but there is only so much we can do and every month isn't going to be a sales bonanza. Bad sales is not an excuse to panic or attack others just because you feel vulnerable.

沒錯，但是我們能做的就是這麼多，不是每個月都可以業績衝上天。只不過因為你覺得脆弱，你也不能拿業績差作藉口來恐慌或攻擊他人。

Chi   I suppose that is true.

我猜大概是沒錯。

Daniel   Being honest with our feelings is a way of <u>putting our lives into perspective</u>. Our individual problems sometimes can cloud our emotions and cause us to overreact. Barbara's acute focus on her problems has caused us, her supportive coworkers, undue stress. My comments may be a bit condescending, but sometimes we need to remind people that these type of

對我們的感覺坦白，其實是一個從更理性、清晰的角度來檢視我們生命的方法，有時候個人的問題蒙蔽了我們的情緒，並導致我們過度反應。芭芭拉過份聚焦在她的問題上面，已經對我們，這群幫助她的工作夥伴，製造了不當的壓力。我的話也許

生活篇 信仰篇 表達篇 外來語篇 文明篇 其它篇

problems are not always as critical as people may think they are.	帶有藐視的意味，但是有時我們必須提醒別人，這種問題並不一定像他們想像的那麼嚴重。
Chi I am sorry you feel this way, Daniel. It's not fair that she puts her frustration on you.	我很抱歉你這麼覺得。她對你出氣是不公平的。
Daniel It's all right. I know her well enough that once she <u>gets it out of her system</u> she will be that funny, nothing-can-ever-bother-me boss again.	沒關係啦。我了解她，一旦把壓力完全釋放出去以後，她就又恢復成那個搞笑、什麼事都難不到我的老闆了。
Chi I agree. Barbara normally is not like that. I know she has had a lot of pressure put on her since the branch was open.	我同意，芭芭拉平常不像那樣。我知道自從分行開幕後她就承受了很多壓力。
Daniel Yeah, guess we all on the same boat so we need to help each other out. Time to make some phone calls and talk to customers!	是啊，我猜我們都在同一條船上所以大家要互相幫忙。該去打些電話跟客戶談談了！

 ## 單字

☑ frivolous [ˈfrɪvələs] *adj.* 瑣碎的

☑ bonanza [boˈnænzə] *n.* 一下子突然的繁榮；一飛沖天的好景氣

☑ acute [əˈkjut] *adj.* 敏感的；事態嚴重的

☑ undue [ʌnˈdju] *adj.* 不適當的；過度的

☑ condescending [ˌkɑndɪˈsɛndɪŋ] *adj.* 藐視的；帶有優越感的

慣用語

☑ in the pipeline 正在進行中；正在發展中
☑ get over something 在經歷某個困難的事件後，重新感覺好過了起來；重新振作
☑ put something into perspective 客觀清晰地審視某個事件
☑ get it out of someone's system 將某人心中的慾望或想法完全釋放出來

日常會話

☑ Shoot me！ 拿把槍射我吧！讓我死了吧！

這句話是這麼說的之一：Oh Boo Hoo, Cry Me a River!

假設你那個家裡超有錢的朋友，某天來跟你抱怨：「我老爸剛幫我買的那部法拉利跑車喔，早就跟他說過我喜歡的顏色，他竟然忘了，買了另外一個顏色的！」

呃... 這個時候，你唯一需要作的，就是舉起你的右手握拳擰淚，一臉假裝要哭出來地對他／她說：Oh, boo hoo, cry me a river!（喂，你到底哭夠了沒？）

一九五五年的一首爵士藍調曲 "Cry Me a River"，歌詞闡述在某段戀情關係中，原本拋棄主角的人之後反悔、痛哭流涕地想要重續舊情，於是主角就在歌裡這麼唱：Well, you can cry me a river, cry me a river. I cried a river over you.（哼，你盡管哭吧，我以前為了你，曾掉了有一條河那麼多的眼淚）表示主角雖然過去被對方傷得很深，但是已堅強地重新站起來，現在面對這個負心的對象，不論他／她給予再多的藉口，主角都一點也不在意了。很難判斷當時寫這首歌的人是否發明了 "cry me a river" 這句話，但是這個用語在歌流行起來後，即被大眾所熟知，有人在前面又加上了一句 "Oh, boo hoo" － "boo hoo" 是擬聲詞，用來模仿人大哭的聲音－就形成目前的用法，來指對對方的抱怨或訴苦感到不耐煩或不屑一顧。

美國人叫愛抱怨的人為 cry baby，這些人最喜歡訴苦，到處跟人家提他的 sob story（為了引人同情或憐憫而說的悲慘故事）。如果你覺得某人對你抱怨的事情，簡直是日子過得太好、沒事在無理取鬧的話，這句 cry me a river 大概就可以派上用場！要特別強調一下，cry me a river 僅限於交情好、不忌諱玩笑的朋友之間使用。如果人家真的有難過的事，說這句話就顯得你沒同情心；要是你是拿這句話來講另外一個人，最好確定那個人不在場，否則你麻煩就大囉！

Chi is reading an article about the 2008 housing market crash in a financial magazine.

季薇在讀一篇財經雜誌中有關二〇〇八年房地產市場崩潰的文章。

Chi　This report brings back so many memories. Merrill Lynch was acquired by Bank of America. Lehman Brothers' was filing for bankruptcy. Every month we kept hearing about more and more of these big financial corporations falling like dominoes.

這個報導帶來許多回憶。美林證券被美國銀行收購。雷曼兄弟申請破產保護。每個月我們持續聽到越來越多這些龐大的財經集團，像骨牌一樣相繼倒下。

Paul　The real amazing part is that there were signs that this was going to happen before it happened. The housing market started to recess because it couldn't maintain Wall Street's ambitious growth expectations. Prices of homes dropped sharply in key areas and then people started missing payments. The government failed to regulate, investigate, and anticipate the burgeoning housing bubble.

真正不可思議的部份是在它發生之前，徵兆早就出現了。房地產市場開始退燒，它無法如華爾街大膽預測的持續成長。許多關鍵地區內的房價直線下跌，人們開始付不出貸款。政府沒有適當地管制、調查，以及預期房地產泡沫的發生。

Chi　Back then the bank was loaning money to anyone who asked regardless of their credit history.

那個時期銀行不管客戶的信用紀錄如何，誰要借錢就貸款給誰。

Paul　That alone should have been a <u>red flag</u>.

光那樣就足以視為危險的徵

Loaning to people with deficient credit histories enable the bank to charge a higher interest rate. This compensated for the additional risk, but made it difficult to pay back the loan due to flexible interest rates. For example, at the beginning of a loan period you might start by paying five hundred dollars a month, however when the rate went up, next month's payment could jump to two thousand dollars or more.

象了。借錢給信用紀錄差的客人，讓銀行有權提高貸款利率。銀行用較高的利息來彌補額外的風險，但其彈性利率的設計則使客戶面臨還款的困難。舉例來說，在貸款的初期你一開始每月支付五百元，但是當利率上漲，你下個月的帳單可能一下跳到兩千塊以上。

Chi　Most people live on a fixed income. No way could they handle that kind of volatility!

大多數人的收入是固定的。沒人能應付那樣的劇烈波動！

Paul　Exactly. The end result was massive foreclosures. When the foreclosure rate sky rocketed, banks panicked and desperately tried to sell their interests before the issue became public. In order to reduce the risks and increase profit, banks bundled their subprime mortgage loans and then sold them to other investors under falsified "A" ratings. At this point everyone everywhere now had toxic investments in their portfolios. It was then that the ground began to shift beneath their feet.

就是說。最後的結果即是大規模的銀行查封或法拍房屋。當法拍率大舉提升時，銀行開始恐慌，並想盡辦法在消息公諸前將它們的資產賣掉。為了降低風險和提高獲利，銀行把它們的次級房貸組合起來，以造假的 A 級評等賣給其他的投資者。到了這個階段，每一個地方，每一個人的資產裡，現在都有了這種有害的投資商品。就是在那時，人們腳下的地面開始大舉移動。

Chi　World governments did everything they could to fix the problem.

世界各地的政府已盡力在解決問題。

Paul　How much a government should do is debatable. After all, when depression-era regulations were removed in the US, it allowed the banks to take unnecessary risk with other people's money. New markets with astronomical gains were created, but proved to be unsustainable. The market shifted to equalize the arbitrage. Government bailouts possibly prevented the inevitable recession from becoming a depression. We got lucky, history almost repeated itself.

政府應該做到什麼程度還有待討論。畢竟，在美國政府取消了經濟蕭條時期的法令限制後，銀行開始可以用別人的錢去冒不必要的險。雖然創造了巨額報酬的新興市場，但是最後證明是無法持續的。市場大量地位移，以平衡那些利用價差以賺取利潤的投機交易。政府提供的財務紓困，極有可能防止了經濟衰退成為經濟蕭條。我們這次運氣好，差一點又重複了歷史的腳步。

 ## 單字

☑ domino [`dɑməˌno] *n.* 骨牌

☑ burgeon [`bɝdʒən] *v.* 發芽；快速出現

☑ deficient [dɪ`fɪʃənt] *adj.* 有缺陷的

☑ volatility [ˌvɑlə`tɪlətɪ] *n.* 上下劇烈變動；反覆無常

☑ foreclosure [for`kloʒɚ] *n.* 法拍；銀行查封房屋並拍賣以討回貸款

☑ subprime mortgage [ˌsʌb`praɪm `mɔrgɪdʒ] *n.* 次級房貸

☑ toxic [`tɑksɪk] *adj.* 有毒的

☑ astronomical [ˌæstrə`nɑmɪk!] *adj.* 天文數字般的；巨大的

☑ arbitrage [`ɑrbətrɑʒ] *n.* 利用市場間的價差，一買一賣以賺取利益的交易行為

☑ bailout [`belˌɑʊt] *n.* 保釋；救援

日常會話

☑ <u>red flag</u> 警告；危險的徵象

這句話是這麼說的之二：The Ground Is Shifting Below Our Feet

在電影《黑心交易員的告白》（*Margin Call*）中，一名年輕的分析員意外地發現公司資產的評估有漏洞，經過他調整後，結果指出公司目前承受的風險過份巨大，任何時刻都可能爆發破產的危機。這個發現撼動了公司高層，老闆和幾位主管在連夜會議後，決定立刻拋售公司股票與債權。隔天在開市前，飾演交易部門經理的名演員凱文‧史貝西說了以下的一句話：

"The ground is shifting below our feet."

這句是在講什麼？

句裡的 "below" 可以用同義字的 "beneath" 或 "under" 來替代。如果你是在地球科學課上聽到這句話，它大概可以照字面翻譯為地殼表面在變動；但是這句拿到政治、經濟或商業的背景裡來用的話，你可就要小心了！這句背後的意思不久的將來，一個或許多巨大、影響深遠、通常是危險、摧毀性的變化即將產生。這句英文 The ground is shifting below our feet. 表示出，除了日常的直接語言外，美國人也擅長用各種隱喻，來描述抽象的概念或表達暗藏的情緒。

要是你在公司會議上聽到上層主管使用這句，哇，那就代表企業近日面臨重大的挑戰，市場趨向轉了一個大彎，以前賺錢的產品現在沒人要買；也或許公司將要展開大規模的裁員，你很有可能就是捲鋪蓋走路的其中之一。若是在全球經濟展望會上聽到專家這樣說，Brace Yourself！（戴好你的鋼盔，可要準備好了！）下一季或下一年，經濟風暴即將掀起，整個商業的面貌會完全改觀，舊有的觀念或系統面臨崩台，失業率提高，貨幣通膨…總之這句話嚴重的很，絕對要謹慎使用！

13° 這句話是這麼說的 [Phrases]

51 That's What She Said

(Probably the most versatile joke ever invented, "That's what she said" can be applied to almost any seemingly innocent statement. What follows is a real-life scenario taken to the extreme. The delivery of this classic joke is presented in a format known as the run-on. David Letterman of the Late Show is famous for frequently using this style of humor.)

（它大概是有史以來用途最廣泛的笑話，「她就是這麼説的」可以應用到幾乎任何原本聽起來相當無辜的話上面。以下是一段強化版的真實生活情境。在這裡，用來呈現這個經典笑話的手法，是所謂重複同樣笑點的模式。深夜脱口秀節目主持人大衛·萊特曼，即以經常使用這種風格的幽默手法而著名。）

In their back yard, Paul and Chi are barbecuing.
保羅和季薇在他們家的後院烤肉。

Chi	Hand me the meat.	把那條肉給我。
Paul	That's what she said.	她就是這麼説的。
Chi	Haha... That's funny. But seriously, hand over the meat.	哈哈！很好笑。但是説真的，把那條肉給我。
Paul	That's what she said.	她就是這麼説的。
Chi	I'll do it myself.	我自己來。
Paul	That's what she said.	她就是這麼説的。
	Paul throws the steak on the grill. Fire flares up.	保羅將牛排丟在烤肉架上。火焰噴上來。
Chi	Jeez, you need to be gentle!	老天，你動作溫柔點！

Paul	That's what she said.	她就是這麼説的。
Chi	Now I need you to give me the sausage.	現在我要你把香腸給我。
Paul	That's what she said.	她就是這麼説的。
	Chi rolls her eyes: You are having way too much fun.	（翻白眼）你玩得未免有點太過火了吧？
Paul	That's what she said.	她就是這麼説的。
	Chi asks Paul to set the table.	季薇要保羅擺設餐具，準備吃飯。
Chi	Honey, are you ready?	親愛的，你好了沒？
Paul	That's what she said.	她就是這麼説的。
Chi	I mean, are you ready to eat?	我的意思是，你準備好來吃了嗎？
Paul	That's what she said.	她就是這麼説的。
Chi	You'd better hurry. The meat looks very tender and juicy.	你最好快一點。這條肉看起來又嫩又多汁。
Paul	That's what she said.	她就是這麼説的。
Chi	You are TWISTED.	你好變態。
Paul	That's what she said.	她就是這麼説的。
Chi	Careful, you spilled the sauce. (Points to a bottle of dipping sauce Paul accidentally tipped over.)	小心，你的醬灑出來了。（指著被保羅不小心翻倒的一瓶沾醬。）

Paul	That's what she said.	她就是這麼説的。
Chi	Goodness gracious. How long do we have to play this game?	我的老天爺啊！我們這個遊戲到底還要玩多久？
Paul	That's what she said.	她就是這麼説的。
Chi	Enough. Stop!	夠了。停！
Paul	That's what she said, too!	她也是這麼説的耶！

❤️ 單字

- ☑ **versatile** [ˋvɝsət!, -ˏtaɪl] **adj.** 用途廣泛的

- ☑ **scenario** [sɪˋnɛrɪˏo] **n.** 劇情；場景

- ☑ **run-on** [ˋrʌnˏɑn] **n.** 以不斷重複某個特定笑話以表示幽默的手法，高明的表演者會使用 run-on joke 來達到多重層次的娛樂效果

- ☑ **grill** [grɪl] **n.** 烤肉架

- ☑ **Jeez** [dʒiz] **interj.**「天哪」。從 "Jesus" 縮簡而來的委婉講法，以避免直呼耶穌名號的不敬。

- ☑ **twisted** [ˋtwɪstɪd] **adj.** （心術）不正的；變態的

- ☑ **goodness gracious** **interj.** 相當於說 "Oh my God"，以表示驚訝或氣餒的語氣，原本指的是 the good（or the grace）of God。

🎈 片語

- ☑ <u>flare up</u> 火焰快速且突然地噴起
- ☑ <u>roll someone's eyes</u> 翻白眼
- ☑ <u>set the table</u> 擺好餐巾、杯盤及餐具等以準備進食

這句話是這麼說的之三：**That's What She Said**

以上標題裡的四個字，讓愛搞鬼的美國人把幾乎任何一句日常生活中，平淡無奇的對話，都可能變成讓人笑到不行的淺黃色笑話！

容我解釋 That's what she said 怎麼作用：首先，你要有一顆邪惡的腦袋，和兩隻很尖的耳朵。TWSS（也就是這四個神奇英文字的縮寫）的前提為，當有人講了某句話，而想像那句話如果換了時空背景，可以是從一位曾跟你有親密行為的女生口中說出的相同用語，在這個關鍵的時刻，你就可以立刻接著宣布：That's what she said！

舉個例子，一群剛從考場出來的死黨好友，其中有人問另一人覺得試題的內容程度如何，而被問的人誠實地回答："Oh, it was really hard." 話一說完，有人冒出一句："That'vs what she said." 眾人皆哄笑。（請自行體會 hard 這個字在閨房中的相關意思）

一個成功的 TWSS 笑話，原來那句被斷章取義、單挑出來的無心之語，其引申含意通常必須對那個說 that's what she said 的人，有正面、讚揚的效果（That's what she said—to you—你希望你的女朋友怎麼說你呢？），否則要是用不好，最後被笑的人就是你啦！

當然也有改成從女性觀點發出的版本：That's what he said，但 "she" 的版本還是目前的主流。這句口頭禪在 92 年的經典搞笑電影 *Wayne's World*《反斗智多星》中一爆而紅，而近年來又因為電視劇 *The Office*《辦公室瘋雲》而被推上另一高峰，飾演總經理 Michael Scott 的是大家熟悉的史提夫‧卡爾（Steven Carell），他的角色老是在應該要很正經的場合裡，說出相當不合宜的話，"That's what she said." 就是他最著名的招牌台詞。

YouTube 連結：《辦公室瘋雲》"That's what she said" 爆笑時刻！http://popwatch.ew.com/2011/04/29/the-office-finale-thats-what-she-said/

52 À La Mode

Paul and Chi are at their favorite chain restaurant, Denny's. After being seated, they begin to read the menu.

保羅和季薇在他們最喜愛的丹尼連鎖餐廳。兩人坐定後,他們開始看菜單。

Chi	I am in the mood for something sweet ... Cinnamon brioche, crêpes with mixed berries... What does it mean by apple pie "à la mode"?	我想要吃甜的…肉桂甜麵包、法式薄餅加綜合莓果…嘿,蘋果派 "à la mode" 是什麼意思啊?
Paul	It means that the pie is served with a scoop of ice cream. You've never heard that? It's really good. You should try it!	意思是「蘋果派搭配一勺冰淇淋」。妳沒聽説過嗎?那真的很美味,妳應該嚐試一下!
Chi	I sure will. Tell me more about the expression "à la mode."	我當然會囉!有關這個措辭 à la mode 麻煩再多講一點。
Paul	It's French, means "trendy." "À la" means "in the style of" in English. Sometimes you may also see restaurants indicate "à la carte" on their menu. It means to serve individual dishes separately.	那是法文,指「時髦的」。À la 的意思是「以…的方式」。有時候妳也會看到餐廳在他們的菜單上標示 "à la carte",指的是「個別的菜餚分開點」。
Chi	What do you mean?	那是什麼意思?
Paul	Normally when customers order an entrée, say a steak, it's a set meal. The content includes a salad, bread, a steak, and two	正常情況下當客人點一道主菜,譬如説牛排的時候,端上桌的是一整個套餐。套餐

side dishes such as baked potato and vegetables. But if the restaurant offers the option of à la carte, customers can order the steak, the baked potato, or any of the dishes by themselves without paying for other food they may or may not want.

的內容包括沙拉、麵包、牛排、以及兩樣配菜像是烤洋芋和蔬菜等。但是如果餐廳提供了 à la carte 的選項，那麼客人就可以單點牛排、烤洋芋、或是任何菜餚，而不需要花錢買其他他們可能不想吃的食物。

Chi　Hold on, I think I've seen the expression "chicken à la King" on a TV dinner package. I remember it was diced chicken breast cooked in a cream sauce with bell peppers and mushrooms.

等等，我想起來我曾經在冷凍盒餐的包裝上看到 "chicken à la King" 的字樣。印象中它是雞胸肉切成小塊，跟紅椒還有蘑菇一起煮的奶油醬。

Paul　The recipe of chicken à la King was invented by a chef whose last name was King. So basically chicken à la King means its chicken prepared in a specific style of that cook.

Chicken à la King 這道食譜是一位姓 King 的廚師發明的。所以基本上 chicken à la King 意思就是以那個廚師的獨特方式製成的雞肉料理。

Chi　Back to my desert… May I choose the flavor of ice cream to go with my pie?

回到我的甜點…，請問我可以選擇冰淇淋的口味來搭配我的派嗎？

Paul　Traditionally the ice cream is vanilla, but if you want, you can ask the waiter if he has any other flavors. However this is not an ice cream shop, your choices will most likely be limited to strawberry, chocolate, and vanilla. Put all three together and you have Neapolitan.

傳統上配的冰淇淋是香草口味的，但如果妳想要的話，妳可以問侍者是否有其他的口味。但是這裡不是冰淇淋專賣店，所以妳的選擇很可能就只有草莓、巧克力和香草。把這三種加在一起，就是所謂的那不勒斯三色冰淇淋。

生活篇　信仰篇　表達篇　**外來語篇**　文明篇　其它篇

233

Chi　Neapolitan?

那不勒斯三色冰淇淋？

Paul　A three layered brick of ice cream developed by immigrants of Naples, Italy in the late 19th century. I used to eat it all the time when I was a kid. But if you are looking for that classic Americana experience, then you need to go with the warm apple pie with a scoop of fresh vanilla bean ice cream, drizzled with a dollop of piping hot caramel. Whoa-that's-a-gooooooood!

那是一種三層的塊狀冰淇淋，於十九世紀晚期，由義大利那不勒斯城來的移民發明的。我小的時候經常吃。但是如果妳想要一場經典的美式體驗，那麼妳就必須來一客熱蘋果派，加一匙新鮮的香草冰淇淋，淋上一坨滾燙的焦糖。哇！超超超超好吃的！

 # 單字

- ☑ cinnamon [ˋsɪnəmən] *n.* 肉桂

- ☑ brioche [ˋbrɪoʃ] *n.* 一種法式甜麵包，質地鬆軟

- ☑ crêpe [krep] *n.* 法式薄餅、可麗餅

- ☑ entrée [ˋɑntre] *n.* 主菜

- ☑ à la carte [ˏɑ lə ˋkɑrt] *adj.* *adv.* 單點

- ☑ TV dinner *n.* 冷凍盒餐

- ☑ Neapolitan [ˏniə ˋpɑlətn̩] *n.* 三色冰淇淋。 由義大利那不勒斯移民到美國的人民，將三種口味的冰淇淋組合並作成塊狀，以其顏色及圖案象徵義大利國旗。

- ☑ dollop [ˋdɑləp] *n.* （奶油、黏土等的）一團、一坨

- ☑ piping hot [ˋpaɪpɪŋ ˋhɑt] *adj.* （形容食物）非常燙

- ☑ caramel [ˋkærəm!] *n.* 焦糖

英語中的法文之一：À La Mode

你知道很多今天我們常用的英文字，像是 art、competition、force、machine、police、role、routine 和 table 等，都是由法文演變而來的嗎？（所以別說你完全都不會法文喔！其實日常生活裡你已經不知不覺地在使用大量的法國字彙了。）

英、法兩國自古以來關係密切，其語言間的互換與借用，發生相當頻繁。許多字，像上面列舉的，不但發音已經完全英語化，連其字形也已改——譬如重音標示被取消等。另外有些字，雖然外表的形態仍然保持著，但是意思卻完全不同了！今天，我就要來介紹一個這樣的法文轉英文字：À la mode。

"À la mode" 在平時講話的時候比較少使用，大部份都用在書寫文章一譬如報紙或菜單上會看到，它的意思是「（甜點）加一球冰淇淋」。À la mode 原來法文中的意思是「時髦、符合時尚的」，但是美國人所知道的 à la mode，意思卻大相逕庭，變成了不論男女老少都喜愛的一種享用甜食的方法。

Apple pie à la mode：一塊剛烤好的新鮮蘋果派，加上一大匙香草冰淇淋，熱軟的派跟冰涼香甜的驚喜口感，真是教人一口接一口、意猶未盡呀！

53 RSVP

Paul arrives home with a letter.　保羅帶著一封信回到家。

| Paul | My cousin Amy is getting married. | 我表妹愛咪要結婚了。 |

| Chi | I know. Your Aunt called today. She wants us to RSVP. I am not sure that means. What are we supposed to do? | 我知道。你的阿姨今天打電話來，她要我們 RSVP。我不曉得那是什麼意思。我們應該要做什麼啊？ |

| Paul | I will RSVP either by indicating my intent on the card and mailing it back, or because I have my Aunt's phone number I can just call her to let her know whether or not I will be attending. RSVP means that the host is requesting a confirmation of attendance from whoever received the invitation. The host needs to know how much food and seating is required. It is considered proper etiquette to reply promptly if the invitation is RSVP'ed. I think RSVP is an abbreviation from a set of French words. Look it up. | 要 RSVP 的話，我可以在卡片上註明我的意圖再寄回去，或者，因為我知道我阿姨的電話，所以我可以乾脆打電話跟她講我要不要參加就好。RSVP 的意思是宴會的主人要求收到邀請的客人回應確認是否出席。主人需要知道他必須準備多少食物和席位。如果邀請卡上寫明了 RSVP，儘快地回覆被視為是符合禮節的舉止。我想 RSVP 是從一組法文縮寫成的。去查一下。 |

| Chi | Right away... (Pulls out her laptop.) I've found it. RSVP comes from "Répondez s'il vous plaît." which means "respond, please" in English. It's funny how you used RSVP as a verb. It doesn't make sense when you said "I will RSVP." which translates as "I will respond, please." | 立刻照辦…（拿出她的筆記型電腦）我找到了。RSVP 原來是 "Répondez s'il vous plaît." 意思是「請回覆」。我覺得你把 RSVP 當作動詞用滿奇怪的，因為當你説「我會 RSVP」時，直接的翻譯是「我會請回覆」。 |

Paul	Your definition is incomplete. RSVP means "please respond quickly." My response to the request is used as a verb. I am responding quickly as requested. Responding is a verb.	妳的定義不完整。RSVP 的意思是請儘速回覆。我對這個要求的回應，是一個動詞。我正依照主人的要求，儘快作出回應。回應的這個動作是動詞。
Chi	What about the "please" part?	至於「請」的部份呢？
Paul	Please, is nothing more than a pleasantry given by the requester, it has nothing to do with the response: I will respond quickly.	請，不過是一個主人用來表示好感的字眼，跟回應這個動作沒關係：我會儘速回覆。
Chi	So I tell her two guests?	所以我應該告訴她兩位賓客？
Paul	No! The invitation is to me. The correct response is guest plus one. You are not a guest, but you will accompany me to the festivities. Read the note carefully. See at the bottom?	不對！被邀請的對象是我。正確的回答是一位賓客加一個朋友。妳不是受邀的客人，但是妳會陪著我一同參加這個慶祝活動。仔細地讀這張卡片，看到底下寫什麼？
Chi	I see three check boxes. Will not attend, guest, and guest plus one!	我看到三個打勾的空格。不參加、一位賓客、跟一位賓客加一個朋友！
Paul	Right! If I check guest plus one, it is a subtle reminder to me to not forget who you are and my responsibilities as a guest to the host and my escort.	沒錯！如果在一位賓客加一個朋友上面打勾，等於是在提醒我別忘記妳的身份，以及我的責任包括了自己身為一個客人，以及我的女伴。
Chi	What do you mean?	你的意思是什麼？

生活篇｜信仰篇｜表達篇｜外來語篇｜文明篇｜其它篇

237

Paul	I am the invited guest. You were not invited, but you do have access to the party through me, which means you are my responsibility not the host's. <u>Keeping you in check</u> and informing you of proper etiquette at these proceedings is my responsibility. Any social mistakes you make are my own, because I didn't properly instruct you prior to the engagement, and therefore I will be <u>held accountable for</u> your actions. You are a reflection upon me, not yourself. That's some old-school Victorian age etiquette right there.	我是受邀的賓客。妳雖沒有被邀請，但是由於我的緣故，妳得以參加這場派對，因此妳是我的責任，而不是派對主人的。管理妳的行為舉止，以及告知妳在這些場合上的禮儀是我的責任。任何妳犯的社交錯誤，相當於我自己犯了那些錯誤。因為我沒有在赴約之前好好地教導妳，所以我必須對妳的行為負全責。妳代表了我，而不是代表妳自己。這些都是源自英國維多利亞時期非常傳統的規矩！
Chi	So I will escort you, an honored guest to the ball?	所以我將會伴隨你，也就是一位榮譽的賓客，前往參加舞會？
Paul	Correct.	正確。
Chi	And I am under your authority.	然後我是屬於你的管轄之下。
Paul	Yes.	對。

💜 單字

- ☑ etiquette [ˋɛtɪkɛt] **n.** 禮儀、規矩
- ☑ pleasantry [ˋplɛzntrɪ] **n.** 令人愉悅的東西、給人好印象的物品
- ☑ festivity [fɛsˋtɪvətɪ] **n.** 慶典、慶祝活動
- ☑ escort [ˋɛskɔrt] **n.** 男／女伴、隨伴

☑ **proceedings** [prə`sidɪŋz] **n.** （注意複數形）正式的場合或活動

☑ **engagement** [ɪn`gedʒmənt] **n.** 約定、約會

☑ **Victorian age** [vɪk`torɪən `edʒ] **n.** 維多利亞女王時代

☑ **old-school** [`old `skul] **adj.** 舊制的、傳統的

片語

☑ keep someone in check 管制某人、確定某人不踰矩或惹出麻煩
☑ be held accountable for something 對某件事負有責任

英語中的法文之二：RSVP

大多數人都知道 RSVP 就是印製在邀請卡上的那四個英文字母。但是你知道它代表了什麼意思嗎？

RSVP，或是 R.S.V.P.（即在每個字母後都加個縮寫的點，字間不空格）又是另一個從法文衍生為英文用語的例子。原本法文的整句 "Répondez, s'il vous plaît"，發音近似[rɛpon`dɛˌsɪl vu`plɛ]（註），RSVP 是抓每個字字首的字母來組合而成的。法文 "s'il vous plait" 意思是「請」，"répondez" 相當於英文中的 "respond"，所以整個的意思就是「請回覆（Respond, please.）」。

大部份的 RSVP 邀請函都貼心地附上了是否參加的選項，所以客人只要在所選的空格裡打勾，再寄回去就好。收到 RSVP 如果不回覆，是會被視為不合禮儀的行為，千萬不要以為如果你不寄回你的卡片，就等於是你不想參加的意思，RSVP 已經非常清楚地講了，不論你要不要去，主人都需要你的回覆！

RSVP 這個字深深融入美國人的語言中，許多人甚至把它當作動詞來用！所以除了說 "My friend and I would love to come to your party."（假設說你要帶一位朋友去參加這場宴會），你也可以說 "I would like to RSVP myself and a friend." 或 "I am RSVPing a guest plus one."

註 法文發音的訣竅──絕大時候，在字尾的 z、s 和 t 是不發音的！

生活篇

信仰篇

表達篇

外來語篇

文明篇

其它篇

14 英語中的法文 [French]

54 En Route

Paul and Chi are on their way to a screening of Richard Gere's movie *Arbitrage*. Paul's phone rings.

保羅和季薇在往李察・吉爾的《情慾華爾街》電影試映會的開車途中。保羅的手機響了起來。

Paul	Hello. (Pause) Hey Mike.	哈囉。（停頓）嘿，麥可。
Chi	(Reading their GPS) Tell him we are almost there.	（看著 GPS）告訴他我們就快到了。
Paul	We are en route to the theater. Uh-huh. No problem. Will be there in five.	我們正在到戲院的途中。嗯哼，沒問題，五分鐘內就到。
	Paul and Chi arrive and watch the movie with Mike. The lights come up.	保羅與季薇到達目的地，並與麥可一同看了電影。戲院內的燈光亮了起來。
Hostess	Please remain in your seats. I was told that Mr. Gere is en route and would be here momentarily.	請不要離開座位。我剛獲知吉爾先生正在途中，再一會兒就會到達。
Chi	(Turns to the boys.) Looks like we are not the only ones who are late today.	（轉向男生那邊）看起來今天不是只有我們遲到。
Paul	Guess not.	大概不是。
Chi	Did the host pronounce "en route" as IN root? I thought it should be pronounced as ON root. At least that's how I heard you	剛剛那位主持人是不是把在途中的 "en route" 說成 IN root？我以為應該唸成 ON

240

	say it in the car.	root，至少那是我在車子裡面聽見你說的。
Paul	Some people even pronounce it as IN RAUT. To-MAY-toe, to-MA-toe. Po-TAY-toe, po-TA-toe. They are all the same. E-ther, I-ther way you say it. What's your point?	有些人甚至把它發音成 IN RAUT。蕃茄的英文有人說 To-MAY-toe，也有人說 to-MA-toe；馬鈴薯有人講 Po-TAY-toe，也有人講 po-TA-toe，意思都一樣。Either 妳要唸 E-ther，還是唸 I-ther 都可以。妳的重點是什麼？
Chi	My point is IT IS VERY CONFUSING to us foreigners who are trying to learn the language.	我的重點是這對我們想學好這門語言的外國人來說真是太叫人困惑了。
Paul	A lot of people speak English. Accents, culture and foreign influences cause everyone to speak it a little bit differently. Entire paradigms and vocabulary can arise in different regions. Remember it is a LIVING language, ever changing.	很多人講英文。口音、文化和外來的影響，使得每個人講得都有一點點不一樣。不同的地區裡可能出現整組不同的模式與字彙。謹記英文是一個活生生的語言，不斷地在改變。
Chi	I guess so. Mandarin is the same way. It depends on where you live, your education, background, sometimes even how celebrities say things can affect how people pronounce certain words.	我想也是。國語也是一樣，看你住在哪裡、教育程度、家庭背景，有時候連明星在電視上怎麼說，也會影響人們對某些字的發音。
Paul	However it is important to note that although there are endless variations in America alone, the one that is considered	雖然光是在美國就有數不盡的說話方式，但是注意有一個最主流的形態叫作「中西

生活篇 — 信仰篇 — 表達篇 — 外來語篇 — 文明篇 — 其它篇

241

	the most main-stream is called the "midwest" accent. It is the one I have and it is the one most professional American actors have. Unless there is a specific reason to have a regional accent, say like a Southern drawl which comes in many flavors, a California Valley girl, Brooklyn, Jersey, Boston, Connecticut elite, Texas cowboy, and so on, then the one you hear on TV is typically classified as midwest.	部」口音。這種口音就是我的口音，大多數的專業美國演員都具有這種口音。除非你因為某個特殊原因而帶有某種地區的口音，像是各種風味的南方口音、加州谷區白人女孩、布魯克林、紐澤西、波士頓、康乃狄克州上流社會、德州牛仔等，那麼妳在電視上聽到的通常被歸類為中西部口音。
Chi	(Valley) You mean like when Valley girls like kind of like say like things that like always like end with a like question mark?	（加州谷區口音）你指像當谷區的女生像大概像說話的時候像句子都像以問號結尾？
Paul	(Urban) Fur-reals girl friend!	（城市黑人口音）當然囉女朋友！
Mike	Yo, Mama!	喲，媽媽！
Paul	Fa-sizzle my brother.	的確老兄。
Chi	(Southern) Yall' stop foolin' around. (Squeals) Mr. Geer is here!	（南方口音）全部都給我停止胡搞。（尖聲叫）吉爾先生到了！
Paul	(Italian) Don't worry, I'll make him an offer he can't refuse. <u>Bada bing bada boop</u>!	（義大利口音）沒問題，我會提出一個他無法拒絕的條件。小事一件！

美國各地不同口音

☑ Southern drawl [`sʌðən drɔl] 南方口音，其特徵包括濃厚的喉音，及拉長語調的說話方式。

☑ Valley girl [`vælɪ `gɜl] 南加州谷區白人女孩口音，Valley 是指聖佛南多谷（San Fernando Valley），這個地區包括部份洛杉磯都會區如好萊塢，及媒體重鎮柏本克（Burbank）等。這種說話方式的特色是句子的尾部音調提高，以及談話間不時夾雜 "like" 等字。

☑ Brooklyn [`brʊklɪn] 紐約布魯克林區口音，特徵包括著重嘴唇上的發音、與在許多字的字尾省略掉 r 和 g，譬如 player 唸成[pleə]，going 不唸[goɪŋ]，而唸作[goɪn]或[gon]等。

☑ Jersey [`dʒɜzɪ] 紐澤西口音，受到當地義大利移民影響而演變成的獨特腔調，特色包括強調某些字中的字母 o，誇張地發成 [ɔ] 的音、或把某些字尾的 r 改唸為[ə]，例如 sister 唸成[`sɪstə]等。

☑ Boston [`bɔstn̩] 波士頓口音，特徵為強調 ɑ 的音，並常省略 r 的發音，例如 dark 聽起來像[dɑk]。

☑ Connecticut elite [kə`nɛtɪkət ɪ`lit] 康乃狄克州上流社會口音，這種說話方式強調某些字裡的重音部份，以及句子的抑揚頓挫，聽起來很正式，有點像在演戲和演講，是較不明顯的一種腔調。

☑ Texas cowboy [`tɛksəs `kaʊˌbɔɪ] 德州牛仔口音。德州人發母音有其獨特的發音方式，接近南方口音，但較內斂，口氣也比較簡短。美國前總統小布希曾任德州州長，即為帶有此種說話口吻的代表人物之一。

 日常會話

☑ <u>Bada bing bada boop!</u> 也有人講 "Bada bing bada boom!"，指某件事不費吹灰之力、很容易就做好了。電視和電影中常描述義大利幫派份子使用這類措辭。

生活篇 — 信仰篇 — 表達篇 — **外來語篇** — 文明篇 — 其它篇

英語中的法文之三：En Route

我不只一次聽到，在好萊塢警匪追逐的動作片中，從警察無線電對講機傳出："XX（某部警車代號）is en route..." 在好奇心的驅使下，季薇開始查詢這個詞的意思，結果不出所料，"en route" 又是另一個從法文發源出來的英文句子。

En route 在英文中相當於 "on the way"，所以上面那個情況就是說某輛警車已經在途中。更令我著迷的是，en route 這一句每個人發音都稍有一些不同，有人說[ʌn`rut]，另外一些人唸[ɪn`raut]，我甚至還有一次在電影放映會上聽到某位主持人講[ɪn`rut]（她把那兩個最常用的發音組合起來了！）

目前[ʌn`rut]這個發音佔上多數的優勢，畢竟這詞原本是從法國引入，當然還是遵從法語的發音比較正統。美國人之所以會開始發展出另一種發音，原因可能是 "en" 在單字像 "English"，和 "ou" 在 "house" 裡的唸法的關係。

最後再提一點，route 這個字如果單獨用而且作名詞的話，也是要看上下文有時候唸[rut]，有時候唸[raut]；大致來說，美國人在講道路名稱的時候會唸成[rut]，例如 Route 66、Route 101；而在指一般開車或走路的路徑、路途時，他們會唸做 [raut]，譬如："I took a new route today to get to my office."（我今天換了一條路徑去上班。）

Notes

55 Noel

In the hallway of their apartment building, Chi notices the decorations the landlord has set up for the holidays.

在公寓大樓的走道間，季薇注意到房東為迎接節慶而擺設的裝飾。

Chi	It's very nice of Don to set up a real Christmas tree. I can smell the pine needles!	唐他人真好，特地佈置了一棵真的聖誕樹。我可以聞到松針葉的味道！
Paul	It does have a nice smell. The fake plastic trees can never compare.	它的確有股宜人的氣味。假的塑膠樹根本不能比。
Chi	Who is "Noel?"	誰是「諾埃爾」啊？
Paul	What?	什麼？
Chi	The poster by the tree says "Noel." Is he one of Santa Claus's reindeers? (Singing) Rudolph the red-nosed reindeer...	在樹旁邊的海報寫著「諾埃爾」。他是聖誕老公公的麋鹿之一嗎？（唱著）紅鼻子的麋鹿魯道夫…
Paul	Noel is not a reindeer, or a person! It's French for Christmas.	諾埃爾不是麋鹿，也不是人！那是法文的聖誕節。
Chi	For real?... So that's why the *South Park's* Christmas album has the word "Noel" on it!	真的嗎？…所以那就是為什麼《南方四賤客》的聖誕專輯上面印有「諾埃爾」的原因！
Paul	Remember Hitler singing "O Tannenbaum" on the CD? Well, the word tannenbaum is German for fir tree. The custom of decorating Christmas trees was first developed by the Germans, then the idea	記得 CD 裡面希特勒唱的「喔，塔拿巴」？塔拿巴是德文的樅樹。裝飾聖誕樹的習慣最起先是由德國人開始建立，然後逐漸散播到世界

gradually spread out to the rest of the world.

Chi Hitler was a Christian?

Paul Yes. Although Christians tend to try to forget that part of history by mislabeling him as a pagan or atheist. The point is that Christmas has no set rules per se. It is a hodgepodge of local interpretations shared between subcultures that meshes together into what we now call the mainstream. The variable strengths of unique subcultural influences however ebbs and flows with time. The "French" word Noel, for example, has lost most of its influence in the "American English" language, because Napoleon sold a large parcel of land to the United States called the Louisiana purchase during the French revolution. This single act alone eliminated a significant degree of French presence in that region. So although Noel is still in the language, most Americans prefer to say Christmas instead.

Chi What other subcultures are we talking about?

Paul There are no absolutes, but I also remember having Christmas in Florida and Texas. In Florida the reindeer are replaced by dolphins and in Texas snowmen are replaced by tumbleweed men. Wherever you go, people adapt the

的其他地方。

希特勒是基督徒？

是的，雖然基督徒試圖藉由為他貼上異教徒或無神論者的標籤，來淡忘這段歷史。重點是聖誕節本身沒有固定的規則。它是次文化之間，各地對這個節日的詮釋混合起來的產物，這個大雜燴就是我們現在稱的主流。然而，各種次文化的影響力隨著時間衰退或增強。拿這個「法文」字諾埃爾來講，它在「美式英文」中的影響力已大不如前，導因於拿破崙於法國革命期間把一大片土地賣給美國，也就是所謂的「路易西安那交易」。此一舉動大量地削減了法國文化在那個區域裡的能見度。因此雖然諾埃爾仍然在我們的語言裡，多數的美國人還是比較喜歡說聖誕節。

還有什麼其他的次文化嗎？

沒有一定，但是我還記得以前在佛羅里達州跟德州度過聖誕節。在佛羅里達麋鹿被海豚取代，而在德州雪人被換成風滾草人。不管你身在何處，人們修改聖誕節的主

247

	main theme to meet local culture. But there is one thing that everybody does, no matter where they are from or what they believe.	題以適應當地的文化。可是有一件事是每一個人都會做的，不論人們是從哪裡來，或是信仰什麼宗教。
Chi	What is that?	那是什麼？
Paul	LIGHTS! Everyone puts up lights. In some areas the town hall will draw up a map of the best houses to see.	聖誕燈！每一個人都裝飾彩燈。有些地方的市政廳甚至繪製地圖，介紹當地燈光設計最美麗的房子。
Chi	Yes, I remember the light parade in Florida. I really liked how they modified the theme by decorating their yachts.	對耶，我記得在佛羅里達的燈車遊行。我真的很喜歡那些人藉由裝飾他們的遊艇，以達到改造主題的目的。
Paul	Exactly, rich and poor alike, everybody loves the holidays. Except for people who are alone. They commit suicide. Suicide rates are highest around the holidays.	的確，不論貧富每個人都愛聖誕節。除了孤獨的人。這些人會自殺。自殺率在聖誕假期間是最高的。
Chi	PAUL!! Do you have to ruin everything all the time? You are awful!	保羅！！你非得老是破壞情緒不可嗎？你真壞！
Paul	Just saying ...	不過是說說罷了…

 單字

☑ fir [fɝ] **n.** 樅、冷杉	☑ pagan [ˋpegən] **n.** 異教徒
☑ atheist [ˋeθɪɪst] **n.** 無神論者、不信神的人	☑ per se [ˋpɝˋse] **adv.** 本質上、就本身來說
☑ hodgepodge [ˋhɑdʒ͵pɑdʒ] **n.** 雜燴、混雜物	☑ ebb [ɛb] **v.** 退潮、衰退

☑ parcel [`pɑrs!] **n.**（土地的）一區、一片

☑ tumbleweed [`tʌmb!ˌwid] **n.** 風滾草。乾燥氣候地區中，植物除了地表以下的根部，其他部份例如莖、葉、甚至花的部分，經乾燥後與主體分離，受風吹聚集成團狀的毛絮物。在風大時常見於地面上滾動（tumble），因而得名。

英語中的法文之四：Noel

在美國，一過完感恩節（十一月的第四個星期四）大家就幾乎都開始為聖誕節準備了。在接下來整整一個月裡，到處都可以看到各種象徵佳節到來的裝飾：聖誕樹、裝禮物的襪子、麋鹿……以及無數張的大小卡片，上面寫著祝賀的字樣，如 Peace、Joy 等等。今年，其中一個字特別吸引了我的注意力，那個單字就是 Noel。

不清楚其中典故的人，大概會以為某個叫 Noel 的人跟聖誕節特別有關聯。Noel 這字在用於名字的時候，兩性皆可，作男生名字時通常發音為 [nol]，女生則唸[noˋɛl]（當女生名時，有時候也會拼為 Noelle)。

但是在聖誕節的背景裡，Noel 這個字其實是法文的「聖誕節」。它原來的寫法是 Noël，在法語裡，在字母 e 的上面加兩點，（這個符號叫做 trema）意思是 e 的母音，跟前面的母音 o 要分開、一個一個清楚唸，所以發音為 [noˋɛl]（註一）。這個法文字傳到美國後，有時 e 上那兩點就省略不打了。跟 "Christmas" 這字同樣，Noel 的字首 N 也一定要大寫。美國人把 Noel 寫在卡片或海報上，就相當於寫 Christmas。

說到 Christmas 的同義字，另外還有一個字 Yule（註二），意思也是聖誕節。Yule 這個字通常跟 log 連在一起，Yule log 是指歐美國家人民於聖誕節期間，在壁爐裡燒的一大塊樹幹。美國電視頻道中有一台，到了聖誕節時就專門播放 Yule log 在火爐中緩慢燃燒的情景，據說起因是頻道的老闆，為了慰藉居住在紐約公寓或大樓，家中沒有壁爐的人，所創立的一個節目；另一個理由則是能讓電視台的員工回家渡假，不用為跑節目而留守公司。

註一 美國人有時候為了順口，會在兩個連續的母音中間加一個 w 的音，把 Noel 這個字唸成 [noˋwɛl]。

註二 Yule 不是法文起源。

56 Rendezvous

At the mall.　在購物中心。

| Paul | I'm going to check out the RPG games. |
| | 我要去看看有哪些新上市的 RPG 遊戲。 |

Chi　Urrrg. I'm not interested in those video games. I want to go to Pottery Barn to look at their new furniture designs.

呃，我對那些電動遊戲沒興趣。我想去陶瓷工場看他們最近推出的傢俱設計。

Paul　First of all, RPG's are NOT video games. A role-playing game's character development is directly dependent on non-linear story choices. Video games are not. Video games may have a story, but game play is not affected by it and vice versa. Second, I am not going to Pottery Barn. You and I can rendezvous at the food court at four.

第一，RPG 跟電動遊戲不一樣。角色扮演遊戲中主角性格的建立，主要決定於非線性的故事情節選擇。電動遊戲則不同。電動遊戲裡可能也有個故事背景，但是遊戲的玩法不受故事的影響，反之亦然。第二，我不要去陶瓷工場。妳我可以四點的時候在美食街 rendezvous。

Chi　Ren-de-what?

Ren-de- 什麼？

Paul　RON-DAY-VU! Why can't you pronounce French words? (Sighs) It means to split up and later on meet at a predetermined time and place. It can also be used as a noun. Rendezvous may mean the location or the act of meeting itself. In our case, the food court is the "rendezvous" point and our "rendezvous" will take place at four o'clock.

RON-DAY-VU！為什麼妳一碰到法文字就沒辦法了？（歎氣）它的意思是「分頭出發，稍晚於某個預先指定的時間和地點上會面」。這個字也可以當作名詞用，可指地點或那個集合的行為本身。以我們的例子來說，美食街是我們的 rendezvous 點，而我們的 rendezvous 將在四點發生。

Chi　I like this word! You're absolutely right.

我喜歡這個字！你説的對，

We should rendezvous. That way we both get to do what we want.

Paul　You need to watch more *Star Trek* with me. Characters in Star Trek are always rendezvousing somewhere. (Pulls out his imaginary communicator and flips it open) "Bleep-bloop... Spock let's rendezvous on the bridge in five... tsch... Aye, captain... click... Khannnnnnnnnnnnnnnnn"!

Chi　Haha... I would love to. Let's change our rendezvous to the arcade. We can play the one with the guns.

Paul　You mean the shooter.

Chi　The what?

Paul　Seriously, are you joking?

Chi　NO!

Paul　There are endless variations of possible video games. "Shooter" is just one of them. There is also "driving," "single screen," "scrolling platforms," "fighters," and so on. For example, Pac Man has a classic single screen while Mario Bros uses a scrolling platform design.

Chi　Do Mario Bros ever rendezvous like Kirk and Spock?

我們應該 rendezvous。這樣一來我們兩人都可以做自己想做的事。

妳應該多跟我一起看《星際爭霸戰》。《星際爭霸戰》裡的角色老是在某個地方 rendezvous。（保羅掏出隱形的通訊器，並假裝掀開蓋子）「嗶剝…史巴克我們五分鐘後在艦橋上 rendezvous…沙沙聲…是，艦長…咔嗒…可汗汗汗汗汗汗汗汗！」

哈哈…樂意之至。這樣好不好我們把 rendezvous 的地點改在遊戲館。我們可以玩那個有槍的遊戲。

妳指射擊遊戲。

什麼？

講真的，妳在開玩笑嗎？

沒有！

電玩遊戲有無窮無盡的不同形態。「射擊遊戲」只是其中一種，其他還有「賽車」、「單一畫面」、「移動式平台」、「搏鬥遊戲」等等。舉例來說，「小精靈」具有經典的單一畫面，而「瑪莉兄弟」則使用了移動式平台的設計。

瑪莉兄弟曾經像寇克艦長與史巴克一樣 rendezvous 過嗎？

生活篇　信仰篇　表達篇　**外來語篇**　文明篇　其它篇

Paul	Not that I know of, but in a lot of console games, multiple players will coordinate an attack, and rendezvous somewhere in the 3D environment to either resupply ammo, repair equipment, heal wounds, or assess the battlefield prior to moving into a new area. Those games are far more complicated than a typical video game. Most video games today are used to supplement the gaming experience. My feelings will dictate what type of game I want to play that day. But never mind that... you're wasting time. Go.
Chi	When I get back we're going to play that "shooter" and I'm gunna kick... your... ass!
Paul	In... your... dreams!

據我所知沒有，但是在許多線上互動遊戲中，多位玩家會協調組織攻擊行動，之後在 3D 的環境裡某個地點 rendezvous 以補充彈藥、修復裝備、急救療傷，或者在移入新的地區前勘察戰場。這些遊戲比傳統的電動遊戲要複雜得許多，今天大多數的電動遊戲被用來填補遊戲經驗間不足的空隙。我的心情會決定當天我想要玩什麼樣的遊戲⋯。但那不重要⋯。妳在浪費時間。快走吧！

當我回來的時候，我們要玩那個「射擊遊戲」。然後我會把你打得落—花—流—水！

妳—作—夢！

 # 單字

☑ **linear** [`lɪnɪɚ] **adj.** 線性的、直線的

☑ **bridge** [brɪdʒ] **n.** 艦橋。為艦長指揮、發號施令之處。

☑ **arcade** [ɑr`ked] **n.** 室內遊戲館、電動玩具店

☑ **console game** [`kɑnsol `gem] **n.** 一種多媒體互動遊戲，其影像及聲音由連接到電視或電腦螢幕的遊戲主機所輸出，玩家利用鍵盤、滑鼠或搖桿來操作遊戲。Console 指的就是遊戲主機。

☑ **coordinate** [ko`ɔrdnet]] **v.** 協調、組織整合

☑ ammo [`æmo] *n.* 子彈、彈藥。為 ammunition 非正式的說法。

☑ dictate [`dɪktet] *v.* 指使、決定

 片語

☑ kick someone's ass 把某人打得落花流水

 日常會話

☑ Aye!「是！」海軍士兵對長官（有時也見海盜對船長）的回答語。

 英語中的法文之五：**Rendezvous**

　　Rendezvous 的發音為 [`rɑndɛˏvu]，其中的 z 跟字尾的 s 都不發聲。中文的意思是「在預先約好的地點和時間見面」。

　　這個字，其實是由兩個法文單字組成：rendez 跟 vous。"Rendez" 就是英文裡的 "render"，意思是「使……發生／出現」，也就是 to present 的意思；"vous" 是 "you"，合起來看 "render yourself" 中文解釋即為「使你出現」或「呈現你自己」。如果你叫某人在某個地方和時間跟你 "rendezvous"，意思不就是要他在那個特定點「呈現自己」嗎？很好想像吧？這個字好玩的地方就在這兒！

　　Rendezvous 的用法在 21012 年的兩部電影《惡靈古堡 5：天譴日》（*Resident Evil: Retribution*)與《超時空徵友啟事》（*Safety Not Guaranteed*）中都有出現過。劇情內主角們按照先前的計畫，分頭進行任務，最後再到指定的地點會合。

　　美國人在用 rendezvous 時，多作為動詞，例如 "We can rendezvous at the bar around 2." 和 "The plan was to rendezvous on Sunday afternoon." 偶爾也可見當名詞用，譬如軍事術語的 "rendezvous point"（會合點）。

15 英語中的西班牙文 [Spanish]

57 Hasta La Vista, Baby

Chi is reading her e-mails.　季薇在讀她的電子郵件。

Chi	PAUL.	保羅。
Paul	What?	什麼事？
Chi	The editor rejected our last draft.	編輯把我們上次寫的草稿退回來了。
Paul	Why?	為什麼？
Chi	It's because of the "special part."	都因為「特別部份」。
Paul	What "special part"?	什麼「特別部份」？
Chi	You know (tilts her head), the "special part."	你知道的（頭歪向一邊），那個「特別部份」。
Paul	Oh.	噢。
Chi	She liked your tongue-in-cheek delivery, but thought that the double entendre was too much.	她喜歡你輕鬆幽默的筆調，但認為雙關語的部份有些太過份。
Paul	My innuendoes were subtle and vague. You translated it poorly.	我作的暗示既微妙又帶有朦朧美，是妳翻譯的不好。
Chi	I did not.	才不是我翻譯的問題。

Paul	Tell me what you did.	告訴我妳是怎麼翻的。
Chi	It doesn't matter anymore. The fact is that she thinks the remarks you wrote were inappropriate for kids.	那已經不重要了。事實是，她覺得你寫的意見不適合小孩子看。
Paul	Kids? This is an advanced-level English textbook. Our target audience is adult learners.	小孩子？這是一本進階級的英文參考書，針對的是成人讀者。
Chi	Our book will be accessible to everyone who is in a bookstore. You don't want parents to complain. We want to maximize our audience, not limit it. One of the key reason author J. K. Rowling is so successful is because ANYONE can read her books. You ought to be more careful in the future.	任何人都能在書局裡買到我們的書，你不會希望招致家長的抗議。我們的目的是儘量擴大，而非限制，讀者的範圍。作者 J.K.羅琳之所以如此成功，其中一個關鍵因素是任何人都可以看她的書。你以後應該更加小心。
Paul	I thought the con-FAB-ulation was FAB-ULOUS.	我以為那段談話很精彩。
Chi	I warned you ahead of time not everyone wants to read that type of discourse. You have the bad habit of treating everything as a joke.	我先前就警告過你，不是每個人都會想讀那樣的對話。你的一個壞習慣是不管什麼事你都把它當成笑話。
Paul	It WAS a joke! And a good one at that.	它本來就是個笑話嘛！而且還是個很不錯的笑話説。
Chi	I think you overstepped our cultural boundaries this time. From this point on, you need to take a step back and re-think	我認為你這次踰越了文化的界限。從今起，你必須暫緩腳步並重新思考你寫出來的

生活篇 信仰篇 表達篇 **外來語篇** 文明篇 其它篇

255

	about what you are writing.		東西。
Paul	I suppose you're right. I can either rephrase the dialogue or shift the tone altogether.		我想妳是對的。我可以用較適切的措辭來重寫那段對話，或者徹底改變文章的語調。
Chi	What do I do to the old draft?		那舊的草稿怎麼辦？
Paul	(Imitating Arnold Schwarzenegger.) "Hasta la vista, baby!" You can tell editor "special parts" she'll have a re-write this weekend.		（模做阿諾‧史瓦辛格）「再見啦，寶貝！」妳可以告訴編輯「特別部份」這個週末她會收到一份新的稿子。
Chi	Don't call her that!		別那樣叫人家！
Paul	Oh, come-on, THAT'S FUNNY!		噢，拜託，那真的很好笑好不好！
Chi	Ok, maybe a little bit, but don't do it again. She's only doing her job.		也許有一滴滴，但是下次不准再這樣子了，人家很認真在做她的工作。
Paul	Fine!		好啦！

♥ 單字

☑ tilt [tɪlt] *v.* 傾斜	☑ **double entendre** [ˋdʌbḷ ɑnˋtɑndrə] *n.* 雙關語
☑ innuendo [ɪnjʊˋɛndo] *n.* 諷刺、暗示	☑ remark [rɪˋmɑrk] *n.* 意見、評論

☑ confabulation [kənˌfæbjəˈleʃən] **n.** 談笑、閒談

☑ fabulous [ˈfæbjələs] **adj.** 非常好的、精彩的

☑ discourse [ˈdɪskors] **n.** （正式的）對話、會話

☑ rephrase [rɪˈfrez] **v.** 以不同的用語表示、換個說法（尤其以更恰當的措辭表示）

 片語

☑ tongue-in-cheek 以輕鬆、不嚴肅之方式呈現的（喜劇或笑話）
☑ take a step back 暫停（以思索計畫的下一步）

 英語中的西班牙文之一：Hasta La Vista, Baby.

　　Hasta la vista 這句話的發音為 [ˈɑstɑˌlɑˈvɪstɑ]，西班牙文中的 H 一般說來不發聲，中文的意思是「再見」。

　　"Hasta la vista, baby!" 這句話之所以會融入美國人的英語體系，主要是歸功於好萊塢電影《魔鬼終結者 2：審判日》。影片中，阿諾・史瓦辛格飾演的機器人魔鬼終結者，從未來回來，目的是要保護當時還是青少年的約翰・康納（John Connor）；在開車的途中，約翰康納教終結者怎麼使用一些日常用語，其中一句，就是這句著名的台詞。而在電影的結尾，當魔鬼終結者要開槍幹掉 T1000 之前，阿諾一副酷極了地在鏡頭前說："Hasta la vista, baby!"

　　西班牙文中 hasta 是「直到」，而 vista 有「看（seeing; vision）」、「景觀（view)」的意思，"hasta la vista" 直接翻成英文，就等於 "until the seeing"，也就是 "see you later"。這邊特別要一提的是，vista 這個字不僅是一個西班牙文的單字，它也是一個英文字，字面跟西班牙文裡的意思類似，有「景觀」的涵義。所以在美國公路上開車，或許偶爾會看見一兩個路標，寫著 Vista Point 或 Vista Way 等，這時你大概就可以猜到，往那個方向開過去會有個景點或可供瞭望的景觀台喔！

　　YouTube 連結：聽阿諾講 "Hasta la vista, baby!" http://www.youtube.com/watch?v=D_7vVOnpyJY

生活篇

信仰篇

表達篇

外來語篇

文明篇

其它篇

257

Chi	Jason invited us to his baby sister's quinceañera!	傑森邀請我們參加他妹妹的十五歲生日舞會！
Paul	So.	所以哩。
Chi	We should go.	我們應該去參加。
Paul	Do I have to go?	我一定要去嗎？
Chi	I've never been to a quinceañera. Pleeeeeeease?	我從來沒去過拉丁女孩的十五歲生日舞會，拜託跟我一起去啦？
Paul	I don't know anyone there.	那邊我一個人也不認識。
Chi	Me, neither. But Jason says there will be music, dancing, and food.	我也一樣啊。但是傑森說會有音樂、跳舞和食物。
Paul	If the party gets dull, I'm leaving.	如果舞會變得無聊，我就走人。
	At the party.	在舞會上。
Chi	Wow, Vicky, you look stunning! That purse is so cute.	哇，維琪，妳今天好漂亮！這個手提包好可愛。
Vicky	Thank you. Miriam and I went shopping and then we had makeovers. It was so much fun.	謝謝。蜜莉安跟我去逛街購物，然後我們互相幫對方改變造型，好玩極了。

Paul	Jason.	傑森。
Jason	Paul.	保羅。
Chi	Ooooh Jason, you look awesome too. How are you doing tonight?	噢噢噢傑森，你也看起來容光煥發，你今晚好嗎？
Jason	Good.	很好。
Vicky	I'm so glad you two could make it to Miriam's quinceañera. The first game starts now.	很高興看到你倆能來參加蜜莉安的十五歲生日舞會。現在我們來開始第一個遊戲。
Chi	What game?	什麼遊戲？
Vicky	Here ... wear this lei. You too, Paul.	來…把這條花環掛上。你也是，保羅。
Paul	Mmmp.	嗯噗。
Vicky	If you see someone crosses their legs then you get to take their lei. Whoever snags fifteen leis first wins.	如果你見到有人雙腳交叉，你就可以把他的花環佔為己有。第一個搶到十五個花環的人就算贏了。
	Miriam enters the banquet hall.	蜜莉安進入宴會廳。
Chi	Isn't she beautiful? I remember the first time I saw Miriam. She came to the bank with Jason to make a deposit to her "little savers" account. She looks all grown-up.	你看她美不美？我記得我初次見到蜜莉安的時候，她跟傑森到銀行來在她的兒童帳戶裡存錢。現在看來就像個大人一樣。

生活篇 — 信仰篇 — 表達篇 — 外來語篇 — 文明篇 — 其它篇

259

Paul	What? You talking to me?	什麼？妳在對我說話？
Chi	Yes!	沒錯！
Paul	(Paul walks away.) Excuse me, ma'am, but your legs are crossed and your lei is mine.	（離開座位）抱歉，女士，但妳的腳交叉起來所以妳的花環是我的了。
Lady	You got me!	被你抓到！
Chi	Wow, you're quick. (Looks around the room.) My turn... Jayyy-sonnn!	哇，你動作好快。（向房間四周環顧）輪到我…傑森森森！
Jason	Hahaha, you totally <u>caught me off guard</u>!	哈哈哈，我完全沒想到會被妳逮到！
Chi	<u>You snooze you lose.</u>	如果眼睛不睜大一點，你就只好準備認輸吧。
	The party reaches a high point as Jason hosts the party games.	當傑森主持遊戲時，宴會到達了高潮。
Jason	Stand behind the line and place the potato in between your knees. When I blow the whistle, waddle your way to the other end, loop around the pole, come back, and then be the first person to drop it into the cup. If you drop the potato or miss the cup then YOU'RE OUT! <u>On your marks, get set</u>...... GOOOOOO!	站在這條線後面，把馬鈴薯夾在兩個膝蓋中間。當我吹哨，快步到達另一端，繞過竿子，回來，第一個將馬鈴薯置入杯子裡的人獲勝。如果你在中途把馬鈴薯掉落在地上，或無法瞄準杯子就算出局！就定位，預備…開始始始！

260

Crowd	Ooooo, Yeah, Ohhhhhh!	嗚～耶～噢噢！
	Potatoes roll everywhere as the guys bump into each other on the turn.	當參賽男士們轉身回返時互相碰撞，造成馬鈴薯掉落了一地。
Chi	There's only two left. Go Paul, go! Who's gonna make it?	只剩下兩名參賽者了，加油，保羅，加油！最後誰會贏？
	Paul approaches the cup.	保羅逐漸接近杯子。
Paul	(Briefly stumbles giving the old man the lead.) Whoops.	（短暫地露出跟蹌狀，讓另一位年紀較大的男士搶先）噢。
	The old man drops his potato into the cup. The crowd goes wild.	那位年紀大的男士將馬鈴薯掉入杯子中，圍觀的人群發出歡呼。
Paul	You got me!	被你打敗了！
Chi	(Whispers to Paul.) You let him win.	（小聲地向保羅説）你故意讓他贏的。
Paul	He's the father to the birthday girl, of course I'm going to let him win.	他是壽星女孩兒的父親，我當然要讓給他。
Chi	How many leis do you have?	你有幾條花環了？
Paul	Eight.	八條。
Chi	Here's seven more. Go collect your prize.	我這裡有七條。快去領獎吧。

Paul	OK.	好。
	(Jason hands Paul an envelope.)	（傑森交給保羅一個信封）
Chi	What'd we get?	我們贏到什麼？
Paul	"Fifteen" free tacos!	「十五」個免費的墨西哥塔克餅！

 單字

☑ makeover [ˋmekˌovɚ] *n.* 利用不同的服飾或化妝以完全改變外貌、重新改造（人的形象或家居裝潢等）

☑ lei [le] *n.* 夏威夷人掛在對方頸上以表示友好的花圈

☑ snag [snæg] *v.* 迅速抓到

☑ banquet [ˋbæŋkwɪt] *n.* 宴會

☑ waddle [ˋwɑdl̩] *v.* （像鴨子）搖擺地走

☑ loop [lup] *v.* 沿著一圈走、環繞

☑ taco [ˋtɑko] *n.* 墨西哥塔克餅。以烘軟的麵粉餅皮或油炸的玉米脆餅，夾入調味過的碎肉、生菜及起司末食用。

 片語

☑ caught someone off guard 趁某人沒有警戒心的時候（做出某件事）、乘人不備

日常會話

☑ You snooze you lose. 要是你偷懶或降低警備，成功的機會就只好拱手讓人。

☑ On your mark(s), get set, go! 「就定位，預備，開始！」賽跑時通用的三句指令。On your mark(s) 意思是到你指定的跑道及起跑點上；get set 是進入開跑的姿勢。

英語中的西班牙文之二：Quinceañera

Quinceañera 這個單字，以西班牙文的正統發音來唸，是讀成 [ˌkɪnsɛˋɪɛnlɑ]，但是就好像原來美國人叫名演員的名字 Tom Cruise，然而同樣的名字拿到中文裡，中國人就改唸成「湯姆克魯斯」一樣，美國人不發 quinceañera 的西班牙原文，而把它按照英文的發音方法，照著字面唸作 [ˌkɪnsiˋnɛrɑ]。

Quinceañera，按照拉丁美洲裔的習俗，是指「一個女孩子到了她十五歲生日那天，所特別舉辦的成人禮」。Quinceañera 也可以用來指「那個正在舉辦十五歲生日宴會的女孩」。

在美國，尤其是在墨西哥人多聚集的大城市如洛杉磯等，街頭上有時可見穿著晚禮服的年輕女子，身旁跟隨著幾個年紀相近的同伴，也是盛裝打扮地，在互相交談或嬉戲——不要懷疑，你大概正好親眼目睹了一位 quinceañera，在慶祝她的十五歲生日。在這一天中，這位「公主」會戴上皇冠，穿上之前挑選好的高貴禮服，第一次在眾人面前跳舞，她會首先與父親跳一支華爾滋曲，然後跟其他人，像是她的主要護從／男伴（main escort）以及家族成員等共舞。

這一天也是她第一次穿上高跟鞋。她的父母親會幫她換掉平底鞋、變成高跟鞋—這是最後一次她的雙親幫她穿鞋，象徵小女孩已經長大成人。在儀式中，她也會將代表童年的洋娃娃，送給家族裡年幼的女孩子，以示世代交替、薪火相傳。

Chi	Crossing the border into Mexico was easier than I thought it would be.	通過邊境進入墨西哥比我想像中的還容易。
Paul	Wait till we try to get back! The San Ysidro Port is the busiest land-border crossing station in the world. It accounts for 30,000 daily crossings between the city of San Diego and Tijuana.	等我們要回去美國的時候妳就知道了！聖伊希卓站是世界上最繁忙的陸上出入境管制站，平均每天有三萬人次在聖地牙哥市和提華納之間穿梭來回。
Chi	Consider my mind blown! What do we do now?	令人無法置信！接下來我們要做什麼？
Paul	After we settle down in the hotel, let's take a walk. You're gonna love the street food here.	在旅館把行李放下來以後，我們就到外面散個步。妳會愛死這裡街上的小吃。
	Later that afternoon.	當天下午稍晚。
Chi	I want one of those! They're called churros, right?	我要一支那個！它們叫做吉拿棒，對吧？
Paul	Yup, freshly-made churros. They are mmm... "delicioso."	沒錯，現做的吉拿棒，它們可說是嗯…人間美味。
	Music fills the air.	音樂充滿於空氣中。
Chi	No way! A MARIACHI BAND! Right here!	怎麼可能！墨西哥式樂團！就在這裡！

Paul	What do you mean "right here"?	妳說「就在這裡」是什麼意思？
Chi	I thought they only showed up in fancy backdrops like high-end restaurants and private parties. Like in the movies. Like those fiddlers and Italian sopranos!	我以為他們只出現在華麗的背景裡譬如高級餐廳或私人派對等，就像電影裡面演的，就像那些小提琴手跟義大利女高音歌手！
Paul	Dear, you're in Mexico now. They're everywhere, especially here in Tijuana. What would you like to hear?	親愛的，妳現在人在墨西哥了，他們到處都是，尤其在提華納這裡。妳想聽什麼歌？
Chi	I don't know. Anything.	我也不知道，什麼都好。
	Paul approaches one of the musicians.	保羅探詢其中一位樂師。
Band	La cucaracha, la cucaracha, ya no puede caminar. Porque no tiene, porque le falta. una patita para andar.	這隻蟑螂，這隻蟑螂，再也沒法走路了。因為牠沒有，因為牠缺少了，一條後腿。（西班牙文）
Chi	That was wonderful! I love it!	太棒了！我好喜歡這首歌！
Paul	Your first official mariachi song; it's very famous.	妳的第一首官方墨西哥式樂團歌曲；非常著名的歌。
Chi	What's it called?	這首歌叫什麼？
Paul	"La Cucaracha."	「啦酷卡拉恰」。
Chi:	La... kak-ro...cha? What does it mean?	啦…卡克若…恰？那是什麼意思？

生活篇 信仰篇 表達篇 外來語篇 文明篇 其它篇

265

Paul	"The Cockroach."	「這隻蟑螂」。
Chi	You mean the giant, disgusting, flying pest with hairy legs, that cockroach?	你指的是巨大、噁心、長著毛茸茸的腳還飛來飛去的害蟲，那個蟑螂？
Paul	Unhuh!	嗯哼！
Chi	Great. My first mariachi song is about a cockroach. What fond memories we're building.	太好了，我的第一首墨西哥式樂團歌是關於一隻蟑螂的故事。多麼溫馨美好的記憶。
Paul	I knew you'd love it. Let's go grab a beer. Today's Cinco de Mayo, or as my Navy buddies used to say, "Drinko de Mayo." You pick the first bar, then we'll work our way down the street!	我就知道妳會喜歡。我們去喝杯啤酒吧，今天是五月五日節，或者，就如我以前海軍裡的同袍講的：「五月喝酒節」。由妳來挑第一間酒吧，然後我倆就沿著這條街一路喝下去。
Chi	(Points.) That one.	（指向）那間。
Paul	Humph ... are you sure?	哈…妳確定？
Chi	Why not?	何不？
Paul	Look around you. Notice anything unusual?	妳看看四周，注意到有什麼異常的景象了嗎？
Chi	What?	什麼？
Paul	Some of these establishments contain adult entertainment.	這邊其中一些設施包含成人娛樂。

Chi	I'm not shy.	我才不會害羞。
Paul	Great! Neither am I.	太好啦！我也不會。
	Paul and Chi enter the club. Girls are dancing everywhere.	保羅和季薇走入酒吧。到處可見跳舞的女孩子。
Paul	I should come here more often!	我應該多來光顧這個地方！
Chi	We're leaving.	我們走人吧！
Paul	Awww... but we just got here.	噢…可是我們才剛到而已。
Chi	I'm kidding! Let's get a beer.	我開玩笑的！咱們點啤酒吧。
Paul	Now you're talking. (Turns to bartender.) Hola, dos cervezas por favor.	這才像話。（轉向酒保）哈囉，麻煩兩杯啤酒。（西班牙文）
	Two beers roll up onto the bar.	兩杯啤酒端上吧台。
Paul	Cheers!	乾杯！
Chi	Cheers, babe! (Takes a swig of beer. Spit-take.) Whoa ... look, a midget mariachi band!	乾杯，寶貝！（喝下一大口啤酒。突然噴出來）嘩…看，一個墨西哥式侏儒樂團！
Paul	I told you they're EVERYWHERE, plus they're not midgets ... they're little people.	我就跟妳說了他們到處都是，況且你不能叫他們侏儒…他們只是小一號的人。

267

單字

☑ Tijuana [tɪəˈwɑnɑ] 提華納市。隸屬墨西哥，與美國加州聖地牙哥市相鄰，由於地理及距離因素，成為加州旅客經常拜訪的邊境城市，觀光事業發達。

☑ churro [ˈtʃʊros] ***n.*** 吉拿棒，又稱西班牙甜式油條。麵糊由擠筒推出，經油炸後灑上砂糖（有時加入肉桂粉）食用。

☑ delicioso [ˌdɛlɪsɪˈoso] ***adj.*** 西班牙文中的「美味」，相當於英文的 delicious

☑ backdrop [ˈbækˌdrɑp] ***n.*** （舞台後垂掛的）背景布幕，繪有遠景等以襯托故事情節

☑ fiddler [ˈfɪdlɚ] ***n.*** 小提琴手

☑ soprano [səˈpræno, -ˈprɑno] ***n.*** 女高音歌手

☑ pest [pɛst] ***n.*** 害蟲

☑ Cinco de Mayo [ˈsɪngo dəˈmajo] ***n.*** 墨西哥五月五日節。Cinco de Mayo 就是西班牙文中「五月五日」的意思。一八六二年五月五日，法國殖民軍逼近墨西哥普埃布拉市（Purbla），當地軍隊以寡擊眾，贏得那場戰爭的勝利。在美國 Cinco de Mayo 廣泛被視為慶祝墨西哥傳統及文化的一個重要節日。

☑ establishment [əsˈtæblɪʃmənt] ***n.*** 企業、設施（如餐廳、店家、學校、醫院等）

☑ swig [swɪg] ***n.*** 豪飲、大口喝酒

☑ spit-take [ˈspɪt ˈtek] ***n.*** 在聽到某件事後噴出口中飲料的驚訝反應。

 片語

☑ account for 為⋯負責、構成（某個特定數量或比例）
☑ blow someone's mind 使某人無法置信或異常驚訝

英語中的西班牙文之三：Mariachi Band

當一個美國男士想要對他的女伴表示愛意時，除了送鮮花到她辦公室，或在香檳酒杯裡藏枚戒指之外，他還可以做甚麼事呢？答案是：

請一個 Mariachi 樂隊到他們約會的地點演奏浪漫的音樂！

Mariachi 這個字的英文發音為 [mɛrɪˈɑtʃɪ]，在電影《全民情獸》（*Zookeeper*）中，男主角就運用了以上這個技巧，在黃昏中的沙灘上向女友求婚。（很不幸沒有成功，但那卻是劇情需要的轉折點。背景裡震天的煙火，和 mariachi 誇張的音樂表現，成功地調侃了戲中的諷刺及尷尬場面）。而在另一部動畫電影《飆風雷哥》（*Rango*）裡，從頭到尾導演運用了一組說話帶有西班牙口音的貓頭鷹 mariachi 樂團，來串場、敘述變色龍雷哥的故事。由這兩個例子中（註），可以一窺 mariachi band 是多麼具有異國情調，並因而深深獲得美國人的青睞。

Mariachi 這個特殊形式的音樂，據傳是從墨西哥的 Jalisco 州發源的（西班牙文中 J 發音類似英文的 H，所以 Jalisco 唸為[hɑˈlɪsko]，中文譯為哈利斯科州，美國酒吧每家必備的龍舌蘭酒 Tequila，也是這個州的特產！）原來是一種當地的民俗音樂，隨著時間漸漸演變成我們今天熟悉的模式：樂師們穿著色彩鮮艷的傳統牛仔／牧馬人服裝、頭上戴巨大的寬邊墨西哥帽、除了主唱（人聲）外，常見的演奏樂器包括：吉他、小喇吧和小提琴。

註 兩部電影中包含 Mariachi band 的片段：
http://www.youtube.com/watch?v=7i5FiIW8sKc、
http://www.youtube.com/watch?v=rHm5-av1Uks

Paul	What are you reading?	妳在讀什麼？
Chi	The latest news on the government shutdown. It's all I've heard about in the last few days.	有關政府關閉的最新報導。過去幾天每個人都在講這件事。
Paul	Boooor-ring!	無～聊！
Chi	But our retired customers are rushing in to make sure that their social security has been deposited on time.	可是好多退休的客人專程跑到銀行來，確認他們的社會福利退休金有準時存入帳戶。
Paul	Lame. The government is required by law to pay their bills on time every time. They would never miss a deposit without the fear of invoking a justified rebellion or massive lawsuit.	缺乏新意。依照法律，美國政府必須毫無例外地準時付款。他們不敢少存任何一筆款項，否則叛亂或大規模的訴訟就隨時可能興起。
Chi	I suppose having a government shutdown is not as bad as it sounds.	我猜政府關閉其實不像它聽起來那麼糟。
Paul	Ehh, they happen all the time.	這種事常常發生的啦！
Chi	So, it's a sign of properly functioning republic.	所以說，這象徵了共和政體仍舊正常運作中。
Paul	In a way, yes. Engaging in civil debate in order to work out our differences is fundamental to a healthy and productive relationship. Besides, Chicken Little, it just goes to show you how much we DON'T need the government involved in the day-to-day running of this country.	從某種角度來看，沒錯。進行理性的公民對話以解決彼此的歧見，是讓關係變得更健康與富建設性的一個基本原則。此外，小雞，這次的事件也顯示出這個國家的日常運作是多麼不需要政府的

The sky is NOT falling.

Chi According to this article, "...House Republicans are on a 'kamikaze' crusade, led by a suicide caucus within the GOP, to extend the shutdown and force a White House showdown over the debt ceiling, Republican Rep. Peter King said Sunday."

Paul A "kamikaze crusade?" Uhhhh!

Chi Evidently, King does not agree with his party's use of the "kamikaze" strategy to force their opponents' hand.

Paul Both sides are fighting hard to do what they think is right. Republicans don't want the debt ceiling to be raised, because they don't want the Affordable Care Act to be funded. After decades of trying, democrats have finally managed to pass health care reform legislation and they are moments away from having it officially implemented. The president is in a unique situation. He is in his second term, he will not be up for reelection and therefore he can dig in his heels and take the issue to the mat.

Chi If the government remains shut down then no one wins.

Paul Someone will blink eventually, until then the stalemate continues.

介入。天不會塌下來的啦。

根據這篇文章，「…共和黨的眾議員正在打一場『自殺式』的聖戰，由黨內一群有自我毀滅傾向的幹部領軍，目標是延長關閉的期限，並迫使白宮對舉債上限的議題攤牌，共和黨代表彼得・金於週日表示。」

「自殺式的聖戰」？噁！

明顯地，這位金先生不同意他所屬的黨使用「自殺式的」策略來逼迫敵人作決定。

這兩方都為了本身的信念而奮戰。共和黨員不希望提高舉債上限，因為他們不想為平價醫療法編納預算。而民主黨在數十年不斷努力後，終於通過了改革醫療制度的法令，只差一點點就可以見到它正式落實。總統目前則處於一個特殊的情況中，現在他在他的第二個任期內，下回的總統大選他反正也不能參加，所以他更是鐵了心、立志要支持這個議題。

如果政府持續關閉，沒有人能贏。

有人終究會眨眼的，不過在任何一方讓步前，這種僵持

Chi	How long do you think this will last?
Paul	As long as it takes! The last one was thirteen years ago and it lasted for twenty-one days. We are only on day nine so far.
Chi	I hope someone can come up with a solution soon, otherwise vampires and zombies may take over the world!
Paul	What do you mean "may take over," the democrats and republicans are already here!

的局面將繼續下去。

你認為它會維持多久？

需要多久來達成協議就會維持多久！上一次政府關閉是十三年前，持續了二十一天。我們才在第九天而已。

我希望有人能趕快想出解決之道，否則吸血鬼與殭屍可能會跑出來佔領世界！

什麼叫「可能會出來佔領世界」，民主黨跟共和黨早就在這裡了！

 ## 單字

☑ **Chicken Little** [ˋtʃɪkɪn ˋlɪt!] *n.* 為著名民間故事中，一隻擔心天要塌下來的小雞的名字。含義類似中國寓言裡的「杞人憂天」。

☑ **House** [haʊs] *n.* （常用 the House，集合名詞）眾議院、眾議院議員

☑ **crusade** [kruˋsed] *n.* 十字軍東征、聖戰

☑ **caucus** [ˋkɔkəs] *n.* 政黨內部一群代表某個特殊議題的人員

☑ **GOP** *n.* 共和黨。GOP 為美國共和黨之綽號 Grand Old Party 的縮寫。

☑ **showdown** [ˋʃoˌdaʊn] *n.* 亮牌、一決勝負

☑ **stalemate** [ˋstelˌmet] *n.* （西洋棋中的）僵局、雙方都沒有棋步，比賽打成平局的僵持狀態

 ## 片語

☑ <u>force someone's hand</u> 強迫某人做出某事

☑ dig someone's heels in 堅持某人的立場、固執己見
☑ take something to the mat 強烈地支持某件事。此用語中的 mat 指的是拳擊擂台表面的墊子；如果某人擁護某個主張的程度到了他願意上擂台去為之戰鬥，則表示他的決心十分強烈。

英語中的日文之一：**Kamikaze**

Kamikaze，中國人所知的「日本敢死隊」，是指第二次世界大戰末期，日本空軍飛行員駕駛戰機，企圖撞毀盟軍大型船艦的一種自殺式行動。

Kamikaze 的平假名是かみかぜ，日文真正的唸法近似 [ˌkɑmiˈkɑzɛ]，但是美國人一般都唸成 [ˌkɑmiˈkɑzɪ]，字尾唸 ɪ（伊）、不唸 ɛ（欸）。日文的寫法是漢字的「神風」，kami 的意思為「神(God)」；而 kaze 指「風(wind)」。「神風」原來是一個颱風的名字，這場颱風在西元 1281 年的海上發生，阻止了當時忽必烈蒙古大軍對日本國的侵略，日本人認為那是上天送來的神風，名稱因此而起。

原來在二次大戰期間，日本人只有在非正式的場合中用 "kamikaze" 來稱呼那些自殺式的攻擊空軍隊，日文的正式名稱其實是「神風特別攻擊隊」，唸 shinpu tokubetsu kogeki tai，但是在大戰結束後，kamikaze 這個字在國際間被廣泛使用，最後反而再傳回日本國內，重新被日本人採用。

與 kamikaze 相連的那段戰爭歷史，是相當震撼人心且殘酷的。使用 kamikaze 戰略，代表著犧牲那些隊上最出色的精英份子，不僅難以找尋質量相等的人才來替代，在戰爭中更等於宣告了自己的死期，意思要不斷消耗僅有的資源、直到最後一兵一卒。日本在大戰末期，軍備武器上不如盟軍的先進與強大，面臨敵方威脅要攻到本國國土，迫不得已才會使用這種軍事策略。

Kamikaze 可以單獨當名詞，如 "The ship was attacked by a kamikaze in the gulf."（船艦在波斯灣受到自殺式的攻擊。）也可以作形容詞使用。美國人用這個字，一般僅限於描述第二次世界大戰裡的自殺攻擊，但是有時候在政治與商業領域中也會提到這種策略，譬如："In the campaign's final days, the politician adopted what the press called a kamikaze strategy by initiating a series of falsehoods and sleazy attacks, in a desperate attempt to win the election."（在宣傳活動的末期，這位政治人物為贏得選舉，情急下採取了媒體所謂的自殺式策略，向敵手發出一連串不實與拙劣的言論攻擊。）

生活篇

信仰篇

表達篇

外來語篇

文明篇

其它篇

61 Sumo Wrestler

Chi	You're watching sumo wrestling ... again!	你又⋯在看相撲摔角！
Paul	What do you mean "again?" Sumo is awesome.	妳講「又」是什麼意思，相撲很酷的。
Chi	I don't get it. What's so interesting about watching two fat dudes push each other around?	我不懂，兩個大胖子互相推來推去有什麼好看的？
Paul	Excuse me, but they are not "fat." They're professional athletes with a highly calculated weight distribution.	不好意思，他們不是「胖」，他們是體重分佈高度精確的專業運動員。
Chi	I'm sorry. Guess my question should have been: What do you find so fascinating about the sport?	對不起，我猜我原來應該這麼問才對：你為什麼會這麼喜歡這項運動？
Paul	It's FUN! I would really like to have front row seats to a tournament someday.	因為它很有趣！真希望有天我可以坐在前排的座位上觀賞大相撲賽。
Chi	Mmm... Front row seats? I have to warn you though, you're going to get sticker shock when you see the price of a ticket. They are very expensive.	嗯⋯前排的座位？我得事先警告你，當你見到一張門票要花多少錢的時候，你大概會吐血。那些票很貴的。
Paul	Well, I'm sure we'll be able to work something out. I managed to get decent seats at the Muay Thai kickboxing	我確定我們應該可以想出一些辦法。我們去泰國玩的時候，我不就在那場泰拳錦標

tournament when we were in Thailand. Although I presume those tickets were relatively inexpensive by comparison.

賽裡為我倆弄到還不錯的位置了嗎，雖然我猜想看泰拳賽大概比看相撲要便宜許多。

Chi When I went to Japan with my college friends, I wanted to go to a tournament. But they told me that since I didn't understand the language, or the culture behind sumo wrestling, I wouldn't be able to enjoy the event. So I never went.

記得我跟我大學同學去日本的時候，我原本想去觀賞大相撲賽。但是他們告訴我，既然我一來不懂語言，二來不了解相撲背後的文化，我不會懂那些比賽在做什麼，所以去的計畫就作罷了。

Paul That's too bad, forget them, now you can do it with me.

太可惜了。忘掉妳那些同學，現在妳可以跟我一起去。

Chi I'd love to. Much has changed since then. Soon after that trip I took a two-year course in Japanese and I learned about some aspects of the sport. For example, do you know why those wrestlers clap their hands before each bout?

樂意之至。那次旅遊之後很多事都有所改變，回國後我唸了兩年的日文，並對這項運動有了一些認知，舉例來說，你知道為什麼那些摔角手在每回比賽前都要擊掌？

Paul To intimidate their opponent?

阻嚇對手？

Chi No, to attract the attention of the gods. Then they open their hands up to show their opponent that they don't have any hidden weapons.

不是，擊掌的目的是要吸引天神的注意力。之後他們會打開他們的掌心，向敵手顯示他們沒有隱藏任何武器。

Paul Fascinating!

酷斃了！

生活篇　信仰篇　表達篇　外來語篇　文明篇　其它篇

275

TV	SUMO! SUMO! SUMO! Come on down and get your tournament tickets as the grand yokozunas from the far east visit Honolulu, Hawaii. This Thanksgiving only. Tickets are going fast. Call 1-800-BUY-SUMO. That's 1-800-BUY-SUMO. Order yours NOWWWWWWWWW!	相撲！相撲！相撲！橫綱力士自遠東而來拜訪夏威夷的檀香山，趕快獲得親身體驗大相撲賽的門票。只限今年感恩節期間。預購從速。請撥 1-800-BUY-SUMO，1-800-BUY-SUMO。現在就立刻訂票！
Pau	Wait... What? Did you hear that?	等等…什麼？妳聽到了嗎？
Chi	Are they serious? Hawaii? That would be perfect. Hawaii is much closer than Tokyo. Plane tickets from LAX to Honolulu are only a hundred bucks. Plus it might be in English so we can both enjoy the game!	不是開玩笑的吧？夏威夷？那就太完美了。夏威夷比東京近得多，機票從洛杉磯國際機場到檀香山才一百塊，而且他們有可能用英文播報賽事，這樣子我們兩個都可以聽得懂！
Paul	Quick, gimme the phone!	快，把電話給我！
Chi	Wait, I'll have to take some time off from work.	等等，我得跟公司請假。
Paul	Yeah, yeah, whatever. Gimme the phone!	好啦，隨便啦。把電話給我！
Chi	Whee! This is going to be so much fun.	耶！這趟一定會很好玩。

 # 單字

☑ dude [djud] *n.* （俚語）男子、年輕男人

☑ tournament [ˈtɝnəmənt] *n.* 錦標賽、大賽

☑ sticker shock [ˋstɪkɚ ˋʃɑk] **n.** 發現某樣你原來想買的東西價格超出預期的震撼心理

☑ Muay Thai [ˋmoɛˋtaɪ] **n.** 泰式拳擊

☑ kickboxing [ˋkɪkˏbɑksɪŋ] **n.** 踢拳道。一種結合了踢腿和拳擊的自由搏擊術。

☑ presume [prɪˋzum] **v.** 推測、猜想

☑ bout [baʊt] **n.** （拳擊的）一回比賽

☑ Honolulu [ˏhɑnəˋlulu] **n.** 檀香山。音譯為火奴魯魯，為夏威夷州的首都

☑ LAX [ˏɛlˋeˋɛks] **n.** 洛杉磯國際機場的機場代碼（美國人一般皆以 LAX 來稱呼這個機場。）

 # 英語中的日文之二：Sumo Wrestler

Sumo 是日文「相撲」的英文，所以 sumo wrestler 就是相撲摔角手。

美國人對於相撲這項日本傳統競技的著迷程度，於 1993 年達到高峰，因為那年是歷史上第一次，日本相撲界的最高頭銜「橫綱」由一名美國人取得。這位 sumo wrestler 的原名是 Chad Rowen，後改名為曙太郎，出生於夏威夷，獲選為日本第 64 代橫綱，造成轟動國際的新聞。

值得順道一提的是，橫綱的英文為 yokozuna。yoko 是「橫」；zuna或 tsuna，是「綱」，意思也就是「繩子」，橫綱英文直接翻譯成 horizontal rope，原指角力士腰際上綁的那條粗麻繩。橫綱腰間繫的繩子有其特殊的綁法，前面垂繫著「之」字或閃電形的白紙片，象徵潔淨和避邪的作用。要成為全日本推崇的 yokozuna，「橫綱」，除了要連續贏得兩次相撲大賽的冠軍外，選手個人的品格還要通過審核的標準，這一點跟美國的運動界就很不同，對美國人來說，如果比賽打贏了，冠軍就是冠軍，個人的行為操守跟運動場上的表現是兩件分開的事。

跟美國來的曙太郎經常比賽、一決高下的另一名日本相撲手，名字叫「貴乃花」。對啦！他就是那個曾經跟名女星宮澤理惠訂婚，舊名「貴花田」的 sumo wrestler，繼曙太郎之後，他成為第 65 代橫綱。

生活篇　信仰篇　表達篇　外來語篇　文明篇　其它篇

277

Chi	After doing research on samurais, I now feel like I'm seeing them everywhere!	在對武士這個主題做過一些資料的蒐集後，我現在覺得好像不管往哪裡看去都會發現他們的影子！
Paul	You're experiencing the "Baader-Meinhof" phenomenon.	妳正在體驗「巴德-邁恩霍夫」現象。
Chi	The what?	什麼？
Paul	Baader-Meinhof is the act of becoming familiar with a previously unknown experience, event, or object and then, due to our egocentric nature, we suddenly become more aware of emerging examples in our local environment. What once was just a part of the background noise, is now in the forefront of our conscious minds.	巴德-邁恩霍夫現象是描述人們在學習了某個新的經驗、事件或東西以後，由於其自我中心的本性，我們突然在周遭的環境裡察覺到層出不窮的類似例子。過去本來只是背景一部份的東西，如今被推到了我們意識的最上層。
Chi	For example?	舉例説？
Paul	You hurt your leg and are temporarily required to use a wheelchair for a few days. Over those few days you will have a noticeable shift in perspective, and you will become more aware of others around you who are also physically vulnerable. The thing is that they were always there, you just didn't notice them until your ego was able to identify with them.	假設妳的腳受傷，所以接下來的幾天妳必須使用輪椅行動。這段期間內妳的觀點會出現非常明顯的轉變，妳將注意到周遭其他身體不便的人。事實是，那些人一直都存在著，妳只是從來不曾注意到他們，直到妳的自我意識能夠認同這群人。

Chi Well, my "Baader-Meinhof" moment focuses on the term "corporate samurai." Suddenly it occurred to me that the characters Dom Cobb in *Inception*, and James Bond of *007* fame fit the description quite well.

嗯，我的「巴德-邁恩霍夫」時刻目前集中在「企業武士」這個名詞上。我突然發現，電影角色如《全面啟動》中的唐姆・柯比，跟以《007》系列著名的詹姆士・龐德，都相當符合這個名詞的描述。

Paul OK. Give me the definition of what a corporate samurai is.

告訴我「企業武士」的定義是什麼。

Chi "A person in a conflict-oriented profession (i.e. assassin, negotiator, etc.) who follows a samurai-like code of ethics. This generally means limiting collateral damage, treating their job as 'just business (not bringing personal animosity into competition),' and respecting competitors in their profession." These samurai work for mega corporations and interact at the executive level.

「某人所從事的工作，其內容著重於衝突的協調與處理（例如：刺客、談判專家等），並遵循一套武士的職業道德；大體上包括將間接損失控制到最低、用『純粹職責所需』的眼光看待自己的工作（意即把個人的仇怨排除在外）、以及尊重競爭對手。」這些武士為規模龐大的企業集團效命，並直接與總裁等級的人物交涉。

Paul I think Dom is more like a ronin. He is a former corporate samurai, working abroad independent of a patron due to a pending murder charge. Nevertheless, he is a freelance extractor of information, with an expertise in corporate espionage. 007, on the other hand...

我認為唐姆比較像浪人。他曾經是一名企業武士，後來因為殺人罪嫌潛逃，在海外獨立作業。不管怎麼說，他是個竊取機密的自由情報員，專門從事商業的間諜活動。至於 007 嘛⋯

Chi What about 007?

007 怎樣？

Paul Although he is a high-profile, executive-level informant and assassin, he doesn't

雖然他是盛名遠播的高階情報員與殺手，他並不幫企業

生活篇 — 信仰篇 — 表達篇 — 外來語篇 — 文明篇 — 其它篇

279

work for a corporation. He works for a government. However, governments typically control about 20% of their economy directly, and they legally control, tax, legislate, and regulate the rest. So 007 could fit into a broader definition of a corporate samurai.

賣命。他為政府工作。不過，一般說來政府直接控制了大約百分之二十的國內經濟，並能合法地對剩下的百分之八十加以操控、課稅、立法與管制，所以妳大概可以說 007 符合企業武士較廣義的解釋。

Chi I thought so.

我也是這麼想。

Paul What about ninjas? Have you thought about doing some research on ninjas? They are very popular in the US.

那忍者呢？妳有想過對忍者這個主題做些研究嗎？他們在美國很受歡迎的。

Chi I don't want to start seeing ninjas everywhere.

我不想突然到處都看得到忍者的蹤影。

Paul You don't see ninjas... they "see" you!

妳看不見忍者…他們「看見」妳！

 ## 單字

☑ Baader-Meinhof [ˈbɑdɚˈmaɪnˌhɑf] 巴德-邁恩霍夫現象。一種認知偏差的心理經驗，描述當人在學到某種新的概念或字彙後，接下來的幾天甚至幾週內，會發現那個概念重複地在生活中出現。

☑ egocentric [ˌigoˈsɛntrɪk] *adj.* 自我中心的

☑ forefront [ˈforˌfrʌnt] *n.* 最前方、最前線

☑ code of ethics [kod əvˈɛθɪks] *n.*（公司、工作的）道德標準或規範

☑ collateral damage [kəˈlætərəl ˈdæmɪdʒ] *n.* 附帶損失、間接傷害。常作為軍事用語，指戰爭中意外造成的百姓傷亡、或建築物受到摧毀（原先並非包括在軍事行動內）等的損害。

☑ animosity [ˌænəˈmɑsətɪ] *n.* 敵意、憎恨

☑ patron [`petrən] *n.* 資助者、贊助者

☑ espionage [ˌɛspɪəˈnɑʒ] *n.* 間諜行為、諜報活動

☑ informant [ɪnˈfɔrmənt] *n.* 情報提供者、告密者

英語中的日文之三：Samurai

　　Samurai 的英文發音為 [`sæmʊraɪ]，指日本封建時期的武士。這個字的單複數同形，也就是說不管是一名武士，或是多名武士，英文都用 samurai，不用加 s。

　　Samurai 原來在日文中寫做「侍」，對於懂漢字的我們來說，一看就可以望文生義：「侍」這個字在中文裡有「服侍」的意思，所以 samurai 就是稱呼那些服事、效忠皇族的士兵。

　　國際知名的日本導演黑澤明，生前執導的黑白電影「七人の侍」，英文片名為 *Seven Samurai*，是首部將 samurai 這個概念介紹給美國觀眾的影片。電影在 1954 年全球首映後，立即造成轟動，故事敘述七個無主的武士（註）幫助一個村莊的村民抵禦強盜。美國人後來將這部片子改編成西部牛仔片 *The Magnificent Seven*，結果新的電影也成為另一部經典片！

　　西方世界對 samurai 的熱愛從未中斷，除了女星鄔瑪‧舒曼在《追殺比爾》（*Kill Bill*）片中揮舞鋒利的武士刀（samurai sword）大砍敵人、以及湯姆‧克魯斯於《末代武士》（*The Last Samurai*）裡飾演一名洋人軍官，從被某群日本 samurai 俘虜，到後來深受武士道精神鼓舞，進而與他們並肩作戰之外，另一個電影界中明顯的例子是喬治‧盧卡司(George Lucas)的《星際大戰》（*Star Wars*），當大導演在構思絕地武士（Jedi）這個關鍵的角色時，他坦承擷取了三種性格：西部拓荒時期保護人民的警長、中世紀勇敢的圓桌武士、與嚴守紀律、不斷訓練技巧的日本 samurai。仔細觀察 Jedi 手上的光劍，以及其使用的刀法，你看見日本武士刀的影子了嗎？

註 日文中稱呼這種沒有主子、到處流浪的武士為「浪人」(ronin)，其主人可能已死亡、或是武士受到懲罰被驅逐、或他自己選擇了不附屬於任何人或政府的生活。

第五篇　文明篇 Civilization

Paul and Chi are listening to talk radio in the car.
保羅和季薇在車裡聆聽政治談話性廣播節目。

Host	The latest thing out of Washington is crazy. Goofy. They're <u>off their rocker</u>.	最近華府裡發生的事情真是瘋狂。莫名其妙。那些人都精神有問題。
Co-host	What do yah mean? What are they say'n?	你什麼意思？他們說了什麼？
Host	We are in the middle of a budget crisis, yes?	我們目前正處於預算危機之中，對吧？
Co-host	Right!	對！
Host	We need to cut something somewhere, correct?	不管從哪裡，我們都必須砍一些預算下來，是吧？
Co-host	Absolutely!	當然！
Host	So get this, TODAY the Democrats said don't fret the budget. The fact that we want to continue borrowing more money is not the issue. After all we only want to spend a dollar thirty-five for every dollar we bring in. This is ten cents down from last year.	聽好了，今天那些民主黨員說別再削減預算了，我們希望再借更多錢的構想其實不成問題，畢竟，我們只是想在賺得的每一塊錢之外，花掉一塊三毛五，跟去年比較，我們還少花了一毛錢。
Co-host	That's awful.	有夠差勁的理由。

Host	BUT WAIT THERE'S MORE! The Republicans came out later on and said that the Democrats were being fiscally reckless amid the recent recession recovery.	等等更精彩的還在後頭！共和黨員接著從後面冒出來說，國內的經濟衰退情形還沒有完全復甦，這些民主黨的人真是亂花錢。
Co-host	Sounds reasonable.	聽來很合理。
Host	Oh, don't get ahead of me. I'm not done yet. They then stated that they are going to "draw a line in the sand, here, and now."	噢，別太快下結論，我還沒講完。然後他們說他們要「此時此地、劃清界線」。
Co-host	Powerful stuff.	相當強而有力的說法。
Host	Spending a dollar thirty-five is too much. TOO MUCH!	一塊三毛五太多了，太多了！
Co-host	Indeed!	的確！
Host	The Republican budget only calls for a dollar TWENTY-SIX spending package for every dollar we have.	共和黨提出的預算計畫是，在每一塊錢之外，只花一塊二毛六。
Co-host	WHAT?	什麼？
Host	Yeah! So, that is what they are arguing about today on Capitol Hill. Is it just me or does that sound retarded to you too? If I ran my company or family budget this way we'd be bankrupt soon after, and yet the government talks about this level of spending like it's normal.	沒錯！這就是今天他們在國會山莊爭論不休的議題。你覺得是我還是他們腦袋有問題？如果我照他們這種作法來經營公司或編列家庭預算，很快我就得宣告破產了，然而政府官員卻把這種花錢的方式不當一回事。

生活篇

信仰篇

表達篇

外來語篇

文明篇

其它篇

285

Chi	Hahaha... they're arguing over how to spend the money they DON'T have?	哈哈哈…這些人在吵該怎麼花他們沒有的錢？
Paul	That's not funny! This is a real problem.	不好笑！這真的是一個很嚴重的問題。
Chi	The Tea Party must be going nuts over this.	要是茶黨聽到他們的對話一定會抓狂。
Paul	I can hear them now "At most... ONE DOLLAR is all you should be allowed to spend." In fact, we should probably spend only eighty cents on the dollar. We still need to pay back the interest and principal of the last loan we took out.	我現在就可以聽到他們大吼：「最多…一塊錢是你們能夠花的上限。」事實上，我們大概每賺一塊錢只應花八毛錢，因為我們還得償付之前貸款的本金和利息。
Chi	Is "Living within your means" a cliché, a lost guideline to living a sober life? Have Americans become habitual borrowers, addicted to a seemingly limitless year-round shopping spree?	難道「量入為出」已經變成老掉牙的一句話，而不再是人們生活的指導方針了嗎？美國人真的都對借錢這種事習以為常，非得要一年到頭，每天都毫無限制地瘋狂購物才滿足？
Paul	(Sarcastically) Mm'merica, the only place where you can party hard for decades and then leave the bill to your grandkids. How is it that "the Greatest Generation" produced the worst generation in American economic history?	（諷刺地）美利堅，是世界上唯一一個能讓你大肆揮霍數十年，然後要你後代子孫幫你付賬單的地方。怎麼搞得「最偉大的世代」竟然製造出美國經濟史上最糟糕的世代？（作者按："Merica"是保羅在模倣南方老粗（rednecks）口音）

Chi	Can our generation clean up this mess?	我們這一代能解決這個困境嗎？
Paul	Yes... but it's not going to be easy.	可以…但不容易。

 ## 單字

☑ **talk radio** [`tɔk `redɪˌo] *n.* 談話性廣播節目，其內容多著重於社會及政治議題。

☑ **fret** [frɛt] *v.* 使磨損、逐漸侵蝕

☑ **Capitol Hill** [`kæpətəl `hɪl] *n.* 國會山莊。美國國會大廈（the Capitol）所在的山丘。

☑ **habitual** [hə`bɪtʃʊəl] *adj.* 習慣性的

☑ **spree** [spri] *n.* 在某一段期間內毫無節制地做某種行為、狂歡

☑ **means** [minz] *n.* （視為複數）資產、財產

☑ **the Greatest Generation** [ðə `gretɪst ˌdʒɛnə`reʃən] *n.* 最偉大的世代。此名詞乃由新聞主播及作者湯姆・布羅考（Tom Brokaw）所創造。他的書 The Greatest Generation 描述上一代的美國人，在歷經經濟大蕭條後，接著又投入第二次世界大戰。他們具備了堅毅不拔的工作態度，及為正義而戰的精神，堪稱是美國史上「最偉大的世代」。

 ## 片語

☑ off someone's rocker 某人做出瘋狂的舉動、精神不正常。對於這句俚語中的 rocker 究竟指什麼，說法有很多，其中較流行的一種解釋稱 rocker 是搖椅，藉由人從舒適的搖椅裡摔落下來的不安狀態，引伸為瘋狂或怪異的表現。

☑ draw a line in the sand 清楚地定下門檻或界線，並表明如果對方踰越了這條線，則將會受到懲罰

生活篇　信仰篇　表達篇　外來語篇　**文明篇**　其它篇

政治與社會之一：Tea Party

Tea Party 這個名詞用在今天的美國政治會話裡，可不是你所想像的浪漫畫面：優雅的英國仕女邀請客人吃點心、飲紅茶的下午宴會… No。

美國的政客、新聞記者、或是任何對政治稍有關心的人，在談到 Tea Party 的時候，他們所指的是從 2009 年開始興起的一股政治運動，參與的抗議群眾大多傾向節制、保守的想法，其主要訴求為：降低政府的支出、控制預算、裁稅、減少國債及聯邦政府的龐大赤字。

Tea Party 這個名稱，是從 1773 年波士頓茶葉事件（Boston Tea Party）衍義過來的。（現在季薇要喚醒你沈睡已久的記憶…還記得高中唸的美國歷史嗎？）那一年，在麻省波士頓的殖民地居民因不滿英國政府在茶葉上徵稅，而將船上裝箱的茶葉全數倒進波士頓港以示抗議，即為著名的「波士頓茶葉事件」。殖民地的人民認為，如果他們在英國國會裡沒有代表的席位，就不應該繳稅，這個概念是英文中相當重要的一句口號：No taxation without representation.

現代的 Tea Party 支持者有著類似的想法，他們看到美國政府不斷增加支出及稅收，認為政府利用通過新的法律，來改變稅制，是沒有徵得人民同意的作法。

當然，從 Tea Party 這麼大的抗議運動中，也不可避免地產出一些新的英文字，其中最突出的一個名詞叫做 teabagger， 因為 tea-bag 這個動詞含有性意味，是政治評論者及深夜脫口秀主持人最喜歡拿來稱呼 Tea Party 參與群眾的玩笑話。

Notes

Chi It's TWO MONTHS before the presidential election and the news is filled with talking heads debating the possible outcome of the vote in each state!

距離總統大選還有整整兩個月，新聞裡不管什麼時段，淨是專家學者們在爭辯每一州選舉結果的畫面！

Paul Not every state. The swing states will get the most attention. Ohio, Pensilvania, and Florida could go either way. This also explains why the candidates are spending most of their money in battleground districts.

並不是每一州喔。通常只有搖擺州會受到各方的關注。俄亥俄州、賓州跟佛羅里達都不一定會往哪邊倒。這也解釋了為何候選人都將大部份選舉經費花在那些主要戰場區上。

Chi Speaking of which, can you explain to me why the states are colored red and blue?

既然提到這個，你可不可以解釋一下為什麼有些州畫紅色，有些州又畫藍色？

Paul The press have always used colored maps to indicate the demographics of a voting block; however they didn't become standardized until the 2000 election. From that point on, a blue state meant that the majority of its voters were Democrats. Red states have a majority of Republicans and third party candidates are often labeled white.

新聞媒體向來就有使用不同顏色的地圖來表示選區統計資料的習慣，但是這種作法一直到兩千年的總統大選才開始有了標準的格式。自那時起，藍色的州指它的大部份選民是民主黨。紅色的黨指共和黨佔多數，而第三黨候選人通常以白色標示。

Chi Now the host is talking about purple states! What party is purple?

主持人現在提到紫色的州！什麼黨是紫色的？

Paul None. "Purple states" is slang for swing states. The potential votes are so evenly divided between the major parties that it is incredibly difficult to anticipate the outcome with any reasonable certainty.

沒有黨是紫色的。「紫色的黨」是搖擺州的俗稱。這些州內分屬兩大黨派的可能選票數剛好一半一半，沒有人能信心十足地預測選舉結果。這也就

Which is why they are so interesting and why everyone talks about them. Nobody wonders which party Texas or California will vote for.

Chi So can Ohio, as a "swing state," be called a purple state?

Paul Yes. It's a lot of words that essentially all mean the same thing ... opportunity!

Chi It sounds like each party's degree of influence there is equally matched. It will be interesting to see if either party can manage to garner an advantage over the other.

Paul We'll see. The candidates are pushing hard to sway the public to their cause. Every person they meet is a potential voter who could give them the edge they need.

Chi They just indicated North Carolina as a red state. Isn't that where your cousin Amy lives?

Paul No surprise there, North Carolina is on the edge of the Bible belt. People in this area are usually conservative. They promote small government, capitalism, low taxes, and reserved values. Amy is all these things. She has a deep faith, growing business, and a quiet strength.

是為什麼每個人都對這些州深感興趣並大加議論的原因，沒人會去費心猜想德州或加州會投哪一黨。

所以像俄亥俄州這種「搖擺州」，也可以稱作是紫色的州囉？

對。其實這麼多不同的名稱，指的都是同一件事…機會！

聽起來在這些州裡各黨勢均力敵。兩黨之間誰會勝出，相當耐人尋味。

我們等著瞧。這些候選人正使出全力說服選民支持他們的主張。他們遇見的每一個人都有可能是那張幫助他們取得優勢的選票。

電視上剛指出北卡羅萊納州是個紅色的州，你表妹愛咪不就住那裡嗎？

一點也不令人感到驚訝。北卡羅萊納州處於聖經帶的邊緣上，這個區域裡的人民通常相當保守，他們主張縮小政府規模、提倡資本主義、低稅率，以及內斂的價值觀，這些特質愛咪全都具備，她有虔誠的信仰、日漸茁壯的公司，及一份沈靜的力量。

生活篇　信仰篇　表達篇　外來語篇　**文明篇**　其它篇

Chi	Grandpa says she is launching her fourth store!	阿公提到她準備要開第四家店了！
Paul	Plus a kiosk in the mall.	加上一個購物中心裡的販售亭。
Paul	If you are a conservative, a red state is probably where you wanna be. If you are a liberal, states in the northeast and the west coast might fit your personality and life style better. However, national statistics is not necessarily an indicator of local politics. There are pockets of conservatives in blue states and pockets of democrats in red states.	如果你是保守主義者，你大概會想住在紅色的州。如果你是自由主義者，東北邊和西岸上的州可能比較符合你的個性和生活方式。然而全國性的統計結果不盡然代表小區域內的政治傾向，藍色的州裡可能包含了四處分散的保守派團體，而紅色的州裡則有獨立的民主黨人士。
Chi	So if these pockets grow big enough then the state might become purple. Right?	所以如果這些獨立的團體長得夠大了，整個州就可能變成紫色的，對吧？
Paul	Exactly!	正是！

♥ 單字

☑ **talking head** [`tɔkɪŋ `hɛd] **n.** 新聞節目的主持人、來賓或專家。這個名詞來自於新聞或政論節目裡，電視鏡頭通常只播出談話者的臉或胸部以上的部份。

☑ **swing state** [swɪŋ stet] **n.** 搖擺州、游離州

☑ **battleground** [`bæt! ˌgraʊnd] **n.** 戰場

☑ **demographics** [ˌdɛmə`græfɪks] **n.** （視為複數名詞）某一群人的背景資料，其內容可能包括年齡、教育程度、政治偏好等

☑ **sway** [swe] **v.** 影響、動搖（人心、意見等）

☑ **edge** [ɛdʒ] **n.** 優勢、比…有利的部份

☑ **the Bible belt** [ðə`baɪb! `bɛlt] **n.** （非正式用語）聖經帶。指美國中南部及東南部的地區。

☑ reserved [rɪ`zɝvd] **adj.** 謹慎的、內斂的

☑ kiosk [`kiɑsk] **n.** 小亭式的報攤或販售點

☑ pocket [`pɑkɪt] **n.** 孤立的地區或團體

 # 政治與社會之二：Blue States

藍色的州？

如果美國人在談政治時，提到藍色、紅色、甚至是紫色的州時（blue states, red states, and purple states），他們的意思是什麼呢？

Blue states 指的是，在總統大選時，住在這個州的居民，大多數會投票給民主黨（Democratic Party) 的候選人。

相對而言，紅色的州就是選民偏好共和黨（Republican Party）的州（註）。這個「藍州→民主黨」，與「紅州→共和黨」的正式定名，大家公認是從已故資深新聞記者 Tim Russert 開始的。2000 年總統大選的一週前，他在收視率極高的《今天》*Today Show* 晨間新聞節目上，使用這兩個對比強烈的顏色，來區分並稱呼那些傾向投票給美國兩大黨的州。

由於民主黨偏好社會自由主義（Social Liberalism），美國人在說 blue states 的時候，多少都有點暗示這個州是傾向自由派（相對於保守的 red states）。支持自由主義想法的人，我們稱為 Liberals，大致上他們認為政府應該要積極管理並適度地干預經濟，保障每一個小市民，尤其是弱勢族群的權益。舉例來講，他們主張制定最低工資（minimum wage）、分級所得稅率（即收入超過某程度須繳付更高的稅率）、支持墮胎、同性戀結婚等議題，提倡全民醫療服務（universal health care）、並減少軍備支出。

註 提供一個我個人的記憶小祕訣：紅色英文 red 的開頭兩個字母 re 跟共和黨人 Republicans 前面兩個字母一樣，所以 red = republicans！

生活篇 信仰篇 表達篇 外來語篇 文明篇 其它篇

Chi	Amy, it's such an honor to be Jacob's godparents. The ceremony was beautiful! I was so moved.	愛咪，我們感到很榮幸能成為雅各的教父母。這場儀式優美極了，我覺得好感動。
Amy	We are glad that you guys can be here for our baby's baptism. Go make yourselves comfortable. It has been a long morning. Can I get you two something to drink? They made some Kool-Aid in the back. Would you like a cup? Paul, you too?	很高興你倆能前來參加我們小寶貝的受洗儀式。快找個舒服的地方坐下來，大家都折騰一整個早上了。你們需不需要喝點什麼？他們在後頭調了一些酷愛牌果汁，妳想喝一杯嗎？保羅，你也來一杯？
Paul	Uh, no... I think I'll have the water instead.	呃，不用了…我想我喝水就好。
Chi	I'll have water, too. Thanks, Amy.	我也是喝水，謝謝，愛咪。
	Amy leaves.	愛咪轉身離開。
Chi	(Chuckling and jabs Paul in the side.) Haha ... I know what you are thinking!	（竊笑並從旁邊戳了戳保羅）哈哈... 我知道你在想什麼！
Paul	What am I thinking? (Winks.)	我在想什麼？（眨眼）
Chi	You know I just learned that expression.	你知道我才剛學到這個講法。

Paul   (Smirking) What expression?   （假笑）什麼講法？

Chi: Stop pretending that you didn't know what I'm saying! We are in a religious setting and they just suggested we drink the Kool-Aid!   停止假裝你不曉得我在說什麼！我們現在在一個宗教的場合，而他們剛剛建議我們來喝酷愛牌果汁！

Paul   Yeah, I'd rather not. You know me, I prefer to find my own path!   對啊，我還是不喝比較好。妳是了解我的，我寧願找出屬於自己的路！

Chi   Are you saying the guests here who drank the Kool-Aid are all conformists?   難不成你認為在這裡只要是喝了酷愛牌果汁的賓客，就都是沒有自己的主張、盲目地遵從社會規範的人嗎？

Paul   Not necessarily; however it is easier to have someone give you a set of rules to follow than going out to the world and discover the truth for yourself. Maybe you should try their Kool-Aid, too. It's very tempting, you have to admit. There is comfort in solidarity.   不盡然；不過，比起你自己一人到世界上尋覓真理，遵循別人給你一套既定的規則來活，相較下要簡單得多。也許妳也應該喝喝看他們的酷愛牌果汁。妳得承認，它非常誘人，認同感給人安全感。

Chi   Speaking of truth, as a physicist, how do you know you're not drinking the Kool-Aid already? A kind of "science" Kool-Aid?   說到真理，身為一位物理學者，你怎麼知道你不是在喝酷愛牌果汁？也就是說，一種標榜「科學」的酷愛牌果汁？

Paul   Ha! "Science Kool-Aid"? That's an oxymoron. Science by definition, is the   哈！「科學的酷愛牌果汁」？這句話前後矛盾。科

生活篇 信仰篇 表達篇 外來語篇 文明篇 其它篇

opposite of faith. Anything in the scientific community can be challenged at any time by anyone willing to do the work and produce verifiable observations that support new or modified ideas. When you drink the Kool-Aid, you are embracing an idea without questioning. You accept it on faith alone. For a religious person, that is the end of the journey. For a scientist, that is the beginning of a long series of questions, experiments, and investigations.

學，就定義上而言，正好是信仰的相反。在科學領域中的任何一件事，不論何時任何人都能對之挑戰，只要你願意進實驗室，深入研究並提出可驗證的觀察報告來支持全新或修正過的主張。當你喝下酷愛牌果汁時，你毫無疑問地接受了某種主張，你接受的理由完全只是因為你相信它。對一個宗教徒來說，這裡即是旅程的終點；然而對一個科學家來說，這是一長串提問、實驗和調查的開始。

Amy　(Returns with two bottles of water.) What are you two talking about?

（帶了兩瓶水回來）你們倆個在談什麼啊？

Paul　Nothing important. So what are our plans for later tonight?

沒什麼。晚上我們有計劃要做什麼嗎？

Amy　Well, TJ just purchased a new pair of sneakers, and he wants to break them in so he suggested that we go for a hike.

提傑剛買了一雙新的運動鞋，他想要把鞋子穿鬆一點，所以他建議我們等下一道去健行。

Paul and Chi both turn and notice Amy's husband's footwear.

保羅和季薇同時轉頭注意到愛咪老公腳上的鞋子。

Paul　Black-and-white Nike's... interesting choice.

黑白相間的耐吉跑鞋…有意思。

Chi	NO WAY!	不會吧！
Paul	(Turns quickly towards Chi.) CHI! We would love to. It sounds like fun. I look forward to racing you to the top. Can we bring the dogs?	（快速轉向季薇。）季薇！我們樂意之至；聽來很有趣。我會跟妳比賽誰先到達山頂。我們能帶狗去嗎？
Amy	Sure!	當然！

（作者按：除了衍生出 "drinking the Kool-Aid" 這個用語的人民聖殿教自殺事件外，在美國史上另一起著名的宗教集體自殺案「天堂之門（Heaven's Gate）」中，死去的教徒被發現皆身穿黑色的運動衣褲及黑白相間的耐吉運動鞋。）

 # 單字

- ☑ godparents [`gɑd͵pɛrənt] *n.* 教父母（協助親生父母提供孩子生活上指導的另一對配偶）、乾爸乾媽

- ☑ baptism [`bæptɪzm̩] *n.* 浸禮、受洗的儀式

- ☑ jab [dʒæb] *v.* 戳、刺入

- ☑ smirk [smɝk] *v.* 假笑、傻笑

- ☑ conformist [kən`fɔrmɪst] *n.* 對既有社會規範毫不懷疑就遵從的人、迎合大眾潮流的人

- ☑ tempting [`tɛmptɪŋ] *adj.* 有誘惑力的、動人的

- ☑ solidarity [͵sɑlə`dærətɪ] *n.* 身為團體中一份子的認同感、向心力

- ☑ oxymoron [`ɑksɪ͵mɔrɑn] *n.* 將兩個互相矛盾的概念組合在一起的說法、前後邏輯相反的組合詞

- ☑ sneakers [`snikɚ] *n.* 運動鞋。Sneakers 這個字的由來，是因其鞋底由橡膠製成，穿著這種鞋子走起來聲音很輕，可用以偷襲某人（sneak up on someone）。

片語

☑ <u>break in</u> (new shoes) 把（新鞋）穿鬆，使其更合腳

政治與社會之三：Drinking the Kool-Aid

電影《選戰風雲》（*The Ides of March*）中有一幕，在民主黨競選團隊裡擔任重要職務的史帝芬，向精明的女記者表示自己堅決支持自家候選人的立場後，女記者瞪著他、並點頭說："You really have drunk the Kool-Aid."（你的確有喝過 Kool-Aid。）而史帝芬也毫不猶豫地回應："I have drunk it. It's delicious."（我喝了。真好喝。）

到底這兩個人之間你來我往的，是在說什麼呀？

首先，Kool-Aid 是一個飲料的品牌，製造這種飲料的公司，把果汁口味的濃縮粉末，裝在紙包裡，美國人買來後加糖和水調成一大壺，冰涼後飲用。然而，今天我們用 drinking the Kool-Aid 這句話，來諷刺某人全心全意地接受了某項信仰或概念，其虔誠的地步甚至到了盲目的境界。

這句話的由來要推溯至 1978 年，那年一個起源於美國印第安納州，後來遷移到南美洲蓋亞那，建立起瓊斯鎮的宗教團體人民聖殿（The People's Temple），在 11 月 18 日下午，於教主吉姆‧瓊斯（Jim Jones）的指示下，九百多名的教徒，喝下滲有毒藥、葡萄口味的飲料（註）集體自殺。此後，人們若是想要警告彼此不要太相信某件事，就用 "Don't drink the Kool-Aid!" 來提醒對方要想清楚、對提倡單一信念的事物要抱持適當的懷疑態度，不可一頭熱掉入陷阱。

註 在事後官方調查的紀錄中，實際上被使用的飲料是另一個比 Kool-Aid 便宜的品牌，叫作 Flavor Aid，但是因為 Kool-Aid 在粉末飲品市場中的知名度比較高，美國人對這個牌子熟悉，所以就一直沿／誤用下來。

Notes

Chi	This is the letter I want to send to the New Hampshire Property's management. Would you please read it through and sign on the bottom?	這是我準備寄給新罕布夏公寓管理維護公司的信，請你看過後在底下簽名好嗎？
Paul	Sure. So we've decided to sue?	沒問題。所以我們準備提出控告了嗎？
Chi	As I stated in the letter, if they don't respond by the 15th of next month, we will take our case to court. I also said that we would notify the Los Angeles Renters' Association of their failure to return our security deposit and refund eleven days of overpaid rent.	我在信裡指出，如果他們沒有於下個月十五日前回覆的話，我們就上法院。我在信中也提到我們將向洛杉磯租屋者協會告知，這間公司沒有歸還我們的押金以及多付的十一天房租。
Paul	Good, and how was your trip to the county courthouse?	很好，妳到地方法院去的那一趟怎樣？
Chi	Productive. The volunteers at the Self-Help Center were very informative. I also met a pro-bono lawyer.	收穫很大。在自助服務區的義工都非常樂意提供他們的知識，我還遇到了一位義務律師。
Paul	Oh?	喔？
Chi	While we were standing in line, he shared with me his experience of representing clients in court. Although he vented about how some court proceedings can take up to two months before moving onto the next stage, he was grateful for the valuable courtroom experiences he had	我們在排隊等待的時候，他跟我分享代表客戶出庭的經驗。雖然他稍微抱怨了一下有些法院程序要花上兩個月的時間才能進到下個步驟，他還是很高興自己從能這些案件中學到許多寶貴的實戰

	gained by taking up these cases.	經驗。
Paul	What he does is quite admirable. Although our case is too small for a lawyer.	他所做的事相當令人敬佩。不過我們的案子太小了，不需要用到律師。
Chi	Right, we can represent ourselves in small-claims court. With the information I've gathered, I'm sure we'll win. However, I really hope that our ex-landlord comes to their senses before that happens.	對，在小額索償法庭上我們可以代表自己出庭辯護。根據我收集到的這些資料，我確定我們一定會勝訴。可是我真心希望我們的前任房東能在那之前就瞭解到他們是錯的，儘快把錢還回來。
Paul	Agreed. Remember when I sued Bruegger's Bagel's manager for not paying me the negotiated amount in transportation costs?	同意。妳記不記得有回我告上布氏培果的餐廳經理，因為他拒絕支付原先講好的交通費用？
Chi	Yeah, that was unpleasant.	對呀，那一點也不好玩。
Paul	For him! Ha! I loved it.	對他來說是不好玩！哈，我可開心的。
Chi	Didn't he get fired after that?	他不是後來被開除了？
Paul	Yup. It was the straw that broke the camel's back. Upper management had been looking for an excuse to fire him for years and I gave it to them.	沒錯。那次事件是壓垮駱駝的最後一根稻草。上層的管理部門多年來一直找藉口想炒他魷魚，我給他們了一個理由。
Chi	Don't you feel bad about that?	你難道不會覺得心裡過意不去嗎？
Paul	Not really. He was a jerk and the court agreed. I stood proudly on the steps of the courthouse knowing that I had won a clear victory. Afterwards I gave a victory	才不會。他對待員工的方式惡劣，這點法庭也同意。我驕傲地站在法院前的階梯上，明瞭自己打贏了一場清

生活篇　信仰篇　表達篇　外來語篇　**文明篇**　其它篇

speech to the press. They gave me a wondrous ovation—for <u>justice had been served</u>.

Chi (Skeptically) Reeeeeeeeally... and how much did you win?

Paul Twenty-five dollars.

Chi And the press showed up for that.

Paul (Smiles) Of course. I am very camera-friendly.

楚的勝仗。隨後我向記者群發表一篇勝利的感言，他們讚歎不已地為我鼓掌—因為正義終於獲得伸張。

（懷疑地）真真真真真的噢…那你贏回多少錢？

二十五元。

新聞媒體為了區區二十五塊出來採訪你。

（微笑）當然囉，我這人非常配合記者們的拍照。

♥ 單字

☑ security deposit [sɪˋkjʊrətɪ dɪˋpɑzɪt] *n.* 押金、擔保金

☑ courthouse [ˋkortˌhaʊs] *n.* 法院

☑ informative [ɪnˋfɔrmətɪv] *adj.* 知識性高的、資訊豐富的

☑ vent [vɛnt] *v.* 發洩、抒發不平

☑ courtroom [ˋkortˌrʊm] *n.* 法官聽證及審理案件的大廳、法庭

☑ admirable [ˋædmərəbl̩] *adj.* 令人佩服的、值得尊敬的

☑ small-claims court [smɔl klemz kort] *n.* 專門處理小額訴訟及案件性質單純的法院、小額索償法庭

☑ jerk [dʒɝk] *n.* （通常用來形容男性）以無禮或傲慢態度對待他人的人

☑ wondrous [ˋwʌndrəs] *adj.* 驚歎的、佩服不已的

☑ ovation [oˋveʃən] *n.* 大喝采、熱烈地鼓掌

片語

☑ come to someone's sense 某人領悟到過去做的事是錯的，而開始做出明智的舉動；某人恢復理智，開始能腦筋清楚地想事情

日常會話

☑ Justice is served 正義終於獲得伸張（壞人已得到應有的懲罰）。

法律之一：Pro Bono

電影《第六感生死緣》（*Meet Joe Black*）開場的一幕戲中，剛展開律師職業生涯的年輕男子裘 Joe，在咖啡店裡邂逅了女主角蘇珊 Susan。以下是他們對話的內容：

> *Joe：It's kind of a pro bono job.*
> Susan：*"Pro bono"?*
> *Joe：Yeah.*
> Susan：*Meaning, doing good?*
> *Joe：That's me！*

蘇珊猜的意思大概很接近了，pro bono 這句拉丁文原來稍長的版本是 pro bono publico，英文翻譯為 for (the) public good。"Pro" 這個常在英文字裡作字首的字，意思是 "for"，而 "bono" 是一個名詞，翻譯為「最好、極佳」。簡單說來，如果有人說他的工作性質是 pro bono，意思是他做的工作是志願性的、根本不支薪或僅收取極少的費用，其出發點基本上是為社會大眾服務。

Pro bono 這句形容詞尤其在法律界中常被引用，律師在他們一般日常的工作之外，如果能夠抽出時間來作志願性的法律顧問服務，這種行為是相當被讚許、鼓勵的（註）。尤其在美國這個崇尚司法、訴訟頻繁的國家裡，pro bono 的概念更是重要，因為若是只有有錢人能請得起律師、上法庭打官司，那這個社會還有什麼司法正義可言！所以在美國很多機構都會提供免費的 pro bono 法律服務，能讓負擔不起的窮人也能獲得法律諮詢、確保其基本權利不會受到損害。

註 美國律師協會（American Bar Association，簡寫 ABA）鼓勵執業律師們每年提供至少 50 小時的 pro bono 工作時數。

67 Lemon Cars

Paul I took our car to the garage today.

Chi Again? What did the mechanic say?

Paul Three-hundred diagnostic dollars later he told me that the transmission was beyond repair. To replace the whole system, it would cost us three-thousand dollars.

Chi WHAT?

Paul I'm sick of having to constantly fix and re-fix this piece of junk. Let's face it, we bought a lemon. The car overheats daily. Yesterday it stalled in the middle of traffic. It's dangerous. We've had numerous issues since the day we drove it off the lot.

Chi If we're to get another car, this time I want a brand new one. The last three used cars we've had all started to break down shortly after a year. The money we thought we saved ended up going into repairs. Not to mention all the headache and time we spent on taking them to the shop.

我今天把車子送到修車廠。

又有問題了？車廠的技師怎麼說？

在花了三～百塊的診斷費後，他告訴我傳動系統是不可能修好的。要更換整套系統，我們要再花三～千塊錢。

什麼？

我覺得這部廢物老是要修這修那的煩死了。認清事實吧，我們買到了一部檸檬車。這部車每天都出現過熱的現象，昨天在路上開到一半竟然給我熄火，危險得要命。從我們把這台車開回家的那天起就問題不斷。

如果我們要再買一部車，這次我要買全新的。我們過去的這三部二手車，買回來一年以後就都開始壞。本來以為省下來的錢，結果都花到修理費用上去，更別提車子出狀況時導致的煩惱焦慮，還有我們送去給人修理所花的時間。

Paul	The warranties on new cars normally run for at least three years. Tomorrow I'll go look around the dealerships. If I like anything, then I will trade in our old car before it becomes completely undrivable.	新車的保固期限正常來說至少都有三年。明天我會到幾家經銷商去逛逛，如果看到喜歡的，在我們這輛舊車完全沒辦法開以前，我會拿它去抵新車一部份的價錢。
Chi	See if you can find us a hybrid. With the price of gas rising, we don't want to be tied down with a gas-guzzler!	看看能不能找到油電混合動力的。現在汽油一天到晚漲價，我不想要被一台很耗油的車給套住！
Paul	I should be able to find something online. I also think we should go with a four-door this time.	我應該能在網路上找到一些資料。另外我覺得這次我們應該買四門的。
Chi	I want the color to be "earthy," yah know like black, silver-gray, brown, deep dark green, navy blue, or tan.	我想要「大地色系」，你知道的像黑色、銀灰、咖啡、暗綠、深藍、或淡褐色。
Paul	So no pink?	所以不能買粉紅色的？
Chi	Uh, no.	呃，不。
Paul	Fine. I know they also offer additional insurance on the tires for potholes. Do you want that?	好吧。我知道汽車業者還針對路面的坑洞提供額外的輪胎保險，妳想保這部份的險嗎？
Chi	Definitely. However the trunk should be big enough to carry our barbecue supplies.	一定要。還有車後廂一定要夠大才能裝得下我們的烤肉用具。
Paul	Indubitably. Do we want any special features?	無疑地。還有其他我們想要的特殊配備嗎？
Paul and Chi	GPS!	衛星導航系統！
Paul	Got to have that, but do you know what I	絕對要有那一項。你知道我

| | would really like even though I know they won't have it? | 還希望我們的新車有哪種配備，雖然我曉得目前市面上還沒有這種東西嗎？ |

Chi　What?

什麼樣的配備？

Paul　Steering-based headlights. If I turn the car in the middle of the night, the lights turn with me. Lights that work only when you move in a straight line are pointless.

配合方向盤轉動的大燈。晚上開車的時候，如果我轉車子方向盤，前面的頭燈會跟著一起轉。如果車燈只限於直線開的時候照亮前方的路面，根本就沒有意義。

Chi　You would think that would be a popular option.

這個配件應該會有很多人買。

Paul　I know, right? But somebody must have a strong hold on an expensive patent, otherwise I think most car makers would have already put them on all their cars by now.

對吧？但是大概哪個人正緊抓著這個專利權不放，要不然我認為多數的製造廠早就把這項裝置加到所有的車子上面去了。

Chi　Sounds like we've got a plan.

聽起來我們準備好了。

Paul　"New car smell" here we come!

「新車的味道」我們來囉！

♥ 單字

☑ **garage** [ɡəˋrɑʒ] *n.* 汽車修理廠

☑ **mechanic** [məˋkænɪk] *n.* 技師、機械維修師

☑ **diagnostic** [ˌdaɪəɡˋnɑstɪk] *adj.* 診斷的、檢查的

☑ **stall** [stɔl] *v.* （汽車）無法開動、（引擎等）停止轉動

☑ **dealership** [ˋdiləˏʃɪp] *n.* 經銷商、業者

☑ **gas-guzzler** [gæsˋgʌzləˊ] *n.* 消耗大量汽油的車種、費油的車

☑ navy blue [`nevɪ `blu] n. 深藍色（源自英國海軍制服的顏色）

☑ tan [tæn] n. 淡棕色、淺褐色

☑ Indubitably [ɪnˋdjubɪtəblɪ] adv. 不容置疑地

☑ steer [stɪr] v. 掌控（車等的）方向盤、操舵

片語

☑ drive (a car) off the lot （把車子）從經銷商的停車場開出來、新車落地

法律之二：Lemon Cars

為什麼美國人把某些車叫作檸檬？所謂檸檬車又是什麼樣的車子呢？

根據加州的檸檬法案（California' s New Car Lemon Law），如果你買的新車（註），在出廠後不久就開始出現狀況，這部車就可能被稱作檸檬—如果車子的問題符合以下三個條件：

1. 這個瑕疵是涵蓋在汽車保固之內。
2. 嚴重地縮減了這部車的使用、價值、以及安全性。
3. 在經過「合理的」修理次數後，問題仍然存在。

目前在加州，車商僅有 4 次的機會（在以前，所謂「合理的」進廠維修次數可多達 30 次！）把你車子的問題修好；另外，若是顧客決定告公司，而且勝訴的話，所有法律訴訟的相關費用都由汽車公司負擔，所以檸檬法的目的是保護消費者權利，也讓路上交通更安全，因為有了這項法律，製造廠商一旦發現自家出產的汽車有瑕疵，都會盡速召回不良品。

美國人把品質差的東西稱為檸檬，原因是這種水果會在人嘴裡留下酸味（leaves a sour taste）， 要是買到了不良品，他們說：You got a sour deal! 看看這一句極有名的諺語：When life gives you lemons, make lemonade. 譯作「當人生給你檸檬（比喻問題或困難的事），就榨成檸檬汁吧（將危機變成轉機）！」

註 除了新車外，二手車也有檸檬法（Used-Car Lemon Laws）來保障消費者，但這種法律在美國尚不普遍，目前只有六個州實施二手車檸檬法。

68 Miranda Rights

Paul and Chi are watching the movie *21 Jump Street*.
保羅季薇正在看電影《龍虎少年隊》。

Chi　Huuhmah. Jenko fumbled the reading of the Miranda rights. He's making it up as he goes... in front of his chief!

哼嘛，強哥把「米蘭達權利」亂唸一通，他…居然在局長的面前編造條文！

Paul　IT'S A MOVIE. Real cops are not that stupid. Most police officers even carry a copy of it in their pocket just in case they need it. English on one side, Spanish on the other.

那只是電影啦！真的警察才沒那麼笨。多數的警察甚至在口袋裡攜帶一份複本以備不時之需，一面是英文，一面是西班牙文。

Chi　I have a customer who is a retired detective and he said Hollywood often reads a suspect their Miranda rights too soon. That typically isn't done unless that person is going to be immediately interrogated.

我有位客戶是退休的警探，他說好萊塢常常太早對嫌犯宣讀米蘭達權利。一般情況下，除非那個人馬上就要接受偵訊，否則警察是不用讀他的權利的。

Paul　Correct. Suspects are not read their Miranda rights until they are in custody. However, if a deputy asks someone about a recent crime on a street, and they blurt out incriminating statements, then since that person is not in a state of formal custodial questioning, the officer doesn't have to read them their rights. Anything they say can and will be used against them in a court of law.

正確。直到嫌犯正式被拘留之前，警察都不需要宣讀米蘭達權利。然而，如果警察在路上針對最近發生的一項犯罪對某人進行詢問，而這人不經思索地脫口而出使自己入罪的言詞，由於這個情形並非正式的拘留偵訊，警方不須向他宣讀他的權利，任何他講的話，都有可能在法庭上成為對他不利的證據。

Chi　That does seem like a finer nuance that most people might not <u>pick up on</u>.

這大概是大多數人都不會注意到的小細節。

Paul　Another bad assumption from this movie is that because Jenko forgot to read the suspect their rights, the chief is now required to have the department drop all charges. In real life, if the Miranda rights are not read, then statements gathered prior to the reading are inadmissible as evidence at trial. Prosecutors do not drop the charges.

這部電影中另一個錯誤的假設是，因為強哥忘記對嫌犯宣讀權利，局長現在必須使部門撤銷所有的控訴。在真實生活中，如果警方忘了唸米蘭達權利，只有那些在嫌犯權利被正式宣讀前所蒐集的證據會失去效力，檢察官其實不會撤銷控告。

Chi　So a difference in pay is not the only distinct difference between TV cops and real cops.

所以電視警察跟真的警察之間的區別，不是只有薪資這一項。

Paul　Facts don't always push a linear storyline forward efficiently, so writers <u>take necessary liberties</u> in order to focus a story's continuity, tone, and flow. Shows like Law and Order and CSI keep the action moving by leading you to believe that cases are worked on one at a time, but the truth is investigators are working many cases simultaneously.

事實不一定能夠有效率地推進劇情，因此編劇採取了必要的手段來改寫，以加強故事的連續性、氣氛和節奏。節目像《法網遊龍》跟《CSI犯罪現場》，為了維持故事的緊湊，他們會特意讓妳以為警方都是一次辦一件案子，事實上，調查人員都是好幾件案子同時進行。

Chi　Or the lab work! They make it seem like you could get the test result back in a few minutes or by the end of the day.

還有實驗室作業！他們拍得好像你可以在幾分鐘或是一天之內就拿到測試結果。

Paul　Yeah... real lab analysis takes weeks or longer depending on how complex the crime scene evidence is! You have to allow yourself to accept the timeline's

是啊…真正的實驗室分析，視犯罪現場證據的複雜程度而定，得花上幾週甚至更久的時間才能完成！妳必須接

生活篇　信仰篇　表達篇　外來語篇　文明篇　其它篇

premise, otherwise you'll pull yourself out of the picture.

受情節裡設定的時間表，要不然妳會很容易從故事中脫離出來。

Chi　Ooooo... I hate that. Does knowing too much about science ruin a scene for you?

唔…我不喜歡那樣。知道太多科學事實會不會破壞你欣賞電影的情緒啊？

Paul　Occasionally, just try to remember it's entertainment. If you think too much about it, you'll ruin the moment. It need only sound plausible to pass.

有時候。盡量提醒自己這不過是一種娛樂形態啦！如果想得太多是會煞風景的。只要情節還算講得過去就好了。

 單字

☑ fumble [ˋfʌmb!] **v.** 摸索、笨拙地弄

☑ custody [ˋkʌstədɪ] **n.** 拘留、拘捕（形容詞為 custodial [ˌkʌsˋtodɪəl]）

☑ deputy [ˋdɛpʊtɪ] **n.** 代理人、代表（在本文中指一般的「警察」，意即「代表警長的人」）

☑ blurt [blɝt] **v.** 不加思索地說出、衝口而出

☑ incriminate [ɪnˋkrɪməˌnet] **v.** 使（人）入罪

☑ nuance [ˋnjuˌɑns] **n.** 細微的差異

☑ inadmissible [ˌɪnədˋmɪsəb!] **adj.** （證據）無法使用的、沒有證據效力的

☑ prosecutor [ˋprɑsɪˌkjutɚ] **n.** 檢察官

☑ lab [læb] **n.** 實驗室。Lab 為 laoratory 的口語

☑ plausible [ˋplɔzəb!] **adj.** （話、辯解等）好像是有道理的、表面上講得通的

片語

☑ pick up on something 注意到某個訊息或某種知識、察覺到某事
☑ take liberties (with something) 為符合需要而擅作主張地改寫（某段史實或小說情節）

法律之三：**Miranda Rights**

"You have the right to remain silent.
Anything you say or do can and will be held against you in a court of law.
You have the right to an attorney.
If you cannot afford an attorney, one will be provided for you.
Do you understand these rights I have just read to you?"

以上這一段，包括了四個陳述句、跟一個問句作結尾的宣言，是所有美國警察在逮捕嫌犯後，要進行偵訊前一定要讀給犯人聽的 Miranda rights。中文譯作「米蘭達權利」。

米蘭達權利的內容，相信看過許多好萊塢警匪電影和電視影集的人都滿熟悉的，但是對米蘭達權利的這個名稱，以及它的由來，大概就不是那麼清楚了。時間要回溯至 1963 年，一個名叫 Ernesto Arturo Miranda（以下簡稱米蘭達）的男子遭警方扣押，在審問的過程中他簽署了一份自白書，供稱自己十天前強暴了一名少女。地方法庭將這篇自白作為證據，把他定罪。米蘭達的律師不服，認為警察在偵訊他的時候，從未告知他有保持沈默和諮詢律師的權利，因此那份自白不能算是完全在米蘭達的自由意志下寫的，不能納入證據。

米蘭達的案子一直上告到美國聯邦最高法院，1966 年聯邦法院聲明了地方法院的判決無效，理由是根據美國憲法第五修正案：人民不能被強迫證明自己有罪（避免警察濫用私刑及冤獄！）；以及第六修正案中，人民有取得法律諮商、協助自己辯護的權利。從此之後，美國警察就都要向嫌疑犯宣讀他們的權利。

米蘭達權利是這樣，如果你光是閉嘴、什麼也不講，是不能算成立的，警方一定要確定你瞭解他們在說什麼，而且你要清楚地聲明你是要使用或放棄這份權利才可以。所以，要是哪天你運氣不好，剛好跟真正的罪犯穿了一模一樣的外套，開著同一款、同樣顏色的車…，在警察伯伯宣讀你的 Miranda rights 後，一定要這麼清晰肯定地回答：Yes. I am exercising my right to remain silent, and I want my lawyer!

Chi stumbles into the kitchen with a big white goldendoodle.
季薇跌跌撞撞地帶著一隻大白色黃金貴賓狗進入廚房。

Paul	What are you doing? Who's dog is this?	妳在幹什麼？這是誰的狗？
Chi	His name is Rover. He is Barbara's dog. Barbara is leaving town with her family for two week so I volunteered to dog-sit Rover for her. I told you about the dog a few days ago but I think it <u>went in one ear and out the other</u>!	牠的名字是來福。牠是芭芭拉的狗。芭芭拉跟她的家人要出城兩個禮拜，所以我就志願幫忙她看顧來福。幾天前我就跟你提過這隻狗，但是我看我的話對你是左耳進右耳出！
Paul	Is Barbara paying for him to stay at our place?	芭芭拉有沒有付錢讓牠待在我們家啊？
Chi	I know I work for Barbara, but she is also my friend! There is no way I would take money from her. Besides, haven't we talked about getting a dog for the longest time? I think you and I can practice with Rover before we get a dog of our own. Barbara has supplied us with a big bag of dog food and some of his toys. All we need to do is to walk him twice a day. It shouldn't be that hard.	我知道芭芭拉是我的老闆，但她也是我的朋友！我不可能會跟她算錢。況且，我們不是說要養條狗說了好久嗎？我認為你跟我在養我們自己的狗之前，可以拿來福來練習。芭芭拉提供了一大袋狗食跟牠的一些玩具。我們必須做的，就只是每天帶牠出去散步兩次。這應該不難吧。
Paul	You mean "you" will walk him twice a day.	妳的意思是「妳」會每天帶牠出去散步兩次。
Chi	Fine. I don't see why not. Rover is "MY" buddy. Come here, Rover! See how well-	好啦。我才不介意。來福跟我是好兄弟。過來這邊，來

	trained he is?	福！看到牠多麼訓練有素了嗎？
Paul	We'll see.	我們等著瞧。
	(A week later) Chi is cleaning in the kitchen.	（一週後）季薇在清理廚房。
Chi	Paul, will you please take the garbage out?	保羅，請你把垃圾拿出去倒好嗎？
Paul	...	...
Chi	Paul, did you hear me?	保羅你聽見我說的話了嗎？
Paul	...	...
Chi	(Takes off her gloves and walks over to the living room.) Paul, I need help with the garbage.	（脫掉手套並走到客廳）保羅，我要你幫我處理垃圾。
	Chi notices that Rover is on the couch.	季薇注意到來福躺在沙發上。
Chi	Rover, get off the couch. That's my seat!	來福，從沙發下來。那是我的位子！
	Rover rolls his head over onto Paul's lap.	來福轉頭趴到保羅的大腿上。
Paul	I don't see your name on it.	我沒看到這個位子寫了妳的名字。
Chi	Rover get off!	來福下來！
	Chi pulls on Rover's legs. Rover rolls over onto his back. His four legs now pointing straight up. Paul does the same.	季薇拉著來福的腳。來福翻了個身，四腳直直朝天。保羅也有樣學樣，四肢朝上躺著。
Paul	"We" will take out the garbage when "we" are ready. Begone!	等「我們」準備好，「我們」就會把垃圾拿出去。走

生活篇

信仰篇

表達篇

外來語篇

文明篇

其它篇

313

		開！
Chi	(Talking to Rover.) I feed you, bathe you, and walk you every day, but you like him more?	（對來福說）我每天餵你、幫你洗澡、帶你出去散步，但是你卻比較喜歡他？
Paul	Relax. Rover and I will go out for a walk after the show. If you want to join us you can.	放輕鬆啦。來福跟我在節目結束後會出去走走。如果妳也想參加就一起來。
Chi	He won't get out of my seat!	牠霸佔著我的位子不放！
Paul	Fine! Rover down.	好了啦！來福下去。
	Rover haplessly rolls off the couch.	來福狀似悲慘地翻身下沙發。
Chi	Et tu, Brute?	連你都背叛我，布魯士？

 單字

☑ stumble [`stʌmb!] ***v.*** 跌跌撞撞；踉蹌

☑ goldengdoodle [`goldṇ`dud!] ***n.*** 一種黃金獵犬與貴賓狗的混合品種

☑ Rover [`rovɚ] ***n.*** 音譯「來福」。"Rover" 是在美國相當流行的一個狗名字；rove 意思是徘徊、漫遊，狗的習性即是到處走動徘徊，「漫遊者」之名因此而起。

☑ dog-sit [`dɔg,sɪt] ***v.*** 在飼主外出時幫忙看顧狗兒（dog-sit 是由另一個字 babysit 變形而來）

☑ couch [kaʊtʃ] ***n.*** 沙發座椅（美國人很少用 sofa 這個單字，通常講 couch）

☑ begone [bɪ`gɔn] ***v.*** 「走開」、「（請你）離開」的意思，多用於祈使句

☑ haplessly [`hæplɪslɪ] ***adv.*** 不幸地；悲慘地

片語

☑ go in one ear and out the other 左耳進右耳出；有聽沒有到

 ## 因莎士比亞而流行的用語之一：**Et Tu, Brute?**

暢銷情色小說《格雷的五十道陰影》（*Fifty Shades of Grey*）中有一章描述，男主角初次與女主角安娜的母親見面，格雷的魅力，連年紀有一段差距的媽媽都難以招架：

"Please, put these drinks on my tab, room 612. I'll call you in the morning, Anastasia. Until tomorrow, Carla."（格雷向安娜、以及她母親卡拉道別）

"Oh, it's so nice to hear someone use your full name."
（母親聽到格雷使用安娜的全名「安娜塔希婭」，感到很窩心）

"Beautiful name for a beautiful girl," Christian murmurs, shaking her outstretched hand, and she actually simpers.
（母親與他握手後，安娜發現她媽媽居然像個小女孩般地在傻笑）

Oh, Mom—et tu, Brute? I stand, gazing up at him...（以下略）

"Et tu, Brute?" 這個名句，字字皆拉丁文，但是對幾乎每一個受過教育的美國人來說，它的意義卻再清楚也不過：「連你都背叛我？」

這句用語之所以會如此廣為人知，要歸功於莎士比亞的名劇《凱撒大帝》。劇情裡，凱撒看到他的好友布魯士竟然也是刺殺他的人其中之一，絕望地喊出 "Et tu, Brute?" 這段台詞。拉丁字 "et"，我們在另一篇講「符號&」的文章會再提到，它的意思相當於英文的 and；而 "tu"，就是 you；"Brute" 是布魯士的名字 Brutus；整句話直翻英語即為 "And you, Brute?" 或 "You too, Brutus?"

發音為[ɛtˋtuˋbrutɛ]，這句是用在警覺到自己被人，特別是好友或原本忠誠的夥伴，所背叛時說的用語。另外一句，同樣也是出於凱撒大帝劇本的名言："Beware of the Ides of March"（小心三月十五日。Ides 唸[aɪdz]，指月份正中間的那一天），則是在警告人要留意即將到來的危險，尤其提防被同黨友人陷害的情況。

70 Good Riddance

Sunday night Paul and Chi are home watching TV. Paul flips through the channels and momentarily stops on a news station. President Obama is speaking.

星期天晚上保羅與季薇在家看電視。保羅在頻道之間轉來轉去,他短暫地停在某個新聞台上,這時歐巴馬總統正在談話。

Obama	Good evening. Tonight, I can report to the American people and to the world that the United States has conducted an operation that killed Osama bin Laden, the leader of al-Qaeda, and a terrorist who was responsible for the murder of thousands of innocent men, women, and children...	各位晚安。今夜,我可以向美國民眾以及全世界報告,美國已經完成一項殲滅奧薩瑪·賓拉登的軍事行動,此人是蓋達組織的領袖,並且是造成數千無辜成人及兒童死亡的一名恐怖份子...
Paul	Bin Laden is dead? Good riddance!	賓拉登死了?Good riddance!
Chi	Good ... "rhythms"?	Good…rhythms?
Paul	No, "good riddance." It means that it is good to be rid of someone. It is a term used to verbally diminish someone even as they are leaving. In other words an insult added to injury or to kick someone while they are down. The longer version of the original phrase is "Good riddance to bad rubbish." A similar phrase is "Don't let the door hit your ass on the way out."	不是,是 "good riddance"。意思是「慶幸終於可以擺脫某人」。這個措辭是用來口頭上矮化某人,即使是在他們準備要離開的時候。換句話說,在傷口上灑鹽巴,或踹著已經倒下的人。這句長一點的版本是"Good riddance to bad rubbish"(壞垃圾丟掉得好)。另外一個類似的

説法是「出去的時候別給門撞到你的屁股」。

Chi　Isn't that a bit mean-spirited? Lowbrow? Crass?

那會不會有點壞心眼？沒品？惡劣呀？

Paul　Yes it is! Humans are emotional and don't always take the high road especially with people who they "feel" hurt them. Although Osama bin Laden never hurt me directly, I do empathize with his victims. However, on the flip side, if I were to reflect even deeper on the issue I can understand how someone might try to rationalize such an unjustifiable act. America does have a very strong presence in the world. Some people may resent that influence.

沒錯！人類是很情緒化的，而且不一定會選擇做高尚的行為，尤其在面對他們「覺得」嚴重傷害過自己的人時。雖然賓拉登從未直接傷害過我，可是我同情被他傷害過的人們。然而從反面的角度來看，如果我對這個事件做更深層的思考，我可以了解為什麼某些人會試圖把一個如此毫無正義可言的行為合理化。美國的確在世界上具有很大的影響力，有些人也許對這點相當反感。

Chi　Are you saying that Osama bin Laden rationalized his actions?

你是在說賓拉登把他的行為合理化嗎？

Paul　Everyone rationalizes their actions! However, in this particular case, what I am saying is that a unique political perspective as volatile as Osama bin Laden's can be twisted to manipulate and justify any act that promotes his cause. As humans we do this all the time. We do what we do because we are emotional not because it is logical. We justified his

每個人都合理化自己的行為好不好！然而針對這個例子，我的意思是，像賓拉登那麼強烈的獨特政治觀可能會被扭曲，以操縱並合理化任何支持他的理想的行為。人類無時不刻都在這麼做。我們做事是基於情感，不是基於邏輯。我們說因為賓拉

生活篇

信仰篇

表達篇

外來語篇

文明篇

其它篇

state-sanctioned execution as morally correct, because he is a proven mass murderer. From his perspective his actions were justified.

登被證明殺害了許多人，所以美國政府對他的處決是正義的。但是從他的觀點出發，他的行為才是正義的。

Chi Are you trying to legitimize his actions or absolve him of them?

你是在試著把他的行為合法化，還是幫他免除他的責任？

Paul No, I am showing you how people can lawyer their morality into substantiating anything. Remember, everything Hitler did was legal. We say this in order to remind ourselves of the difference between human laws and morality in general. They are not the same thing and we should be mindful in knowing the difference.

都不是，我是要讓妳看見，人們怎麼扭曲自己的道德觀，來為自己做的事找理由。切記... 希特勒所做的每件事都是合法的；我們這麼説，就是要提醒自己人類法律和倫理之間的不同。這兩者不是同一件事，而我們必須清楚地加以區別。

❤ 單字

☑ diminish [də`mɪnɪʃ] *v.* 矮化；醜化	☑ mean-spirited [min`spɪrɪtɪd] *adj.* 心地壞的
☑ lowbrow [lo`brou] *adj.* 沒教養的；文化不高的	☑ crass [kræs] *adj.* 惡劣的；粗野的
☑ cause [kɔz] *n.* 理想；目標	☑ state-sanctioned [stet`sæŋkʃənd] *adj.* 為政府所批准的；國家許可的
☑ lawyer [`lɔjɚ] *v.* 曲解事實以達成特定目的	☑ substantiate [səb`stænʃɪˌet] *v.* 證明（某個事件或主張）有根據

片語

☑ add insult to injury 使某個原本已經很壞的情況更加惡化；在傷口上灑鹽巴
☑ take the high road 不基於報復或怨憎，而選擇做道德上正確的事；採取高尚、正直的行為

 日常會話

☑ On the flip side, ... 從另一面來說；由反面的角度看來
☑ Don't let the door hit your ass on the way out. 出去的時候別給門撞到你的屁股；請立刻離開；快滾吧。

 因莎士比亞而流行的用語之二：**Good Riddance**

不知你有沒有這樣的經驗？你巴不得有些人或事從你生活中永遠消失，他們（或它）不僅讓你心情惡透，有時甚至在你的人格或經濟上造成難以彌補的傷害；而當那個討厭鬼終於滾蛋，或者你總算可以丟掉那件累贅物時，你只想深呼一口氣、關上門、慶幸這輩子再也不會跟他／它扯上任何關係了…。除了 "Thank God!"（感謝老天！）外，你知道英文還可以怎麼說呢？

在美國許多人這時會說：Good riddance!

這個用語的中文意思是「走了最好！」說這話的人，不但表示自己完全不在意對方離開的事實，相反的，還很高興對方再也不會打擾他，是一句帶有挖苦、嘲諷意味的評論。

Riddance 這個字是從 rid 演變出來的名詞，意思是「除去」、「擺脫」。在現代英文中，riddance 的使用已經很少見，百分之九十九的機率你會看到這個單字，就是在 good riddance 這一組用語裡，而第一個把 good 跟 riddance 兩個字連在一起的人，就是我們親愛的莎翁。

Good riddance 出現於莎士比亞較少為人知的戰爭愛情悲劇《特洛伊羅斯與克瑞西達》（*Troilus and Cressida*）」。劇中，Thersites 是希臘王子 Ajax 的奴隸，這個奴隸的口舌十分惡毒，有一幕，Thersites 嘲笑他的主人沒腦袋，這時歷史上最偉大的戰士之一，阿基里斯，和他的好友帕克羅克斯特走進來，竟也受到波及，被 Thersites 無情地批評。這三人都受不了他，在這幕戲最後當 Thersites 離開時，帕克羅克斯特就說了這句流傳至今的話：A good riddance.

聽這句話怎麼用！網友提供的一則 YouTube 連結：https://www.facebook.com/video/video.php?v=528838147141281

生活篇

信仰篇

表達篇

外來語篇

文明篇

其它篇

71 Star-Crossed Lovers

Chi is watching *Bachelor Pad* when Paul comes home from work.
保羅下班回家時,季薇正在看真人節目《單身公寓》。

Paul	Are you watching that bachelor crap again?	妳又在看那個爛節目啦?
Chi	It's NOT crap! These people are real!	它才不是什麼爛節目!這些都是有血有肉的真實的人!
Paul	Uh-huh.	嗯哼。
Chi	I love this one couple in particular: Blake and Holly. You can tell that their feelings are sincere. But because Holly's ex-fiancé, Michael, is also on the show, Blake could not publicly show his affection towards Holly.	我尤其喜愛這一對戀人:布雷克和荷莉。你曉得他們之間的感情是真摯的。但是因為荷莉的前未婚夫,麥克,也在節目裡,所以布雷克沒辦法公開地向荷莉表示他的愛意。
Paul	GAYYYYYYY!	軟弱的傢伙伙伙伙伙伙!
Chi	BUUUUUUUT! Holly is torn also. Michael told her that he had made a terrible mistake and that he now realizes how irreplaceable she is. He wants her back. Michael is jealous and is currently trying to rally support to his cause in order to get Blake off the show. I think he might succeed.	但但但但但是!荷莉也在掙扎。麥克告訴她他之前犯了一個糟糕的錯誤,現在他瞭解到她對他而言是無可取代的。他希望她回到他身邊。麥克起了嫉妒心,目前他正試圖召集其他人的支持把布雷克趕出這個節目。我認為他可能會成功。

Paul If you insist on dragging me into this nonsense, I would say on gut instinct alone that because Michael had a previous relationship with Holly he will most likely <u>win her over</u> due to the fact that they have had a longer history together. Statistically girls tend to lean towards the longer relationship. However, the person who should win is Blake, because he deserves to <u>have a shot</u> without the interference of Michael. Girls are stupid they tend to forget why they dumped their ex-boyfriends <u>in the first place</u>. The reality is that Michael has probably not changed. Men don't really change their core selves.

Chi I feel so bad for Blake. He says he knows that he is probably not the most popular person in the house right now, but he couldn't help being drawn towards Holly. Holly loves Blake, too. Her eyes light up whenever Blake walks into the room. However, due to Michael's presence they can only occasionally steal clandestine glances at each other. I can't help but sympathize with these star-crossed lovers.

Paul Star-crossed lovers? Phshh... WE are more qualified than them to be called star-crossed lovers. I remember briefly after we met you had to go back to

如果妳堅持要把我捲進這個沒營養的話題，我會說，光憑直覺而論，因為麥克和荷莉過去曾經有段關係，他們在一起的歷史比較長，他大概會贏回荷莉的心。統計上來說，女孩子傾向選擇較久的關係。但是布雷克才是應該贏的人，因為他應該要有一次沒有麥克從中作梗的挑戰機會。女生都很傻，她們常忘記為什麼她們起初甩掉舊男友的理由。現實是麥克大概還沒改變。男人不會真的改變他們的核心本性。

我好為布雷克感到難過。他說他知道自己大概現在不是單身公寓裡最受歡迎的人，可是他無法不被荷莉所吸引。荷莉也愛著布雷克。每當布雷克走進來她的眼睛就閃亮了起來。但是，因為麥克的存在，他們只能偶爾祕密地互相偷瞥。我無法克制地同情這一對「受天上星辰阻撓的戀人」。

受星辰阻撓的戀人？噗噓…我們還比他們更有資格被稱作受星辰阻撓的戀人。我記得在我們認識後沒多久妳必

Taiwan. At the airport, I thought we would probably never see each other again. There were so many variables and obstacles between us: Our vastly different backgrounds, language, culture, and the sheer unforgivable distance of thousands of miles. We had no time and no money! Anything could have happened. It is a miracle that we are even together at all.

Chi　If we made it so can they.

(Update: Blake and Holly married after the show.)

須返回臺灣。在機場裡，我以為我們再也不會相見了。我倆之間有太多變數與阻礙：妳我大異其趣的背景、語言、文化、以及數千哩全然殘酷的距離。我們既沒時間也沒金錢！什麼事都可能發生。我們能夠在一起根本是個奇蹟。

如果我們能成功，他們應該也能。

（最新報導：布雷克與荷莉在節目結束之後結婚了。）

 ## 單字

☑ pad [pæd] **n.** （俚語）指「屋子」、「住所」。

☑ rally [`rælɪ] **v.** 召集；集合

☑ gut instinct [`gʌt `ɪnstɪŋkt] **n.** 直覺。美國人說，如果直覺告訴你不好的事將要發生，你會感到肚子裡胃腸翻攪不已，即使表面上的事實或理性分析都找不出徵兆。通常你肚子裡的直覺，也就是 your gut instinct 最後證明都是對的。

☑ clandestine [klæn`dɛstən] **adj.** 祕密的

☑ variable [`vɛrɪəb!] **n.** 變數

☑ sheer [ʃɪr] **adj.** 完全的；全然的

 ## 片語

☑ win someone over 贏取某人的支持或同意

☑ have a shot (at something) 有機會（去做某件事）

☑ in the first place 在一開始；最起先的時候

☑ make it 成功；達到目標

 # 因莎士比亞而流行的用語之三：**Star-Crossed Lovers**

"Star-crossed lovers" 是指「感情路多舛的一對戀人」。

雖然英文字 cross 較為人熟知的意思為「交錯」，但在這句用語裡，cross 的解釋是「阻礙、反對」。古代人相信天上的星星可以決定個人的命運（即使在現代，占星術也還是相當熱門！），star-crossed 的意思就是「被星辰反對（或詛咒）的」，如果你和你所愛的那個人之間受到眾星的阻撓，那麼感情路途中勢必要面對許多挫折，若兩人仍執意要在一起，則可能有不好的結局。

這詞 "star-crossed lovers" 乃源自於莎士比亞最著名的愛情悲劇《羅密歐與朱麗葉》。在開場的序言中間部份，莎翁寫道：

From forth the fatal loins of these two foes
從這兩個世代血仇的家庭中出生

A pair of star-cross'd lovers take their life;
一對情路坎坷的戀人自盡

Whose misadventured piteous overthrows
他們不幸與可悲的抗爭

Doth with their death bury their parents' strife.
用死亡結束了他們父母親彼此的敵恨

在許多影迷的心目中堪稱是最偉大愛情電影的《北非諜影》(*Casablanca*)，片中在法國巴黎認識、戀愛、分離、到北非卡薩布蘭卡意外相聚後，卻又因種種外在因素而無法相守的男女主角，就是一個 star-crossed lovers 的例子。男星亨弗萊・鮑嘉（Humphrey Bogart）在終究理解到對兩人都好的結束方法後，對英格麗・褒曼（Ingrid Bergman）說出這兩句令人心碎的話："We will always have Paris."（巴黎永遠都會是我們的。）以及 "Here's looking at you, kid."（這杯敬你，寶貝。）在觀眾腦海裡刻下不滅的印記。

第六篇 其它篇 Numbers

72 Got Your 6

(Sound of panting)　　（喘息聲）

Chi	I'm scared.	我好害怕。
	(People moaning in pain)	（人們痛苦地哀號）
Paul	Keep quiet.	別出聲。
	Paul signals Chi to follow him. They run to the nearest boulder.	保羅暗示季薇跟隨他，兩人跑到附近的一塊巨石後。
Chi	(Whimpering) I don't want to get shot.	（用哭聲說）我不要被槍打到。
Paul	You'll be all right. You're with me now.	妳不會有事的，有我在。
Chi	What do I do?	我要怎麼辦？
Paul	Do you have your gun up?	妳槍準備好了嗎？
Chi	(Scrambles to lift her gun.) Uh. Yes.	（一陣混亂後把槍舉起）呃，準備好了。
Paul	Stay on my six, cover high. We're going for the flag.	跟在我背後，提防敵人從高處射擊，我們現在要去奪旗子。
Chi	How do I use tttttttthhhis thing? (Teeth chattering)	這個東東東東東西西要怎麼用？（牙齒打顫）

Paul Geez. Weren't you paying attention to the instructor at all? Tuck the bottom of the paintball gun securely into your shoulder. While your right hand is on the trigger, use your left hand to steady the barrel. When you aim, try to keep both eyes open. If you close an eye, you'll lose your peripheral vision. Avoid getting in or creating crossfire. And FOR GOD'S SAKE, don't ever take off your mask!

老天，妳剛剛都沒注意聽指導員講的嗎？緊緊地將漆彈槍的底端靠在肩膀上，用妳的右手搭扳機，左手固定槍管。在瞄準目標的時候，試著同時用兩隻眼睛來對準；如果妳把一隻眼睛閉起來的話會影響妳周邊的視角。小心不要介入或造成向隊友射擊的情況。還有拜託妳，千萬不要把面具拿起來！

Chi (Quickly pulls down her mask.) I just wanted to be able to hear you better, I'm ...

（快速地拉下面具）我只是想聽清楚你說什麼，我…

Paul (Sighs) Just aim and shoot.

（歎氣）反正瞄準跟射就對了。

Several minutes later after advancing deep into enemy territory.

數分鐘後深入敵人陣地。

Paul (Behind a barricade) Can you see the flag?

（在障礙物後面）妳看得到旗子嗎？

Chi (Pokes her head out swiftly.) Yes.

（敏捷地探出頭）看得到。

Paul Run as fast as possible and grab the flag. I've got your six. Now, go!

跑得越快越好把旗子拿到手，我會掩護妳。就是現在，跑！

Chi dashes out. After a few seconds Paul follows.

季薇衝出。幾秒後，保羅尾隨。

生活篇　信仰篇　表達篇　外來語篇　文明篇

其它篇

Paul	Got ya! (Shoots down hidden enemy.)	逮到你了！（將匿藏的敵人射落下來）
Chi	I GOT THE FLAG! WE WON!! What... what is this? (Reaching to her back and finds bright yellow paint dripping down from her shoulder blade.)	我拿到旗子了！我們贏了！什麼…這是什麼？（手伸到背後，發現鮮黃色的漆從肩膀上滴落）
Paul	Sorry, honey, I had to use you as bait to draw out their last sniper.	抱歉，親愛的，我必須利用妳把他們的最後一個狙擊手引誘出來。
Chi	I THOUGHT YOU SAID YOU'VE GOT MY BACK. Oh, ow, that really hurts.	我以為你說你會掩護我。喔，噢，那真的有夠痛。
Paul	I'm sure everyone will appreciate your selfless sacrifice for the team. (Plucks the flag from Chi's hand.)	我確定大家都會感謝妳為本隊做出如此無私的犧牲。（從季薇手裡拔出錦旗）
Chi	You son of a...	你這…

 單字

☑ boulder [`boldɚ] **n.** 大石塊、巨礫

☑ whimper [`hwɪmpɚ] **v.** 哭哭地說、哀鳴

☑ scramble [`skræmb!] **v.** 緊急地做（某事）、手忙腳亂地取（某物）

☑ chatter [`tʃætɚ] **v.** （牙齒因寒冷或恐懼而）咯咯作響、震顫碰觸出聲

☑ barrel [`bærəl] **n.** 槍管、砲管

☑ peripheral [pə`rɪfərəl] **adj.** 周圍的、邊緣的

- ☑ crossfire [ˋkrɔsˏfaɪr] **n.** 由於從不同角度發出的火力集中於同一點上，而造成向自己方隊友射擊的情況

- ☑ barricade [ˋbærəˏked] **n.** 屏障、障礙物

- ☑ shoulder blade [ˋʃoldə bled] **n.** 肩胛骨

- ☑ pluck [plʌk] **v.** 拔出、摘掉

🎩 數字之一：Got Your 6

自 2011 年起，好萊塢演藝圈發起了一項運動，名稱為 " Got Your 6 "，其宗旨是幫助自中東戰區退伍返家的軍人，重新適應平民生活。這個活動由許多名人代言，不用說自然引起社會大眾的注意…但是話說回來，到底 Got Your 6 是什麼意思哩？

Got your 6 是 "I've got your back" 或 "I have your back" 的簡寫。如果你對某人說 I've got your back，你就相當是在跟他保證：不用擔心，我會幫你注意從你「背後」來襲的敵人，有什麼問題我會罩你！

那，又為什麼用數字 6 來表示 back，也就是背後呢？

想像你站在一面有傳統指針的大鐘中心，面向 12 點。如果有人講，啊，有個漂亮的妹妹從你的 3 點鐘方向走過來，你就知道這個女生位在你的右手邊；相對的，9 點是你的左手邊，而我們現在講的 6 點鐘，也就是你的背面。

這種用時間鐘點表示方向的系統，大約是從第一次世界大戰的美國空軍開始的。由於飛行時是處於三度空間，所以駕駛員有時還會加上 "high" 與 "low" 來指示敵機的方位，例如："…incoming 11 o'clock high."

另外一個常用的講法是 watch your 6，或是 check your 6，這下你大概可以猜到這句是在說什麼了─它的意思就是要你注意你自己的背後，說這句話的人想提醒你留心可能問題的發生，所以聽到這一句就請千萬小心、步步為營啊！

生活篇 信仰篇 表達篇 外來語篇 文明篇

其它篇

73 The Whole 9 Yards

Mike	Hey, Chi. Hi, Paul.	嘿,季薇。嗨,保羅。
Paul	Hey, man.	嘿,老兄。
Chi	Nice to see ya.	看到你真好。
Mike	You guys ready for the Super Bowl?	準備好一起來看超級盃了嗎?
Paul	You bet.	當然。
Chi	Uh, can someone please explain the rules for me before the game starts?	呃,能不能在比賽開始以前跟我講一下規則?
Paul & Mike	YOU SERIOUS?	妳是認真的嗎?
Mike	Have you ever watched a game before?	妳沒看過任何一場比賽?
Chi	Nope. This is my first time.	沒有,今天是第一次。
Paul	Come on, everyone watches the Super Bowl!	少來了,哪有人不看超級盃的!
Chi	I guess it's not very popular in Taiwan.	我想超級盃在臺灣不是那麼流行。
Paul & Mike	NOT POPULAR?	不流行?
Paul	Football? That's impossible.	美式足球?不可能。
Mike	What do Taiwanese watch?	那臺灣人都看什麼?
Chi	We love our baseball.	我們熱愛我們的棒球。
Paul	YOUR baseball? Americans invented baseball. You are playing OUR game.	你們的棒球?美國人發明棒球。你們玩的是我們的運動。
Chi	We also like basketball.	我們也喜歡籃球。

Paul	American invented game!
Chi	AND we watch the Olympics.
Paul	An American DOMINATED event! Wooo... That's right... we're AWESOME.
Chi	You still haven't answered my question. What are the rules?
Paul	(Checks the time) All right. We have a few minutes. The rules are simple: The game is played by two teams. Before the game starts, a coin toss decides which team receives the ball. The team that receives is now designated as the offense. They have four downs to advance at least ten yards in order to...
Chi	What? I thought it was nine yards! Isn't football where the expression "the whole nine yards" originated from?
Paul	NO! Because in... FOOTBALL, you need to advance "ten" yards before you can score.
Mike	I think that saying is from World War II. The gun belts on fighter planes were nine yards long. When a pilot was to fire all of his ammunition into a target, he'd be giving it "the whole nine yards."
Paul	That's correct, but can we please focus we only have two minutes left. So, after the team advances ten yards on the field,

美國人發明的競賽項目！

我們**也**觀賞奧運。

一項被美國稱霸的活動！唔唔…沒錯…我們太厲害了。

你還是沒回答我的問題，規則到底是什麼？

（看了看時間）好吧，我們有幾分鐘的時間。規則很簡單：比賽分成兩個隊伍，開打前以擲銅板決定哪一隊先拿到球。拿到球的隊伍為進攻的一方，他們必須在四次的進攻機會內，向對方的得方區推進至少十碼才能…

什麼？我一直以為是九碼！「整段九碼長」的說法難道不是源自美式足球嗎？

不是！因為在…美式足球裡，你必須進攻「十」碼才有機會得分。

我認為那個說法起源於第二次世界大戰。那時戰鬥機上的彈鏈是九碼長，當駕駛決定將機上所有的子彈都往一個目標發射時，相當於他把「整段九碼長」都給了那個目標。

正確，但是能不能拜託大家專心點，我們只剩兩分鐘了。所以，進攻的那一隊在

生活篇｜信仰篇｜表達篇｜外來語篇｜文明篇

其它篇

331

they can either try to score six points with a touchdown, or to get three points by kicking the ball through the goal post. After a touchdown you can then go for the extra point.

Chi　What does "kickoff" mean? I hear that people using that term all the time. When do players get to kick the ball?

Paul　The kickoff is at the beginning and the half. It starts the game.

Chi　Honestly, the reason I agreed to watch the game with you guys is because of the halftime show. I heard it's going to be huge this year. So I'm here ready to tackle the kickoffs and scrimmage the touchdowns. I'm gunna go the whole nine yards!

Mike looks at Paul.

Paul　Close enough.

Paul & Mike　(Raise arms) SUPER BOWL!

場上推進十碼後，他們可以把球帶到敵方的得方區觸地拿到六分，也可以將球踢進球門拿三分。在觸地得點後還有額外的分數可以拿。

「開球」是什麼意思？我常聽到別人使用這個詞。什麼時候球員能踢球啊？

開球這個動作發生在比賽開始跟中場的時候。它標示比賽的開始。

老實說，我會同意跟你們一起看球賽的理由是因為中場的表演節目，我聽說今年會做得很大，所以我已經準備好要擁抱開球跟練習賽達陣，我要從頭到尾給它全部看完！

麥可望向保羅。

差不多了啦。

（舉起手臂）超級盃！

 單字

☑ Super Bowl [`supɚ `bol] *n.* 超級盃、職業美式足球的冠軍賽。這場一年一度的盛大賽事通常在二月的第一個星期天舉行，這天稱為 Super Bowl Sunday。

☑ down [daʊn] *n.* 一次進攻機會。進攻隊伍以跑陣或傳球的方式向敵方的得分區推進，當持球者被擒倒，比賽即暫停，這就是一檔的進攻機會。

☑ advance [əd`væns] **v.** 向前移動、推進

☑ touchdown [`tʌtʃˌdaʊn] **n.** 達陣、觸地得分

☑ kickoff [`kɪkˌɔf] **n.** （足球／美式足球中）開球

☑ tackle [`tæk!] **n.** **v.** 擒抱、抱住帶球跑之對方球員並扭倒的動作

☑ scrimmage [`skrɪmɪdʒ] **n.** 練習賽、非正式的比賽

數字之二：The Whole 9 Yards

以前在紐約上州工作時，一位我很喜歡的老闆，她的口頭禪其中一則是："the whole 9 yards"（結果現在每次有人用到這句話，我就不由自主地想起她！）。既然這個系列是在講英文裡含有數字的俏皮話，我就來解釋一下「這整個九碼長」到底是指什麼。

首先，yard，1 碼，是 0.9144 公尺，所以一碼大約是快一公尺，9 碼差不多 8 公尺。The whole 9 yards 的講法，最流行的解釋是來自第二次世界大戰，那時空軍戰機上配備的機關槍，使用的彈藥匣是 9 碼長，在戰況激烈的當時，美軍攻擊敵人之前，會大喊："Give 'em the whole nine yards!"（給他們嚐嚐這整段九碼長（的子彈）！）今天，如果有人跟你說：「哇，我剛買的那部新車配備有 GPS、自動預熱座椅、電動天窗、iPhone 連接系統…The whole 9 yards!」他指的是這部車「應有盡有、一應俱全」，也就是「全部」的意思。

美式英文中還有另外兩個意義相近的用語，一個是 "the works"，再一個是 "the whole shebang"。跟 "the whole 9 yards" 一樣，前面都要加冠詞 the。The works 常在菜單上可以看到，譬如說點菜時，客人若想要所有的配料及澆料，就可以跟侍者說：The works, please.

Shebang 這個字唸作[ʃə`bæŋ]，拼法也很好記，就是 she + bang（請見瑞奇・馬汀的暢銷歌 She Bangs）。The whole shebang 這個用語通常用在比較花俏、誇張的場合，舉例來講，某位朋友想要開一個很盛大的派對，她請了高級廚師、調酒員、樂團、舞者、魔術師，現場裝飾了鮮花、氣球、燈光、冰雕、香檳塔…，講得累了的時候，你就可以在句子的尾巴總結一句：You know, the whole shebang！

生活篇　信仰篇　表達篇　外來語篇　文明篇

其它篇

333

74 My 2 Cents

Chi is sitting pensively at her writing desk. 季薇若有所思地坐在書桌前。

Paul   Penny for your thoughts.

妳在想什麼？

Chi   (Sighs) I'm worried about my writing career. I'm not sure if it's sustainable. What if I can't find a publisher? What happens between projects? Can I make a livable wage?

（歎氣）我在煩惱我的寫作生涯。我不確定這份工作是否能持久。要是我找不到出版社怎麼辦？在企劃案之間我要靠什麼吃飯？我賺得到足夠的錢來維持生計嗎？

Paul   That's it?

就這樣？

Chi   (Insulted) What do you mean, that's it?

（不甘受辱）你什麼意思，就這樣？

Paul   (Cool and collected) You want my two cents?

（一副冷靜沈著的模樣）想聽聽我的淺見？

Chi   Sure.

好吧。

Paul   You need to keep your day job until you become established. The first few things you write you'll have to give away as a taste to readers. When the readers come back then you can hit'em with a new sticker price. Don't forget, J.K. Rowling raised her daughter and worked when she wrote *Harry Potter*. Nicholas Sparks was selling pharmaceutical products before *The Notebook*. It takes time for a writing career to grow before it'll bear fruit.

妳需要繼續做妳白天的工作，直到妳的地位穩固下來。妳前面寫的東西必須免費送給讀者，讓他們有機會欣賞妳的作品；當人們想要看更多時妳再索取費用。別忘了，J. K.羅琳寫《哈利‧波特》的時候一邊撫養她的女兒並一邊工作。在《手札情緣》出版之前，尼可拉斯‧史派克曾是藥品銷售人員。寫作這項職業需要投注時間去培養才會見到成果。

Chi	I think that if I continue to create a great product, people will buy it. But what if my ideas run out?	我認為，如果我能持續創造出很棒的產品，人們會願意購買。但要是我的創意用盡了怎麼辦？
Paul	You have ideas?	妳這人有創意？
Chi	(Annoyed) YES!	（被激怒）當然有！
Paul	Then come to me. MY ideas are endless. We'll write together. Before you know it we'll have a finished product. Afterwards we'll move on to the next project and the one after that. The key is to quit worrying, quit complaining, and just do the work.	那就來問我，我有無窮無盡的點子。我們會一起寫作，很快我們就可以做出成品。在那之後我們會繼續做下一個企劃，然後接著另一個。關鍵是停止煩惱、停止抱怨、專心寫作。
Chi	It's hard not to worry.	不煩惱很難。
Paul	Oh, boohoo yah cry baby... worrying about running out of ideas is pointless. Just borrow old ideas from the thousands of books already out there and then tweak it, modify it, and mix and match it with other ideas in order to create unique combinations. I'll always be here to help you.	噢，嗚嗚，妳這個愛哭鬼…。擔心點子會用完是沒有意義的。妳可以從成千上百的書籍裡找出舊的點子，加以調整、改造，把它跟其他不同的點子搭配起來，創造出獨特的組合。我永遠會在妳身邊幫助妳。
Chi	That'd be nice... writing together... in English!	那會很美妙…一起寫作…用英文寫！
Paul	Whatever. Translate it, don't translate it. It doesn't matter. JUST WRITE! We can do romance, sci-fi, comedy, political thriller...	什麼都行。翻譯或不翻譯，都是其次。總之寫就對了！我們可以寫愛情、科幻、喜劇、政治驚悚…。
Chi	I don't know how to write a political thriller!	我不知道怎麼寫政治驚悚類的小説！
Paul	You are a writer or not? Research it then write about it. That's what writers do, they	妳到底是不是個作家啊？妳對某個主題進行研究然後針

生活篇 — 信仰篇 — 表達篇 — 外來語篇 — 文明篇

其它篇

335

write about everything and anything everyday... all the time! What's wrong with you? If you spent as much time writing as you spent about worrying you'd be done with your first book by now.	對它來寫，這就是作家的工作，他們每一天每一刻裡都在寫，而寫的可能是關於任何事！妳是怎麼搞的？如果妳把妳花在擔心煩惱上的時間都拿來寫作的話，妳第一本書早就寫完了。
Chi　(Snide) So that's your two cents? Continue to work and write when I can?	（不屑）所以這就是你的個人淺見？繼續我日間的工作並盡量找出時間寫作？
Paul　Actually my advice is worth more like FIVE cents! Now, go write another page.	事實上我給妳的是我個人寶貴的意見！現在，再去寫一篇。
Chi　No break?	不能休息一下喔？
Paul　Does Stephen King takes breaks?	史蒂芬・金有在休息的嗎？
Chi　Guess not.	我猜沒有。
Paul　Of course Stephen King takes breaks ... he's rich. You're not!... Back to work!	當然史蒂芬・金有休息時間…人家有錢，妳沒有…給我回去寫作！

 # 單字

- ☑ pensively [`pɛnsɪvlɪ] *adv.* 沈思地
- ☑ pharmaceutical [ˌfɑrməˋsjutɪkl̩] *adj.* 藥劑的、製藥的
- ☑ tweak [twik] *v.* 做細微的改變、稍加調整
- ☑ snide [snaɪd] *adj.* 譏刺的、挖苦的
- ☑ collected [kəˋlɛktɪd] *adj.* 鎮定的、冷靜的
- ☑ bear [bɛr] *v.* 結（果實）、生出
- ☑ thriller [`θrɪlɚ] *n.* 驚悚作品（如電影、小說等）

片語

☑ <u>mix and match</u> 把風格不同但相襯的物品（例如：衣飾、傢俱等）搭配在一起

日常會話

☑ <u>A penny for your thoughts.</u> 告訴我你在想什麼。

數字之三：My 2 Cents

　　Cent，是美國目前流通貨幣中最小的單位，符號寫法為 ¢（註一），相當於中文裡的「分」，100 個 cents 才等於一元美金，難怪有些人不小心掉了幾個 cents 在地上，連撿也懶得撿，所以如果你到美國超市外面的停車場上到處仔細找，很容易就可以收集一些美分起來。

　　因為它的價值如此地微小，正如中國人有著類似謙虛地表示意見的說法：「容在下淺見…」美國人用兩美分，2 cents，來代表「自己提出的見解有多麼地微不足道、今天這樣講完全是為你好，僅供參考」。

　　一般常見的用法包括：在句首一發表意見前一的 "To add／put in／throw in my 2 cents, …"、"If I may give you my 2 pennies' worth, …"、"Here is my 2 cents …（註二）"、以及在句末一意見發表完畢一加上的 "Just my 2 cents!"

　　雖然大部份人在用這個說法的時候，都是抱著「我的意見沒什麼價值喔，你要聽不聽都無所謂」的禮貌態度，但是老實說，大概有 20% 的機率，說這句話的人其實是利用這個說法表面上不想引發爭議的保護殼，來達到實際影響對方作法的目的，或是藉機會，來雞婆一下、提供對方根本原來就沒想要的意見。也難怪有人在發覺說這句話的人的真正心態後，會大聲反擊："Not interested. Keep your 2 cents!!"（沒興趣啦，你這兩美分就省了吧!!）

註一 美國人用 ¢ 這個符號，剛好跟代表美元，Dollar，的 "$" 相反，是寫在數字的後面，不是前面。例如：2 cents 的標價寫法是 2¢，相較於 2 美元是寫作 $2。

註二 注意英文中「多少錢」都視為單數，所以相接的動詞要用「單數的動詞」，正確說法是：Here "is" my 2 cents，而不是 Here are my 2 cents.

Paul and Chi are in the toy section of the mall.　保羅和季薇在購物商場的玩具部門。

	(Paul grabs a small box from the shelf and starts moving towards Chi, while imitating an electronic sound.)	（保羅從架上拿起一個小盒子朝季薇接近，口中並模擬出電子儀器的聲音。）
Chi	What are you doing?	你在幹嘛？
Paul	What am I doing? You don't know what this is?	我在幹嘛？妳不知道這是什麼嗎？
Chi	(Innocently) What is it?	（無辜地）那是什麼？
Paul	It's a tricorder.	這是一個三度儀。
Chi	What's a tricorder? Does it have anything to do with me?	什麼是三度儀？跟我有關係嗎？
Paul	DOES IT HAVE ANYTHING TO DO WITH YOU? Give me your iPhone. (Chi complies.) THIS, is the modern-day equivalence of a tricorder.	跟妳有關係嗎？把妳的 iPhone 給我。（季薇照做。）這個，就等於是現代版的三度儀。
Chi	Huh?	嗄？
Paul	Members of Starship Enterprise used tricorders to scan their surroundings and gather data for analysis. They went where no one has gone before, using technology that is only now emerging!	星艦企業號上的成員使用三度儀來掃描周遭的環境與收集資料以供分析。他們到達人類足跡從未踏至的領域，使用的是一直到最近才出現的科技！

Chi	*Star Trek*, again?	又是《星際奇航記》喔？
Paul	What do you mean "again"? *Star Trek* has planted the creative seeds of nerdom the world 'round. They saw it on the show first and then engineered it into a real thing. (Pushes button on shirt) "Chirp. Transporter room, one to beam up." The communicator on the show is basically the prototype of a cell phone and bluetooth.	妳什麼意思，「又是」？《星際奇航記》在世界各處種下了科技創意的種籽，科學家和工程師們在電視上看到這些東西以後，把它們做成真的產品。（壓了一下衣服上的按鈕）「吱啾，光波輸送室，準備傳送一人上去。」劇中的通訊器基本上就是手機與藍牙技術的原型。
Chi	It is? Wow, okay. Since you mentioned teletransportation, how soon will we see that happening?	是嗎？哇，好吧，既然你提到了遠距運輸，我們什麼時候可以見到這項技術成真？
Paul	TELE - POR - TATION has already been successfully done by scientists using a photon. After that they will work on an electron, proton, neutron, hydrogen atom, and so on until they reach the testing stages for organic material.	科學家已經成功地運用遠距-傳-輸的技術把光子送到另一地。接下來他們會嘗試傳送電子、質子、中子、氫原子等等，直到能夠開始傳輸有機物體的測試階段。
Chi	So it's going to be a while.	所以那還要再等一陣子。
Paul	You just wait, one of these days we are going to be able to teleport humans.	妳等著瞧吧，有天我們一定可以傳送人類。
Chi	And when that day comes I'll have breakfast in Europe with you, lunch in Asia with my family, and then dinner with your family in America.	當那天到來我就可以與你在歐洲共進早餐，跟我家人在亞洲吃午飯，然後在美國跟你的家人一起用晚餐。
Paul	It's a date. By the way, I'm getting the *Star Trek* special edition drinking glass set.	就這麼約好囉。噢對了，我要買這套《星際奇航記》的

生活篇 信仰篇 表達篇 外來語篇 文明篇

其它篇

339

	紀念版玻璃杯組。
Chi	<u>While you're at it</u>, get the tricorder replica, too. That way, when our kids ask us what it is, we can tell them it was from the pre-smart-phone era.	那你就順便一起把這個三度儀的複製品也買下來吧。這樣，以後當我們的小孩問這個東西是什麼的時候，我們可以跟他們解釋，這個是智慧型手機還沒發明以前的一種儀器。
Paul	Then they would ask, "What's a smart phone? And what does it have to do with me?"	然後他們就會問說：「什麼是智慧型手機？跟我有關係嗎？」

 ## 單字

☑ nerdom [`nɝdəm] *n.*（俚語）由書呆子主宰的世界、書呆子王國。Nerdom 即 nerd 加 kingdom 的字尾所衍生的字，nerd 指熱衷於科學或數學等知識，但缺乏社交技能的人。

☑ prototype [`protə͵taɪp] *n.* 原型

☑ teleportation [͵tɛləpor`teʃən] *n.* 瞬間移動物體、將某物分解成訊息或微小粒子，在另一地重組的遠距傳輸方式

☑ photon [`fotɑn] *n.* 光子

☑ proton [`protɑn] *n.* 質子

☑ neutron [`njutrɑn] *n.* 中子

☑ hydrogen [`haɪdrədʒən] *n.* 氫（元素）、氫氣

☑ replica [`rɛplɪkə] *n.* 複製品、摹本

日常會話

- ☑ It's a date. 約好囉！／就這麼說定了，到時候見！
- ☑ While you're at it, ... 在你做件事的時候（請順便做另外一件事情）。

這個東西的英文是什麼之一：

說說看，圖中這個儀器的英文是什麼？

答案是 "tricorder"。

Tricorder 的中文翻譯為「三度儀」，源自於美國的著名科幻電視影集《星艦奇航記》（*Star Trek*）。劇中的航員，初次到達新的星球時，會使用這種儀器來偵測地表面的生態情形，它也可用來紀錄和分析所讀到的數據。艦上的醫生也會使用 tricorder 來診斷病人，但是醫療用的 tricorder 跟科學家用的稍有不同，它多了一個小小的手持掃瞄器，可以跟主體分開。

Tricorder 這個由影視編劇人員創造出來的單字，是由兩部份組成：形容「三個」的字首 "tri-"，和 "recorder"（紀錄器），它的三個主要功能為掃描地理、氣候與生物的資料。

臺灣人比較熟悉的應該是 *Star Trek* 的第二個系列《銀河飛龍》（*Star Trek: The Next Generation*），台視在民國八十年間有播出過，劇情裡的艦長，就是我們熟悉臉孔的光頭名演員派崔克·史都華（Patrick Stewart）。最近好萊塢重新又把 *Star Trek* 搬上大銀幕，翻拍第一個系列，也就是它最原始的影集，美國人為了把這部份跟其他續集區分，稱其為 *Star Trek: The Original Series*，臺灣片商則將之譯為《星際爭霸戰》。

原始系列的星際爭霸戰帶給美國人許多經典的台詞，最有名的要算是具外星 Vulcan 血統、耳朵尖尖的副艦長史巴克，在銀幕前舉起手，中指和無名指分開的敬禮語 "Live long and prosper"。附帶一個在星艦迷間流傳的笑話：如果看見有穿紅制服的艦員，就代表那個人接下來在劇中一定很快會死！艦內不同部門的人員穿著不同顏色以示區別，像是指揮官是黃綠色、科學家和醫官是藍色，而安全人員則是紅色，在登陸外星球的時候，穿著紅衣（red shirt）的警衛人員經常都是第一個遭遇橫禍的角色。

YouTube 影片連結：http://www.youtube.com/watch?v=L9GTjHEsdhY 讀者可以從中看到史巴克使用 tricorder 研判星球上生物文化的進展。

Paul	(Whines.) We've been here for an hour. HURRY UP. Pick a dress and let's go!	（抱怨）我們已經在這個地方耗了一個鐘頭。動作快點，挑件裙子，我們走人了啦！
Chi	Relax, babe. These are the final two: the one with sunflowers and the one with polka dots. Which one do you think I should get?	放輕鬆，寶貝。我最喜歡這兩件：一件有向日葵的圖案，另一件是小圓點印花，你覺得我應該買哪一件？
Paul	Sunflowers. You'll look sexy in a classic summer floral pattern.	向日葵。妳要是穿上經典的夏日花卉圖樣看起來會很性感。
Chi	Really? But I like polka dots. They are back in fashion again!	真的嗎？但是我喜歡小圓點，這種花色又開始流行了耶！
Paul	I like sunflowers, it reminds me of home.	我喜歡向日葵，它讓我聯想起以前我住的小鎮。
Chi	Micky Mouse's girlfriend Minnie wears a red polka dot dress with a matching bow, and she looks lovely!	米老鼠米奇的女朋友米妮穿著一件紅色的圓點洋裝，頭上戴了相配的蝴蝶結，她看來很漂亮！
Paul	First off, Minnie is just Micky's cross-dressing older brother Oswald and second, that dress in your hand is not	第一，米妮其實是米奇有變裝癖的哥哥奧斯華，然後第二，妳手中的洋裝不是紅色

red, it's black-and-white.

的，它是黑白相間。（作者按：迪士尼曾經畫過一隻名叫幸運兔奧斯華（Oswald the Lucky Rabbit）的動畫主角，這個角色成為後來米老鼠的前身。）

Chi　Marilyn Monroe wore a black-and-white polka dot bikini and she couldn't be sexier.

瑪麗‧蓮夢露穿過一件黑白相間的小圓點比基尼泳裝，她看起來再性感也不過了！

Paul　I don't even like Marilyn Monroe, she was overrated.

我不喜歡瑪麗‧蓮夢露，一般大眾對她的評價過高。

Chi　How about Elizabeth Taylor or Lucille Ball? These iconic ladies were among some of the polka dot's chief proponents. Kate Middleton recently wore a polka dot dress to Warner Brothers Studios in London. She looked so refined.

那麼伊莉莎白‧泰勒或露西‧鮑兒呢？這些偶像級的女星都是小圓點印花的愛好者。凱特王妃最近穿了一件圓點花色的連身裙拜訪倫敦的華納兄弟製片廠，她看來十分高雅。

Paul　You're trying to persuade an American by using British royalty as an example? Not a good idea. I am not against polka dots. Your closet just needs more color.

妳想用英國皇室成員的例子來說服一個美國人？沒用的啦。我不反對圓點花樣，只是妳的衣櫥需要多一點色彩。

Chi　But black-and-white goes with everything.

可是黑白相間跟什麼都搭。

Paul　Everything you have is black-and-white. WHERE'S THE COLOR? Your wardrobe is boring. I own a pink shirt. Pink, Chi, PINK!

妳擁有的每一件都是黑白相間。顏色都到哪裡去了？妳的衣著有夠乏味，連我都有一件粉紅色的襯衫，粉紅色，季薇，粉紅色的吶！

生活篇　信仰篇　表達篇　外來語篇　文明篇

其它篇

343

Chi	But, I can even wear this dress to work! (Pauses) Hey, listen.	可是，我甚至還可以穿這件去上班！（突然停頓）嘿，你聽。
Paul	What?	什麼？
Chi	Is that Frank Sinatra?	那是法蘭克・辛納屈嗎？
Frank	(Crooning) Suddenly I saw polka dots and moooooonbeams...	（柔情地唱著）突然間我看到小圓花點和月光…
Chi	It's a sign. I'm getting this dress.	這是老天的暗示，我要買這件洋裝。
Paul	Honey, it's YOUR dress. You get whatever YOU WANT.	蜜糖，這是妳的洋裝，妳想要什麼花色就買什麼花色。
Chi	"May I have the next dance?"	「我能有榮幸跟你跳下一支舞嗎？」
Paul	(Takes Chi's hand and swings her around.) Of course, my little pug-nosed dream!	（牽起季薇的手，並拉著她旋轉。）當然囉，我的扁鼻子夢中情人！

❤ 單字

☑ **dress** [drɛs] *n.* 連身裙、一件式的洋裝裙

☑ **floral** [`flɔrəl] *adj.* 花的、以花裝飾的

☑ **bow** [bo] *n.* 蝴蝶結

☑ **cross-dressing** [`krɔs`drɛsɪŋ] *adj.* 有變裝癖的、喜穿異性服飾的

☑ **overrated** [,ovɚ`retɪd] *adj.* 評價過高的、其實並不像大多數人說得那麼好的

☑ **proponent** [prə`ponənt] *n.* 支持者、愛好者

☑ refined [rɪ`faɪnd] **adj.** 優雅的、高尚的

☑ wardrobe [`wɔrd͵rob] **n.** 衣櫥；個人擁有的全部服裝

☑ croon [krun] **v.** 柔情地唱、輕哼

☑ swing [swɪŋ] **v.** 以弧線擺動、轉動

☑ pug-nosed [`pʌg͵nozd] **adj.** 獅子鼻的、塌鼻的

這個東西的英文是什麼之二：

這種小圓點的印花圖案英文是什麼？

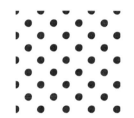

答案是 "polka dot"。

我常常覺得，英文是一種精確的語言，它對物品種類很講究細分，幾乎每一個東西都有一個相對應的英文字；中文則比較像是一種組合式的語言，我們多用既有的形容詞與名詞來稱呼新的事物。拿圖中這種印花圖案來說，中文裡我們就叫小圓（花）點，英文呢，當然就有它自己一個獨特的名字：polka dot。

Polka dot 通常由大小一致、規則排列的圓點組成，因為它在視覺上創造了輕鬆、歡愉的感受，被廣泛應用於青少年服飾、泳衣、玩具和傢俱上。我會學到這個名詞，是某天和一位年輕的女同事聊天時，她提到最喜愛的花色就叫 polka dot！

Polka dot 的名稱由來也挺有趣，它跟同名的波卡舞（polka／polka dance），其實並無直接的關係，只是剛好在十九世紀後期，這種小圓點的印花在英國服裝界開始流行時，正巧也是波卡舞在英國大盛其道的時期，所以人們就稱這個花色圖案為 polka dot。

波卡舞是一種輕快節奏的舞蹈，根據我個人的猜測，男女雙方在跳波卡舞時不斷有轉圈的動作，正符合了波卡圓點帶給人的視覺觀感，可能就是為什麼 polka dot 被取了相同的名字吧？美國 50 年代的經典音樂電影《國王與我》（*The King and I*），其中一幕高潮戲，就是光頭的暹羅國王跟英國教師安娜大跳波卡舞的那段，有興趣的讀者不妨找 DVD 來欣賞一番！

生活篇 信仰篇 表達篇 外來語篇 文明篇

其它篇

At the traffic light. Paul looks out the windshield and points at a small object in the sky.

在紅綠燈前，保羅從擋風玻璃內向外看並指著天空中的某個小物體。

Paul	Do you know what that is?	妳知道那個是什麼嗎？
Chi	That thing? I don't know. What do you call it?	那個東西？我不知道，你怎麼稱呼它？
Paul	It's a "blimp."	那是一個「軟式飛船」。
Chi	A "blimp?" That sounds funny!	「軟式飛船」？聽起來怪有趣的！
Paul	It does, doesn't it? A blimp is a little like a hot air balloon. They both use an envelope to help them float. But a blimp doesn't use heated air to be buoyant. It uses helium.	對吧？軟式飛船有些類似熱氣球，這兩者都使用一個大袋子來幫助它們飄浮，只是軟式飛船用的不是加熱的空氣，而是氦氣來創造浮力。
Chi	Helium. Uh oh, high school chemistry.	氦氣。呃，喔，高中化學課。
Paul	That's right, Missy. How's your high school chemistry?	那就對啦，小姐。妳的高中化學唸得怎樣？
Chi	All right, I guess. I remember helium is on the right side of the periodic table.	我猜還可以吧。我記得氦這個元素在週期表的右邊。
Paul	Not bad. So you know that hydrogen is on the left and it's even lighter than helium.	還不錯喔。所以妳應該知道，氫是在週期表左邊，而且氫比氦還輕。
Chi	Ah, I do remember that.	啊，我的確記得。
Paul	There's another type of airship that looks similar to a blimp but has a rigid frame,	另外一種外型類似軟式飛船，但具有像船身骨架那種

like a keel in a boat. It's called a "zeppelin." They used to fill zeppelins with hydrogen. Compared to helium, not only hydrogen is cheaper to mass produce, it also provides more lift since it's lighter. However, hydrogen has a deadly drawback: it's highly flammable.

Chi I had a bad feeling when you used the past tense: you say they "used" to fill zeppelins with hydrogen. So there was an accident?

Paul Yes, a very famous one called the Hindenburg disaster. You can look up the video on YouTube when we get home. It caught on fire, and within seconds, it was completely engulfed. Almost all of the passengers on the airship died.

Chi Oh, no.

Paul The accident ended the commercial use of large airships. Nowadays, only a handful of blimps and zeppelins are left, and most of them are used for corporate advertisement. I wonder what it is like to ride in an airship. Does a blimp ride differently than a zeppelin? Would they let us drive it?

Chi This summer we could go over to Santa Rosa.

堅硬架構的飛艇,叫做「齊柏林飛船」。以前的人用氫氣來充灌齊柏林飛船。跟氦氣比起來,氫氣不但能夠以較低的成本大量生產,而且因為它比較輕,它還可以提供更多的浮力。然而,氫氣的一個致命的缺點是:高度易燃。

我聽到你剛剛用過去式的時候,就有一種不好的預感:你說「以前」人們用氫氣充灌齊柏林飛船。是曾經發生過意外嗎?

是的,一場非常有名的意外,叫做「興登堡災難事件」。妳回家後可以在YouTube 上調出它的紀錄片。它著火後數秒內就完全被大火吞噬,幾乎所有飛船上的乘客都罹難了。

喔,不。

那場意外結束了使用大型飛船承載旅客的商業活動。今天世界上只剩幾艘軟式和齊柏林飛船還在,而它們多數用來幫企業作廣告。我很好奇搭乘飛船是什麼感覺,在軟式飛船上跟在齊柏林飛船上面的乘坐感不同嗎?這些公司會讓我們駕駛他們的飛船嗎?

這個夏天我們可以去聖塔羅莎市。

生活篇　信仰篇　表達篇　外來語篇　文明篇

其它篇

Paul	Why?	為什麼？
Chi	They have hot air balloon rides.	那裡提供熱氣球之旅。
Paul	One balloon?	就一座熱氣球？
Chi	Yeah so?	是啊，怎樣？
Paul	Back in my home town, we have a hot air balloon festival where hundreds of balloons fill the sky. The problem is they only go up and down. The pilot has no control over the other directions. If I can't pilot a blimp, then I'd rather learn how to fly a plane instead.	我以前住的鎮上每年都會舉辦熱氣球慶典，天際上充滿了數百顆的氣球。問題是它們只能上升或下降，駕駛員無法控制氣球往其他方向走。如果我不能操控軟式飛船，那我寧願學怎麼開飛機。
Chi	Ok, I'll keep looking.	好吧，我會繼續找找看。

♥ 單字

☑ buoyant [ˈbɔɪənt] *adj.* 有浮力的

☑ helium [ˈhilɪəm] *n.* 氦、氦氣

☑ missy [ˈmɪsɪ] *n.* （非正式用語）小姐、用來叫年輕女孩的親暱稱呼，有時帶有輕佻的意味

☑ the periodic table [ðə ˌpɪrɪˈɑdɪk ˈtebl] *n.* （元素的）週期表

☑ keel [kil] *n.* （船的）龍骨、底部支架

☑ zeppelin [ˈzɛpəlɪn] *n.* 齊柏林飛船。得名於德國發明家及飛船設計者齊柏林（Graf Ferdinand von Zeppelin）

☑ drawback [ˈdrɔˌbæk] *n.* 缺點

☑ past tense [ˈpæst ˈtɛns] *n.* 過去式、過去時態

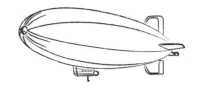

 ## 這個東西的英文是什麼之三

那個在天上飄浮的東西，英文裡叫什麼？

答案是 "blimp"。

美國的天際裡，除了飛機外，偶而會看到一艘展示廣告的氣艇，在天上緩慢地飛行，它就是 blimp！

Blimp 這個英文的由來，主要有兩種說法，第一種是說 blimp 是一個擬聲字，用來形容手指彈在氣艇外表上發出的聲音；另外一個說法是，原本英國海軍在實驗這種軟式飛行器時，初始階段的一批成品被稱為 A-limp（單字 limp 的意思為「軟的」），然而第二批較成功，叫做 B-limp，之後這個名稱就被沿用下來。

Blimp 的飛行原理是在一個大尼龍袋中灌滿比空氣輕的氦氣（helium），利用其浮力來上升。氣球的下方裝置駕駛艙和噴射引擎，尾部加裝翼，駕駛員由操控這些部份來控制進行方向。在大氣球的裡面，前後還有兩個氣囊，如果要降低飛行的高度，就往氣囊裡加灌空氣，如果要升高，就釋放空氣出去（因為空氣比氦氣重），基本原理跟潛水艇利用輸入和排放壓艙水來下降或上升類似。

美國最為一般大眾熟悉的 blimp 廣告來自橡膠輪胎公司 Goodyear，這家公司從 1925 年起，一直到第二次世界大戰期間，為美軍政府製造了數百架以 blimp 為基本架構的軟／硬式飛行器，目的是監控和保護海岸線上的船艦。由於 blimp 主要是用氣體的浮力來飛行，不像飛機或直升機需要消耗大量的燃料，所以可以待在空中較長的時間。今天它們多被用來作為天空上的商業廣告、拍攝球賽及新聞事件、以及學術紀錄和研究。

在 2012 年的卡通電影《羅雷司》（The Lorax）」中，blimp 有著驚鴻一瞥的現身：飾演邪惡市長／企業董事長的 Mr. O'Hare，他的辦公室就位於一艘超級 blimp 的座艙裡，漂浮在半空，日以繼夜地監視市民。在電影的末段，他還駕駛這個 blimp 來追逐男女主角們，真的很有趣呢！

生活篇

信仰篇

表達篇

外來語篇

文明篇

其它篇

It is Saturday night. Paul and Chi are getting ready for their *Star Trek* marathon. After putting in the first DVD, Paul turns on the closed captioning.
週六晚上。保羅和季薇準備開始連續整晚觀賞《星際奇航記》的影集。在放入第一片 DVD 後，保羅開啟顯示字幕的功能。

Chi	Thanks for turning on the subtitles. I noticed that you have been doing it every time we sit down and watch TV together. It's sweet of you.	謝謝你把字幕開起來。我有注意到，每次我們一起坐下來看電視你都會這麼做，你對我真好。
Paul	I did it for myself! I like to have the captions on.	我是為了我自己才這麼做的啦！我喜歡有字幕。
Chi	I thought you found the captioning distracting.	我以為你覺得字幕讓人分心。
Paul	I did at first, but now I actually find it helpful. I like to know what is being said when I have the TV on mute or when characters whisper and it is hard to hear what they are saying. The captions allow me to understand what's going on without pausing the action or rewinding it if I missed something. Plus, in recent years the quality of the subtitles has improved tremendously. It wasn't always like this.	我一開始的確是那麼覺得，可是現在我發現它其實幫助很大。當我把電視消音或劇中人物在講悄悄話、很難聽清楚對話的時候，我會想知道他們在說什麼。有了字幕的輔助，即使我忽略某個細節，我也不需要按暫停或迴轉就能了解正在發生什麼事。加上，最近這幾年字幕大大地有改進。它不是一直都像現在這樣子的。

Chi	What was it like before?	那以前是什麼樣子？
Paul	Closed captioning has had a bad habit of using scrolling text on a black background. Placed at the bottom of the screen. It often covered too much of the scene and was difficult to read since it was moving. The dialogue was usually not in sync with the action and there was a lot of mistakes between what was actually being said and the text being displayed. Overall it was more distracting than helpful.	電視的附加字幕以前常在黑色的背景上使用轉動的文字。它被置於螢幕下方，通常蓋掉太多部份的場景，而且因為它一直動所以很難讀。對話老是跟動作不一致，還有實際講出跟顯示的話之間有很多的錯誤，整體來說它教人分心多於助益。
Chi	Oh, yeah. I remember seeing that style of "scrolling" captions a few years ago. They were like these tapes that roll around. As the new lines appear the old lines disappear at the top. You are right, today's pop-ups are much better.	噢，對耶，我記得幾年前有看過那種「轉軸式」的字幕。它們像捲繞的環帶，新的台詞一出現，舊的台詞就被擠到上方消失。你說的對，目前一段一段跳出來的字幕好太多了。
Paul	The first time I ever see pop-up captions was when I was a kid. Once a month my family and I would go to the opera. Many of the shows were in foreign languages, so in order to prevent alienating the American audience a translation was provided just above the stage. It was easy to read and did not distract from what was happening on stage. The captions on a DVD have been carefully produced in the same way. They don't	我第一次看到整段式的字幕是在我還是小孩子的時候。我們家每個月都會定期去看一齣歌劇。很多歌劇是以外國語言表演的，因此為了要拉近美國觀眾，舞台的上方會提供翻譯。那種字幕很容易讀，而且也不會影響舞台上的演出。DVD 上的字幕也做得一樣地細心，它們不像提字機依然使用老式的轉軸

生活篇　信仰篇　表達篇　外來語篇　文明篇

其它篇

351

use that outdated scrolling method used by teleprompters. Although some live shows, first time broadcasts, the news, and the internet still use the earlier style. Hopefully with time, producers will begin to update the format in order to make it a more enjoyable experience. Anything else?

字幕。然而某些現場實況節目、第一手報導、新聞、以及網路上仍在使用這種早期的風格。希望隨著時間演進，媒體的製作人會開始改善這些格式，以使大眾更能享受觀賞的經驗。還有其他的問題嗎？

Chi　No.

沒有了。

Paul　Are you all set to watch a whole season of *Star Trek* with me?

妳準備好跟我一起看整季的《星際奇航記》了嗎？

Chi　Press "play!"

按「放映」！

Paul　I think there is a Klingon closed cation feature. Want to try it? Qapla'!

我想這套 DVD 上附有克林貢語的字幕。想不想試試看？卡普啦！

 ## 單字

- ☑ marathon [`mærəˌθan] ***n.*** 接連地觀賞某一系列影集的娛樂活動，通常持續數小時至一整天

- ☑ tremendously [trɪ`mɛndəslɪ] ***adv.*** 非常地；極大地

- ☑ sync [sɪŋk] ***n.*** 同步；同時發生（sync 是 synchronization 的簡寫）

- ☑ pop-up [`papˌʌp] ***n.*** 整段對話的字幕一次性地出現於螢幕上、消失、另一段對話再出現的模式

- ☑ alienate [`eliəˌnet] ***v.*** 使疏遠

- ☑ teleprompter [`tɛləˌprɔmptɚ] ***n.*** 顯示演講內容或台詞的提字機

☑ Klingon [ˈklɪnˌɑn] **n.** 克林貢語。克林貢人是星際奇航記裡的一個外星種族，個性好戰殘暴，十分注重榮譽。當時與節目合作的語言學家，為劇中角色發展出一整套虛構的語言系統，熱愛此影集的星迷多可朗朗上口一兩句常用的克林貢語。

☑ Qapla' [kɑpˈlɑ] **n.** （克林貢語）意指「成功」。用以祝福某人成功。

 符號與圖像之一：CC

CC，是 Closed Captioning 的縮寫。

你若是有機會看美國的電視頻道，會常常聽到這句："Closed captioning for this program is brought to you by..."（這個節目的字幕服務是由「某某廣告商或某某公司機構」所提供)。美國為了顧及有聽障功能的觀眾，電視皆附有顯示字幕的服務。字幕就字幕，為什麼要說 "closed" 呢？這是因為美國的電視節目並不像台灣都會主動附加字幕，你如果注意看遙控器上面，會有一個按鈕標示 caption 或 subtitle，按下去螢幕上就會顯示[CC]，再連續按幾次你就可以選擇要看的語言，所以 closed 的意思是一般時是關閉的，只有你在選擇使用這項服務時，它才會開　。

我剛搬到美國時，很不習慣看電視時螢幕下方沒字幕，還好後來發現了遙控器上的這個功能，可以「看」到從演員口中講出的話，對學習英文用語和單字幫助極大。除了電視，另一個更棒的語言學習工具是電影的 DVD，在字幕服務外，DVD 還提供了反覆觀賞與暫停的功能，便於加深印象或抄寫筆記用。通常在 DVD 的語言主選單裡有兩種英文字幕，一是 English，另一種是 English for the hearing impaired 或 English SDH（註），這兩種字幕的不同之處在於 English 只顯示劇中人物的對話；而選擇 English for the hearing impaired 時，為幫助聽障人士更加瞭解電影中正在發生什麼事，不單包括了對話部份，也會加入對背景動作或聲音的描述，譬如某人轉動汽車鑰匙、及引擎轟轟作響的噪音等。

註 SDH 是 Subtitled for the Deaf and Hard of hearing 的縮寫。

Paul	What are you reading?	妳在讀什麼？
Chi	An article about the looming fiscal cliff and commentary on the revival of the GOP. But, why do they have an image of an elephant here?	一篇有關即將發生的財政懸崖，以及解析如何重整共和黨的文章。可是我不懂，為什麼他們在這裡放了一張大象的圖片？
Paul	It's their mascot.	那是共和黨的吉祥動物。
Chi	Why an elephant?	為什麼是大象呢？
Paul	Thomas Nast of *Harper's Weekly* alluded to the parties by drawing them symbolically. For some reason it <u>caught on</u> and became very popular. It happens. You can't predict it. You can't explain why. People are just attracted to an idea and <u>grab on to it</u>. Many artists have created mesmerizing images that are quickly infused into our culture. For example, picture a beagle wearing pilot goggles sitting on top of his doghouse...	《哈波週刊》的湯瑪斯・奈斯特用動物來暗喻黨派。由於某種未知的因素，它一下變得流行起來。這類的事情不時發生，你沒法預料，也沒法解釋為什麼。有時候人們突然間受到某個概念吸引，並緊抓住那個點子不放。歷史上許多畫家創造出令人著迷的影像，而這些影像在極短的時間內被我們的文化所吸收進去。舉例來說，想像有隻米格魯獵犬，戴著飛行員的護鏡，坐在牠的狗屋上…
Chi	Snoopy!	史努比！
Paul	Charles Schulz created a world war one	查爾斯・舒茲曾寫過一個故

satire of Germany's most notorious and undefeated fighter pilot, the Red Baron. Although Snoopy never wins in a direct fight with the Baron, he is given credit for never quitting in the face of a formidable opponent. His relentless, never die, never surrender attitude is quintessentially American.

事，嘲諷第一次世界大戰中最惡名昭彰、同時也是最難以擊敗的德國戰鬥機飛行員紅男爵。雖然史努比不曾贏過任何一場與男爵直接對決的戰役，大家都讚揚牠在面對可怕敵人時，從未放棄過的勇敢行為。史努比堅毅、不死心、決不投降的態度，代表了美國精神的本質。

Chi   What about comic books then?

那麼漫畫書哩？

Paul Although comic book creators don't focus on politics as a central theme, neither do they shy away from the drama that comes with addressing philosophical questions emerging in the public eye. Ironman, Batman, Superman, and Spiderman have all taken the time to project their unique world view on American life.

雖然漫畫書的作者們不把政治當作主要的題材，妳仍可以在故事情節裡見到他們對社會上發生的哲學議題所作的著墨。鋼鐵人、蝙蝠俠、超人和蜘蛛人，都針對美國社會提出過一套獨特的世界觀。

Chi   And they all have symbols or logos, too.

而他們也都有自己的象徵符號或標誌。

Paul Right. Symbols represent big ideas that can be viewed as pure, uncompromising, ever present, and enduring points of inspiration; unlike mankind which is flawed, vulnerable, and weak. For example, Bruce Wayne is a man like any other; however, when he wears his emblem, he is no longer Bruce. He becomes something more. The bat is a symbol that strikes fear into the hearts of

沒錯。符號背後所代表的主張，被視為純粹、毫無妥協可能、無所不在、恆久且發人心的論點；不像人類，代表的是滿身缺點、脆弱和不堅強。拿布魯斯·韋恩來講，他不過是一個平凡人。但是一旦戴上蝙蝠俠標誌，他就不再是布魯斯，他變成了一個更強壯、更巨大的個

criminals. The symbol alone can stop a crime before it starts. That is a demonstration of its power.

體。蝙蝠的符號讓罪犯心中充滿恐懼，光是那個符號就能遏止不法行為的發生，這正證明了符號的力量。

Chi So, politicians may come and go, but the symbols remain.

所以說，政治人物來來去去，但符號是不變的。

 # 單字

- ☑ fiscal cliff [`fɪsk! klɪf] **n.** 財政懸崖。這個名詞是用來形容一種特殊的經濟現象：人民的稅負增加、加上政府的支出緊縮，而可能導致國內經濟惡化。學者原本預估美國在 2013 年會出現這種現象，原因包括前總統小布希的減稅措施於 2012 年底失效，以及之前通過的控制預算法案開始正式進入實行階段，這兩個事件同時發生的結果，即所謂的「財政懸崖」。

- ☑ mascot [`mæskɑt] **n.** 象徵某個團體，並被認為能為之帶來好運的人物、動物或東西。

- ☑ allude [ə`lud] **v.** 間接地指出、暗指

- ☑ infuse [ɪn`fjuz] **v.** 注入（思想、概念等）、輸入

- ☑ beagle [`big!] **n.** 米格魯。一種小型獵犬

- ☑ Charles Schulz [`tʃɑrlz `ʃɔlts] 查爾斯•舒茲（1922-2000），著名連環漫畫《花生米》（Peanuts）的作者，漫畫中的角色包括查理•布朗、露西及史努比等。

- ☑ satire [`sætaɪr] **n.** 諷刺、諷刺文學

- ☑ Red Baron [rɛd`bærən] **n.** 紅男爵。第一次世界大戰中著名的德軍戰鬥機飛行員 Manfred von Richthofen 的綽號

- ☑ formidable [`fɔrmɪdəb!] **adj.** （敵人等）可懼的、難以對付的

- ☑ relentless [rɪ`lɛntlɪs] **adj.** 堅持的、毫不鬆懈的

- ☑ emblem [`ɛmbləm] **n.** 標記、徽章

片語

- ☑ catch on （某種行為或商品）變得流行起來
- ☑ grab onto something 緊緊抓住不放某個東西
- ☑ give someone credit for 因為... 而稱讚某人、由於（某人做了某件事）而認為他或她值得受到鼓勵

 ## 符號與圖像之二：Donkey vs. Elephant

　　美國的兩大主要政黨分別是民主黨（Democratic Party）和共和黨（Republican Party）；而民主黨的象徵動物是驢子，而共和黨是大象，但你知道他們為什麼用這兩種動物來代表這兩個黨嗎？

　　印在美國人最常用的二十元紙幣上的第七任總統，安德魯・傑克森（Andrew Jackson）在1828 年角逐總統職位時，其對手稱呼他為 Jackass（看到了嗎？他的姓 Jackson=Jackass）。"Jackass" 的意思是「公驢」，傑克森的政治理念是站在人民的一邊，與代表金錢與權勢的銀行家和政界中的精英份子對立，驢子這個動物象徵辛勤工作的大眾勞力階級，所以他不但不以為意，反而還相當喜歡這個新的概念，把驢子加入他競選用的宣傳海報裡。

　　然而真正把驢子這個影像與民主黨緊密結合在一起的，是一位名叫 Thomas Nast 的政論漫畫家。這位畫家從 1870 年起在報紙上發表了一連串的政治漫畫，用驢子來象徵民主黨，其他的漫畫家後來跟進，漸漸地驢子與民主黨就分不開了。Nest 同時也是為什麼美國人一看到大象就聯想到共和黨的始作庸者，1874 年他在某張圖裡把大象的背上寫了 THE REPUBLICAN VOTE（共和黨的選票），從那之後，大家就一致認為大象是共和黨的代表動物。

　　有人說大象的記性非常好，牠象徵不忘記傳統；另外這種動物一般給人的印象是尊嚴及力量；捍衛傳統、保守、高大有力…，這些特性都跟被暱稱 Grand Old Party（簡寫為 GOP）的共和黨形象符合，因此共和黨=大象就這樣逐漸定型下來。

生活篇 — 信仰篇 — 表達篇 — 外來語篇 — 文明篇

其它篇

After dinner, Chi sits by the table and opens the mail.

用過晚飯後，季薇坐在餐桌旁打開信件。

| Chi | Honey, my co-worker Vicky and her fiancé invited us to their baby shower! | 親愛的，我的同事維琪跟她未婚夫邀請我們參加他們的新生兒派對！ |

| Paul | When is it? | 那是什麼時候？ |

| Chi | It's the first weekend of next month. Neither of us works that day, we should go. I think that it will be fun. However, I have a question. | 下個月的第一個週末。你我那天都不用上班，我們應該去。我覺得那一定會很好玩，但是我有個問題。 |

| Paul | I am listening. | 説啊，我在聽。 |

| Chi | In the card, Vicky uses a symbol between her and Jason's name. I think it means "and." Is that correct? | 在卡片裡面，維琪在她與傑森的名字之間用了一個符號。我猜想它的意思是「和」。對嗎？ |

| Paul | Yes. It is called an ampersand. The ampersand symbol actually derives from the Latin word "et" which means "and" in English. If you look closely, you will see that there is the letter "e," with the vertical line representing the letter "t" right next to it. When people combine two or more letters to form a single symbol, it is called | 對。它叫做 ampersand。這個符號實際上是從拉丁文的 "et" 衍生出來的，et 在英文中的意思是 "and"。如果你注意看，你會發現這個符號裡包含了字母 e，而旁邊的直線代表的就是字母 t。當人們把兩個或更多的字母合 |

a ligature. From the early stages of printing, it was discovered that using ligatures was an economical means to save time and money. Ligatures therefore are a very popular way to implement efficiency into acrimoniously long strings of linguistic babble. Initialisms, abbreviations, and acronyms also fit into this paradigm. Eliminating redundant or vestigial letters is still common today. As a living language, slang such as YOLO, You Only Live Once, would be a relevant example. Ultimately this helps us to communicate complex ideas quickly.

在一起形成單獨一個符號時，這個符號就稱為合體字。自印刷工業早期開始，工人就發現使用合體字是種相當符合經濟的辦法，可節省時間和金錢。因此合體字是將效率注入長篇大論的一個非常受歡迎的作法。字首縮寫法、簡體字和由簡稱構成的新字，也都符合這個模式。刪減重複或無用的字母在今天仍然相當普遍。YOLO 這個最近加入的俚語，就是一個證明語言是活的好例子。歸結到底，這種方法幫助我們快速地溝通複雜的理念。

Chi　Wait, I think I also have seen people write a cross sign between names.

等等，我想我也看過有人在兩個名字之間寫個加號。

Paul　Yes. The plus sign symbol used in mathematics could be used to mean "and" in special cases since it is viewed as an additive principle. As a matter of fact, all of mathematics could be viewed as a reduced language of abbreviated symbols translated from text.

是的。數學上使用的加號，由於被視為是一個加法的原理符號，在特別情況內也可以用來指「和」。事實上所有的數學都可被看作是一種從文字翻譯成簡化符號的濃縮語言。

Chi　So that's why. Now I need to practice how to write an ampersand!

喔，原來如此。現在我需要練習怎麼來寫一個 ampersand！

Paul　There are many ways to write an ampersand.

Ampersand 的寫法有很多

生活篇　信仰篇　表達篇　外來語篇　文明篇　其它篇

359

Some more popular than others but you should become familiar with all of them.

種。有些寫法比其他來的流行，但是你應該熟悉所有的寫法。

Chi　Yes, sir!

遵命！

 單字

- ☑ **baby shower** [ˋbebɪˋʃaʊɚ] ***n.*** 新生兒派對；美國人為即將分娩的準媽媽舉行的宴會。派對中客人會攜帶禮物，也就是讓新生兒的母親「沐浴」在眾多禮物中（to "shower" the expectant mother with gifts），此即為什麼這種宴會被稱作 baby shower 的原因。

- ☑ **ligature** [ˋlɪɡətʃɚ] ***n.*** 合體字

- ☑ **acrimoniously** [ˌækrəˋmonɪəslɪ] ***adv.*** 極端地（幾乎到令人痛苦的程度）

- ☑ **babble** [ˋbæb!] ***n.*** 長篇大論、廢話

- ☑ **initialism** [ɪˋnɪʃəlˌɪzəm] ***n.*** 從一組名詞中取每字字首之字母出來講的縮寫法，例 FBI、HTML 等（注意字母是一個一個分開唸）。

- ☑ **acronym** [ˋækrənɪm] ***n.*** 從一組名詞中取每字字首之字母，組合成另外一個單字的方法，例 "laser"、NASA（讀作 [ˋnæsə] 美國太空總署 National Aeronautics and Space Administration 的簡寫）等。

- ☑ **paradigm** [ˋpærəˌdaɪm] ***n.*** 模型

- ☑ **vestigial** [vɛsˋtɪdʒəl] ***adj.*** 退化的；無用的

- ☑ **additive** [ˋædətɪv] ***adj.*** 加法的

 符號與圖像之三：&

相信大家都有看過以上這個符號，也大概知道它代表 "and"，也就是中文「和／跟／與」

的意思。但是你知道它的英文是什麼嗎？美國人在日常生活中又是怎麼寫&這個符號的呢？

答案是 ampersand，發音為 [ˋæmpɚˌsænd]。

& 這個符號之所以會被叫做 ampersand，背後典故還滿好玩的：以前的英文字母，不像我們今天所熟知的有 26 個，原來有 27 個！而&就是那最後一個。十九世紀初，學校裡兒童朗誦英文字母的時候，唸到最後，如果只講...X, Y, Z, &（當時&就唸 "and"）會讓人聽起來很困惑—X, Y, Z, and... XYZ 和什麼呢？後面還有其它什麼忘記了或沒講的字母嗎？於是老師就教導學生們在&的後面加 "per se and"。Per se 是拉丁文，意思是「本身是」，所以以 "& per se and" 中文的解釋，就是「&，本身是 "and" 這個字」。結果大家唸 and per se and 唸得快一點，就唸成 ampersand，久而久之，它居然就變成自己一個字，即使在後來&被從字母表中淘汰出局，人們也已習慣用 ampersand 來稱呼 & 這個符號了。

說到美國人如何寫這種符號，就不能不提到&的歷史，&原本是從拉丁文 "et" 演變而來的，et 的意思就是「and／和」，以前羅馬人常把 e 跟 t 這兩個字母連在一起寫，慢慢地它就形成今天的 & 書寫符號。現在大多數人在寫的時候，會先寫一個 ε 或 3，然後用一條由上往下的直線，從中貫穿過去（範例 1 與 2）。也有人不用一整條直線，而用上下兩點（範例 3），或上下兩條分開、較短的直線來替代（範例 4）。

另外一個美國人常用來表示 and 的符號，就是數學符號裡的加號+，但是他們在寫的時候，跟單純的十字有一點不同，寫法是先從上向下畫一條直線，然後筆順著原來的線回去，往上再往左轉一圈，向右邊劃出一條水平線做結束，是帶了一點花俏的加號（範例 5）。字體要比其他的正常的字要小很多，而且要跟左右兩邊的字保持適當的距離，以表示出一個獨立的符號。

範例 1　　　範例 2　　　範例 3　　　範例 4　　　範例 5

好書報報

心理學研究顯示，一個習慣養成，至少必須重複21次！
全書規劃30天學習進度表，搭配學習，
不知不覺養成學習英語的好習慣！

▲圖解學習英文文法 三效合一！
◎刺激大腦記憶◎快速掌握學習大綱◎複習迅速

▲英文文法學習元素一次到位！
◎**20**個必懂觀念 ◎**30**個必學句型 ◎**40**個必閃陷阱

▲流行有趣的英語！
◎「那裡有正妹！」
◎「今天我們去看變形金剛3吧！」

作者：朱懿婷
定價：新台幣349元
規格：364頁 / 18K / 雙色印刷

要說出流利的英文，就是需要常常開口勇敢說！

國外打工兼職很流行，如何找尋機會？
怎麼做完整的英文自我介紹，成功promote自己？
獨自出國打工，職場基礎英語對話該怎麼說？
不同國家、不同領域要知道那些common sense？
保險健康的考量要更注意，各國制度大不同？

6大主題 **30**個單元 **120**組情境式對話 **30**篇補給站！
九大學習特色：
■主題豐富多元 ■多種情境演練 ■激發聯想延伸
■增強單字記憶 ■片語邏輯組合 ■例句靈活套用
■塊狀編排歸納 ■舒適閱讀視覺 ■吸收效果加倍

作者：Claire Chang & Melanie Venecamp
定價：新台幣469元
規格：560頁 / 18K / 雙色印刷

好書報報 —職場系列

好書報報－生活系列

愛情之酒甜而苦。兩人喝，是甘露；
三人喝，是酸醋；隨便喝，要中毒。

精選出偶像劇必定出現的**80**個情境，
每個情境－必備單字、劇情會話訓練班、30秒會話教室
讓你跟著偶像劇的腳步學生活英語會話的劇情，
輕鬆自然地學會英語！

作者：伍羚芝
定價：新台幣349元
規格：344頁 / 18K / 雙色印刷

全書中英對照，介紹東西方節慶的典故，
幫助你的英語學習一學得好、學得深入！

用英語來學節慶分為兩大部分－東方節慶&西方節慶
每個節慶共**7**個學習項目：
節慶源由－簡易版、精彩完整版＋實用單字、閱讀測驗、
習俗放大鏡、實用會話、常用單句這麼說、互動單元...

作者：Melanie Venekamp、陳欣慧、倍斯特編輯團隊
定價：新台幣299元
規格：304頁 / 18K / 雙色印刷

用現有的環境與資源，為自己的小寶貝
創造一個雙語學習環境；讓孩子贏在起跑點上！

我家寶貝愛英文，是一本從媽咪懷孕、嬰兒期到幼兒期，
會常用到的單字、對話、必備例句，
並設計單元延伸的互動小遊戲以及童謠，
增進親子關係，也讓家長與孩子一同學習的參考書！

作者：Mark Venekamp & Claire Chang
定價：新台幣329元
規格：296頁 / 18K / 雙色印刷 / MP3

國際化餐飲時代不可不學！
擁有這一本，即刻通往世界各地！

基礎應對 訂位帶位、包場、活動安排、菜色介紹...
前後場管理 服務生Must Know、擺設學問、食物管理...
人事管理 徵聘與訓練、福利升遷、管理者的職責...
狀況處理 客人不滿意、難纏的顧客、部落客評論...

120個餐廳工作情境
100%英語人士的對話用語
循序漸進勤做練習，職場英語一日千里！

作者：Mark Venekamp & Claire Chang
定價：新台幣369元
規格：328頁 / 18K / 雙色印刷 / MP3

這是一本以航空業為背景，
從職員角度出發的航空英語會話工具書。
從職員VS同事 & 職員VS客戶，
兩大角度，呈現100% 原汁原味職場情境！

特別規劃→
以Q&A的方式，英語實習role play
提供更多航空界專業知識的職場補給站
免稅品服務該留意甚麼？ 旅客出境的SOP！
迎賓服務的步驟與重點！違禁品相關規定?！
飛機健檢大作戰有哪些...

作者：Mark Venekamp & Claire Chang
定價：新台幣369元
規格：352頁 / 18K / 雙色印刷 / MP3

Learn Smart! 025

美國人為什麼這麼說？
Why Do Americans Say That?

作　　者／季薇・伯斯特 & Paul James Borst
封面設計／高鐘琪
內頁構成／菩薩蠻有限公司

發 行 人／周瑞德
企劃編輯／倍斯特編輯部
執行編輯／劉俞青
校　　對／丁筠馨 徐瑞璞
印　　製／世和印製企業有限公司
初　　版／2014 年 1 月
定　　價／新台幣 349 元

出　　版／倍斯特出版事業有限公司
電　　話／（02）2351-2007
傳　　真／（02）2351-0887
地　　址／100 台北市中正區福州街 1 號 10 樓之 2
E m a i l ／best.books.service@gmail.com

總 經 銷／235 商流文化事業有限公司
地　　址／新北市中和區中正路752號7樓
電　　話／（02）2228-8841
傳　　真／（02）2228-6939

國家圖書館出版品預行編目(CIP)資料

美國人為什麼會這麼說 / 季薇.伯斯特，保羅.詹姆
斯.伯斯特合著 ─ 初版. ─ 臺北市：倍斯特，
2014. 01
　　面；　公分. ─ （Learn smart；25）
　ISBN 978-986-89739-9-2(平裝)

　1. 英語 2. 會話

805.188 　　　　　　　　　　　　　102027525